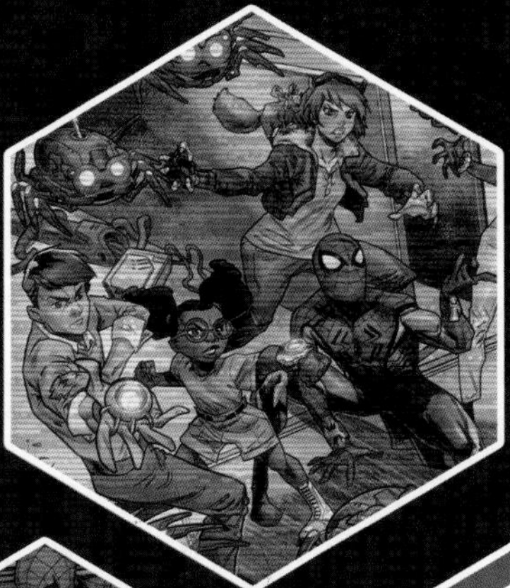

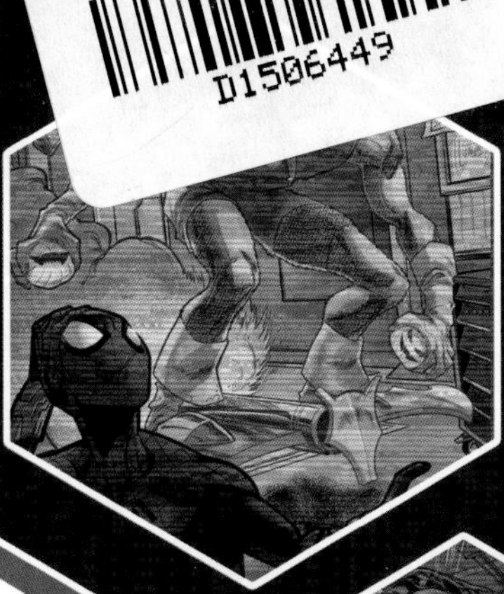

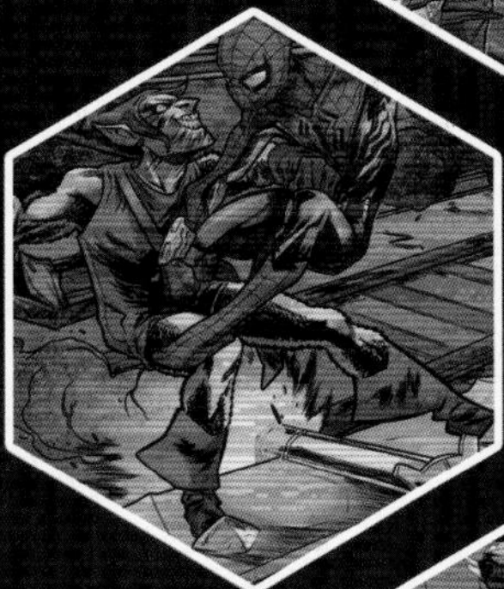

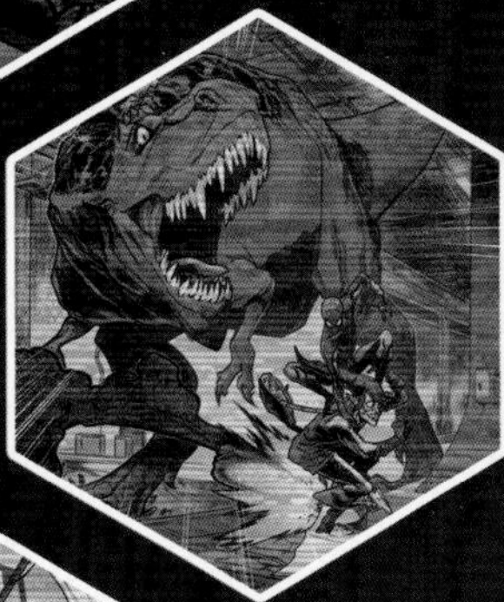

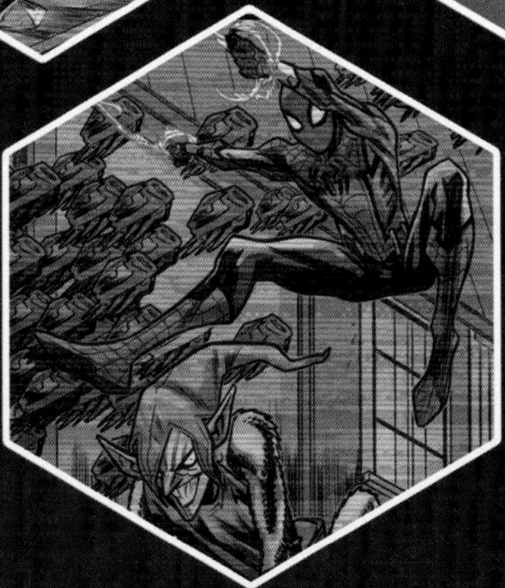

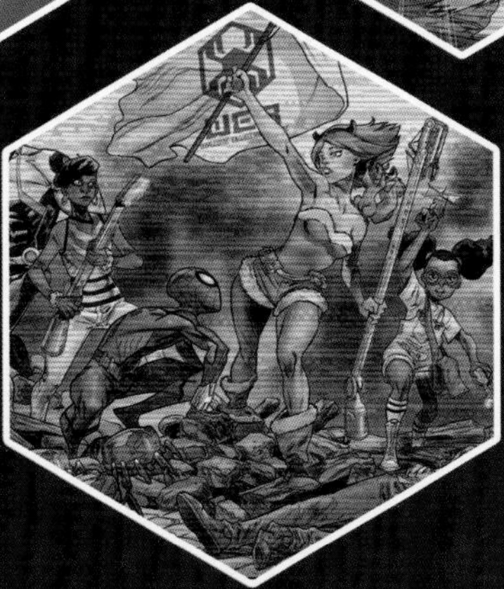

WEB OF SPIDER-MAN

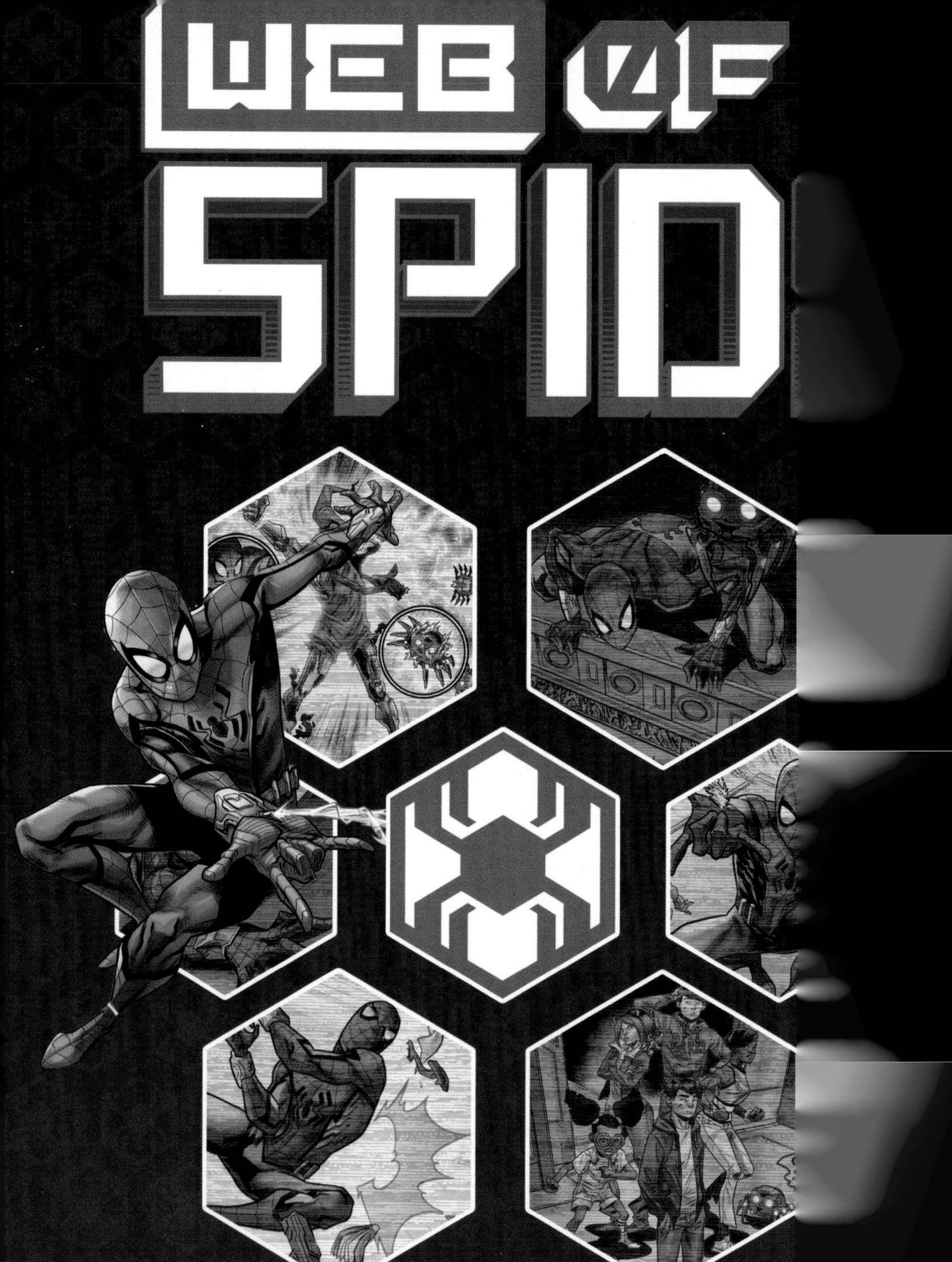
WEB OF
SPID

W.E.B. OF SPIDER-MAN GN-TPB. Contains material originally published in magazine form as W.E.B. OF SPIDER-MAN (2021) #1-5. First printing 2021. ISBN 978-1-302-92306-8. Published by
of MARVEL ENTERTAINMENT, LLC. OFFICE OF PUBLICATION: 1290 Avenue of the Americas, New York, NY 10104. **Printed in Canada.** KEVIN FEIGE, Chief Creative Officer; DAN BU
JOE QUESADA, EVP & Creative Director; DAVID BOGART, Associate Publisher & SVP of Talent Affairs; TOM BREVOORT, VP, Executive Editor; NICK LOWE, Executive Editor, VP of Content, Digital P
Digital Publishing; JEFF YOUNGQUIST, VP of Production & Special Projects; ALEX MORALES, Director of Publishing Operations; DAN EDINGTON, Managing Editor; RICKEY PURDIN, Director of T
Senior Editor, Special Projects; SUSAN CRESPI, Production Manager; STAN LEE, Chairman Emeritus. For information regarding advertising in Marvel Comics or on Marvel.com, please co
Integrated Advertising Manager, at vdebellis@marvel.com. For Marvel subscription inquiries, please call 888-511-5480. **Manufactured between 9/10/2021 and 10/12/2021 by SOLIS**

10 9 8 7 6 5 4 3 2 1

THE AVENGERS ARE SETTING UP NEW HEADQUARTERS AND TRAINING FACILITIES AROUND THE GLOBE TO INSPIRE
POTENTIAL RECRUITS WHO ARE WILLING TO STEP UP AND BECOME A PART OF SOMETHING BIGGER THAN THEMSELVES!
AS PART OF THIS INITIAITVE, TONY STARK FOUNDED THE WORLDWIDE ENGINEERING BRIGADE — W.E.B. FOR SHORT!

R-MAN

KEVIN SHINICK
WRITER

ALBERTO ALBURQUERQUE
ARTIST

RACHELLE ROSENBERG
COLOR ARTIST

VC's TRAVIS LANHAM
LETTERER

JAY BOWEN
LOGO DESIGN

GURIHIRU
COVER ART

**PEPE LARRAZ &
MARTE GRACIA**
COVER ART

DANNY KHAZEM
ASSISTANT EDITOR

DEVIN LEWIS
EDITOR

NICK LOWE
EXECUTIVE EDITOR

SPECIAL THANKS TO **DAVE BUSHORE, SCOT D. DRAKE, JOHN MAURO, CAROLINE MAY,
FRANK REIFSNYDER, STEVEN F. SPIEGEL, BRENT D. STRONG & BRIAN CROSBY**

SPIDER-MAN CREATED BY **STAN LEE & STEVE DITKO**

COLLECTION EDITOR: **JENNIFER GRÜNWALD**
ASSISTANT EDITOR: **DANIEL KIRCHHOFFER**
ASSISTANT MANAGING EDITOR: **MAIA LOY**
ASSISTANT MANAGING EDITOR: **LISA MONTALBANO**

VP PRODUCTION & SPECIAL PROJECTS: **JEFF YOUNGQUIST**
BOOK DESIGNER: **STACIE ZUCKER**
SVP PRINT, SALES & MARKETING: **DAVID GABRIEL**
EDITOR IN CHIEF: **C.B. CEBULSKI**

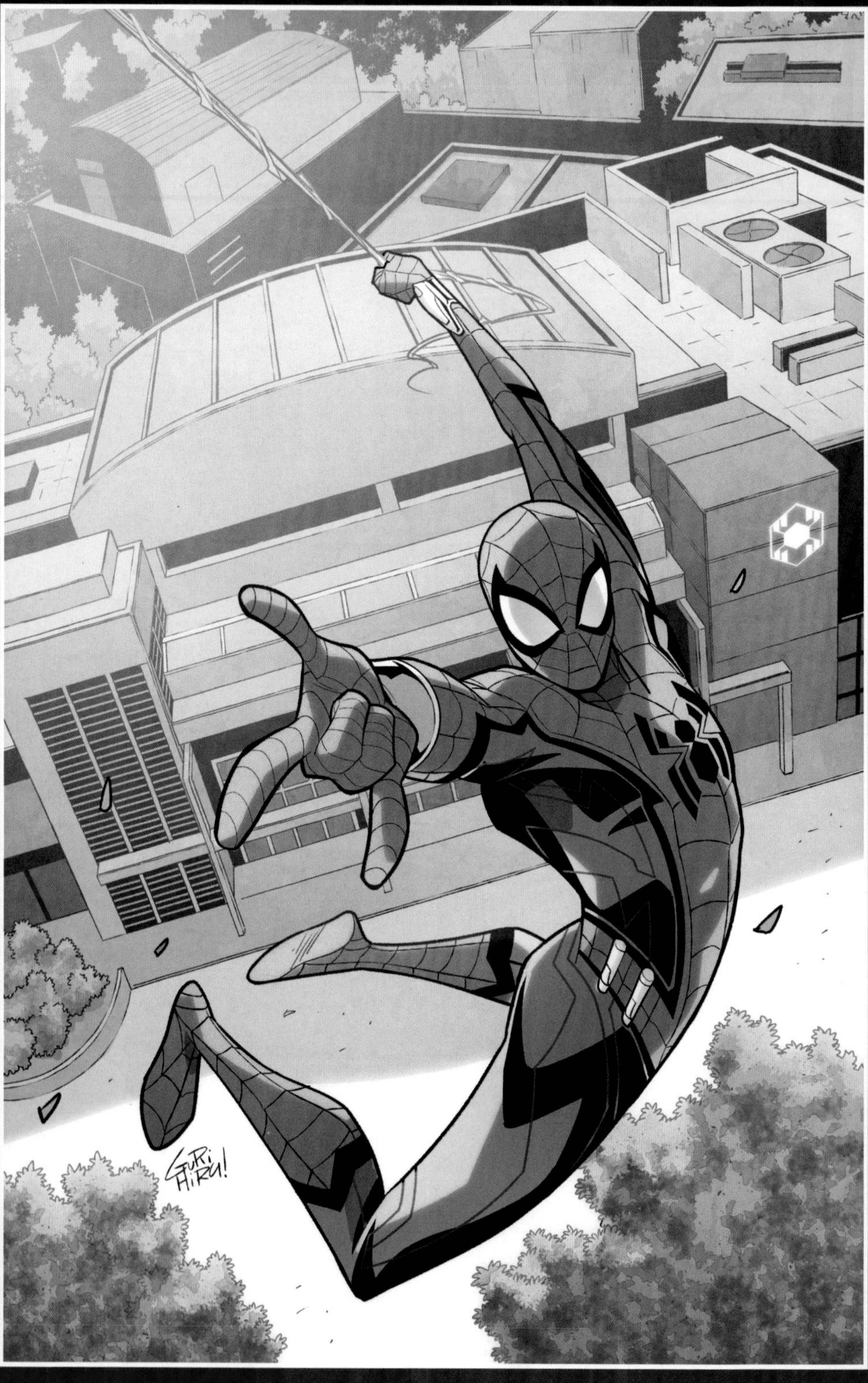
GURI HIRU!

1

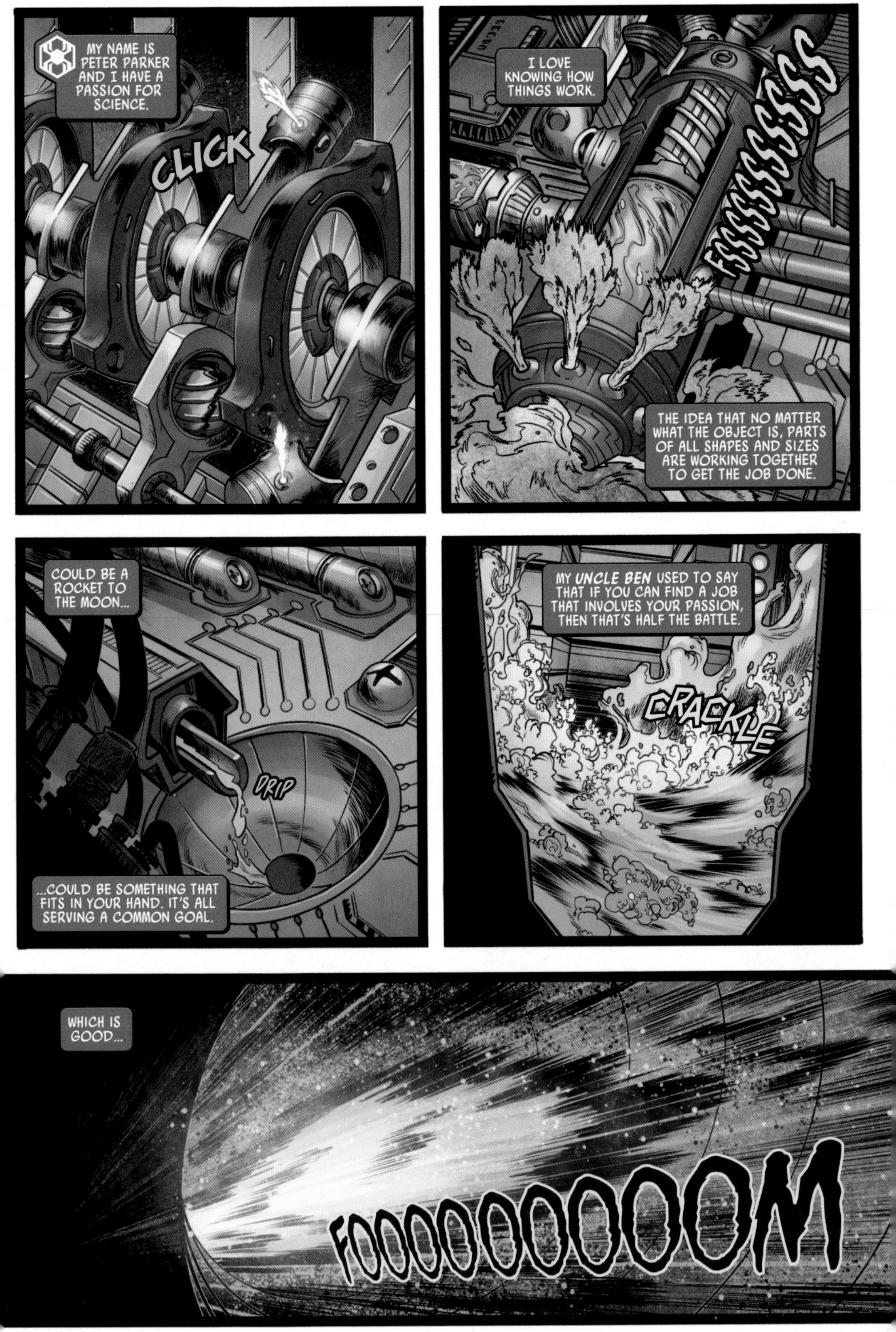
MY NAME IS PETER PARKER AND I HAVE A PASSION FOR SCIENCE.
CLICK
I LOVE KNOWING HOW THINGS WORK.
FSSSSSSSSSSS
THE IDEA THAT NO MATTER WHAT THE OBJECT IS, PARTS OF ALL SHAPES AND SIZES ARE WORKING TOGETHER TO GET THE JOB DONE.
COULD BE A ROCKET TO THE MOON...
DRIP
...COULD BE SOMETHING THAT FITS IN YOUR HAND. IT'S ALL SERVING A COMMON GOAL.
MY UNCLE BEN USED TO SAY THAT IF YOU CAN FIND A JOB THAT INVOLVES YOUR PASSION, THEN THAT'S HALF THE BATTLE.
CRACKLE
WHICH IS GOOD...
FOOOOOOOOOM

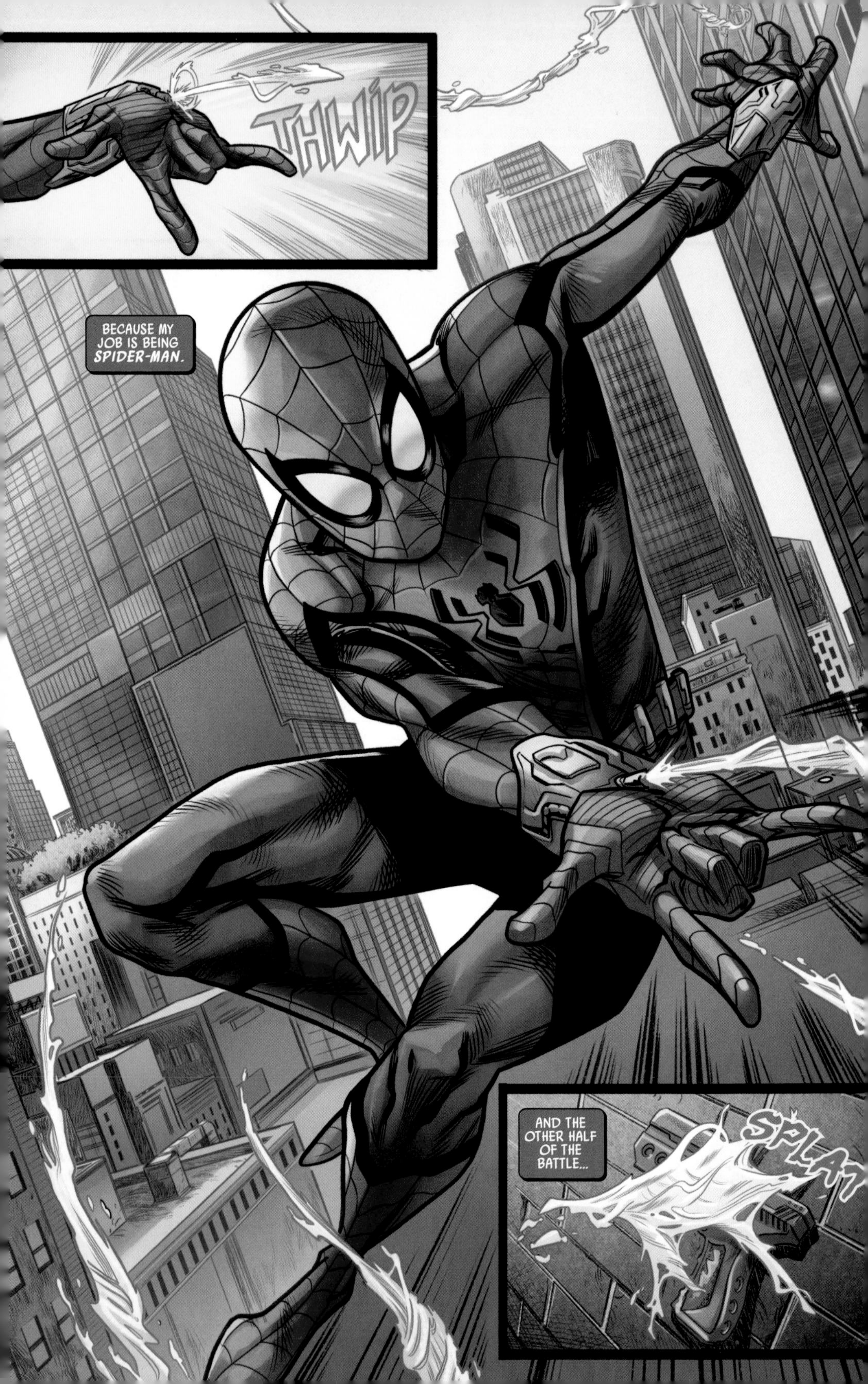
THWIP
BECAUSE MY JOB IS BEING *SPIDER-MAN.*
AND THE OTHER HALF OF THE BATTLE...
SPLAT

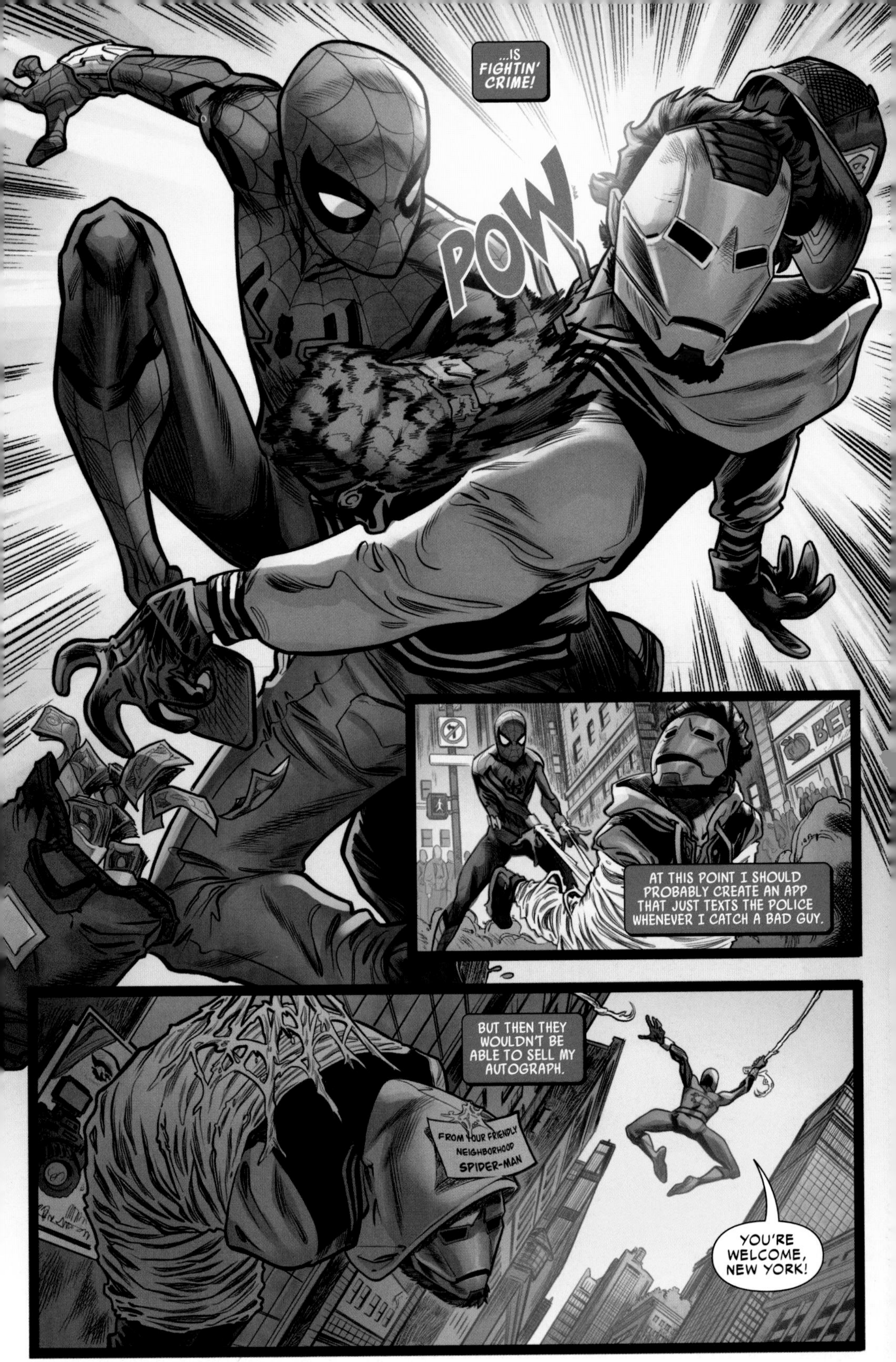
...IS FIGHTIN' CRIME!
POW
AT THIS POINT I SHOULD PROBABLY CREATE AN APP THAT JUST TEXTS THE POLICE WHENEVER I CATCH A BAD GUY.
BUT THEN THEY WOULDN'T BE ABLE TO SELL MY AUTOGRAPH.
FROM YOUR FRIENDLY NEIGHBORHOOD SPIDER-MAN
YOU'RE WELCOME, NEW YORK!

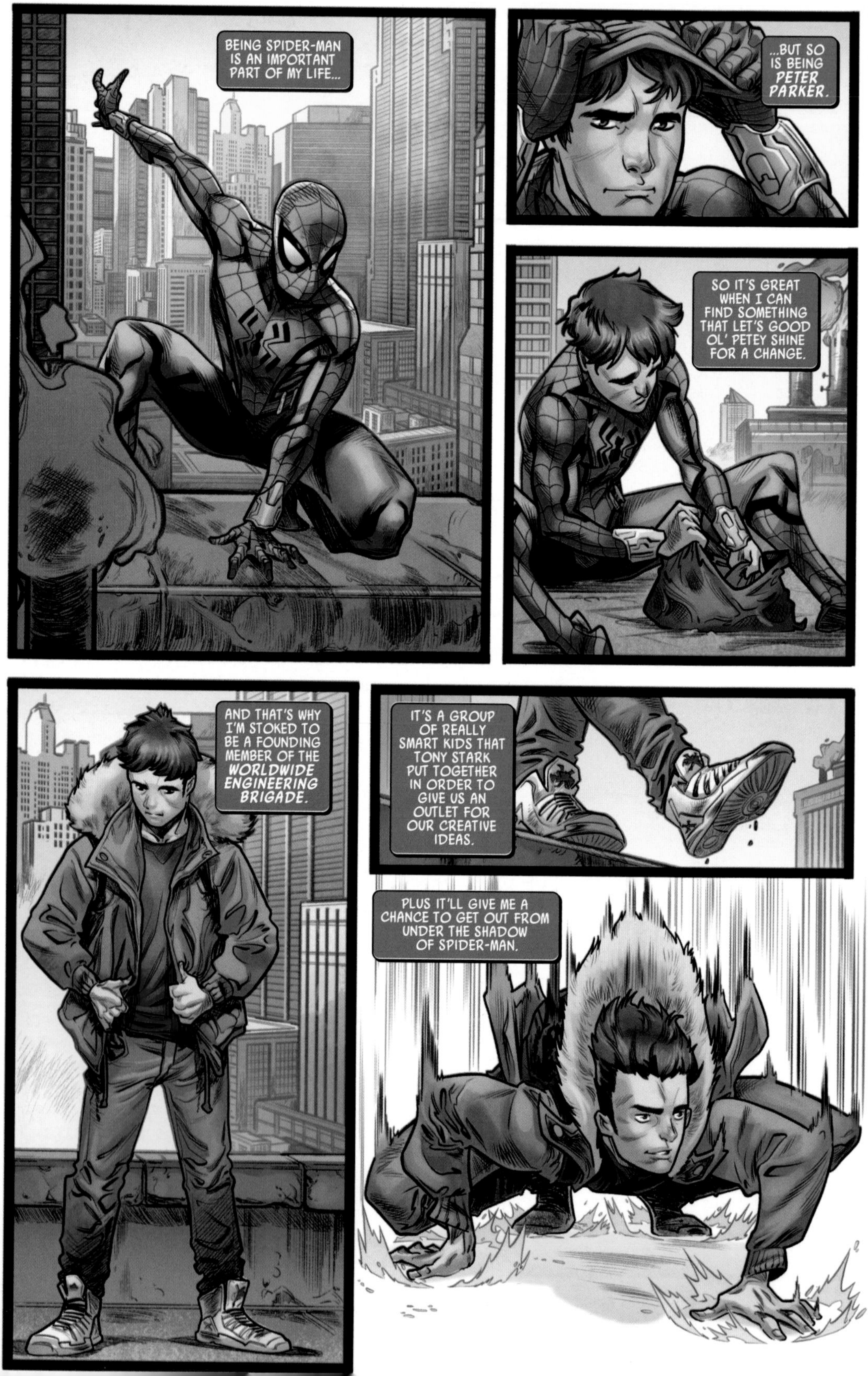
BEING SPIDER-MAN IS AN IMPORTANT PART OF MY LIFE...
...BUT SO IS BEING PETER PARKER.
SO IT'S GREAT WHEN I CAN FIND SOMETHING THAT LET'S GOOD OL' PETEY SHINE FOR A CHANGE.
AND THAT'S WHY I'M STOKED TO BE A FOUNDING MEMBER OF THE WORLDWIDE ENGINEERING BRIGADE.
IT'S A GROUP OF REALLY SMART KIDS THAT TONY STARK PUT TOGETHER IN ORDER TO GIVE US AN OUTLET FOR OUR CREATIVE IDEAS.
PLUS IT'LL GIVE ME A CHANCE TO GET OUT FROM UNDER THE SHADOW OF SPIDER-MAN.

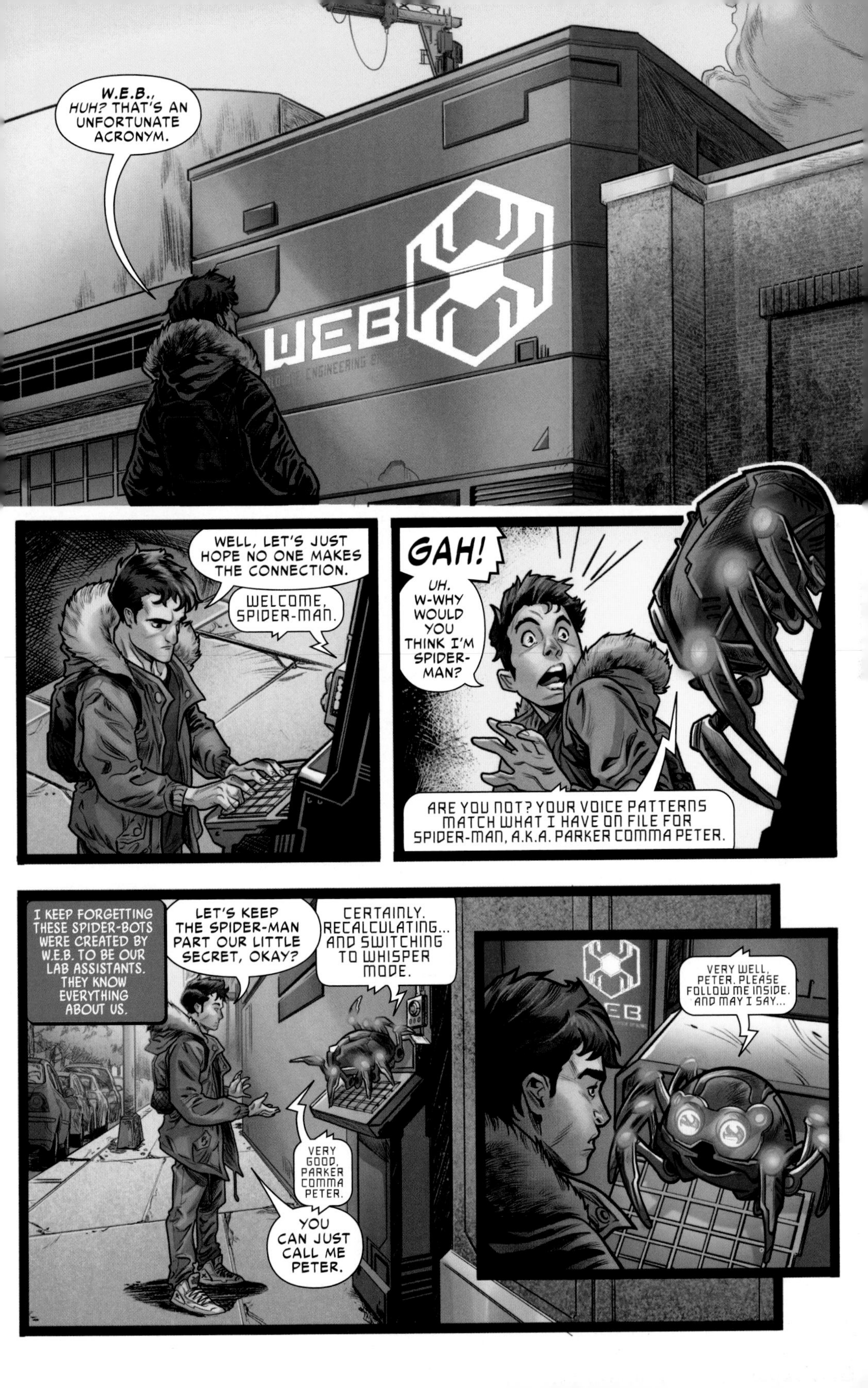
W.E.B., HUH? THAT'S AN UNFORTUNATE ACRONYM.
WEB
WELL, LET'S JUST HOPE NO ONE MAKES THE CONNECTION.
WELCOME, SPIDER-MAN.
GAH!
UH. W-WHY WOULD YOU THINK I'M SPIDER-MAN?
ARE YOU NOT? YOUR VOICE PATTERNS MATCH WHAT I HAVE ON FILE FOR SPIDER-MAN, A.K.A. PARKER COMMA PETER.
I KEEP FORGETTING THESE SPIDER-BOTS WERE CREATED BY W.E.B. TO BE OUR LAB ASSISTANTS. THEY KNOW EVERYTHING ABOUT US.
LET'S KEEP THE SPIDER-MAN PART OUR LITTLE SECRET, OKAY?
CERTAINLY. RECALCULATING... AND SWITCHING TO WHISPER MODE.
VERY GOOD, PARKER COMMA PETER.
YOU CAN JUST CALL ME PETER.
VERY WELL, PETER. PLEASE FOLLOW ME INSIDE. AND MAY I SAY...

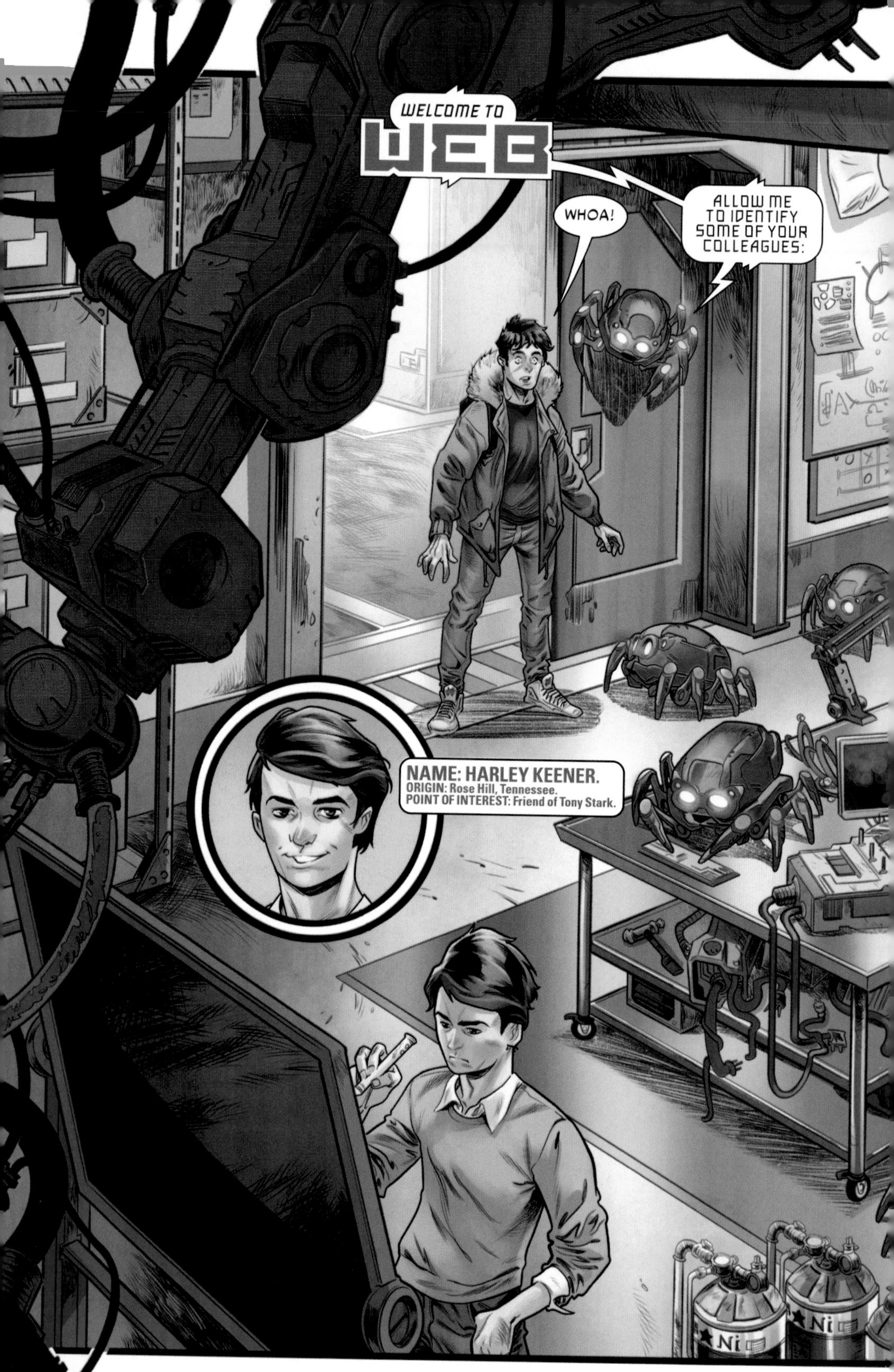
WELCOME TO
WEB
WHOA!
ALLOW ME TO IDENTIFY SOME OF YOUR COLLEAGUES:
NAME: HARLEY KEENER.
ORIGIN: Rose Hill, Tennessee.
POINT OF INTEREST: Friend of Tony Stark.

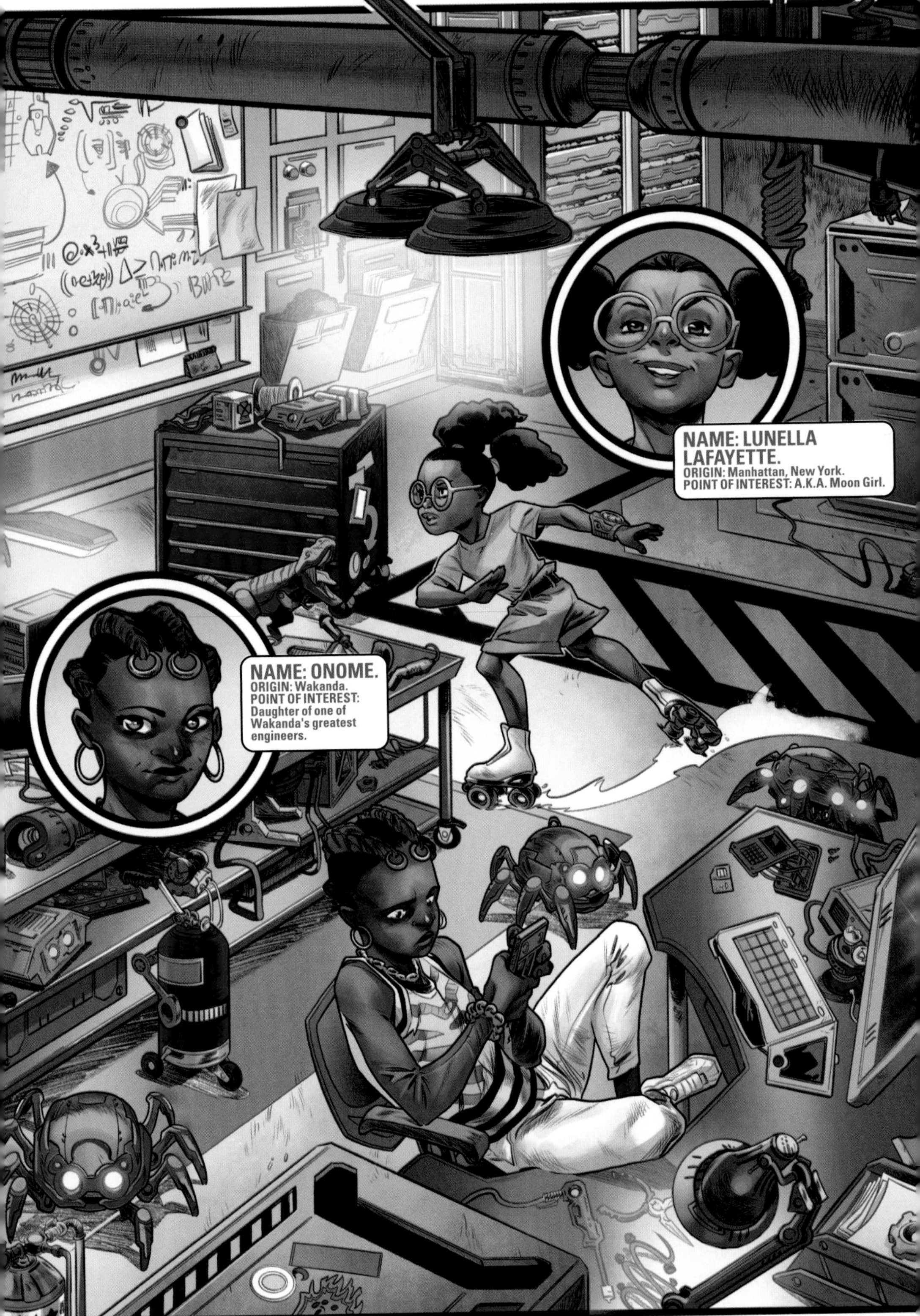
NAME: LUNELLA LAFAYETTE.
ORIGIN: Manhattan, New York.
POINT OF INTEREST: A.K.A. Moon Girl.
NAME: ONOME.
ORIGIN: Wakanda.
POINT OF INTEREST: Daughter of one of Wakanda's greatest engineers.

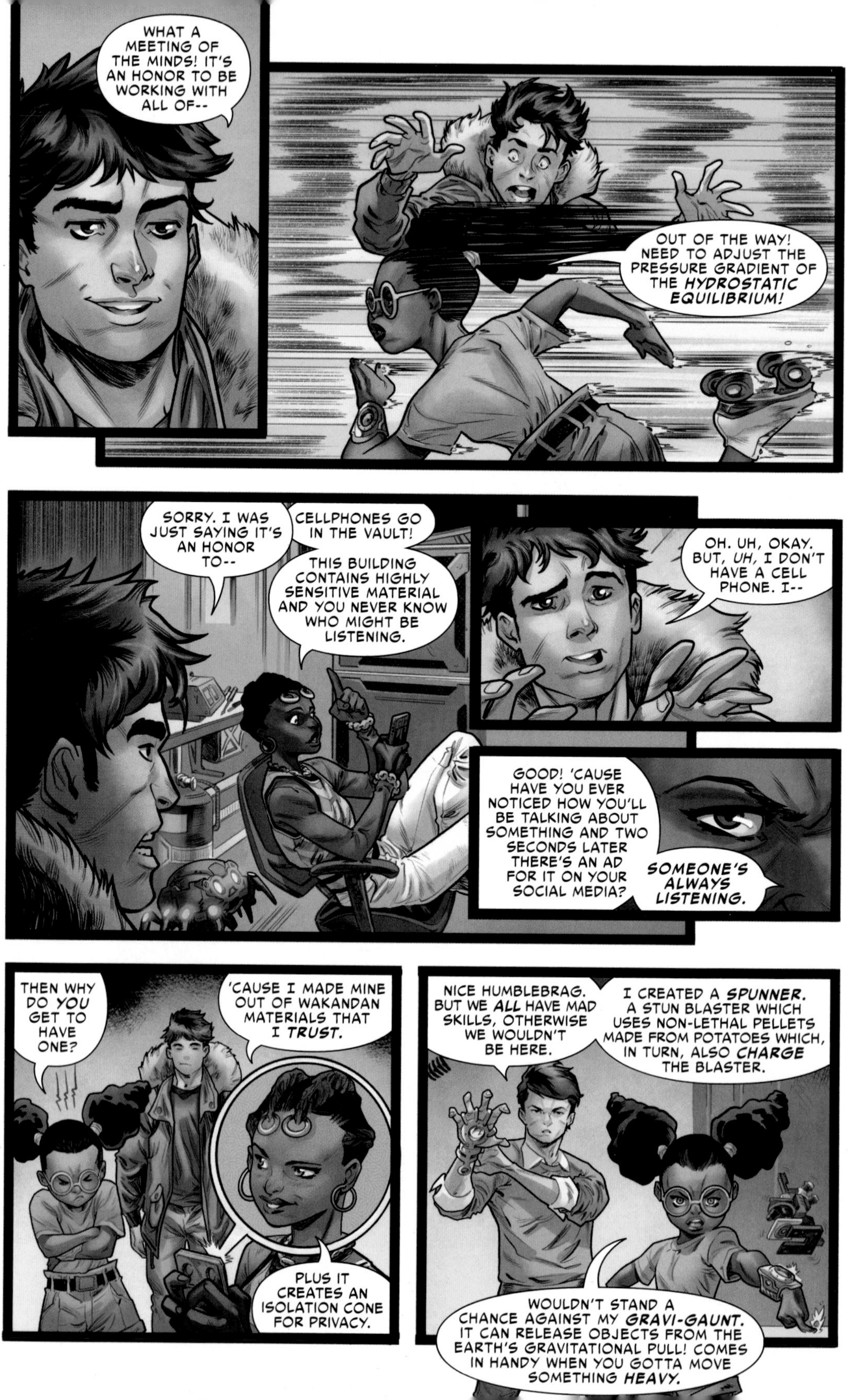
WHAT A MEETING OF THE MINDS! IT'S AN HONOR TO BE WORKING WITH ALL OF--
OUT OF THE WAY! NEED TO ADJUST THE PRESSURE GRADIENT OF THE *HYDROSTATIC EQUILIBRIUM!*
SORRY. I WAS JUST SAYING IT'S AN HONOR TO--
CELLPHONES GO IN THE VAULT!
THIS BUILDING CONTAINS HIGHLY SENSITIVE MATERIAL AND YOU NEVER KNOW WHO MIGHT BE LISTENING.
OH. UH, OKAY. BUT, *UH,* I DON'T HAVE A CELL PHONE. I--
GOOD! 'CAUSE HAVE YOU EVER NOTICED HOW YOU'LL BE TALKING ABOUT SOMETHING AND TWO SECONDS LATER THERE'S AN AD FOR IT ON YOUR SOCIAL MEDIA?
SOMEONE'S ALWAYS LISTENING.
THEN WHY DO *YOU* GET TO HAVE ONE?
'CAUSE I MADE MINE OUT OF WAKANDAN MATERIALS THAT I *TRUST.*
PLUS IT CREATES AN ISOLATION CONE FOR PRIVACY.
NICE HUMBLEBRAG. BUT WE *ALL* HAVE MAD SKILLS, OTHERWISE WE WOULDN'T BE HERE.
I CREATED A *SPUNNER.* A STUN BLASTER WHICH USES NON-LETHAL PELLETS MADE FROM POTATOES WHICH, IN TURN, ALSO *CHARGE* THE BLASTER.
WOULDN'T STAND A CHANCE AGAINST MY *GRAVI-GAUNT.* IT CAN RELEASE OBJECTS FROM THE EARTH'S GRAVITATIONAL PULL! COMES IN HANDY WHEN YOU GOTTA MOVE SOMETHING *HEAVY.*

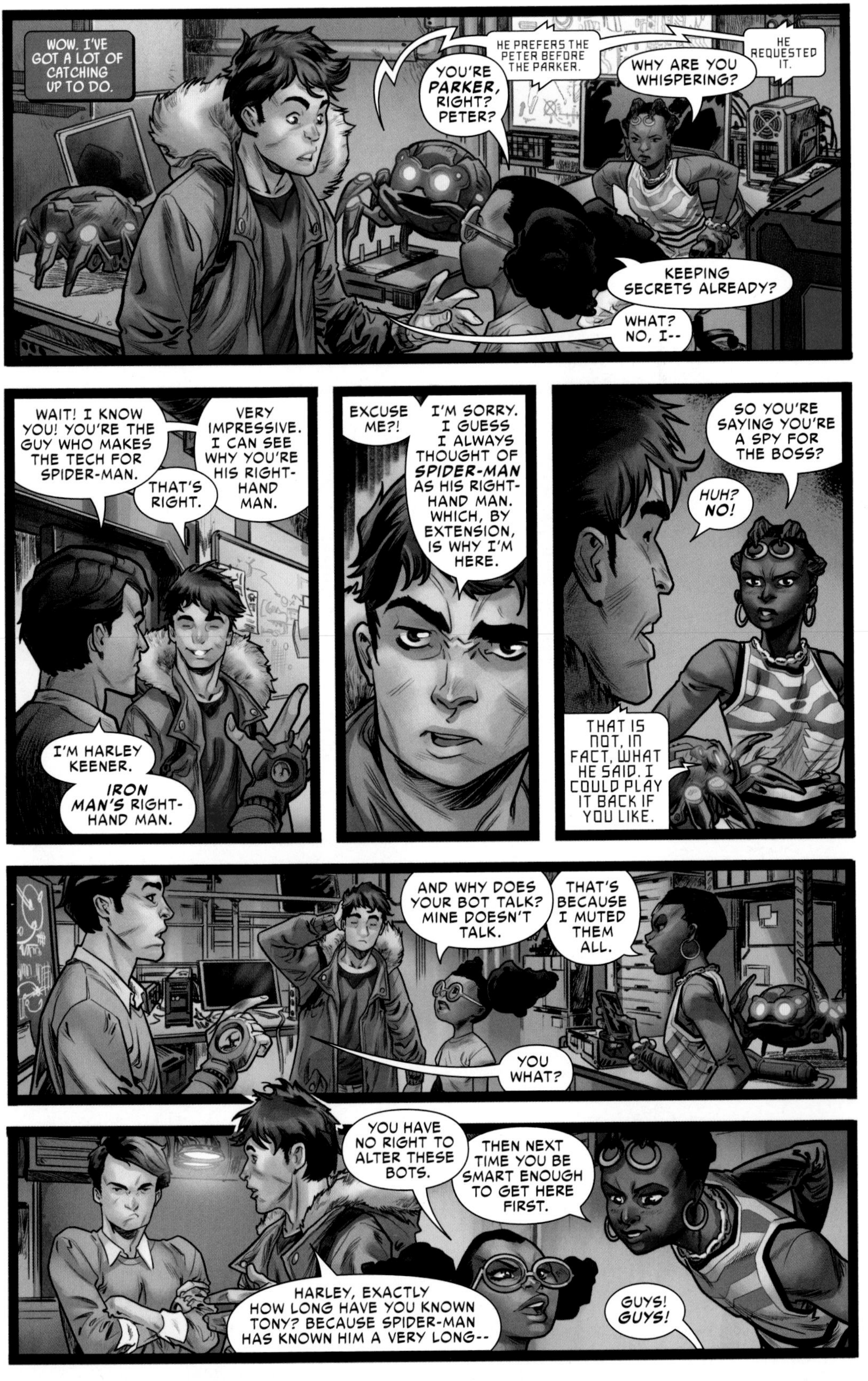
WOW. I'VE GOT A LOT OF CATCHING UP TO DO.
YOU'RE PARKER, RIGHT? PETER?
HE PREFERS THE PETER BEFORE THE PARKER.
WHY ARE YOU WHISPERING?
HE REQUESTED IT.
KEEPING SECRETS ALREADY?
WHAT? NO, I--
WAIT! I KNOW YOU! YOU'RE THE GUY WHO MAKES THE TECH FOR SPIDER-MAN.
THAT'S RIGHT.
VERY IMPRESSIVE. I CAN SEE WHY YOU'RE HIS RIGHT-HAND MAN.
I'M HARLEY KEENER.
IRON MAN'S RIGHT-HAND MAN.
EXCUSE ME?!
I'M SORRY. I GUESS I ALWAYS THOUGHT OF SPIDER-MAN AS HIS RIGHT-HAND MAN. WHICH, BY EXTENSION, IS WHY I'M HERE.
SO YOU'RE SAYING YOU'RE A SPY FOR THE BOSS?
HUH? NO!
THAT IS NOT, IN FACT, WHAT HE SAID. I COULD PLAY IT BACK IF YOU LIKE.
AND WHY DOES YOUR BOT TALK? MINE DOESN'T TALK.
THAT'S BECAUSE I MUTED THEM ALL.
YOU WHAT?
YOU HAVE NO RIGHT TO ALTER THESE BOTS.
THEN NEXT TIME YOU BE SMART ENOUGH TO GET HERE FIRST.
HARLEY, EXACTLY HOW LONG HAVE YOU KNOWN TONY? BECAUSE SPIDER-MAN HAS KNOWN HIM A VERY LONG--
GUYS! GUYS!

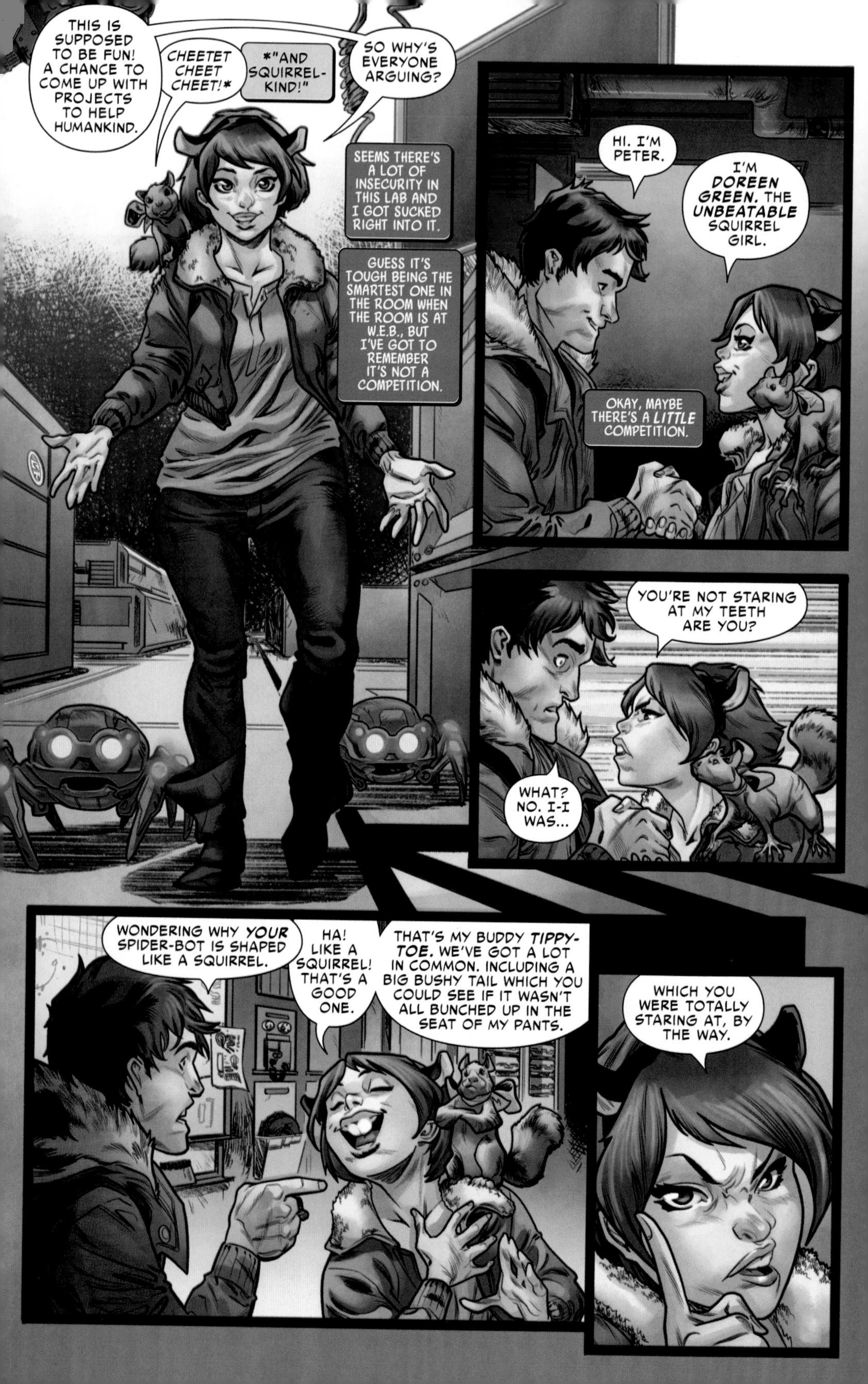
THIS IS SUPPOSED TO BE FUN! A CHANCE TO COME UP WITH PROJECTS TO HELP HUMANKIND.
CHEETET CHEET CHEET!*
*"AND SQUIRREL-KIND!"
SO WHY'S EVERYONE ARGUING?
SEEMS THERE'S A LOT OF INSECURITY IN THIS LAB AND I GOT SUCKED RIGHT INTO IT.
GUESS IT'S TOUGH BEING THE SMARTEST ONE IN THE ROOM WHEN THE ROOM IS AT W.E.B., BUT I'VE GOT TO REMEMBER IT'S NOT A COMPETITION.
HI. I'M PETER.
I'M DOREEN GREEN. THE UNBEATABLE SQUIRREL GIRL.
OKAY, MAYBE THERE'S A LITTLE COMPETITION.
YOU'RE NOT STARING AT MY TEETH ARE YOU?
WHAT? NO. I-I WAS...
WONDERING WHY YOUR SPIDER-BOT IS SHAPED LIKE A SQUIRREL.
HA! LIKE A SQUIRREL! THAT'S A GOOD ONE.
THAT'S MY BUDDY TIPPY-TOE. WE'VE GOT A LOT IN COMMON. INCLUDING A BIG BUSHY TAIL WHICH YOU COULD SEE IF IT WASN'T ALL BUNCHED UP IN THE SEAT OF MY PANTS.
WHICH YOU WERE TOTALLY STARING AT, BY THE WAY.

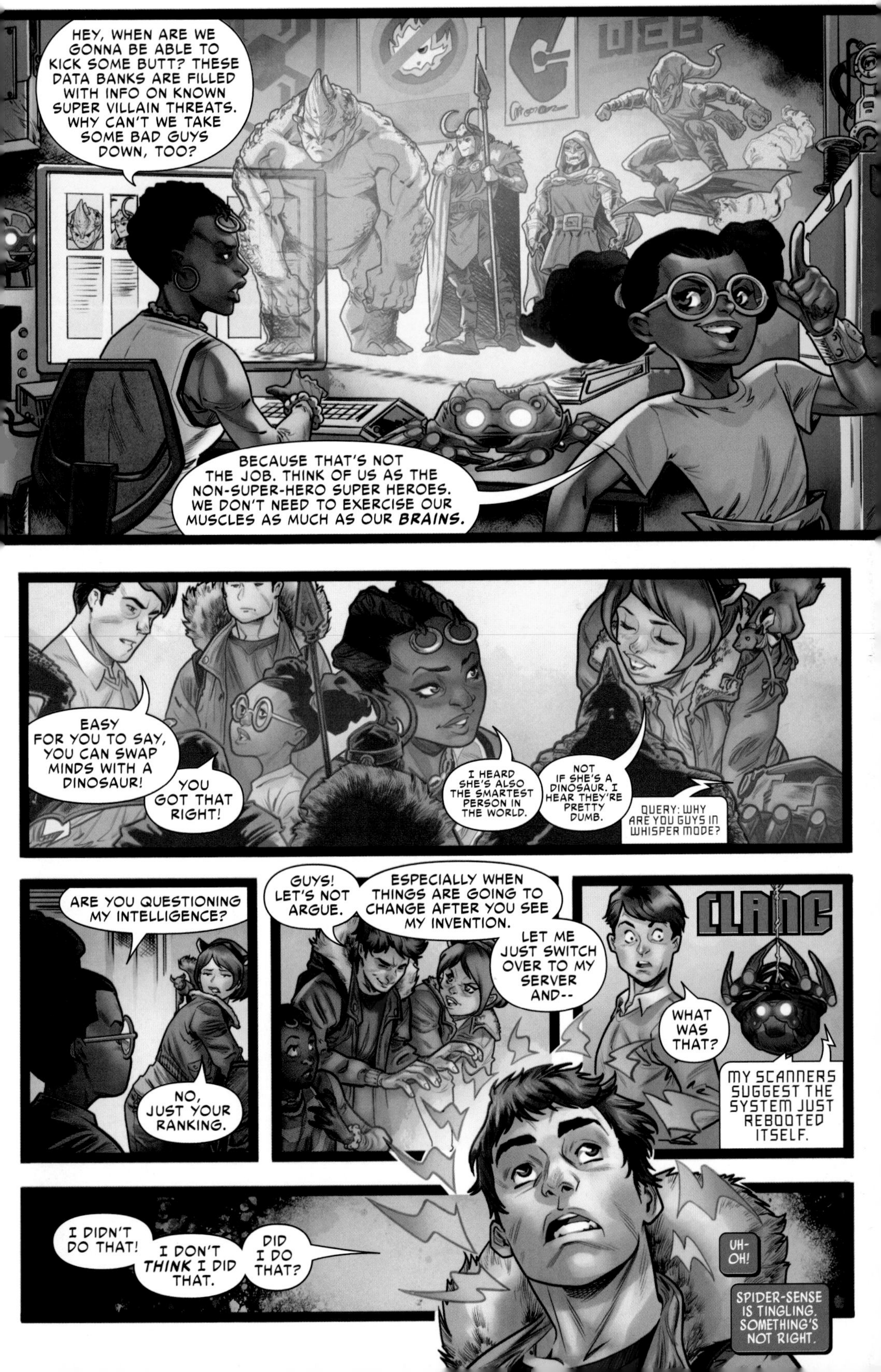
HEY, WHEN ARE WE GONNA BE ABLE TO KICK SOME BUTT? THESE DATA BANKS ARE FILLED WITH INFO ON KNOWN SUPER VILLAIN THREATS. WHY CAN'T WE TAKE SOME BAD GUYS DOWN, TOO?
BECAUSE THAT'S NOT THE JOB. THINK OF US AS THE NON-SUPER-HERO SUPER HEROES. WE DON'T NEED TO EXERCISE OUR MUSCLES AS MUCH AS OUR BRAINS.
EASY FOR YOU TO SAY, YOU CAN SWAP MINDS WITH A DINOSAUR!
YOU GOT THAT RIGHT!
I HEARD SHE'S ALSO THE SMARTEST PERSON IN THE WORLD.
NOT IF SHE'S A DINOSAUR. I HEAR THEY'RE PRETTY DUMB.
QUERY: WHY ARE YOU GUYS IN WHISPER MODE?
ARE YOU QUESTIONING MY INTELLIGENCE?
NO, JUST YOUR RANKING.
GUYS! LET'S NOT ARGUE.
ESPECIALLY WHEN THINGS ARE GOING TO CHANGE AFTER YOU SEE MY INVENTION.
LET ME JUST SWITCH OVER TO MY SERVER AND--
CLANG
WHAT WAS THAT?
MY SCANNERS SUGGEST THE SYSTEM JUST REBOOTED ITSELF.
I DIDN'T DO THAT!
I DON'T THINK I DID THAT.
DID I DO THAT?
UH-OH!
SPIDER-SENSE IS TINGLING. SOMETHING'S NOT RIGHT.

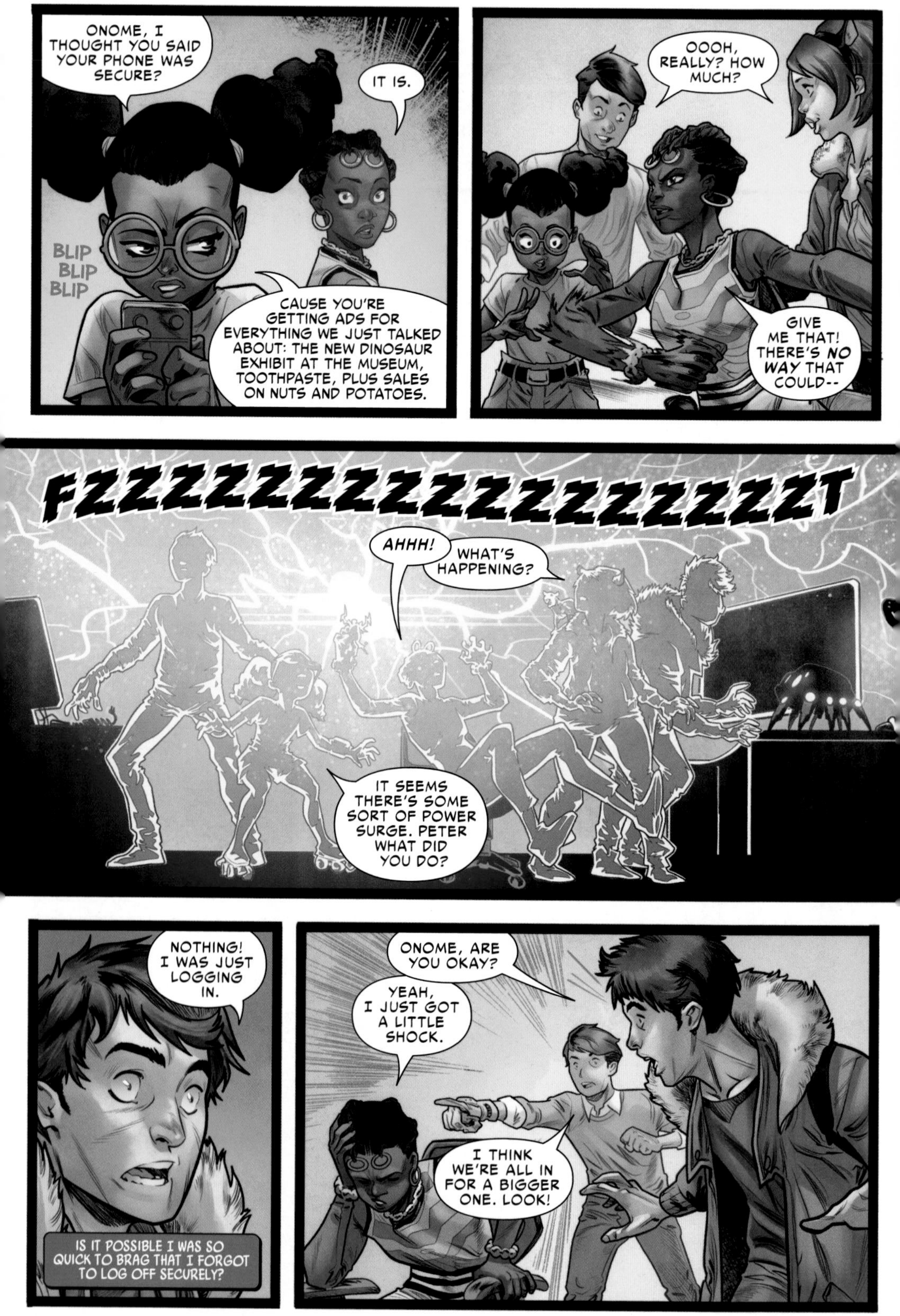
ONOME, I THOUGHT YOU SAID YOUR PHONE WAS SECURE?
IT IS.
BLIP BLIP BLIP
CAUSE YOU'RE GETTING ADS FOR EVERYTHING WE JUST TALKED ABOUT: THE NEW DINOSAUR EXHIBIT AT THE MUSEUM, TOOTHPASTE, PLUS SALES ON NUTS AND POTATOES.
OOOH, REALLY? HOW MUCH?
GIVE ME THAT! THERE'S NO WAY THAT COULD--
FZZZZZZZZZZZZZZZZZZZZT
AHHH!
WHAT'S HAPPENING?
IT SEEMS THERE'S SOME SORT OF POWER SURGE. PETER WHAT DID YOU DO?
NOTHING! I WAS JUST LOGGING IN.
IS IT POSSIBLE I WAS SO QUICK TO BRAG THAT I FORGOT TO LOG OFF SECURELY?
ONOME, ARE YOU OKAY?
YEAH, I JUST GOT A LITTLE SHOCK.
I THINK WE'RE ALL IN FOR A BIGGER ONE. LOOK!

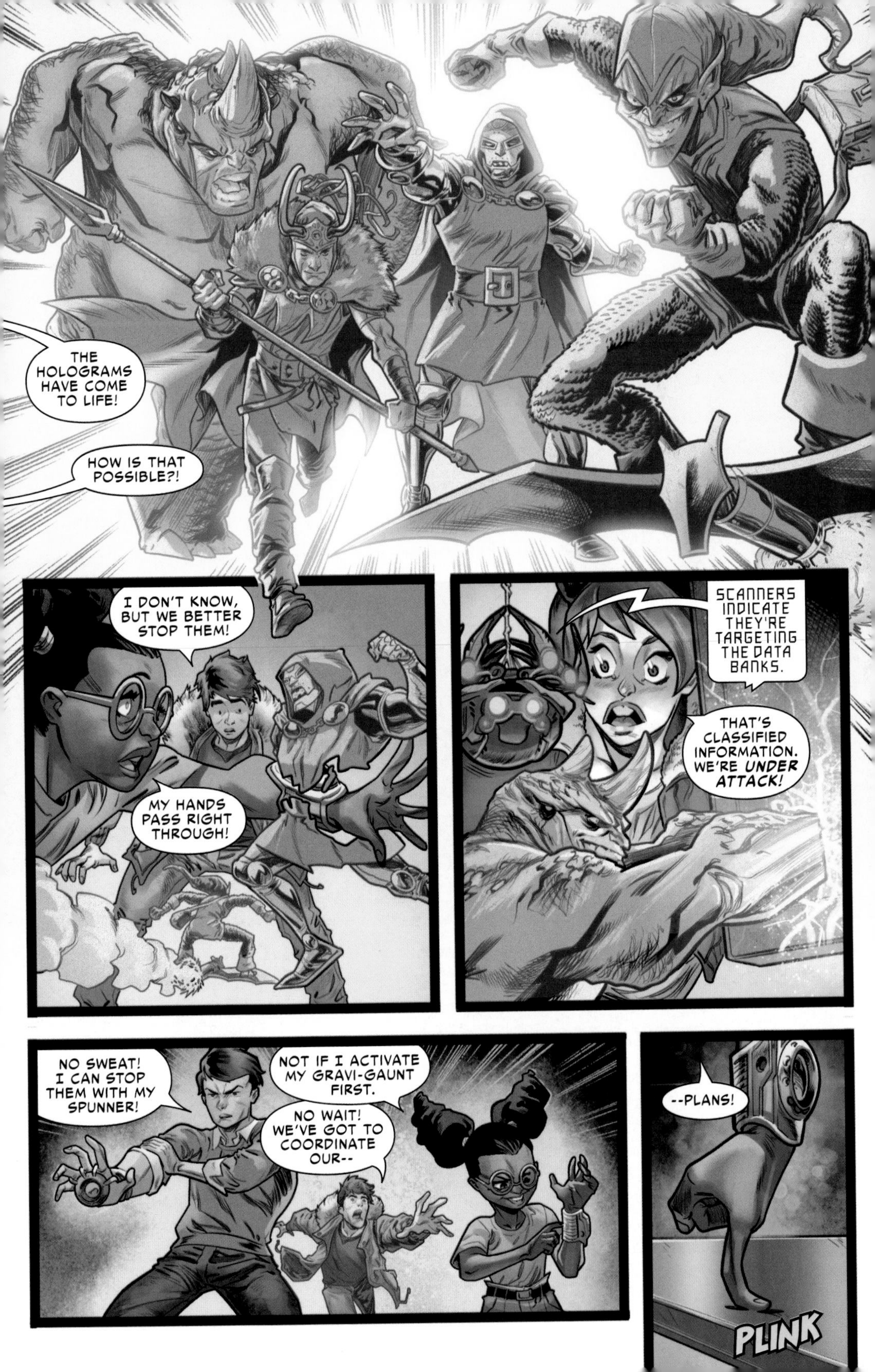
THE HOLOGRAMS HAVE COME TO LIFE!
HOW IS THAT POSSIBLE?!
I DON'T KNOW, BUT WE BETTER STOP THEM!
MY HANDS PASS RIGHT THROUGH!
SCANNERS INDICATE THEY'RE TARGETING THE DATA BANKS.
THAT'S CLASSIFIED INFORMATION. WE'RE UNDER ATTACK!
NO SWEAT! I CAN STOP THEM WITH MY SPUNNER!
NOT IF I ACTIVATE MY GRAVI-GAUNT FIRST.
NO WAIT! WE'VE GOT TO COORDINATE OUR--
--PLANS!
PLINK

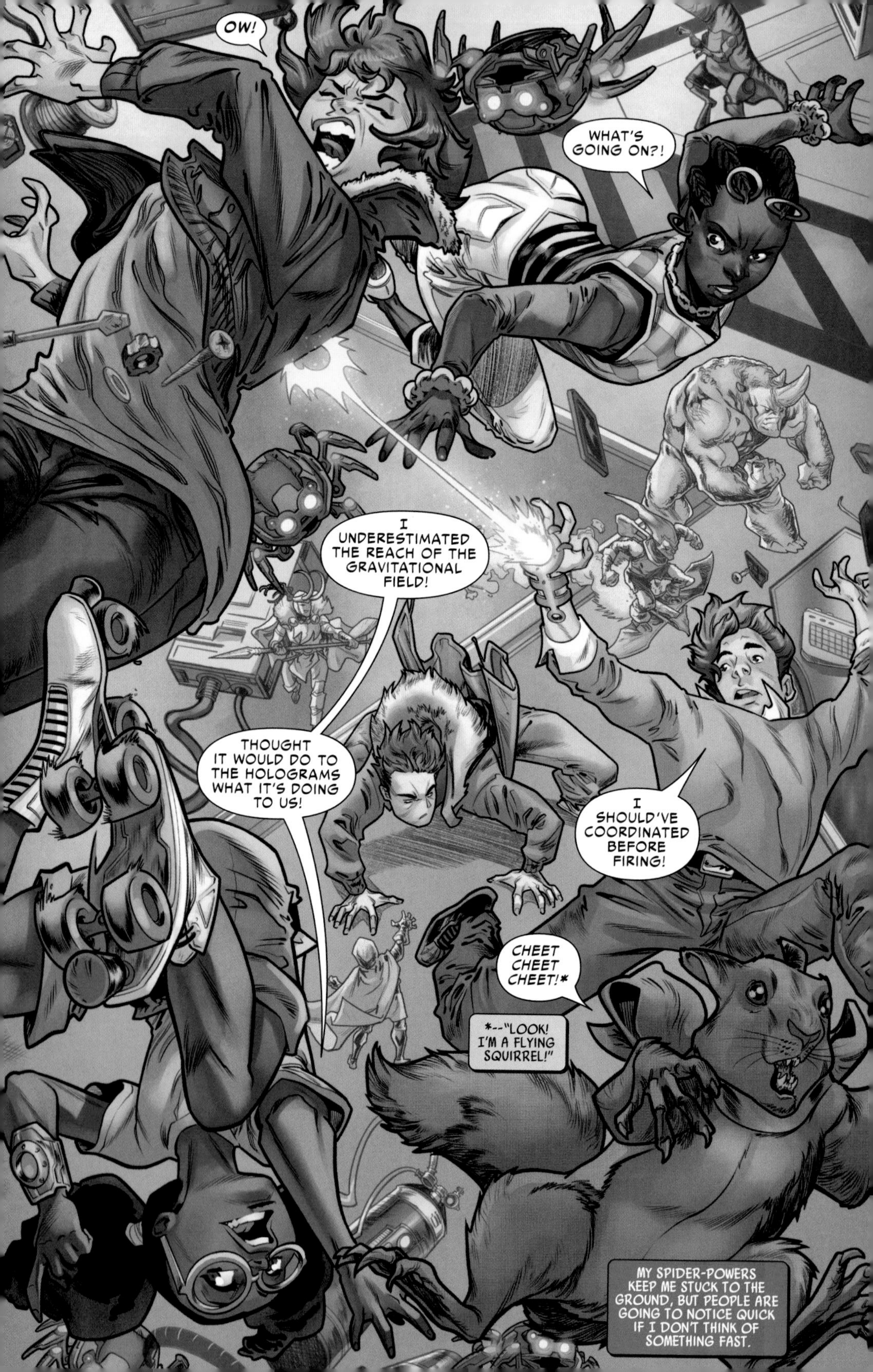
OW!
WHAT'S GOING ON?!
I UNDERESTIMATED THE REACH OF THE GRAVITATIONAL FIELD!
THOUGHT IT WOULD DO TO THE HOLOGRAMS WHAT IT'S DOING TO US!
I SHOULD'VE COORDINATED BEFORE FIRING!
CHEET CHEET CHEET!*
*--"LOOK! I'M A FLYING SQUIRREL!"
MY SPIDER-POWERS KEEP ME STUCK TO THE GROUND, BUT PEOPLE ARE GOING TO NOTICE QUICK IF I DON'T THINK OF SOMETHING FAST.

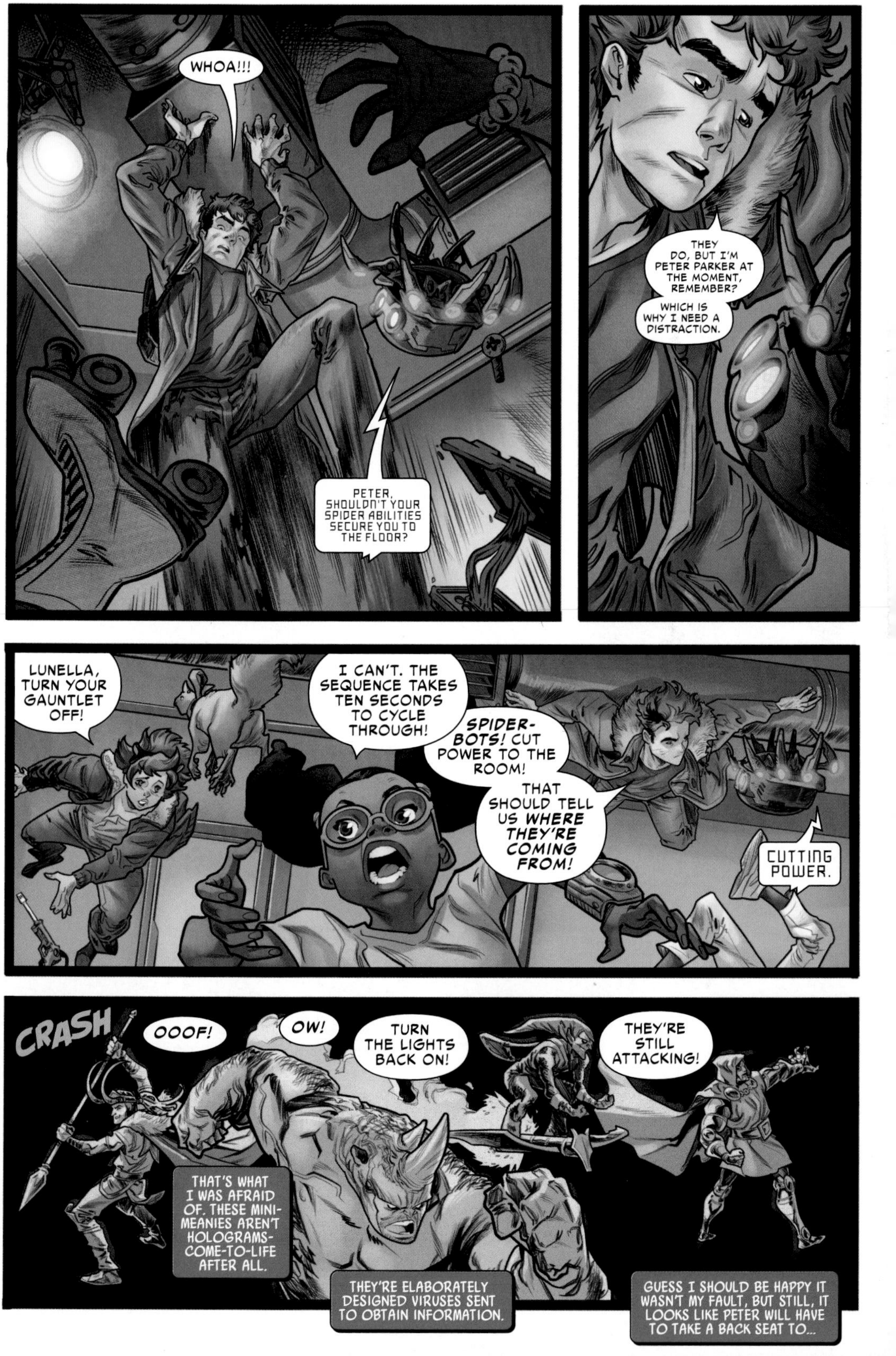
WHOA!!!
PETER, SHOULDN'T YOUR SPIDER ABILITIES SECURE YOU TO THE FLOOR?
THEY DO, BUT I'M PETER PARKER AT THE MOMENT, REMEMBER?
WHICH IS WHY I NEED A DISTRACTION.
LUNELLA, TURN YOUR GAUNTLET OFF!
I CAN'T. THE SEQUENCE TAKES TEN SECONDS TO CYCLE THROUGH!
SPIDER-BOTS! CUT POWER TO THE ROOM!
THAT SHOULD TELL US WHERE THEY'RE COMING FROM!
CUTTING POWER.
CRASH
OOOF!
OW!
TURN THE LIGHTS BACK ON!
THEY'RE STILL ATTACKING!
THAT'S WHAT I WAS AFRAID OF. THESE MINI-MEANIES AREN'T HOLOGRAMS-COME-TO-LIFE AFTER ALL.
THEY'RE ELABORATELY DESIGNED VIRUSES SENT TO OBTAIN INFORMATION.
GUESS I SHOULD BE HAPPY IT WASN'T MY FAULT, BUT STILL, IT LOOKS LIKE PETER WILL HAVE TO TAKE A BACK SEAT TO...

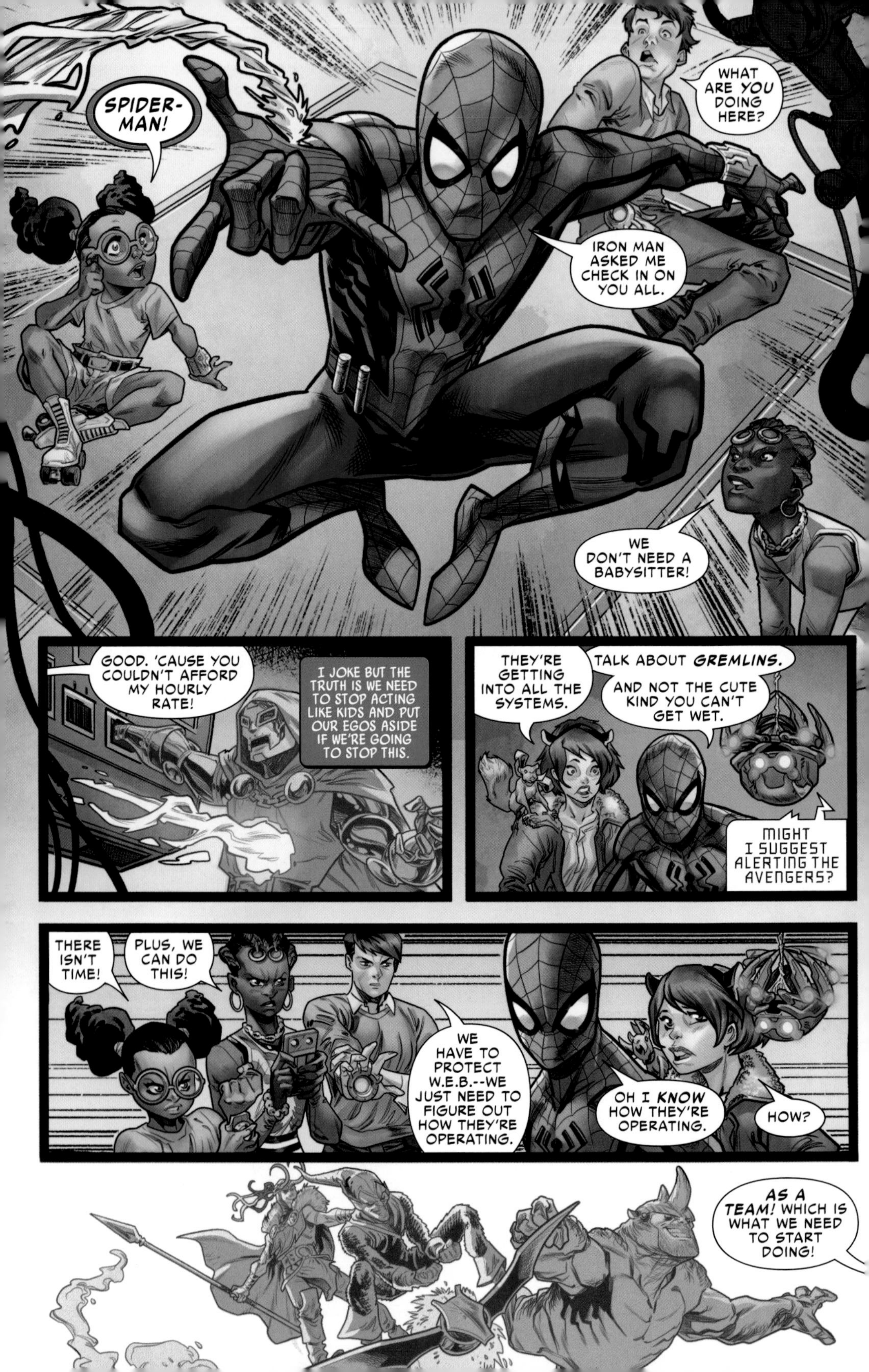

SPIDER-MAN!
WHAT ARE YOU DOING HERE?
IRON MAN ASKED ME CHECK IN ON YOU ALL.
WE DON'T NEED A BABYSITTER!
GOOD. 'CAUSE YOU COULDN'T AFFORD MY HOURLY RATE!
I JOKE BUT THE TRUTH IS WE NEED TO STOP ACTING LIKE KIDS AND PUT OUR EGOS ASIDE IF WE'RE GOING TO STOP THIS.
THEY'RE GETTING INTO ALL THE SYSTEMS.
TALK ABOUT GREMLINS.
AND NOT THE CUTE KIND YOU CAN'T GET WET.
MIGHT I SUGGEST ALERTING THE AVENGERS?
THERE ISN'T TIME!
PLUS, WE CAN DO THIS!
WE HAVE TO PROTECT W.E.B.--WE JUST NEED TO FIGURE OUT HOW THEY'RE OPERATING.
OH I KNOW HOW THEY'RE OPERATING.
HOW?
AS A TEAM! WHICH IS WHAT WE NEED TO START DOING!

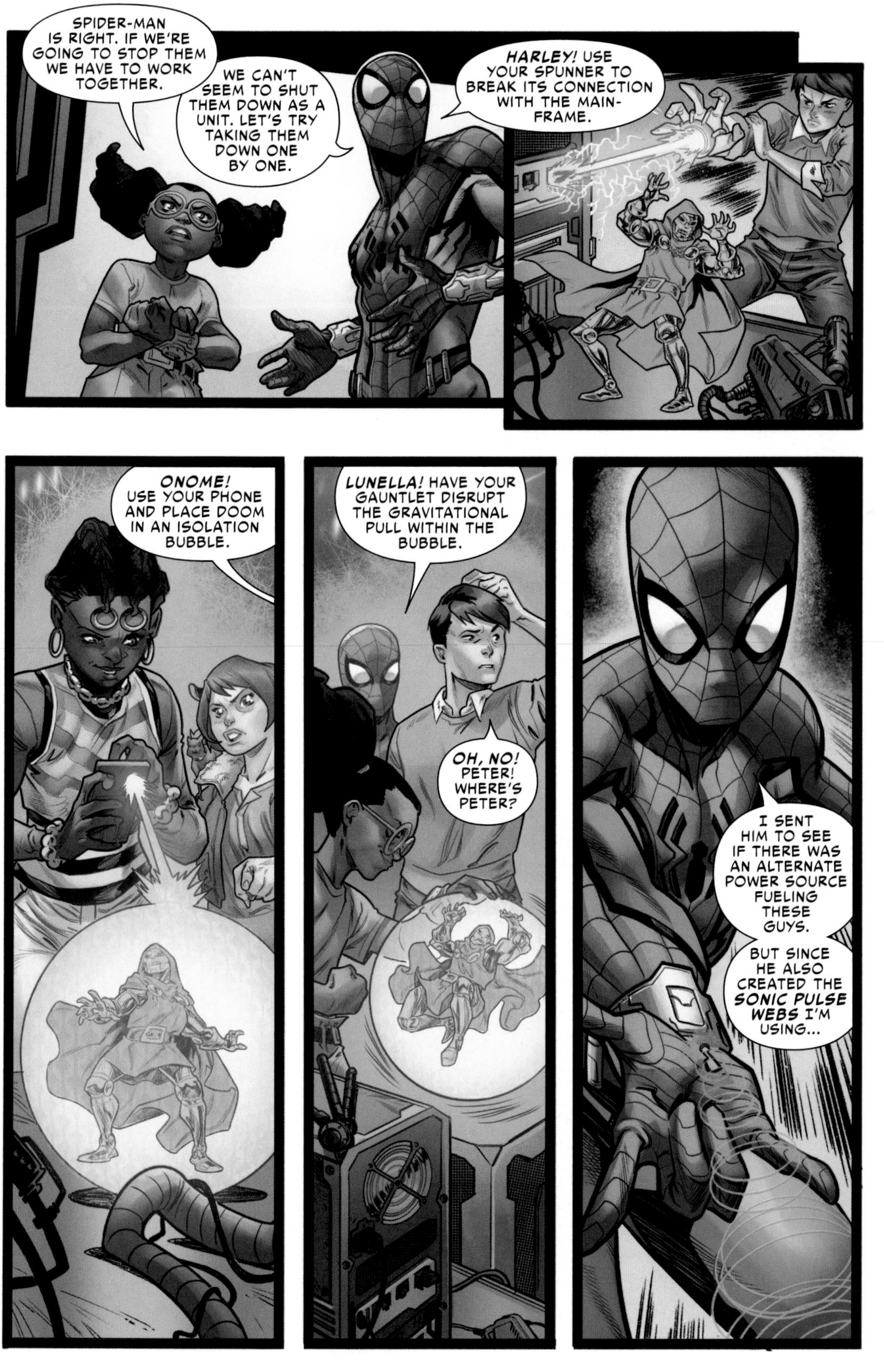
SPIDER-MAN IS RIGHT. IF WE'RE GOING TO STOP THEM WE HAVE TO WORK TOGETHER.
WE CAN'T SEEM TO SHUT THEM DOWN AS A UNIT. LET'S TRY TAKING THEM DOWN ONE BY ONE.
HARLEY! USE YOUR SPUNNER TO BREAK ITS CONNECTION WITH THE MAIN-FRAME.
ONOME! USE YOUR PHONE AND PLACE DOOM IN AN ISOLATION BUBBLE.
LUNELLA! HAVE YOUR GAUNTLET DISRUPT THE GRAVITATIONAL PULL WITHIN THE BUBBLE.
OH, NO! PETER! WHERE'S PETER?
I SENT HIM TO SEE IF THERE WAS AN ALTERNATE POWER SOURCE FUELING THESE GUYS.
BUT SINCE HE ALSO CREATED THE SONIC PULSE WEBS I'M USING...

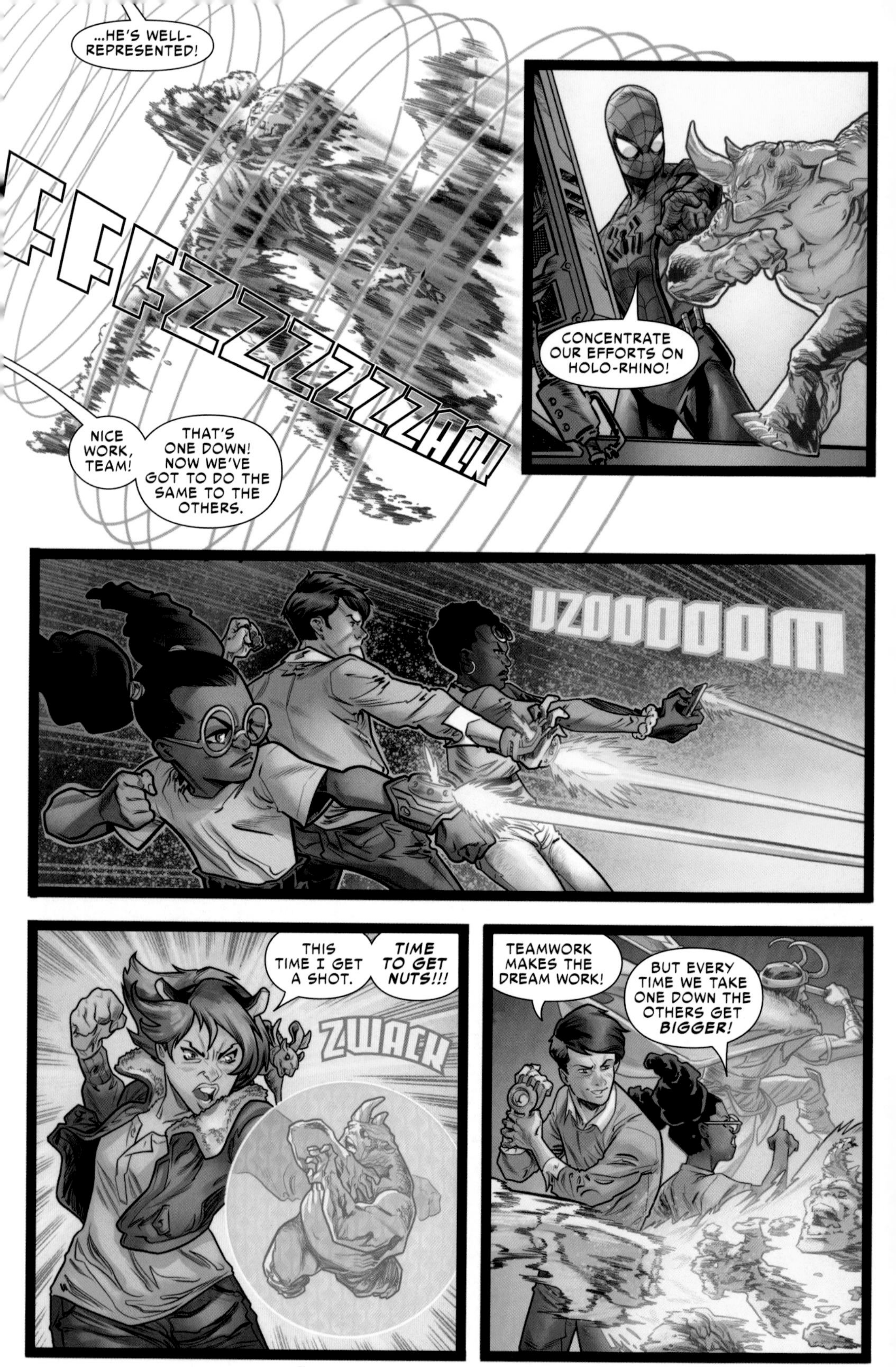

...HE'S WELL-REPRESENTED!
FFFZZZZZZZZACK
CONCENTRATE OUR EFFORTS ON HOLO-RHINO!
NICE WORK, TEAM!
THAT'S ONE DOWN! NOW WE'VE GOT TO DO THE SAME TO THE OTHERS.
VZOOOOOOM
THIS TIME I GET A SHOT.
TIME TO GET NUTS!!!
ZWACK
TEAMWORK MAKES THE DREAM WORK!
BUT EVERY TIME WE TAKE ONE DOWN THE OTHERS GET *BIGGER!*

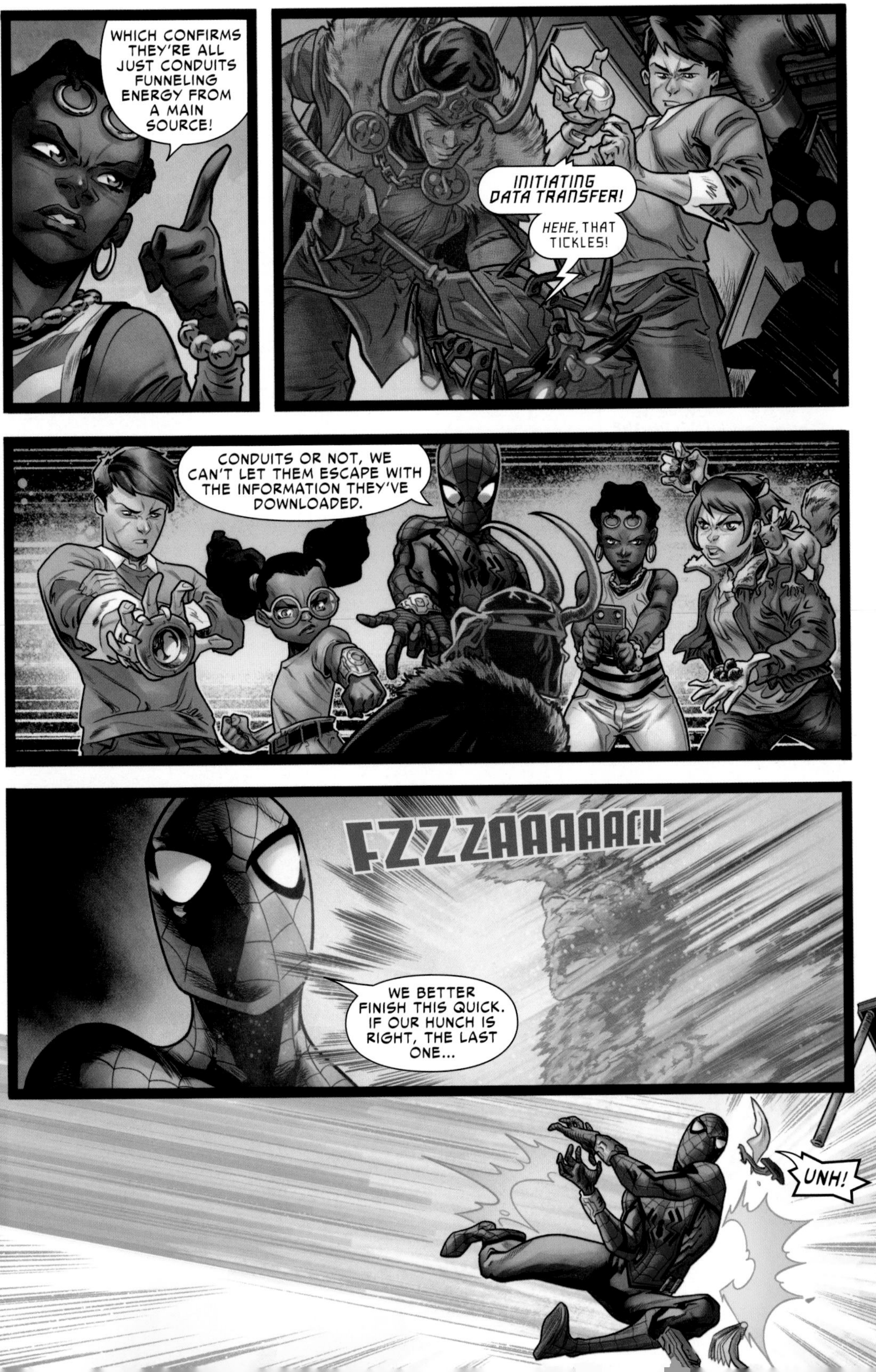
WHICH CONFIRMS THEY'RE ALL JUST CONDUITS FUNNELING ENERGY FROM A MAIN SOURCE!
INITIATING DATA TRANSFER!
HEHE, THAT TICKLES!
CONDUITS OR NOT, WE CAN'T LET THEM ESCAPE WITH THE INFORMATION THEY'VE DOWNLOADED.
FZZZAAAAACK
WE BETTER FINISH THIS QUICK. IF OUR HUNCH IS RIGHT, THE LAST ONE...
UNH!

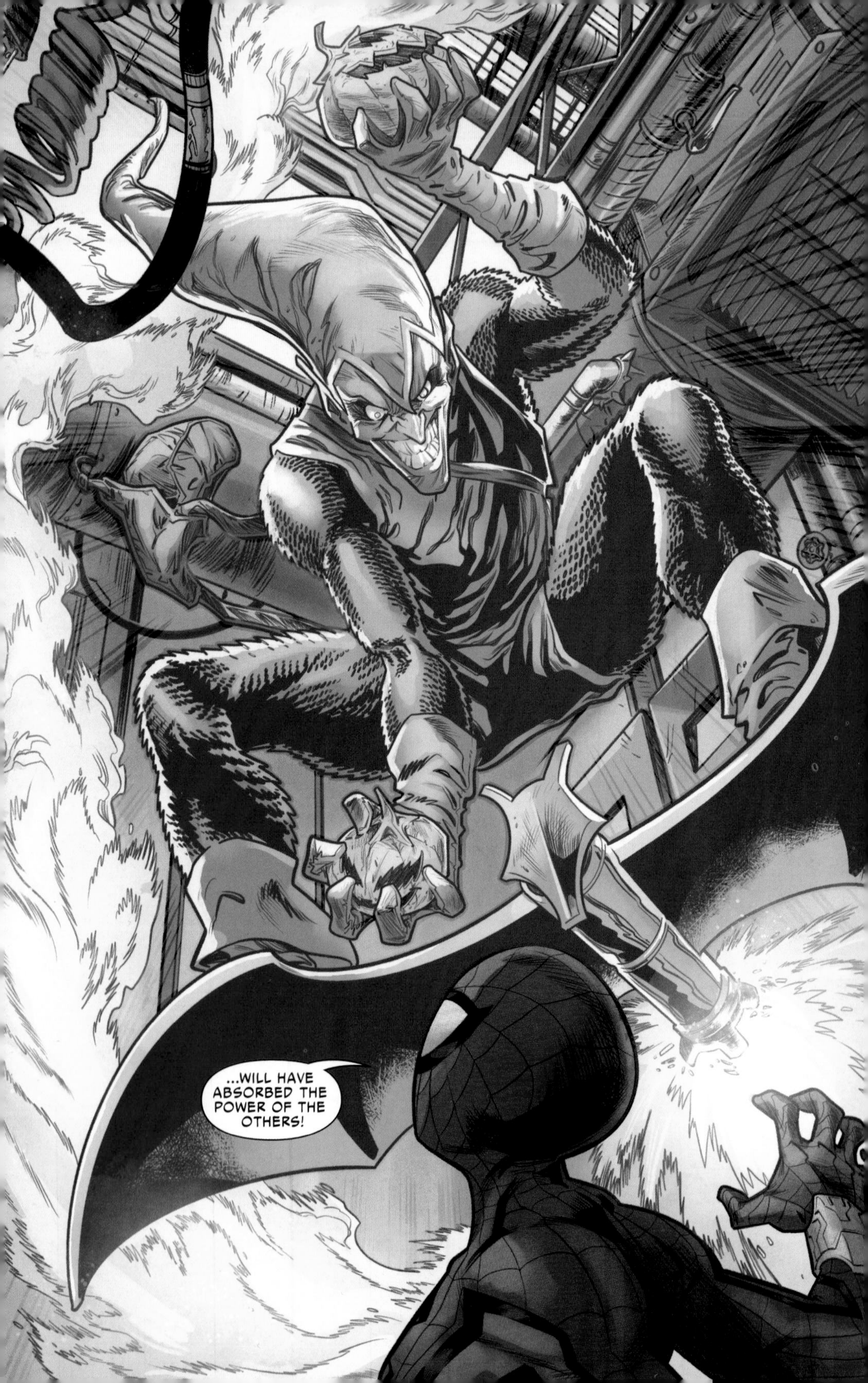
...WILL HAVE ABSORBED THE POWER OF THE OTHERS!

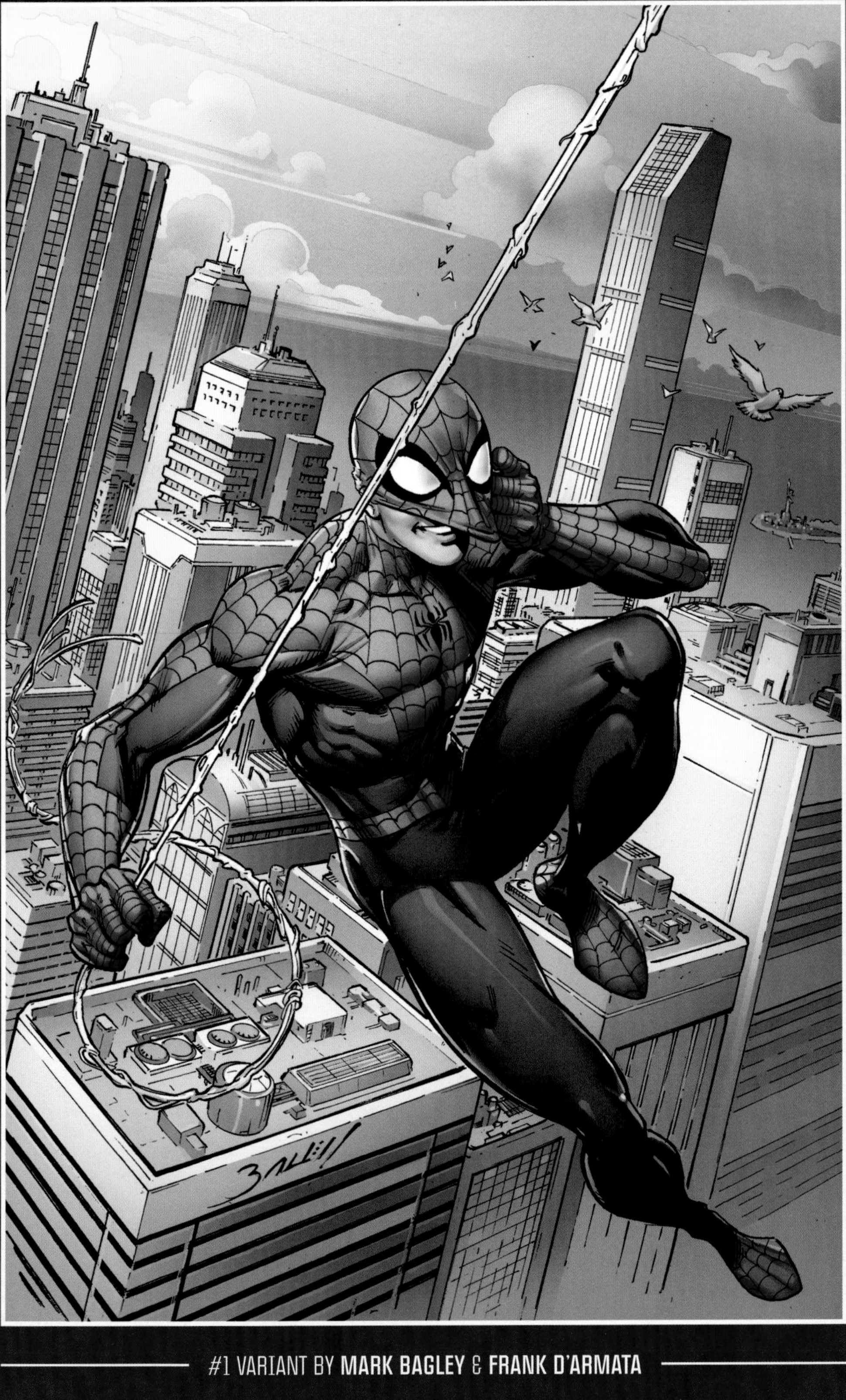

#1 VARIANT BY **MARK BAGLEY** & **FRANK D'ARMATA**

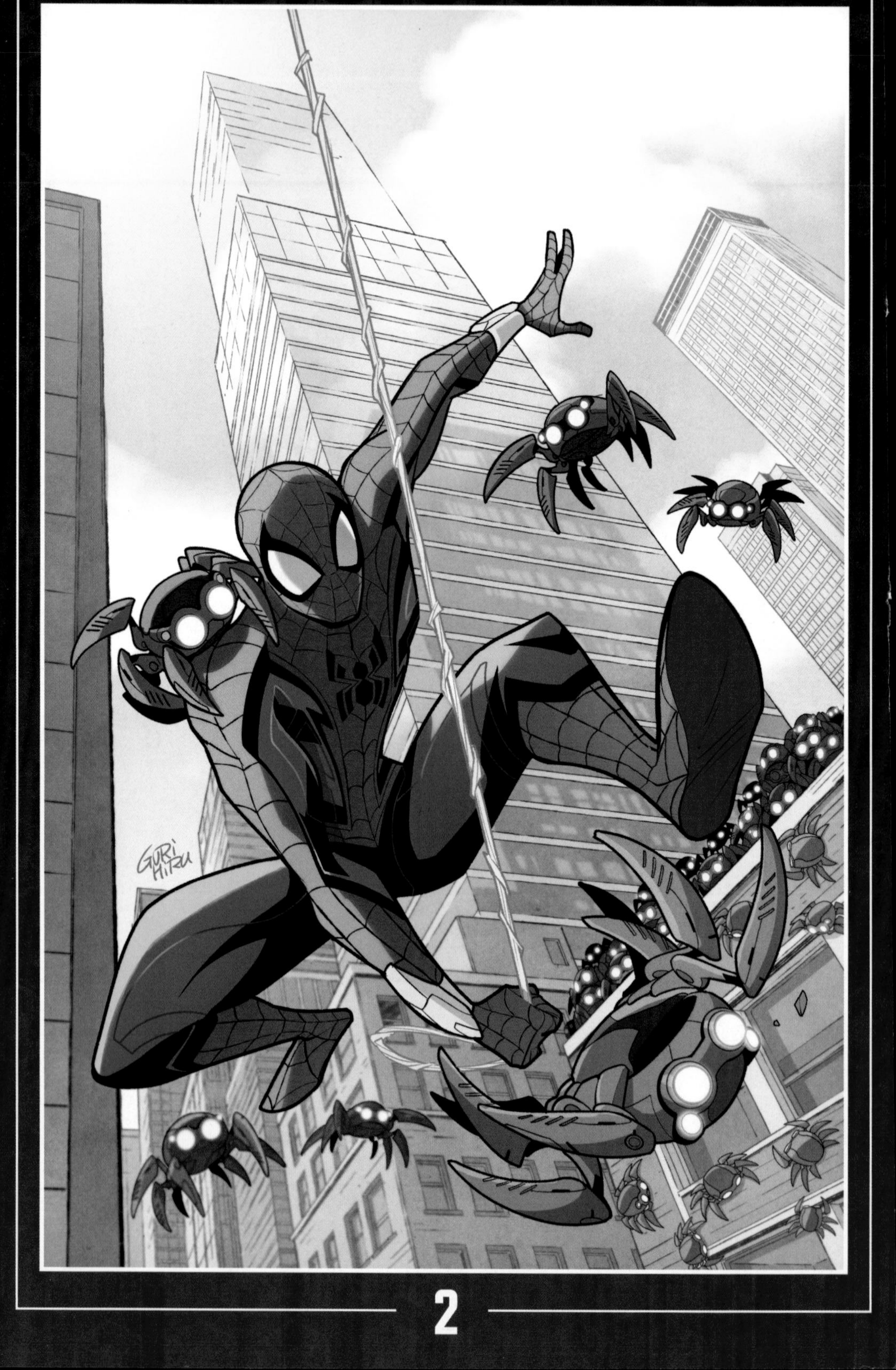
GURIHIRU

2

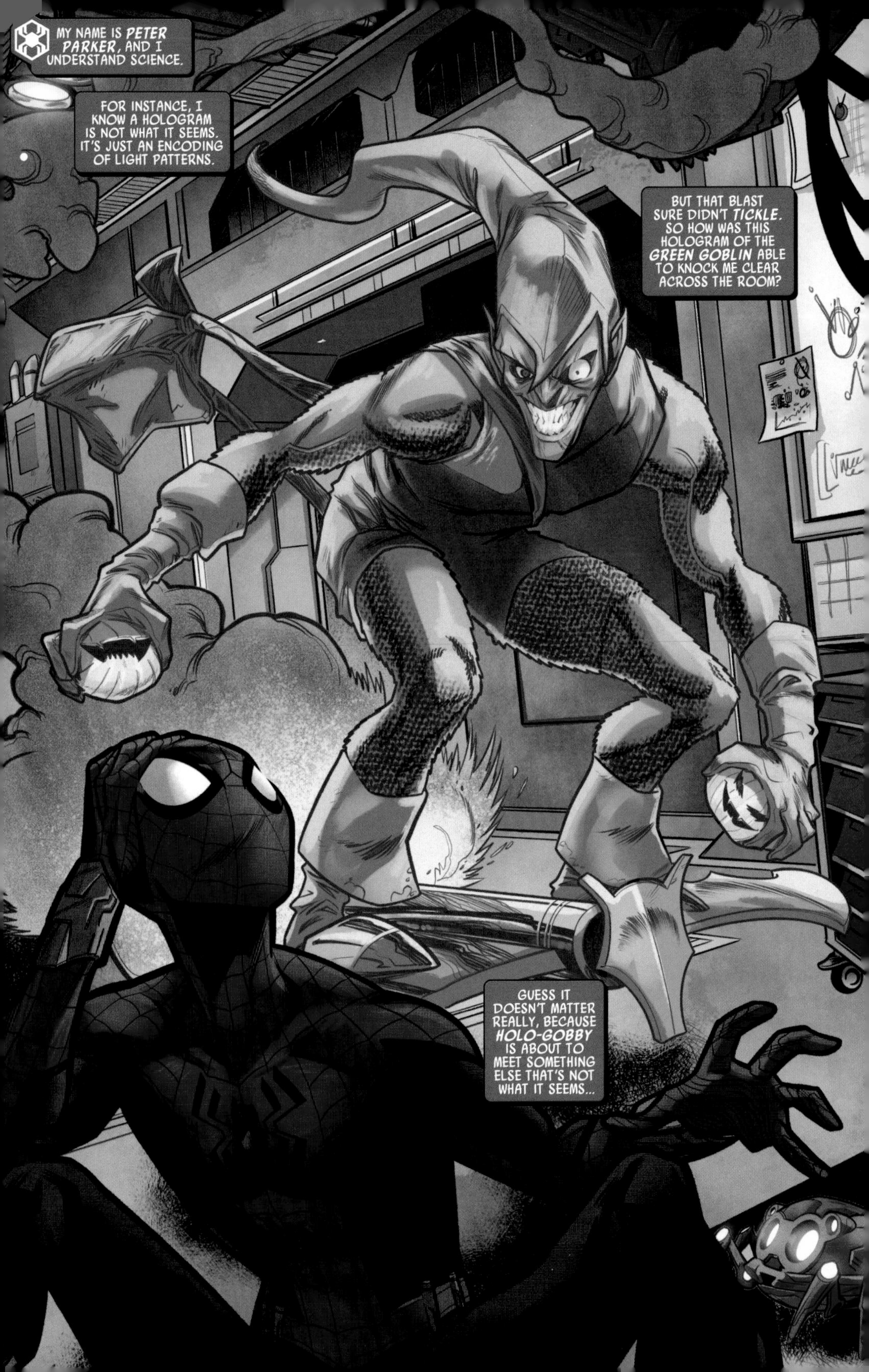
MY NAME IS PETER PARKER, AND I UNDERSTAND SCIENCE.
FOR INSTANCE, I KNOW A HOLOGRAM IS NOT WHAT IT SEEMS. IT'S JUST AN ENCODING OF LIGHT PATTERNS.
BUT THAT BLAST SURE DIDN'T TICKLE. SO HOW WAS THIS HOLOGRAM OF THE GREEN GOBLIN ABLE TO KNOCK ME CLEAR ACROSS THE ROOM?
GUESS IT DOESN'T MATTER REALLY, BECAUSE HOLO-GOBBY IS ABOUT TO MEET SOMETHING ELSE THAT'S NOT WHAT IT SEEMS...

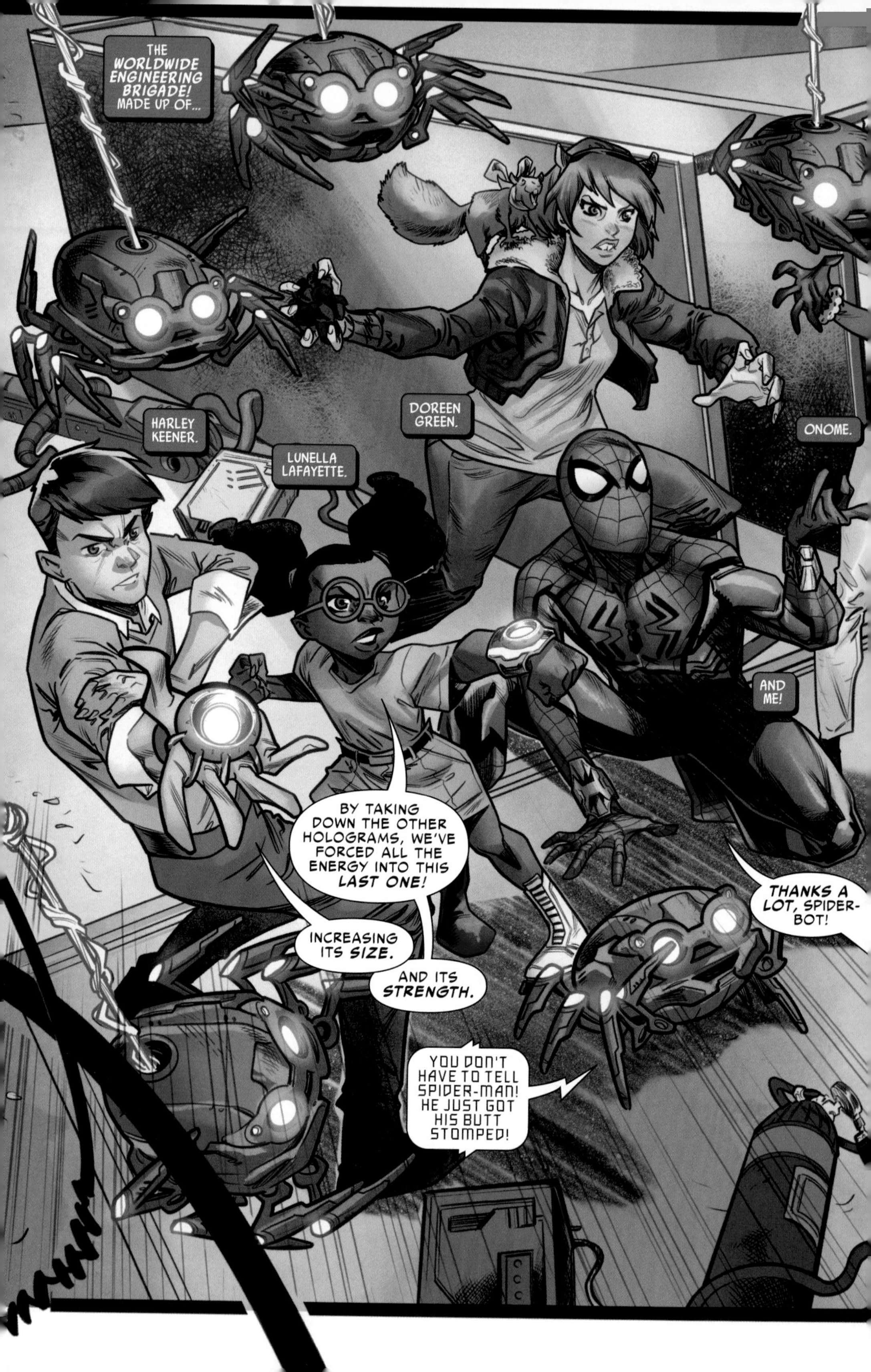

THE WORLDWIDE ENGINEERING BRIGADE! MADE UP OF...
HARLEY KEENER.
LUNELLA LAFAYETTE.
DOREEN GREEN.
ONOME.
AND ME!
BY TAKING DOWN THE OTHER HOLOGRAMS, WE'VE FORCED ALL THE ENERGY INTO THIS LAST ONE!
INCREASING ITS SIZE.
AND ITS STRENGTH.
THANKS A LOT, SPIDER-BOT!
YOU DON'T HAVE TO TELL SPIDER-MAN! HE JUST GOT HIS BUTT STOMPED!

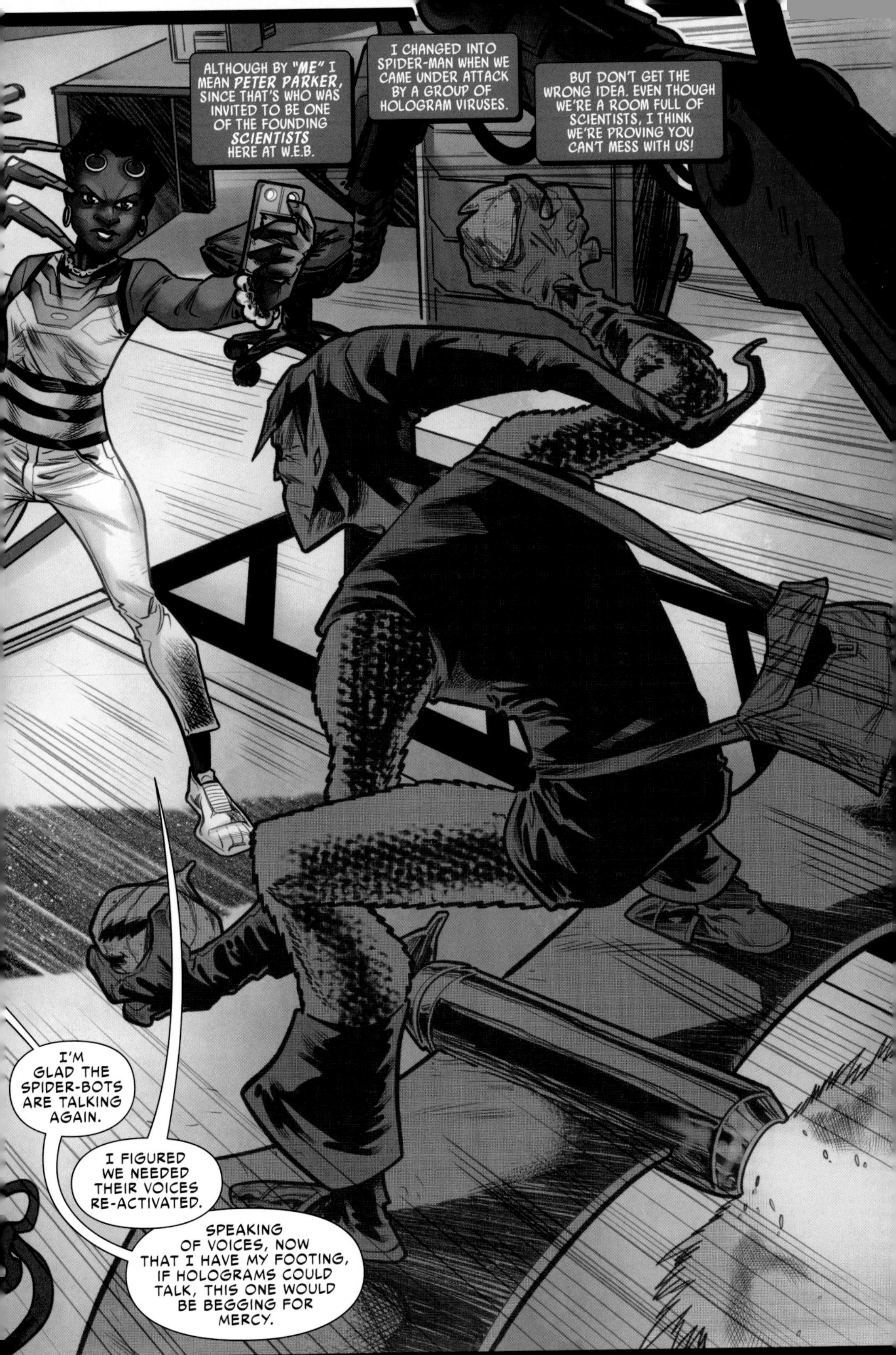
ALTHOUGH BY "ME" I MEAN PETER PARKER, SINCE THAT'S WHO WAS INVITED TO BE ONE OF THE FOUNDING SCIENTISTS HERE AT W.E.B.
I CHANGED INTO SPIDER-MAN WHEN WE CAME UNDER ATTACK BY A GROUP OF HOLOGRAM VIRUSES.
BUT DON'T GET THE WRONG IDEA. EVEN THOUGH WE'RE A ROOM FULL OF SCIENTISTS, I THINK WE'RE PROVING YOU CAN'T MESS WITH US!
I'M GLAD THE SPIDER-BOTS ARE TALKING AGAIN.
I FIGURED WE NEEDED THEIR VOICES RE-ACTIVATED.
SPEAKING OF VOICES, NOW THAT I HAVE MY FOOTING, IF HOLOGRAMS COULD TALK, THIS ONE WOULD BE BEGGING FOR MERCY.

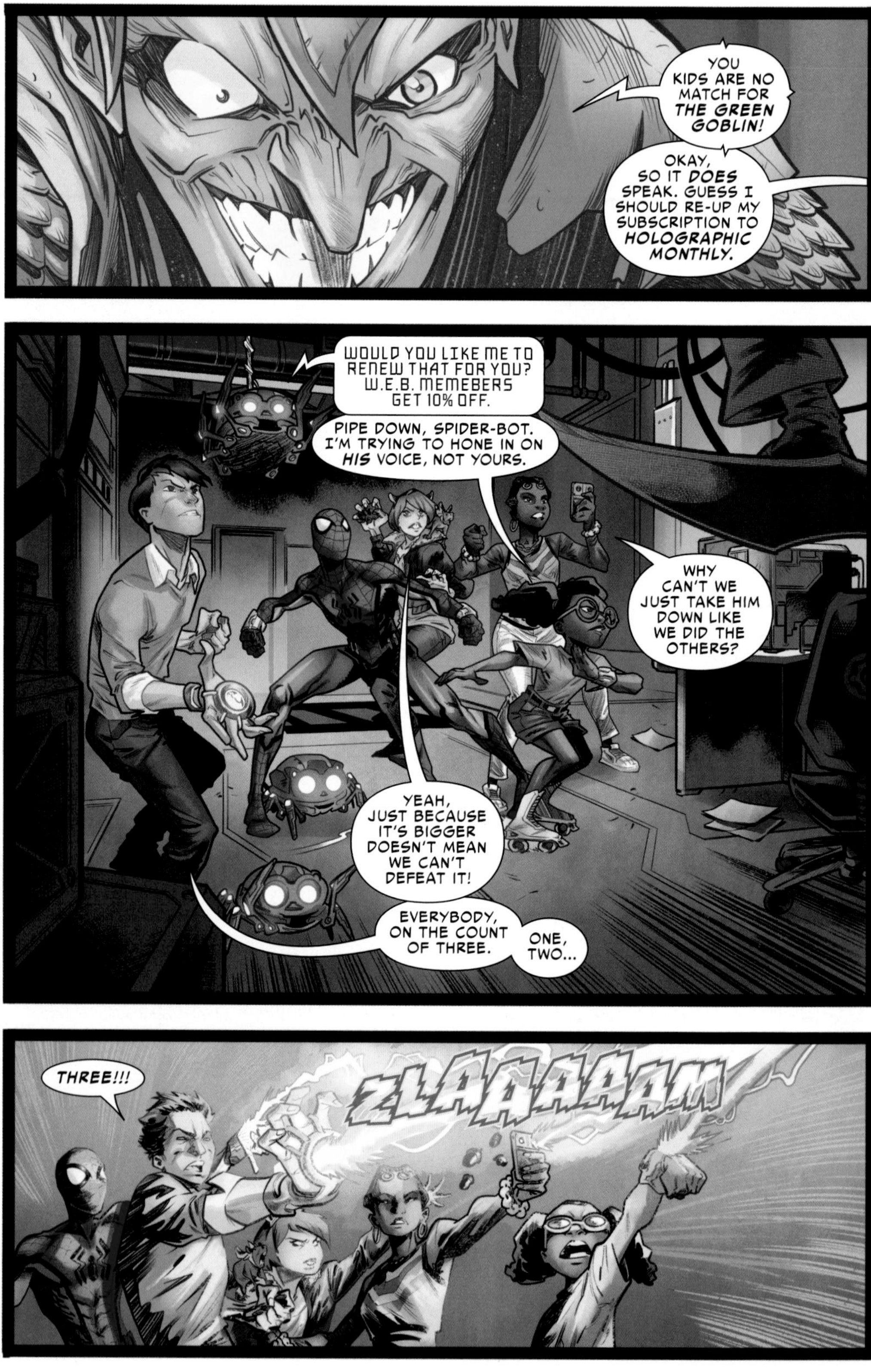
YOU KIDS ARE NO MATCH FOR THE GREEN GOBLIN!
OKAY, SO IT DOES SPEAK. GUESS I SHOULD RE-UP MY SUBSCRIPTION TO HOLOGRAPHIC MONTHLY.
WOULD YOU LIKE ME TO RENEW THAT FOR YOU? W.E.B. MEMEBERS GET 10% OFF.
PIPE DOWN, SPIDER-BOT. I'M TRYING TO HONE IN ON HIS VOICE, NOT YOURS.
WHY CAN'T WE JUST TAKE HIM DOWN LIKE WE DID THE OTHERS?
YEAH, JUST BECAUSE IT'S BIGGER DOESN'T MEAN WE CAN'T DEFEAT IT!
EVERYBODY, ON THE COUNT OF THREE.
ONE, TWO...
THREE!!!
ZLAAAAAAM

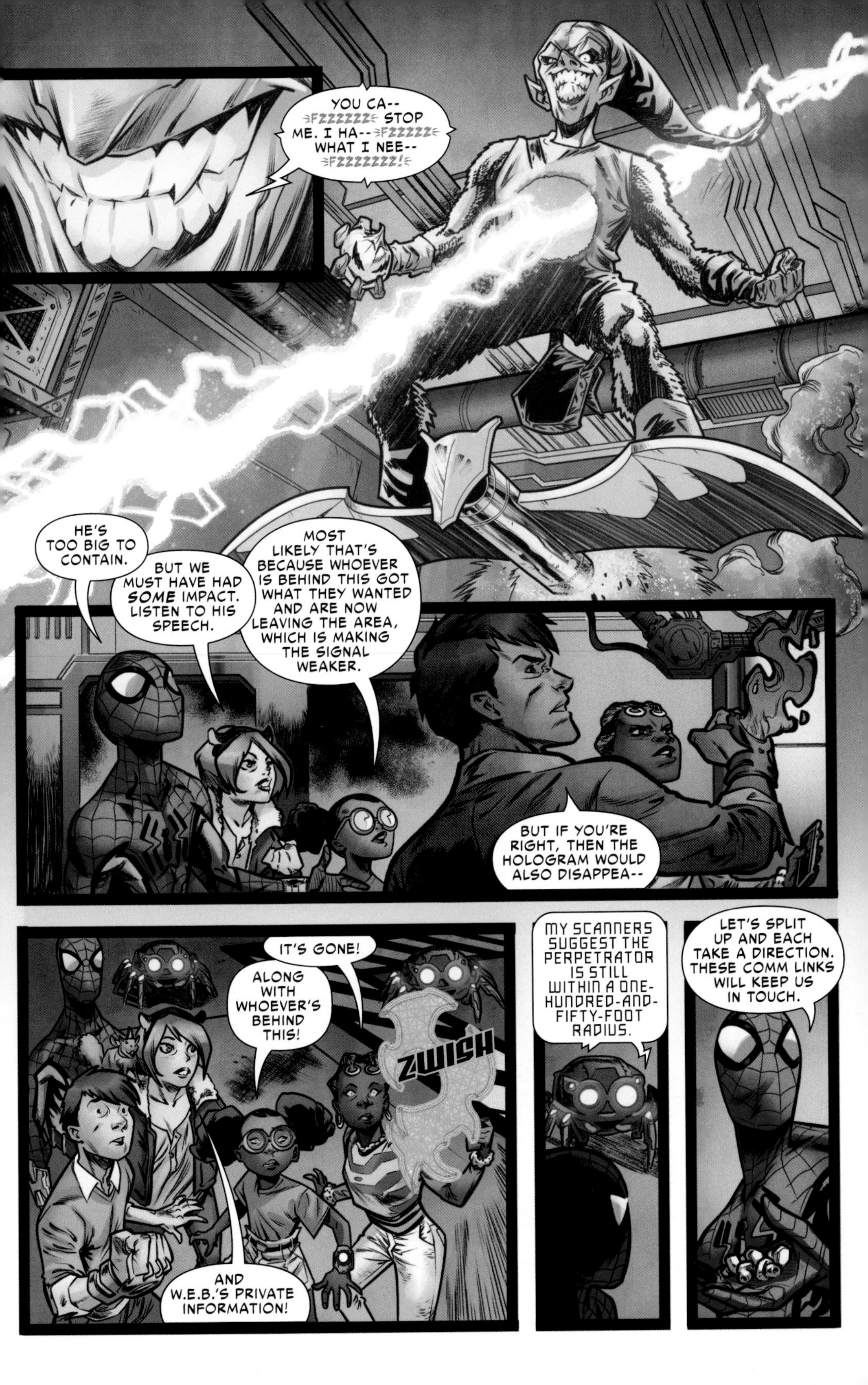
YOU CA-- FZZZZZZZ STOP ME. I HA-- FZZZZZZ WHAT I NEE-- FZZZZZZZZ!
HE'S TOO BIG TO CONTAIN.
BUT WE MUST HAVE HAD SOME IMPACT. LISTEN TO HIS SPEECH.
MOST LIKELY THAT'S BECAUSE WHOEVER IS BEHIND THIS GOT WHAT THEY WANTED AND ARE NOW LEAVING THE AREA, WHICH IS MAKING THE SIGNAL WEAKER.
BUT IF YOU'RE RIGHT, THEN THE HOLOGRAM WOULD ALSO DISAPPEA--
IT'S GONE!
ALONG WITH WHOEVER'S BEHIND THIS!
ZWISH
AND W.E.B.'S PRIVATE INFORMATION!
MY SCANNERS SUGGEST THE PERPETRATOR IS STILL WITHIN A ONE-HUNDRED-AND-FIFTY-FOOT RADIUS.
LET'S SPLIT UP AND EACH TAKE A DIRECTION. THESE COMM LINKS WILL KEEP US IN TOUCH.

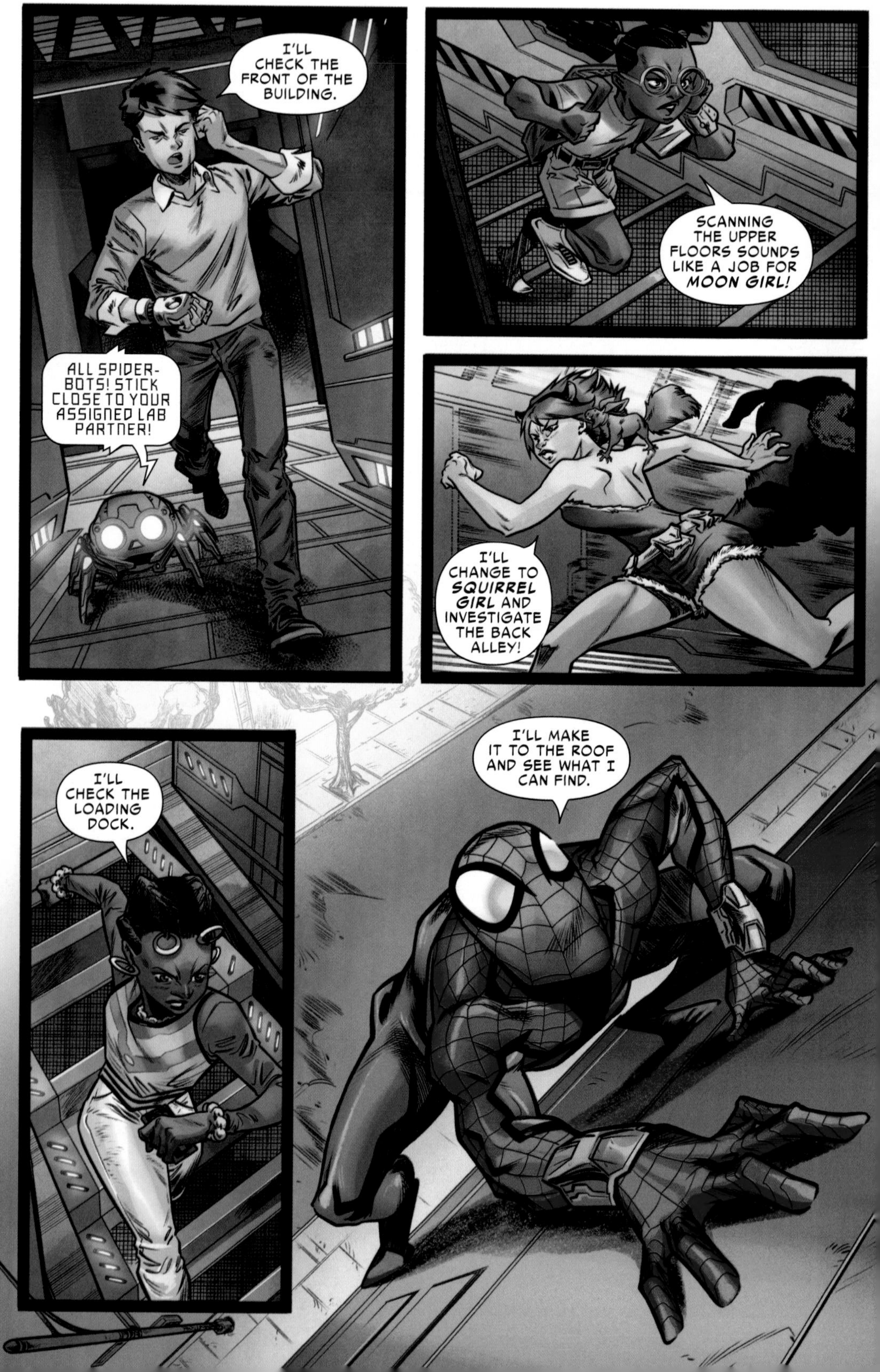
I'LL CHECK THE FRONT OF THE BUILDING.
ALL SPIDER-BOTS! STICK CLOSE TO YOUR ASSIGNED LAB PARTNER!
SCANNING THE UPPER FLOORS SOUNDS LIKE A JOB FOR MOON GIRL!
I'LL CHANGE TO SQUIRREL GIRL AND INVESTIGATE THE BACK ALLEY!
I'LL CHECK THE LOADING DOCK.
I'LL MAKE IT TO THE ROOF AND SEE WHAT I CAN FIND.

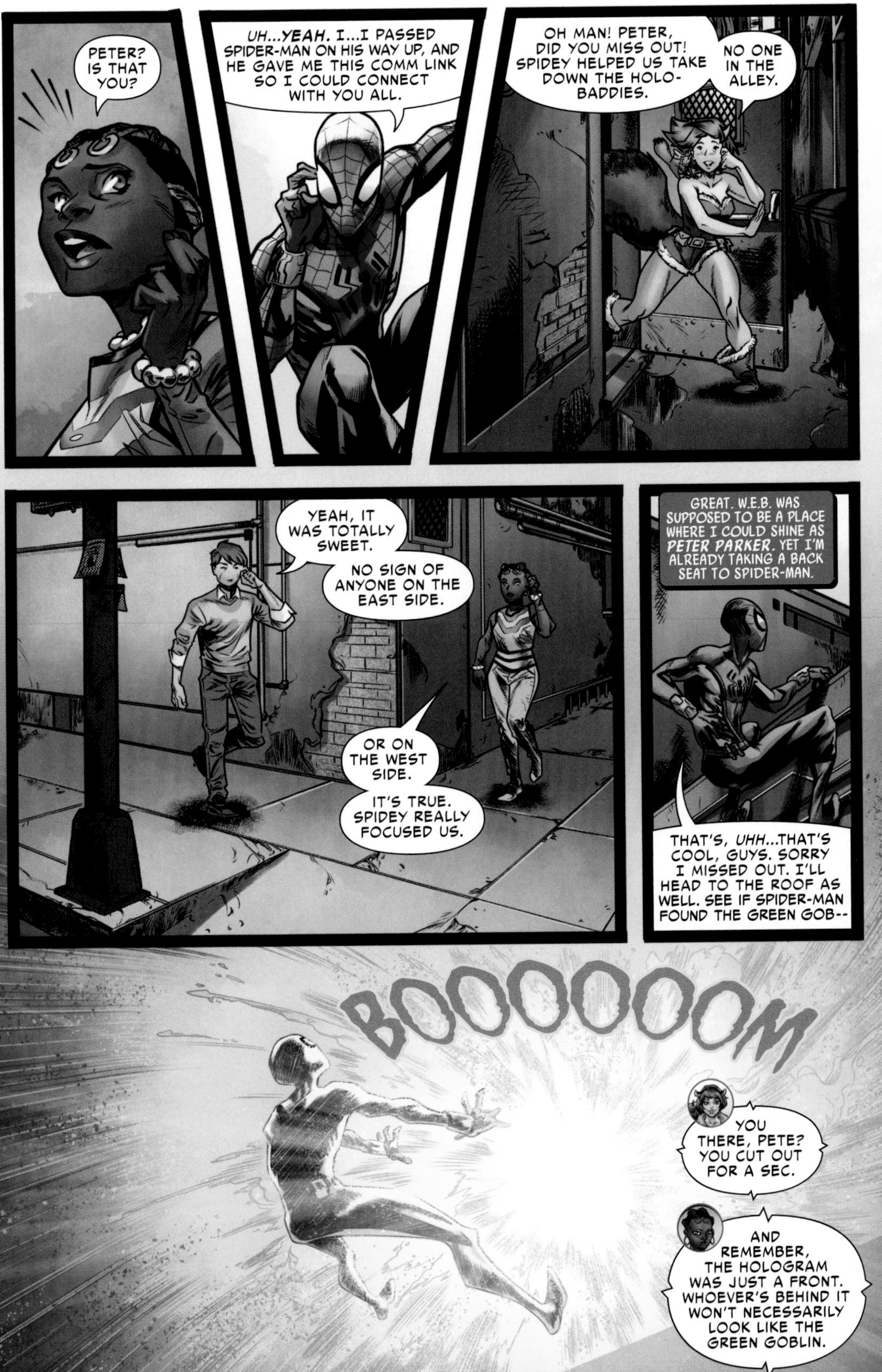
PETER? IS THAT YOU?
UH...YEAH. I...I PASSED SPIDER-MAN ON HIS WAY UP, AND HE GAVE ME THIS COMM LINK SO I COULD CONNECT WITH YOU ALL.
OH MAN! PETER, DID YOU MISS OUT! SPIDEY HELPED US TAKE DOWN THE HOLO-BADDIES.
NO ONE IN THE ALLEY.
YEAH, IT WAS TOTALLY SWEET.
NO SIGN OF ANYONE ON THE EAST SIDE.
OR ON THE WEST SIDE.
IT'S TRUE. SPIDEY REALLY FOCUSED US.
GREAT. W.E.B. WAS SUPPOSED TO BE A PLACE WHERE I COULD SHINE AS PETER PARKER. YET I'M ALREADY TAKING A BACK SEAT TO SPIDER-MAN.
THAT'S, UHH...THAT'S COOL, GUYS. SORRY I MISSED OUT. I'LL HEAD TO THE ROOF AS WELL. SEE IF SPIDER-MAN FOUND THE GREEN GOB--
BOOOOOOM
YOU THERE, PETE? YOU CUT OUT FOR A SEC.
AND REMEMBER, THE HOLOGRAM WAS JUST A FRONT. WHOEVER'S BEHIND IT WON'T NECESSARILY LOOK LIKE THE GREEN GOBLIN.

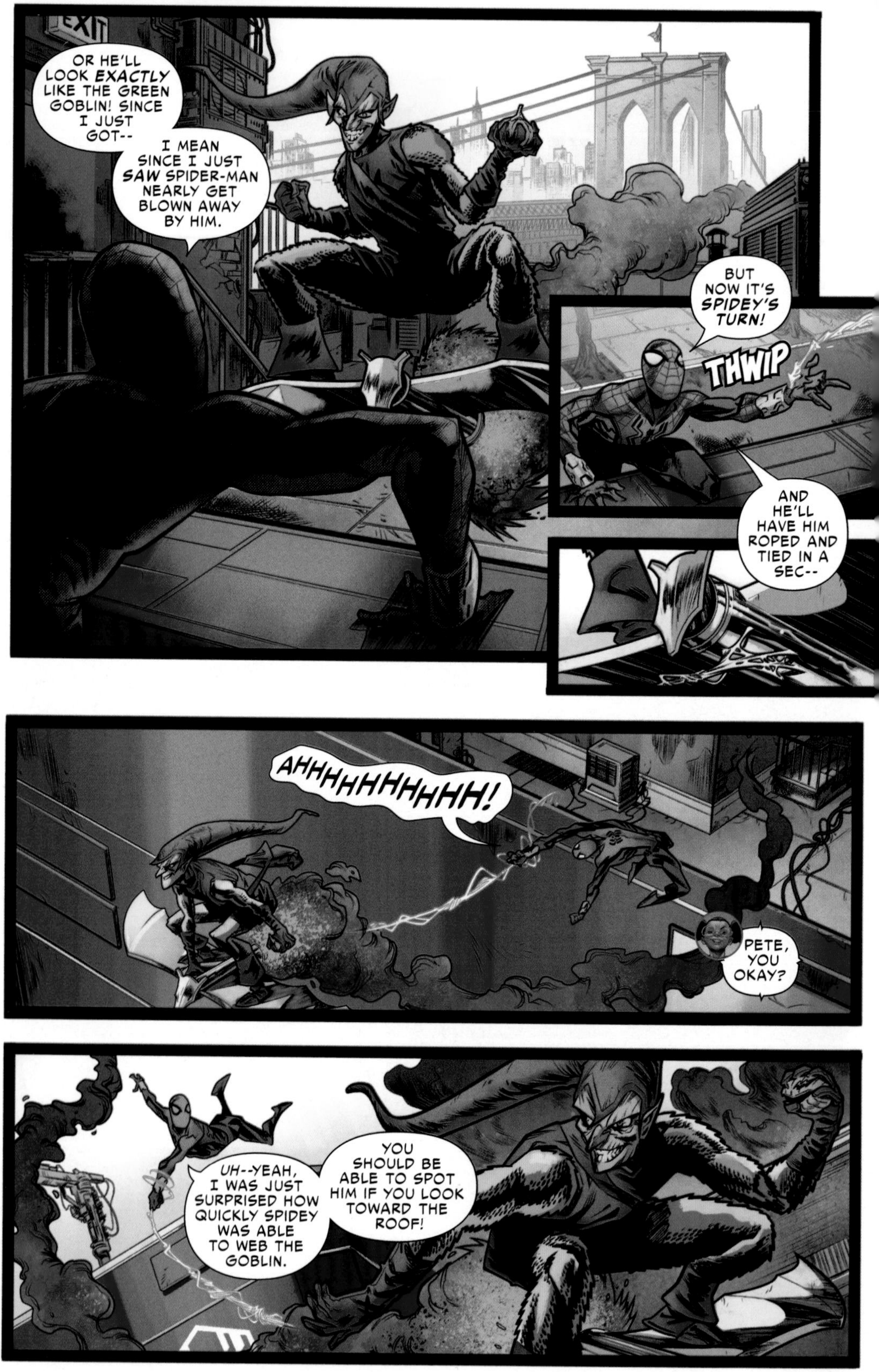

OR HE'LL LOOK EXACTLY LIKE THE GREEN GOBLIN! SINCE I JUST GOT--
I MEAN SINCE I JUST SAW SPIDER-MAN NEARLY GET BLOWN AWAY BY HIM.
EXIT
BUT NOW IT'S SPIDEY'S TURN!
THWIP
AND HE'LL HAVE HIM ROPED AND TIED IN A SEC--
AHHHHHHHHHH!
PETE, YOU OKAY?
UH--YEAH, I WAS JUST SURPRISED HOW QUICKLY SPIDEY WAS ABLE TO WEB THE GOBLIN.
YOU SHOULD BE ABLE TO SPOT HIM IF YOU LOOK TOWARD THE ROOF!

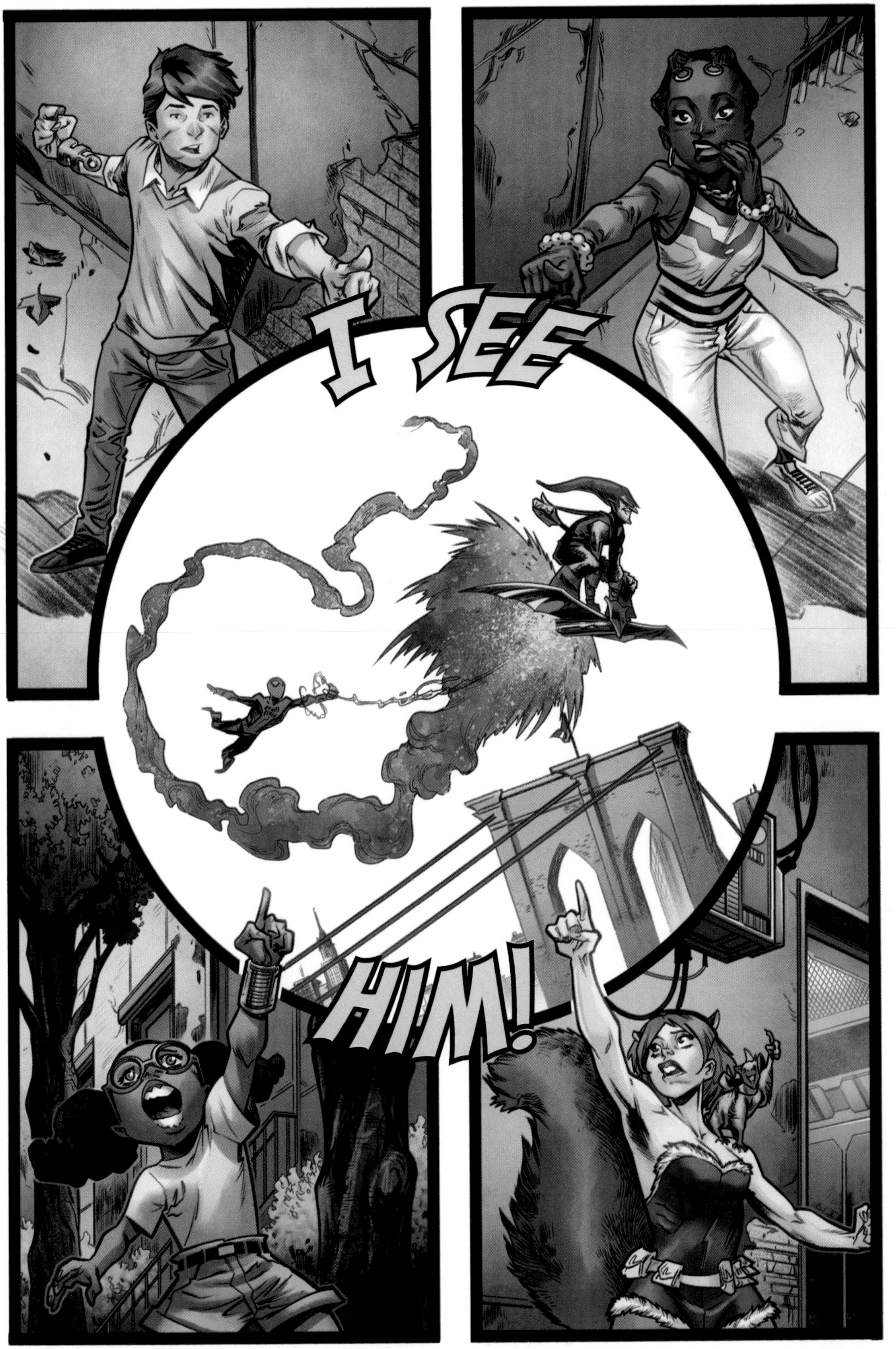
I SEE
HIM!

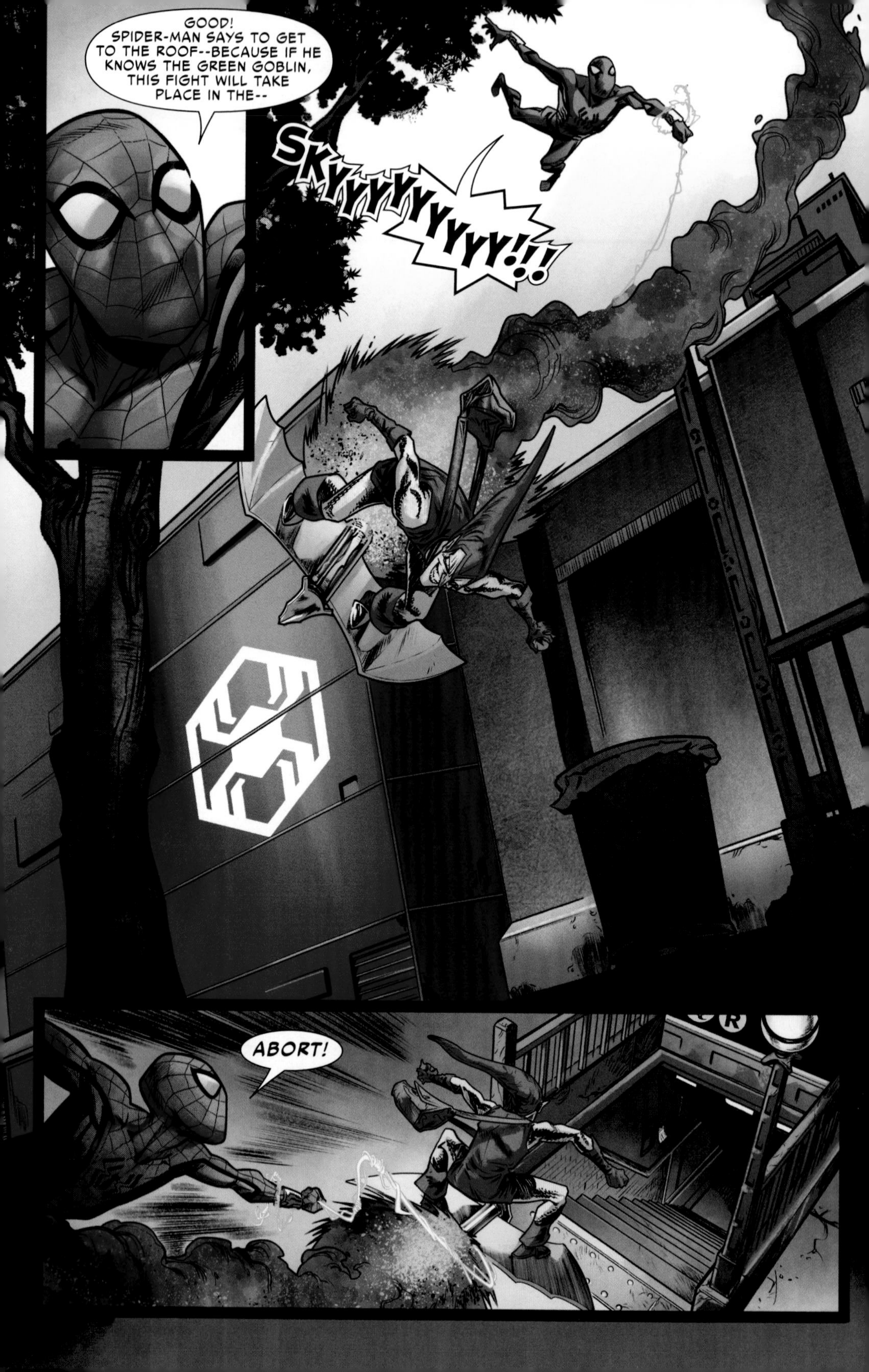
GOOD! SPIDER-MAN SAYS TO GET TO THE ROOF--BECAUSE IF HE KNOWS THE GREEN GOBLIN, THIS FIGHT WILL TAKE PLACE IN THE--
SKYYYYYYYYYY!!!
ABORT!

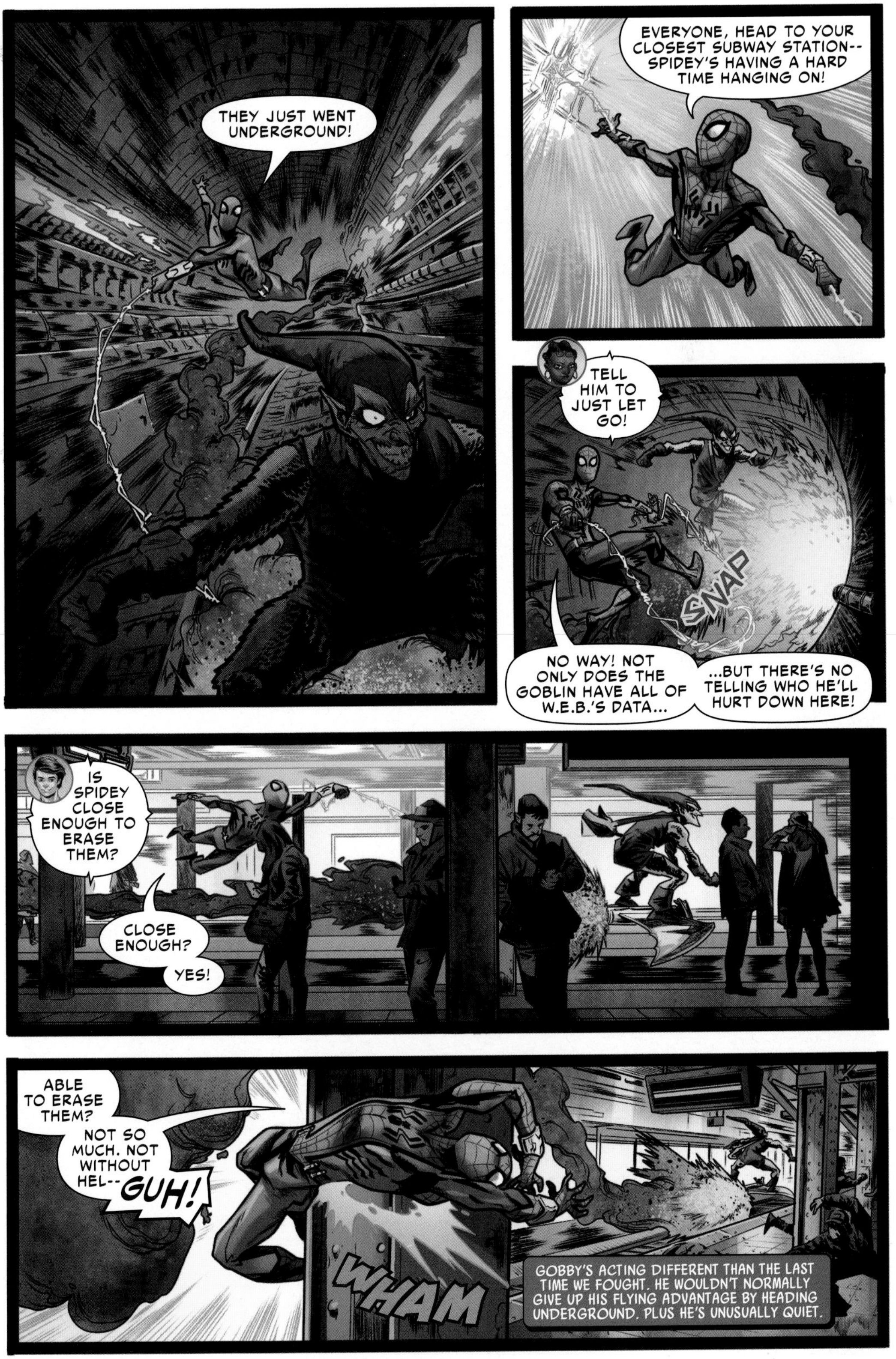
THEY JUST WENT UNDERGROUND!
EVERYONE, HEAD TO YOUR CLOSEST SUBWAY STATION-- SPIDEY'S HAVING A HARD TIME HANGING ON!
TELL HIM TO JUST LET GO!
SNAP
NO WAY! NOT ONLY DOES THE GOBLIN HAVE ALL OF W.E.B.'S DATA...
...BUT THERE'S NO TELLING WHO HE'LL HURT DOWN HERE!
IS SPIDEY CLOSE ENOUGH TO ERASE THEM?
CLOSE ENOUGH?
YES!
ABLE TO ERASE THEM?
NOT SO MUCH. NOT WITHOUT HEL--GUH!
WHAM
GOBBY'S ACTING DIFFERENT THAN THE LAST TIME WE FOUGHT. HE WOULDN'T NORMALLY GIVE UP HIS FLYING ADVANTAGE BY HEADING UNDERGROUND. PLUS HE'S UNUSUALLY QUIET.

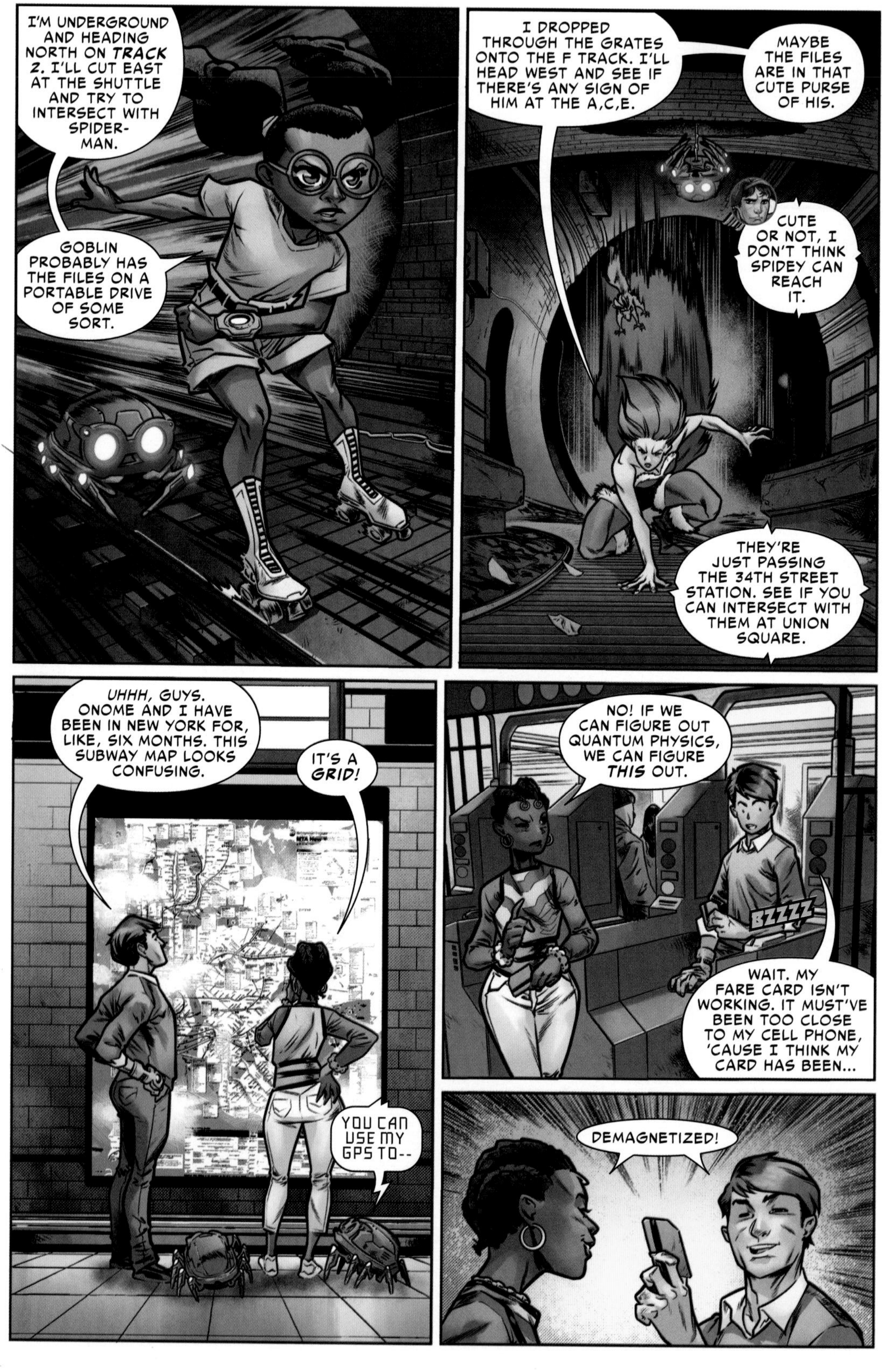

I'M UNDERGROUND AND HEADING NORTH ON *TRACK 2.* I'LL CUT EAST AT THE SHUTTLE AND TRY TO INTERSECT WITH SPIDER-MAN.
GOBLIN PROBABLY HAS THE FILES ON A PORTABLE DRIVE OF SOME SORT.
I DROPPED THROUGH THE GRATES ONTO THE F TRACK. I'LL HEAD WEST AND SEE IF THERE'S ANY SIGN OF HIM AT THE A,C,E.
MAYBE THE FILES ARE IN THAT CUTE PURSE OF HIS.
CUTE OR NOT, I DON'T THINK SPIDEY CAN REACH IT.
THEY'RE JUST PASSING THE 34TH STREET STATION. SEE IF YOU CAN INTERSECT WITH THEM AT UNION SQUARE.
UHHH, GUYS. ONOME AND I HAVE BEEN IN NEW YORK FOR, LIKE, SIX MONTHS. THIS SUBWAY MAP LOOKS CONFUSING.
IT'S A *GRID!*
YOU CAN USE MY GPS TO--
NO! IF WE CAN FIGURE OUT QUANTUM PHYSICS, WE CAN FIGURE *THIS* OUT.
BZZZZ
WAIT. MY FARE CARD ISN'T WORKING. IT MUST'VE BEEN TOO CLOSE TO MY CELL PHONE, 'CAUSE I THINK MY CARD HAS BEEN...
DEMAGNETIZED!

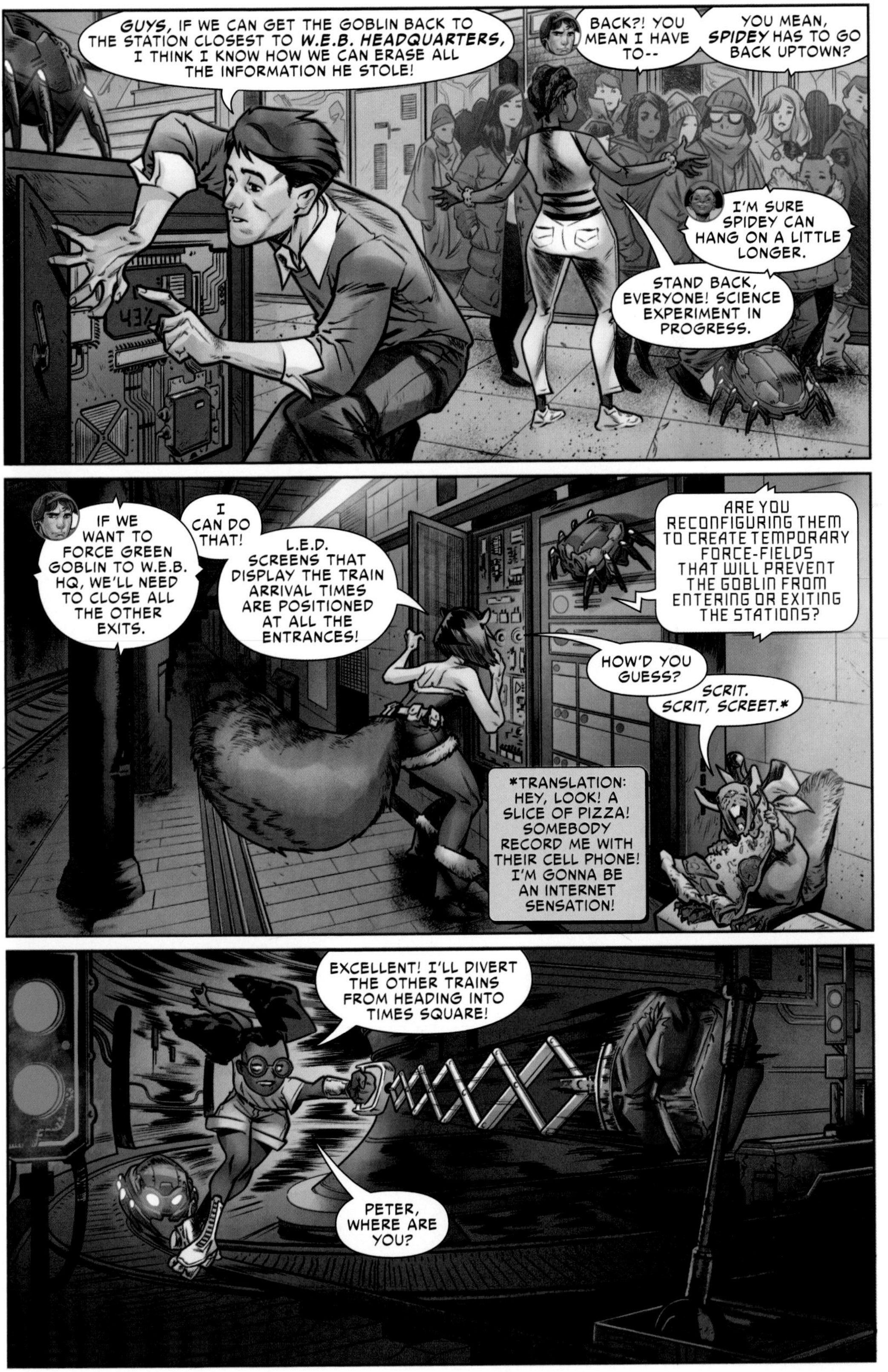
GUYS, IF WE CAN GET THE GOBLIN BACK TO THE STATION CLOSEST TO W.E.B. HEADQUARTERS, I THINK I KNOW HOW WE CAN ERASE ALL THE INFORMATION HE STOLE!
BACK?! YOU MEAN I HAVE TO--
YOU MEAN, SPIDEY HAS TO GO BACK UPTOWN?
I'M SURE SPIDEY CAN HANG ON A LITTLE LONGER.
STAND BACK, EVERYONE! SCIENCE EXPERIMENT IN PROGRESS.
43%
IF WE WANT TO FORCE GREEN GOBLIN TO W.E.B. HQ, WE'LL NEED TO CLOSE ALL THE OTHER EXITS.
I CAN DO THAT!
L.E.D. SCREENS THAT DISPLAY THE TRAIN ARRIVAL TIMES ARE POSITIONED AT ALL THE ENTRANCES!
ARE YOU RECONFIGURING THEM TO CREATE TEMPORARY FORCE-FIELDS THAT WILL PREVENT THE GOBLIN FROM ENTERING OR EXITING THE STATIONS?
HOW'D YOU GUESS?
SCRIT. SCRIT, SCREET.*
*TRANSLATION: HEY, LOOK! A SLICE OF PIZZA! SOMEBODY RECORD ME WITH THEIR CELL PHONE! I'M GONNA BE AN INTERNET SENSATION!
EXCELLENT! I'LL DIVERT THE OTHER TRAINS FROM HEADING INTO TIMES SQUARE!
PETER, WHERE ARE YOU?

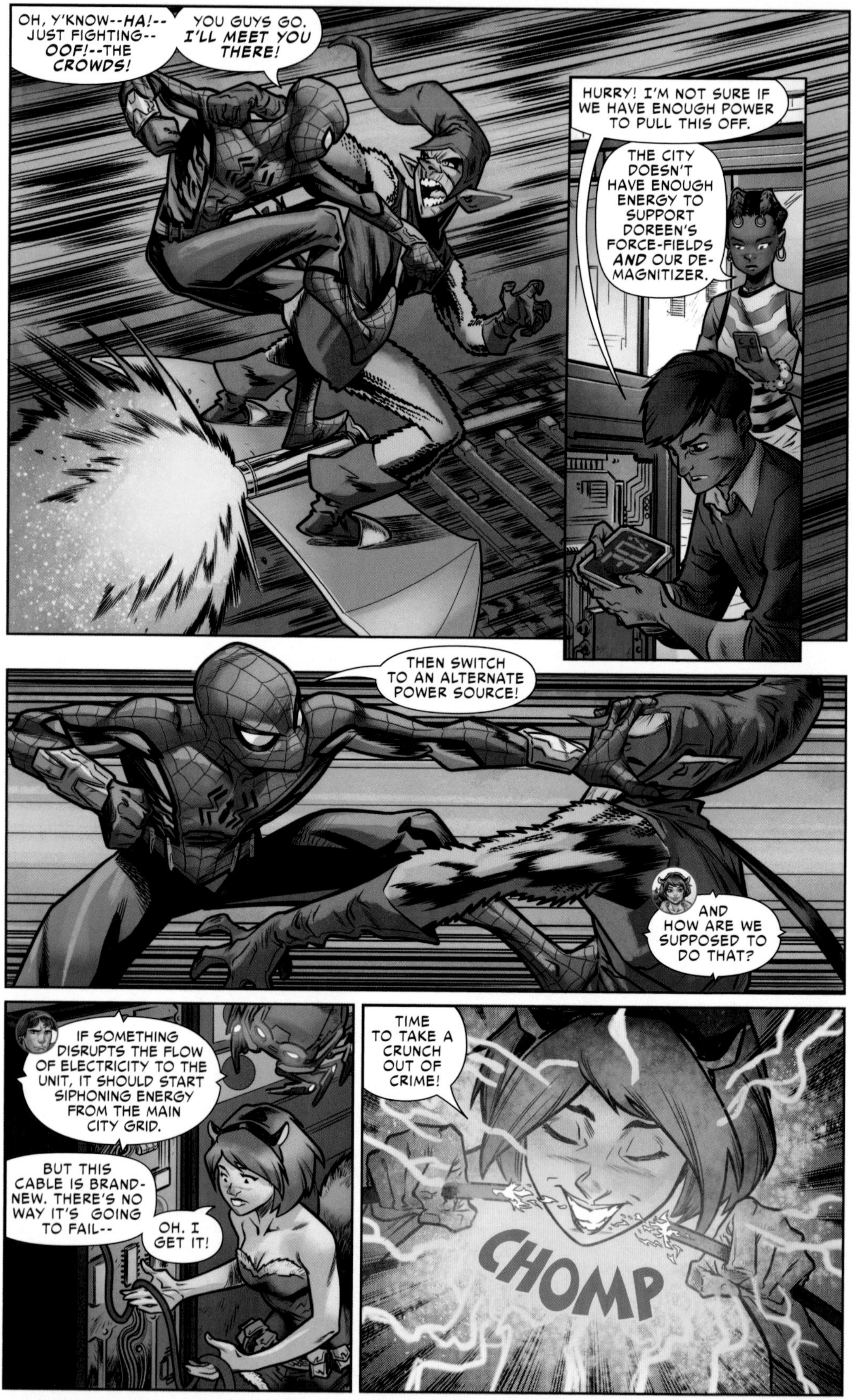
OH, Y'KNOW--HA!--JUST FIGHTING--OOF!--THE CROWDS!
YOU GUYS GO. I'LL MEET YOU THERE!
HURRY! I'M NOT SURE IF WE HAVE ENOUGH POWER TO PULL THIS OFF.
THE CITY DOESN'T HAVE ENOUGH ENERGY TO SUPPORT DOREEN'S FORCE-FIELDS AND OUR DE-MAGNITIZER.
THEN SWITCH TO AN ALTERNATE POWER SOURCE!
AND HOW ARE WE SUPPOSED TO DO THAT?
IF SOMETHING DISRUPTS THE FLOW OF ELECTRICITY TO THE UNIT, IT SHOULD START SIPHONING ENERGY FROM THE MAIN CITY GRID.
BUT THIS CABLE IS BRAND-NEW. THERE'S NO WAY IT'S GOING TO FAIL--
OH. I GET IT!
TIME TO TAKE A CRUNCH OUT OF CRIME!
CHOMP

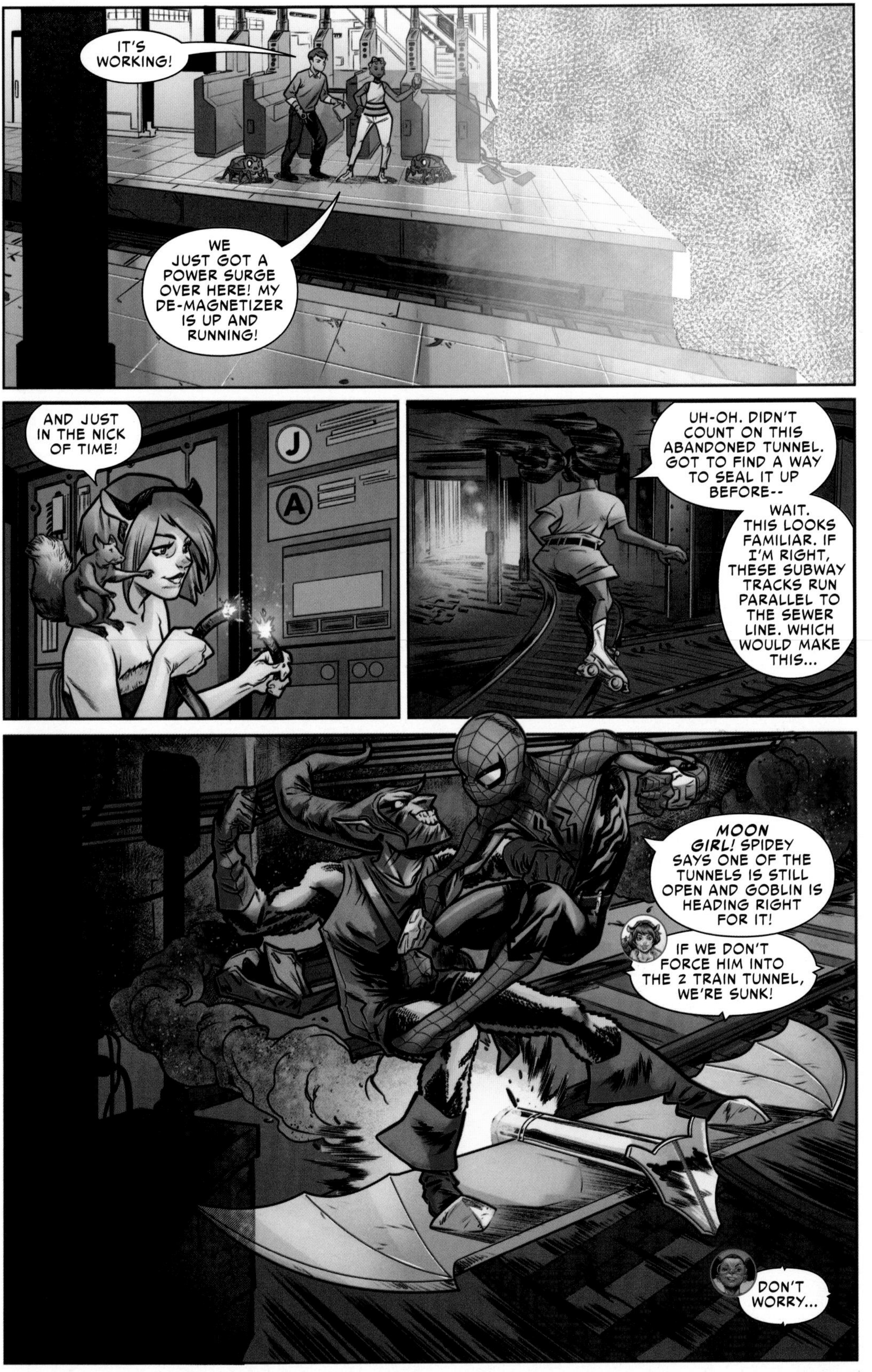
IT'S WORKING!
WE JUST GOT A POWER SURGE OVER HERE! MY DE-MAGNETIZER IS UP AND RUNNING!
AND JUST IN THE NICK OF TIME!
UH-OH. DIDN'T COUNT ON THIS ABANDONED TUNNEL. GOT TO FIND A WAY TO SEAL IT UP BEFORE--
WAIT. THIS LOOKS FAMILIAR. IF I'M RIGHT, THESE SUBWAY TRACKS RUN PARALLEL TO THE SEWER LINE. WHICH WOULD MAKE THIS...
MOON GIRL! SPIDEY SAYS ONE OF THE TUNNELS IS STILL OPEN AND GOBLIN IS HEADING RIGHT FOR IT!
IF WE DON'T FORCE HIM INTO THE 2 TRAIN TUNNEL, WE'RE SUNK!
DON'T WORRY...

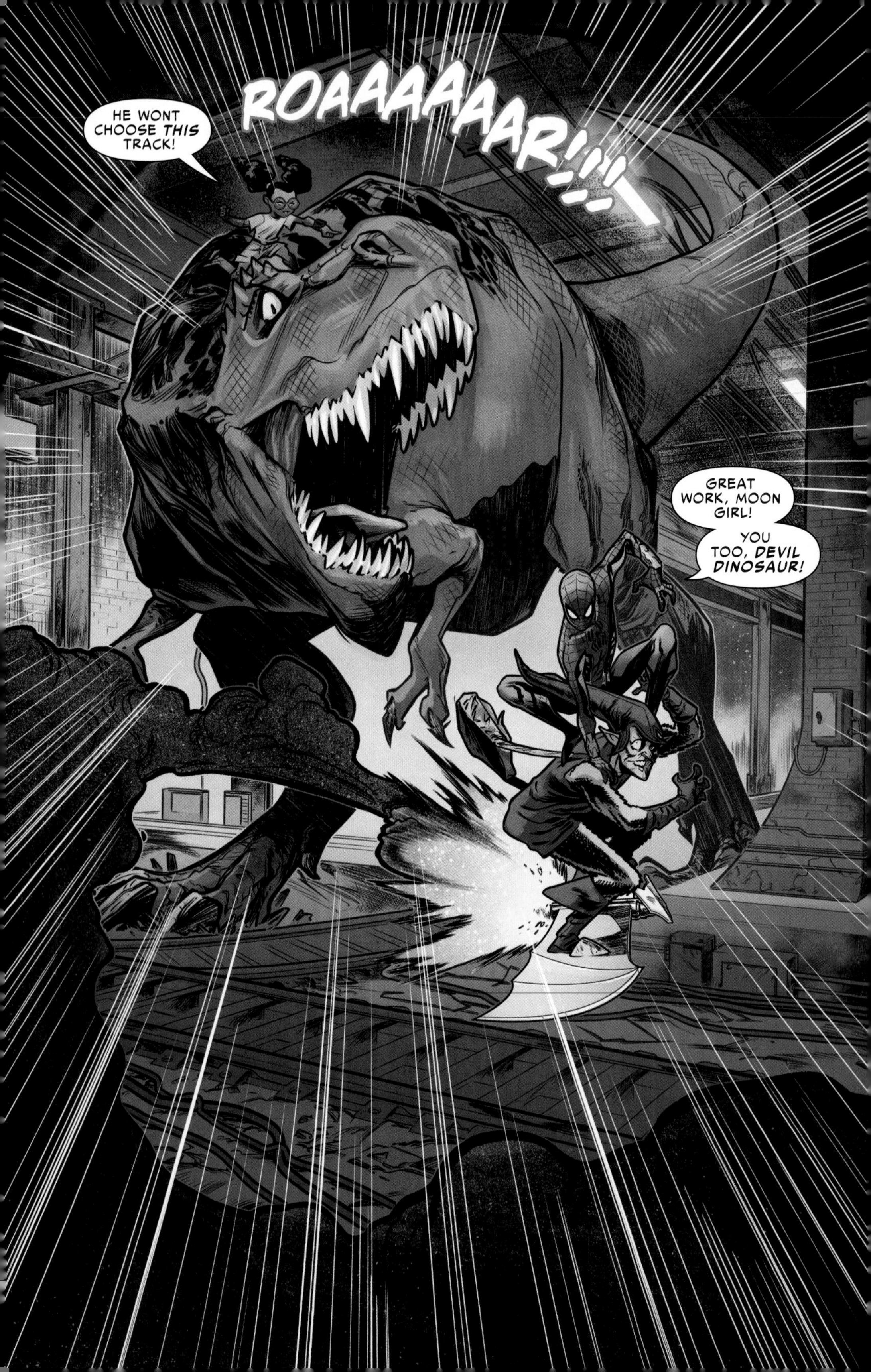
HE WONT CHOOSE THIS TRACK!
ROAAAAAAAR!!!!!
GREAT WORK, MOON GIRL!
YOU TOO, DEVIL DINOSAUR!

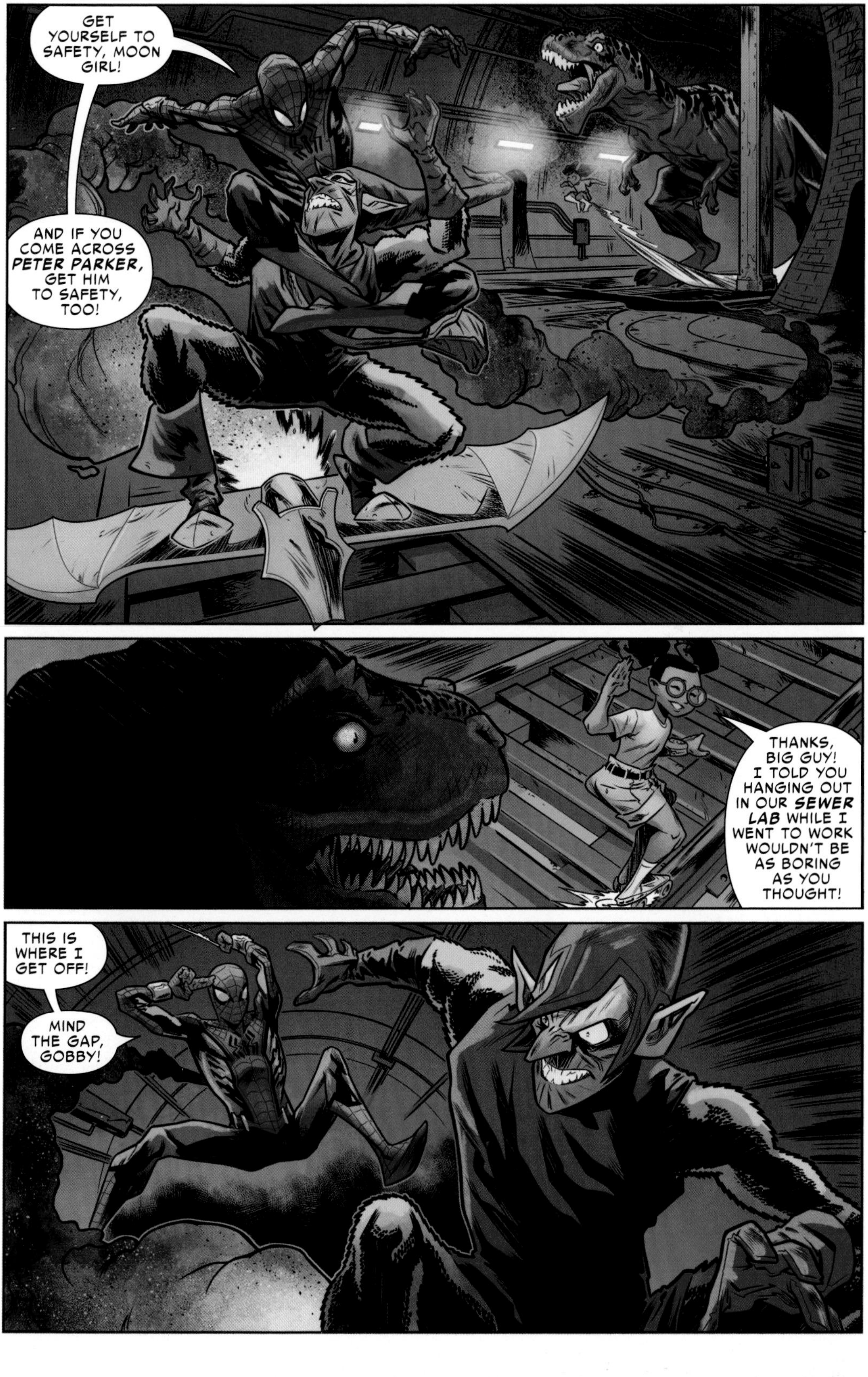
GET YOURSELF TO SAFETY, MOON GIRL!
AND IF YOU COME ACROSS **PETER PARKER,** GET HIM TO SAFETY, TOO!
THANKS, BIG GUY! I TOLD YOU HANGING OUT IN OUR **SEWER LAB** WHILE I WENT TO WORK WOULDN'T BE AS BORING AS YOU THOUGHT!
THIS IS WHERE I GET OFF!
MIND THE GAP, GOBBY!

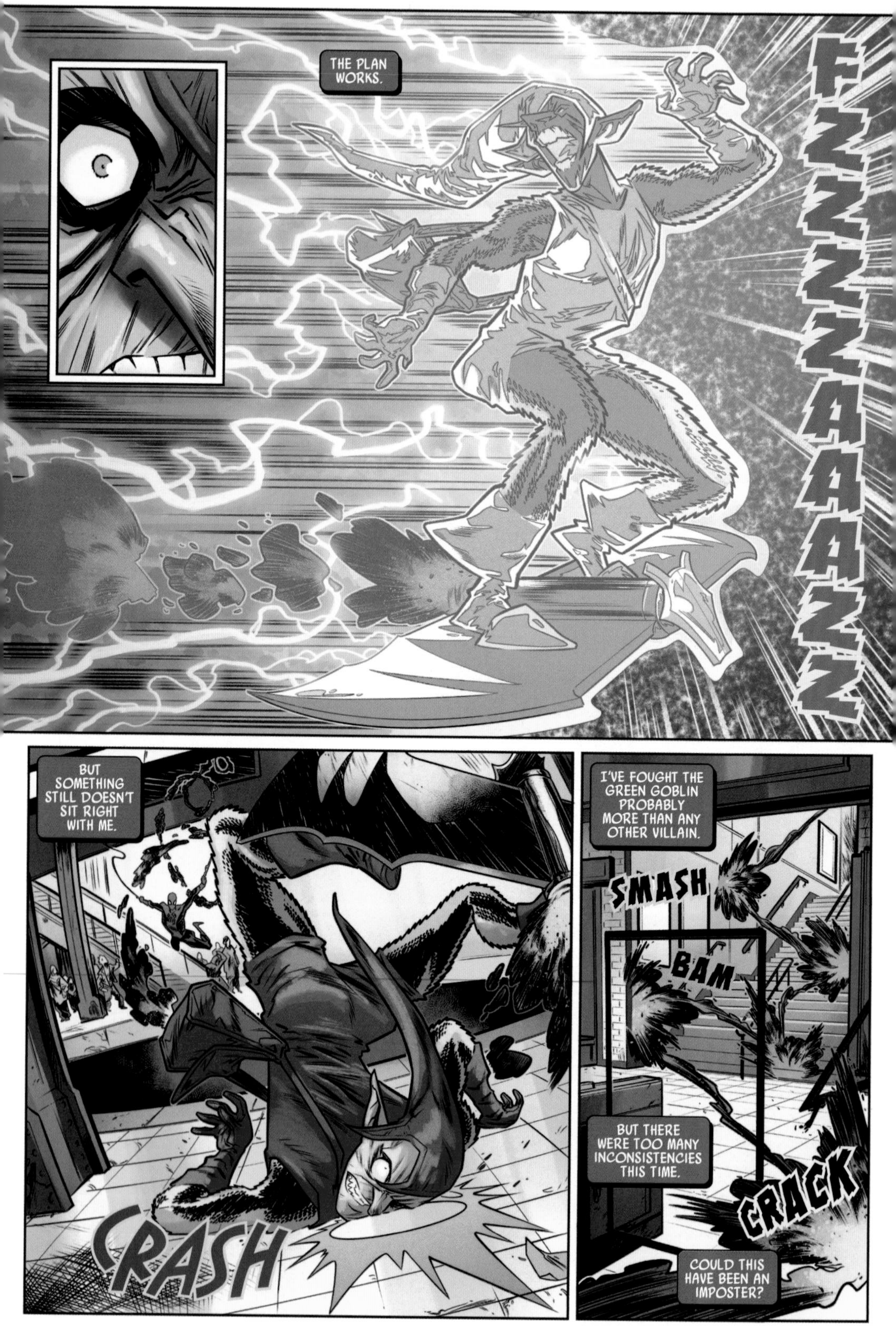
THE PLAN WORKS.
FZZZZAAAAZZ
BUT SOMETHING STILL DOESN'T SIT RIGHT WITH ME.
CRASH
I'VE FOUGHT THE GREEN GOBLIN PROBABLY MORE THAN ANY OTHER VILLAIN.
SMASH
BAM
BUT THERE WERE TOO MANY INCONSISTENCIES THIS TIME.
CRACK
COULD THIS HAVE BEEN AN IMPOSTER?

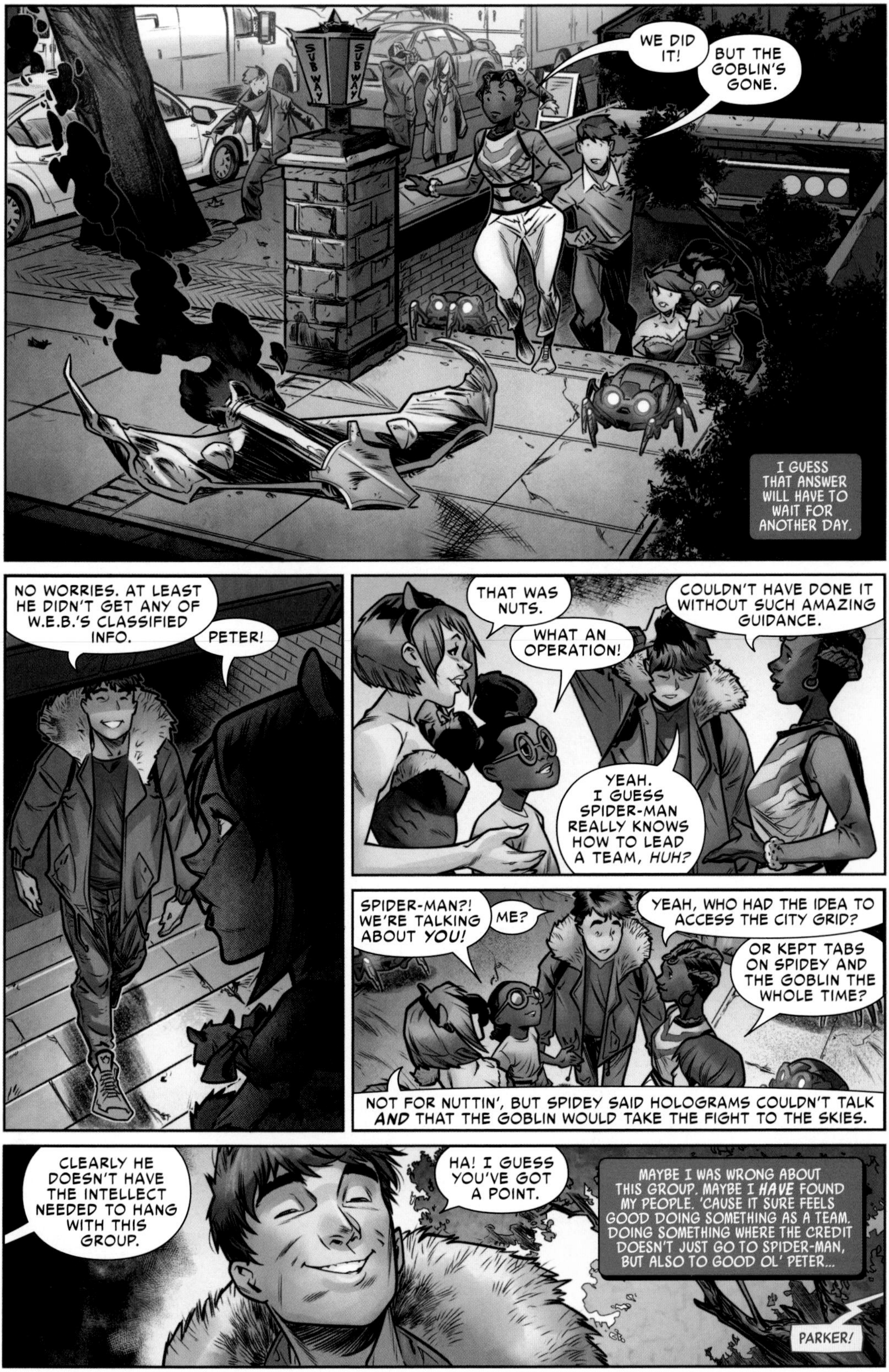
SUB WAY
SUB WAY
WE DID IT!
BUT THE GOBLIN'S GONE.
I GUESS THAT ANSWER WILL HAVE TO WAIT FOR ANOTHER DAY.
NO WORRIES. AT LEAST HE DIDN'T GET ANY OF W.E.B.'S CLASSIFIED INFO.
PETER!
THAT WAS NUTS.
WHAT AN OPERATION!
COULDN'T HAVE DONE IT WITHOUT SUCH AMAZING GUIDANCE.
YEAH. I GUESS SPIDER-MAN REALLY KNOWS HOW TO LEAD A TEAM, *HUH?*
SPIDER-MAN?! WE'RE TALKING ABOUT *YOU!*
ME?
YEAH, WHO HAD THE IDEA TO ACCESS THE CITY GRID?
OR KEPT TABS ON SPIDEY AND THE GOBLIN THE WHOLE TIME?
NOT FOR NUTTIN', BUT SPIDEY SAID HOLOGRAMS COULDN'T TALK *AND* THAT THE GOBLIN WOULD TAKE THE FIGHT TO THE SKIES.
CLEARLY HE DOESN'T HAVE THE INTELLECT NEEDED TO HANG WITH THIS GROUP.
HA! I GUESS YOU'VE GOT A POINT.
MAYBE I WAS WRONG ABOUT THIS GROUP. MAYBE I *HAVE* FOUND MY PEOPLE. 'CAUSE IT SURE FEELS GOOD DOING SOMETHING AS A TEAM. DOING SOMETHING WHERE THE CREDIT DOESN'T JUST GO TO SPIDER-MAN, BUT ALSO TO GOOD OL' PETER...
PARKER!

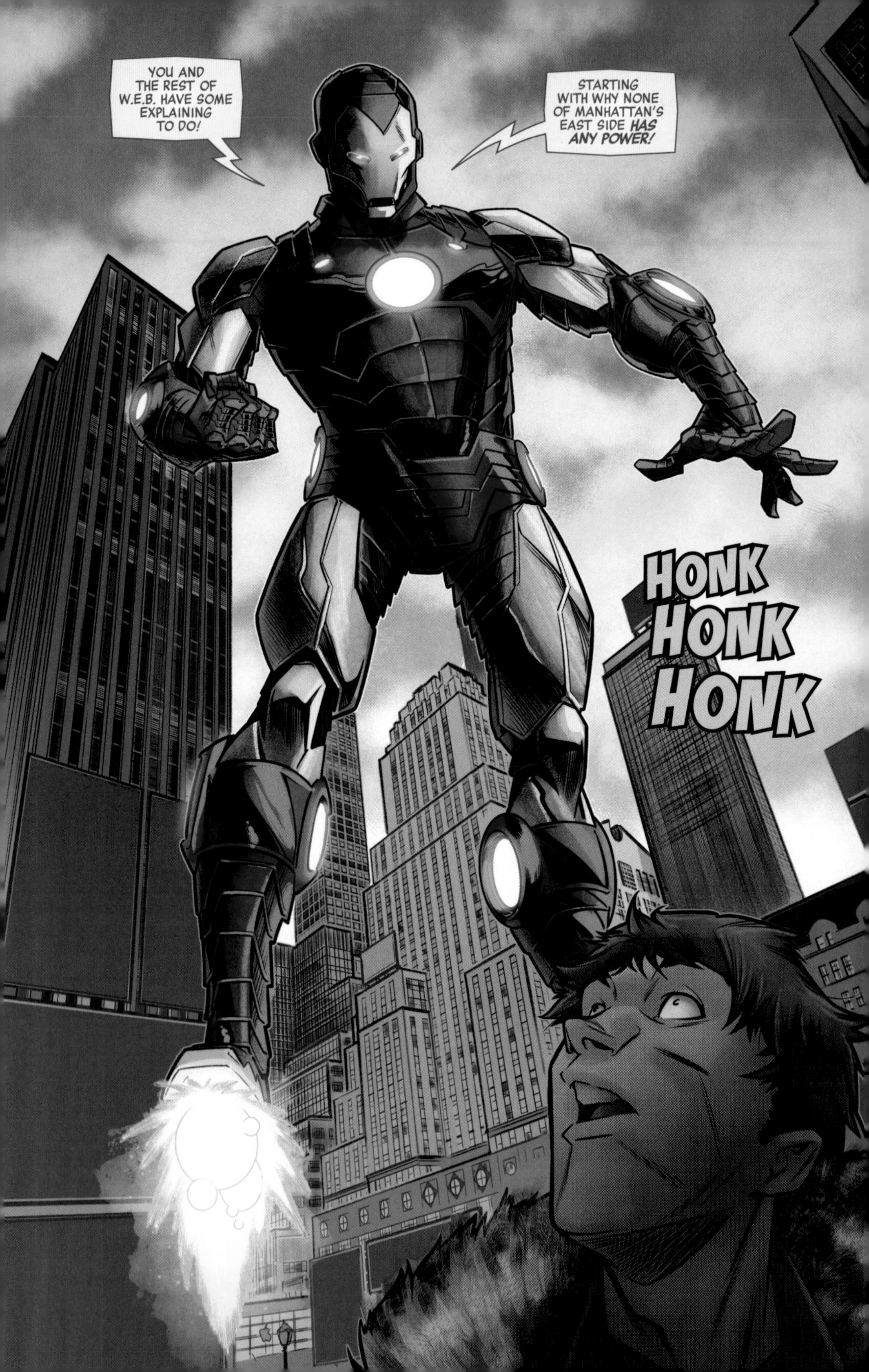
YOU AND THE REST OF W.E.B. HAVE SOME EXPLAINING TO DO!
STARTING WITH WHY NONE OF MANHATTAN'S EAST SIDE HAS ANY POWER!
HONK HONK HONK

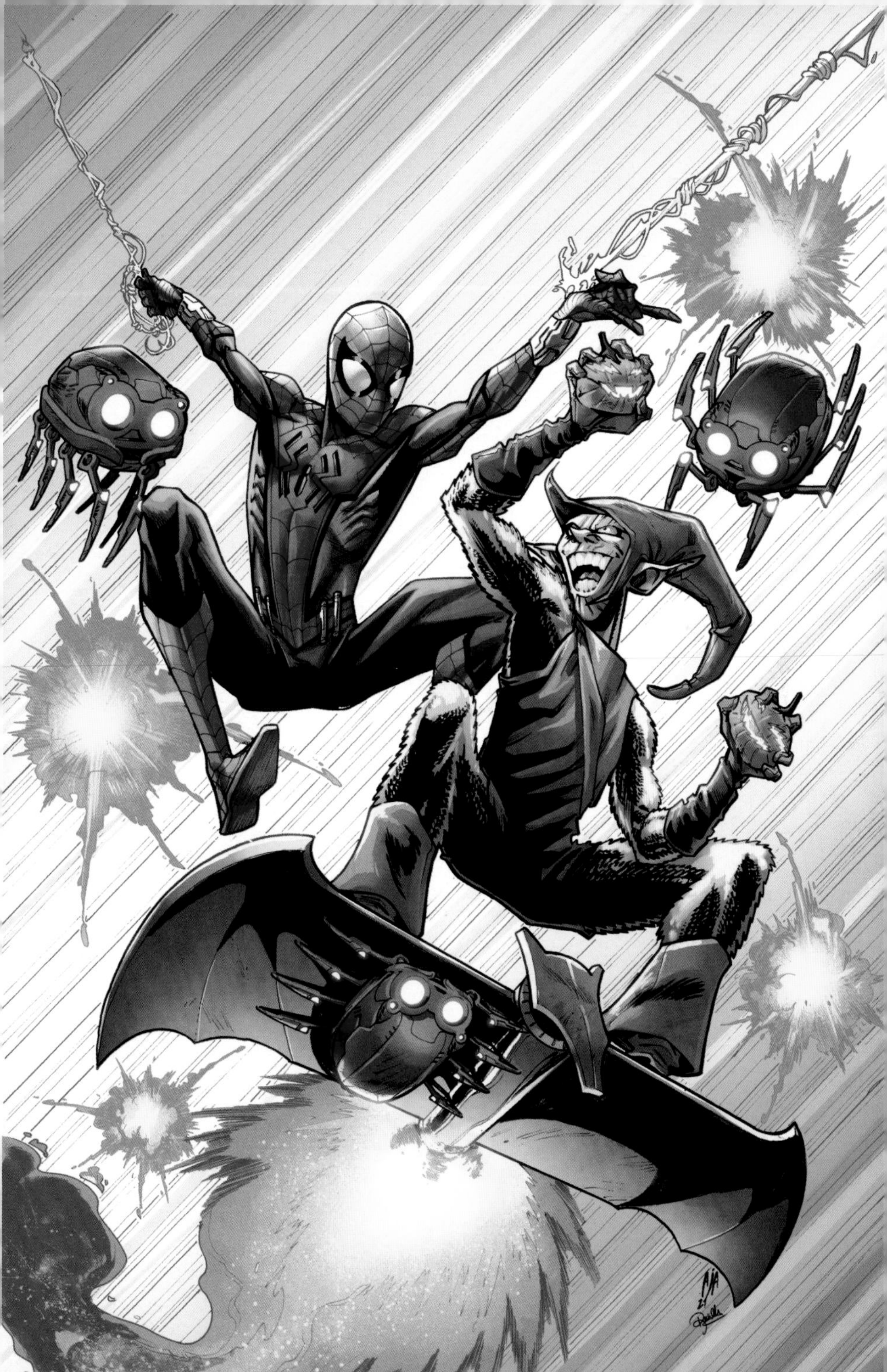

#2 VARIANT BY **ALBERTO ALBURQURQUE** & **RACHELLE ROSENBERG**

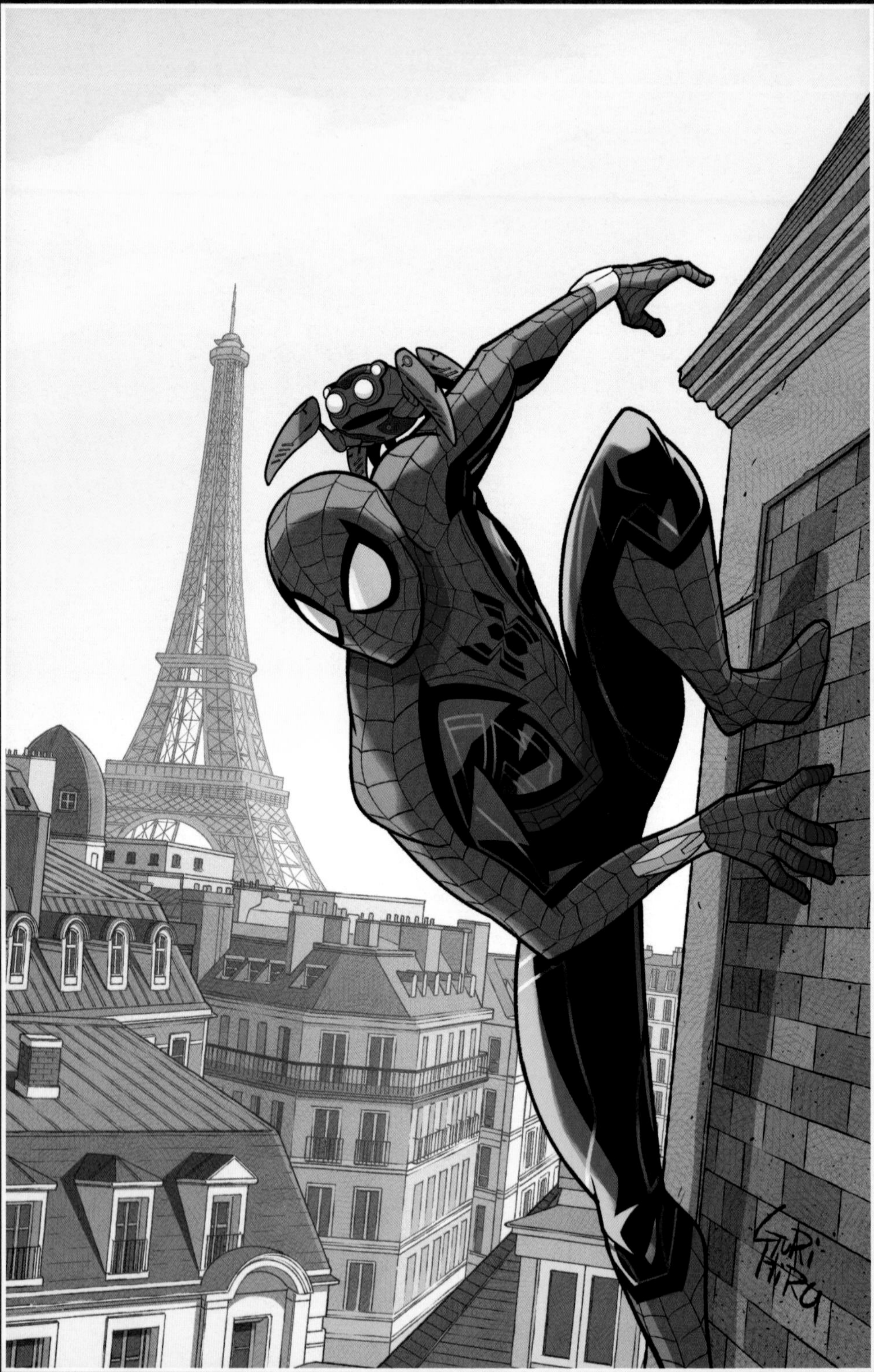

3

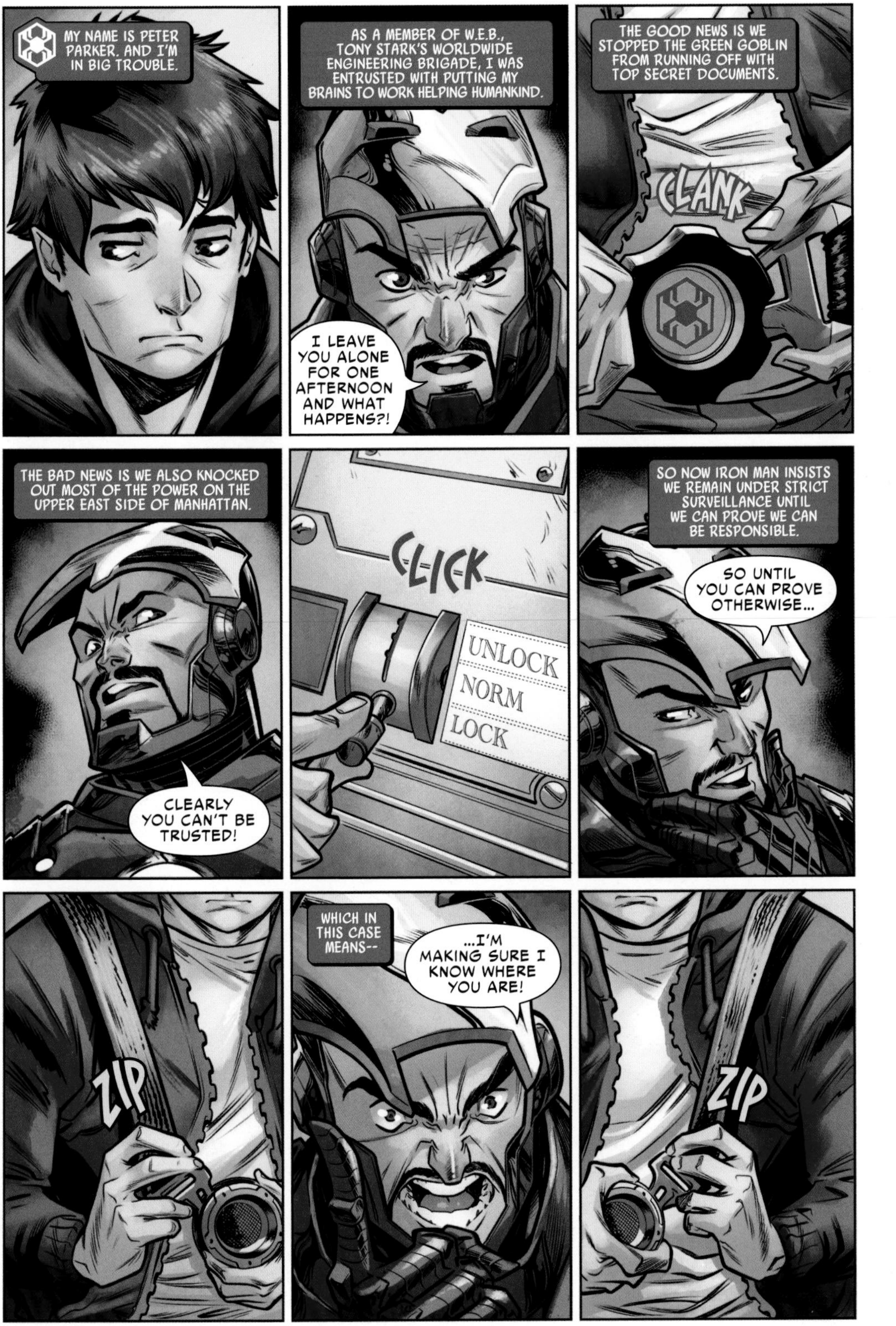
MY NAME IS PETER PARKER. AND I'M IN BIG TROUBLE.
AS A MEMBER OF W.E.B., TONY STARK'S WORLDWIDE ENGINEERING BRIGADE, I WAS ENTRUSTED WITH PUTTING MY BRAINS TO WORK HELPING HUMANKIND.
I LEAVE YOU ALONE FOR ONE AFTERNOON AND WHAT HAPPENS?!
THE GOOD NEWS IS WE STOPPED THE GREEN GOBLIN FROM RUNNING OFF WITH TOP SECRET DOCUMENTS.
CLANK
THE BAD NEWS IS WE ALSO KNOCKED OUT MOST OF THE POWER ON THE UPPER EAST SIDE OF MANHATTAN.
CLEARLY YOU CAN'T BE TRUSTED!
CLICK
UNLOCK
NORM
LOCK
SO NOW IRON MAN INSISTS WE REMAIN UNDER STRICT SURVEILLANCE UNTIL WE CAN PROVE WE CAN BE RESPONSIBLE.
SO UNTIL YOU CAN PROVE OTHERWISE...
ZIP
WHICH IN THIS CASE MEANS--
...I'M MAKING SURE I KNOW WHERE YOU ARE!
ZIP

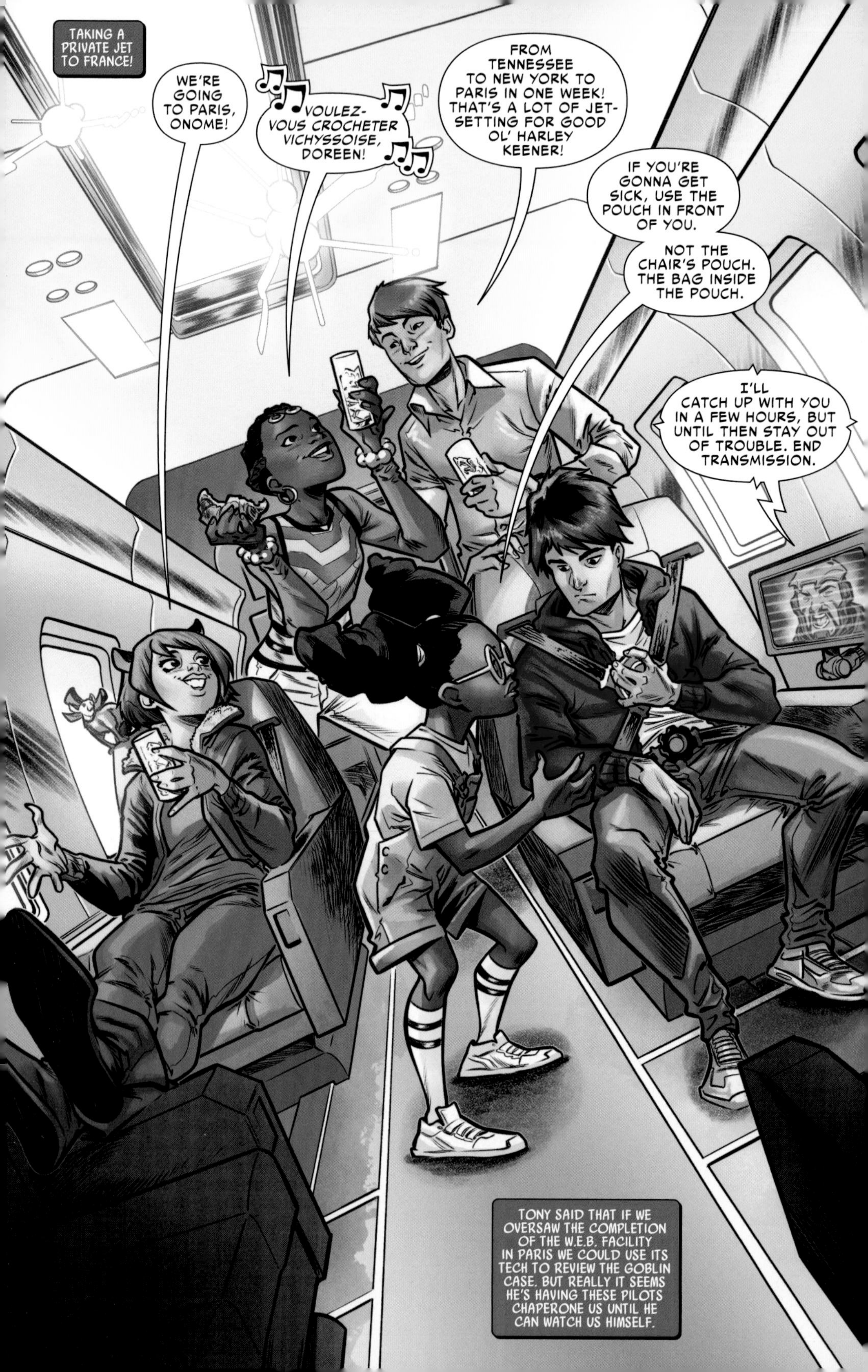
TAKING A PRIVATE JET TO FRANCE!
WE'RE GOING TO PARIS, ONOME!
VOULEZ-VOUS CROCHETER VICHYSSOISE, DOREEN!
FROM TENNESSEE TO NEW YORK TO PARIS IN ONE WEEK! THAT'S A LOT OF JET-SETTING FOR GOOD OL' HARLEY KEENER!
IF YOU'RE GONNA GET SICK, USE THE POUCH IN FRONT OF YOU.
NOT THE CHAIR'S POUCH. THE BAG INSIDE THE POUCH.
I'LL CATCH UP WITH YOU IN A FEW HOURS, BUT UNTIL THEN STAY OUT OF TROUBLE. END TRANSMISSION.
TONY SAID THAT IF WE OVERSAW THE COMPLETION OF THE W.E.B. FACILITY IN PARIS WE COULD USE ITS TECH TO REVIEW THE GOBLIN CASE. BUT REALLY IT SEEMS HE'S HAVING THESE PILOTS CHAPERONE US UNTIL HE CAN WATCH US HIMSELF.

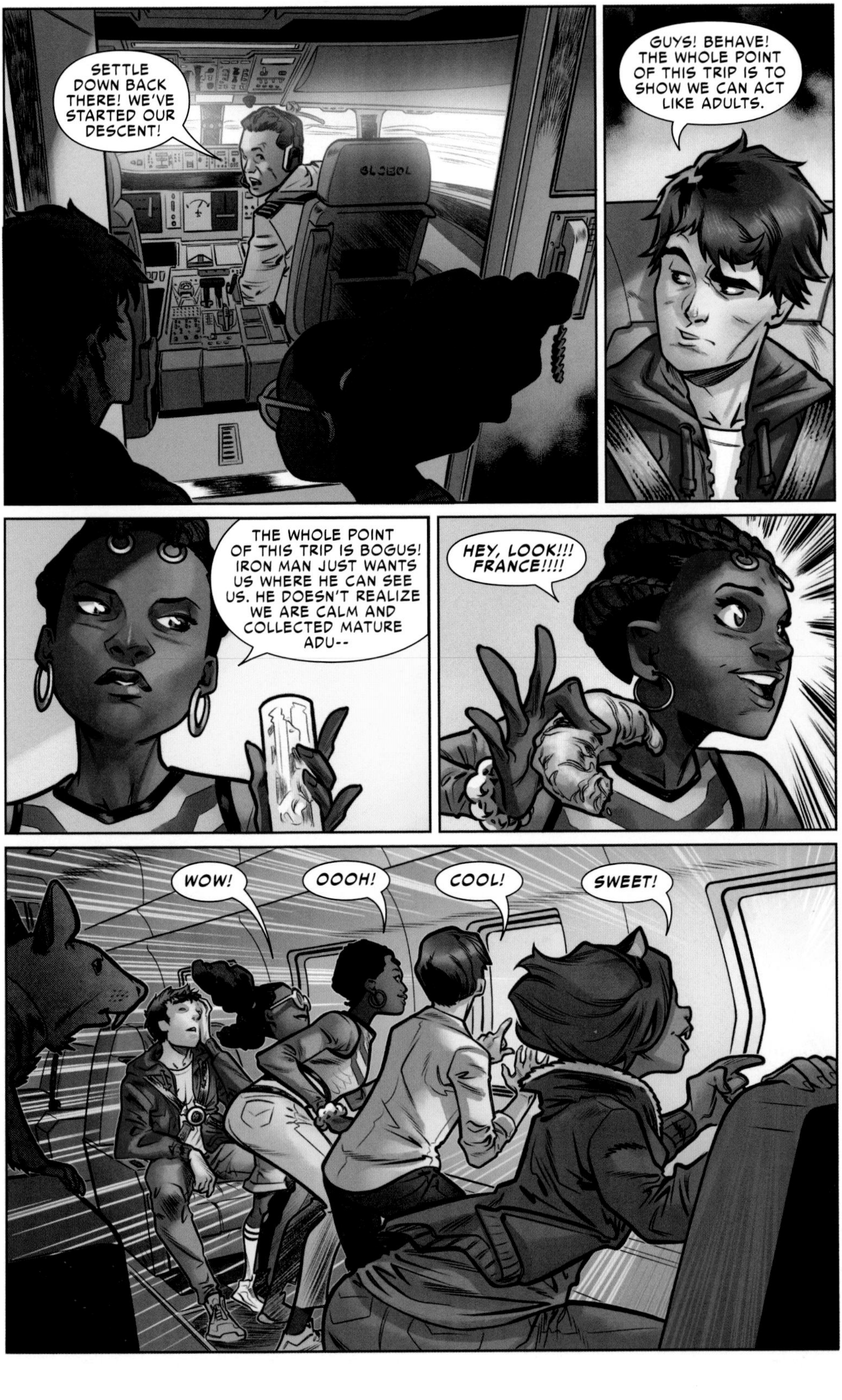
SETTLE DOWN BACK THERE! WE'VE STARTED OUR DESCENT!
GLOBOL
GUYS! BEHAVE! THE WHOLE POINT OF THIS TRIP IS TO SHOW WE CAN ACT LIKE ADULTS.
THE WHOLE POINT OF THIS TRIP IS BOGUS! IRON MAN JUST WANTS US WHERE HE CAN SEE US. HE DOESN'T REALIZE WE ARE CALM AND COLLECTED MATURE ADU--
HEY, LOOK!!! FRANCE!!!!
WOW!
OOOH!
COOL!
SWEET!

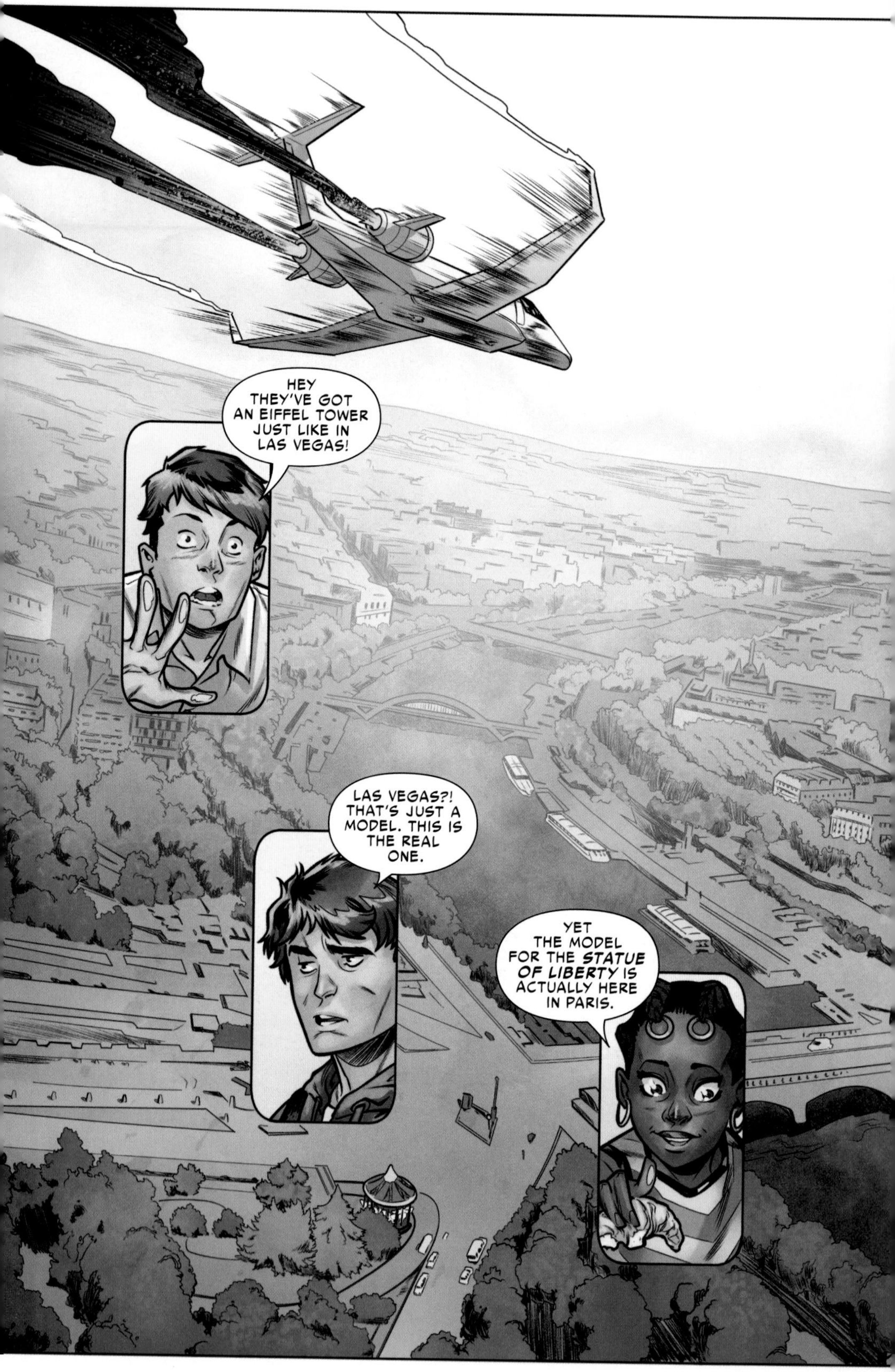
HEY THEY'VE GOT AN EIFFEL TOWER JUST LIKE IN LAS VEGAS!
LAS VEGAS?! THAT'S JUST A MODEL. THIS IS THE REAL ONE.
YET THE MODEL FOR THE STATUE OF LIBERTY IS ACTUALLY HERE IN PARIS.

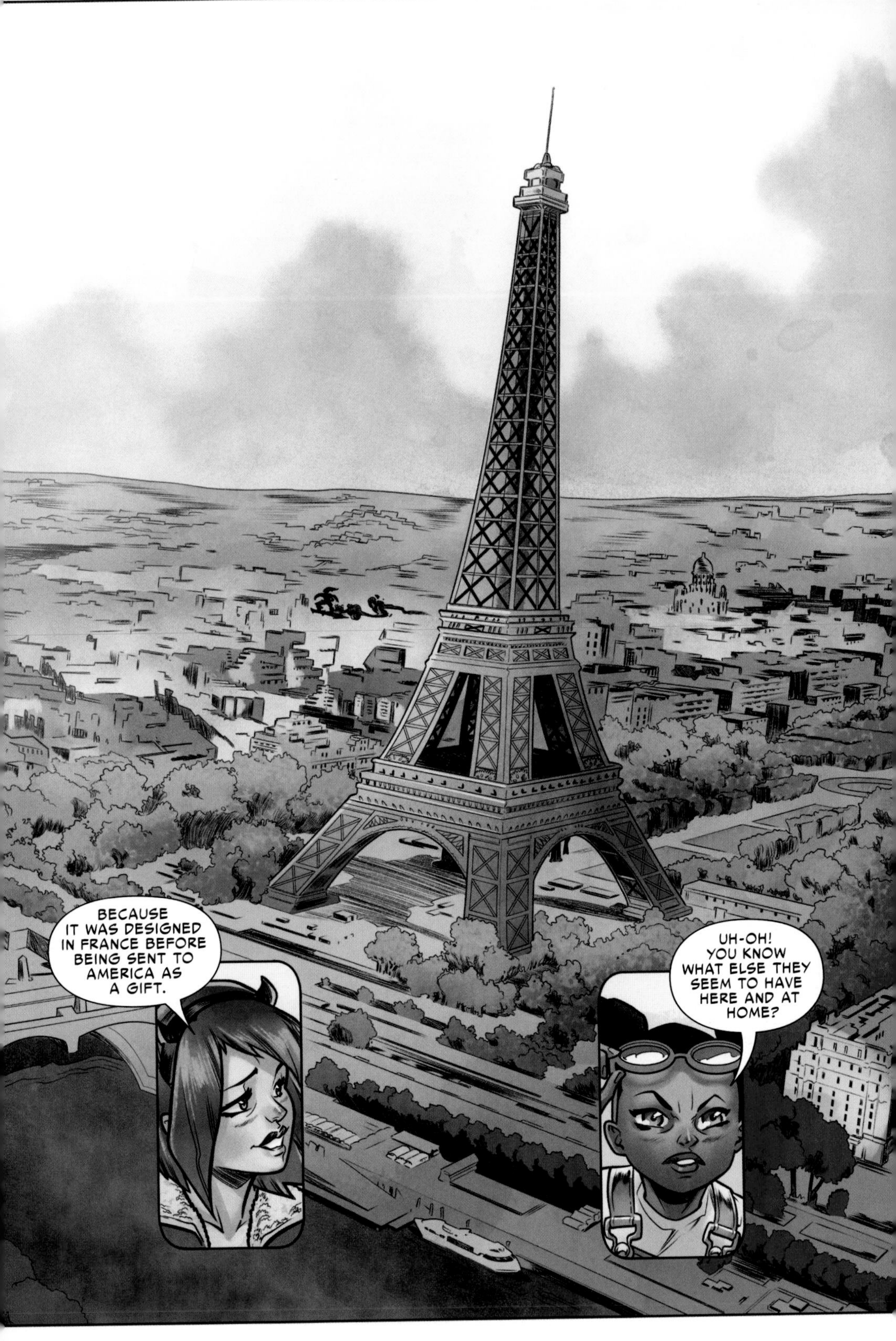
BECAUSE IT WAS DESIGNED IN FRANCE BEFORE BEING SENT TO AMERICA AS A GIFT.
UH-OH! YOU KNOW WHAT ELSE THEY SEEM TO HAVE HERE AND AT HOME?

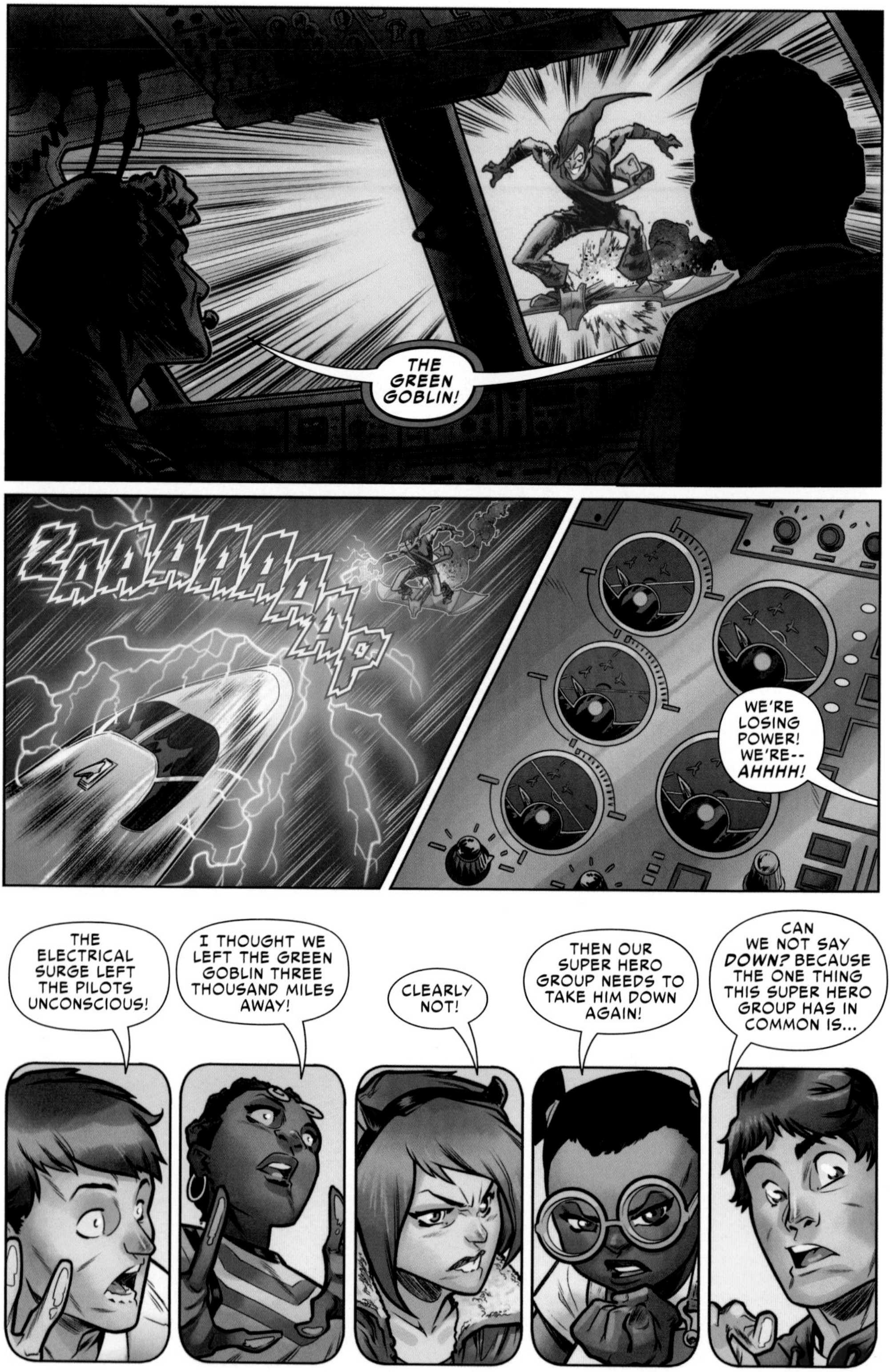
THE GREEN GOBLIN!
ZAAAAAAAAP
WE'RE LOSING POWER! WE'RE-- AHHHH!
THE ELECTRICAL SURGE LEFT THE PILOTS UNCONSCIOUS!
I THOUGHT WE LEFT THE GREEN GOBLIN THREE THOUSAND MILES AWAY!
CLEARLY NOT!
THEN OUR SUPER HERO GROUP NEEDS TO TAKE HIM DOWN AGAIN!
CAN WE NOT SAY DOWN? BECAUSE THE ONE THING THIS SUPER HERO GROUP HAS IN COMMON IS...

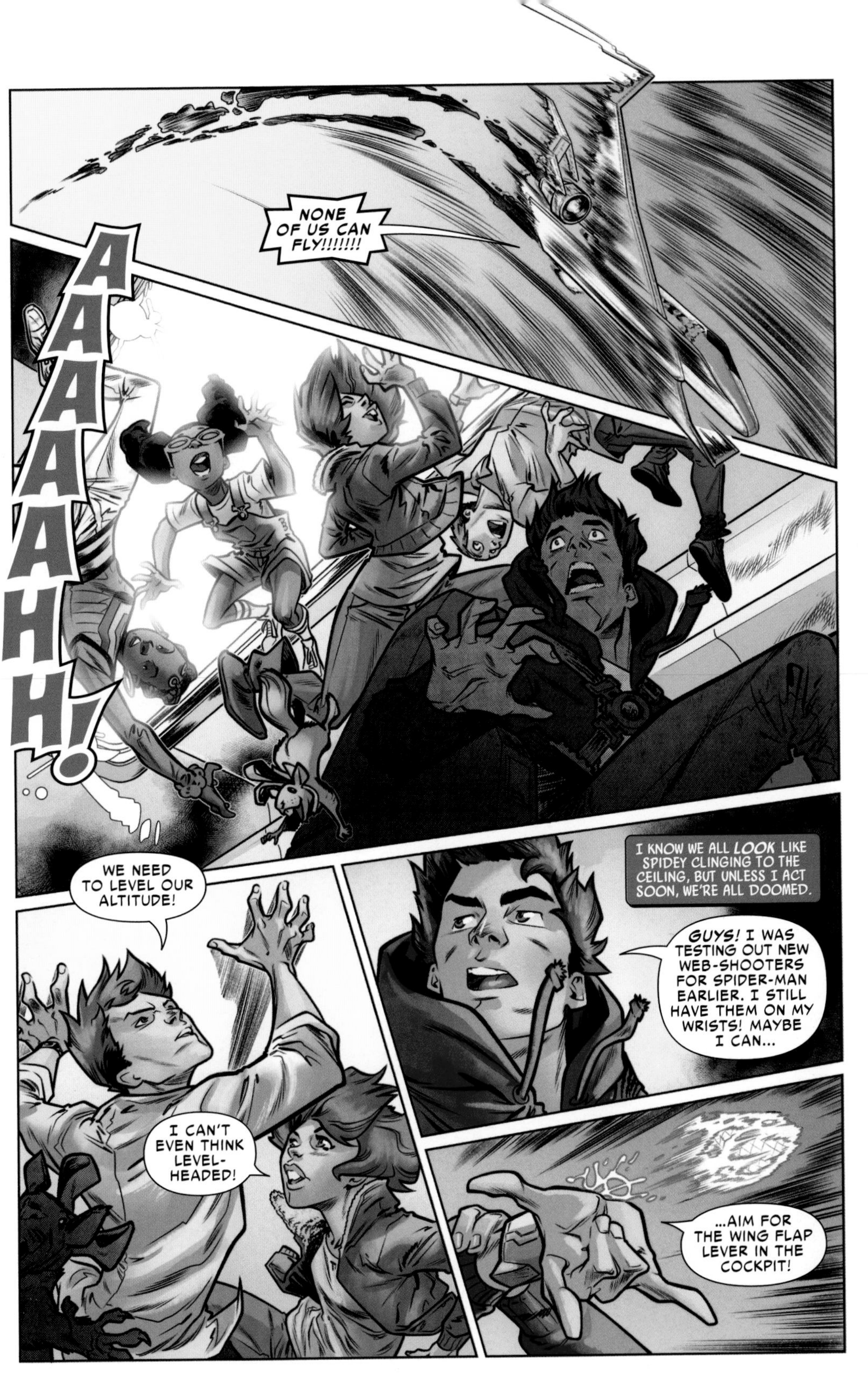
NONE OF US CAN FLY!!!!!!!
AAAAAAHHH!
WE NEED TO LEVEL OUR ALTITUDE!
I KNOW WE ALL LOOK LIKE SPIDEY CLINGING TO THE CEILING, BUT UNLESS I ACT SOON, WE'RE ALL DOOMED.
GUYS! I WAS TESTING OUT NEW WEB-SHOOTERS FOR SPIDER-MAN EARLIER. I STILL HAVE THEM ON MY WRISTS! MAYBE I CAN...
I CAN'T EVEN THINK LEVEL-HEADED!
...AIM FOR THE WING FLAP LEVER IN THE COCKPIT!

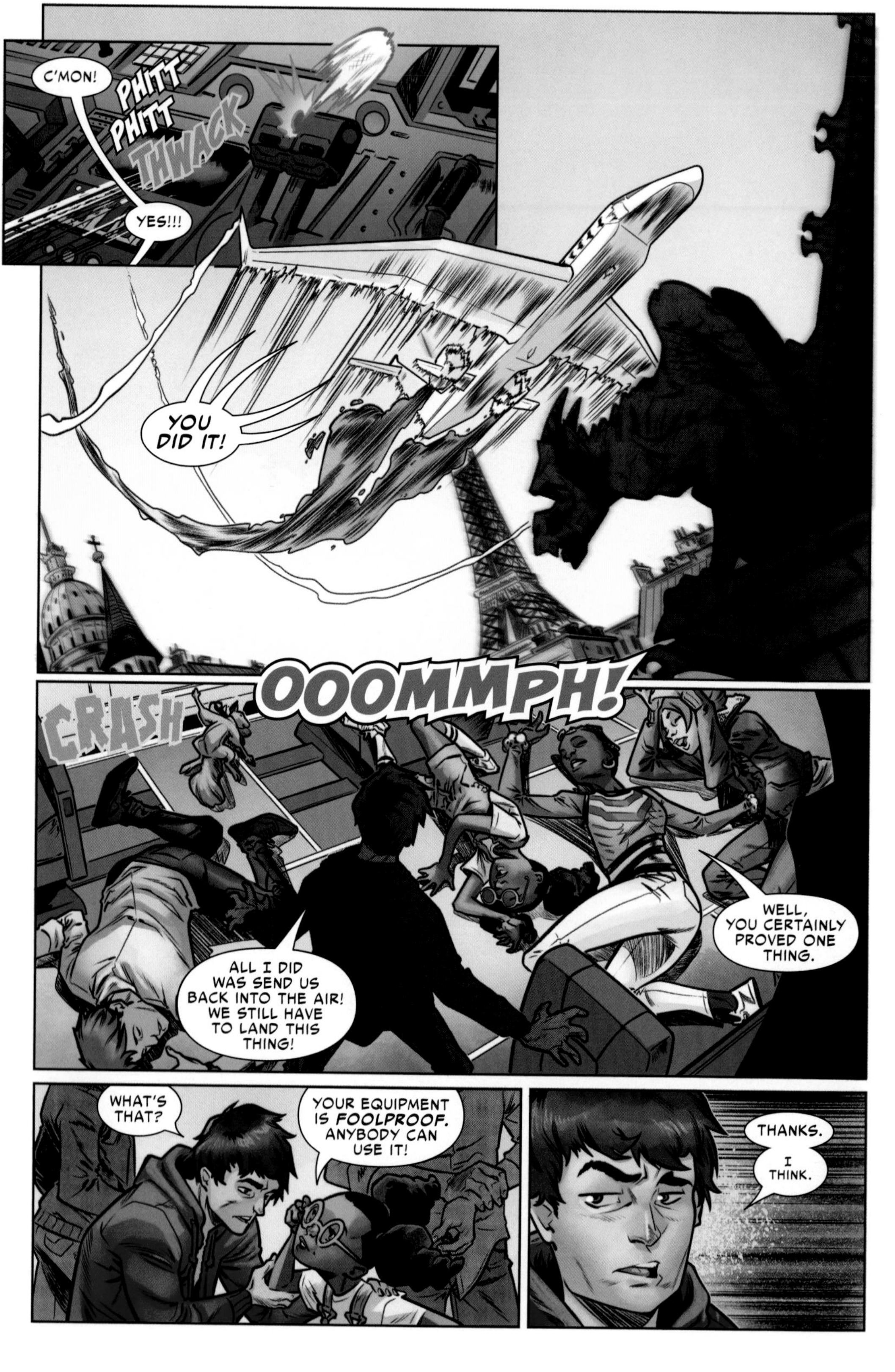
C'MON!
PHITT
PHITT
THWACK
YES!!!
YOU DID IT!
CRASH
OOOMMPH!
ALL I DID WAS SEND US BACK INTO THE AIR! WE STILL HAVE TO LAND THIS THING!
WELL, YOU CERTAINLY PROVED ONE THING.
WHAT'S THAT?
YOUR EQUIPMENT IS FOOLPROOF. ANYBODY CAN USE IT!
THANKS.
I THINK.

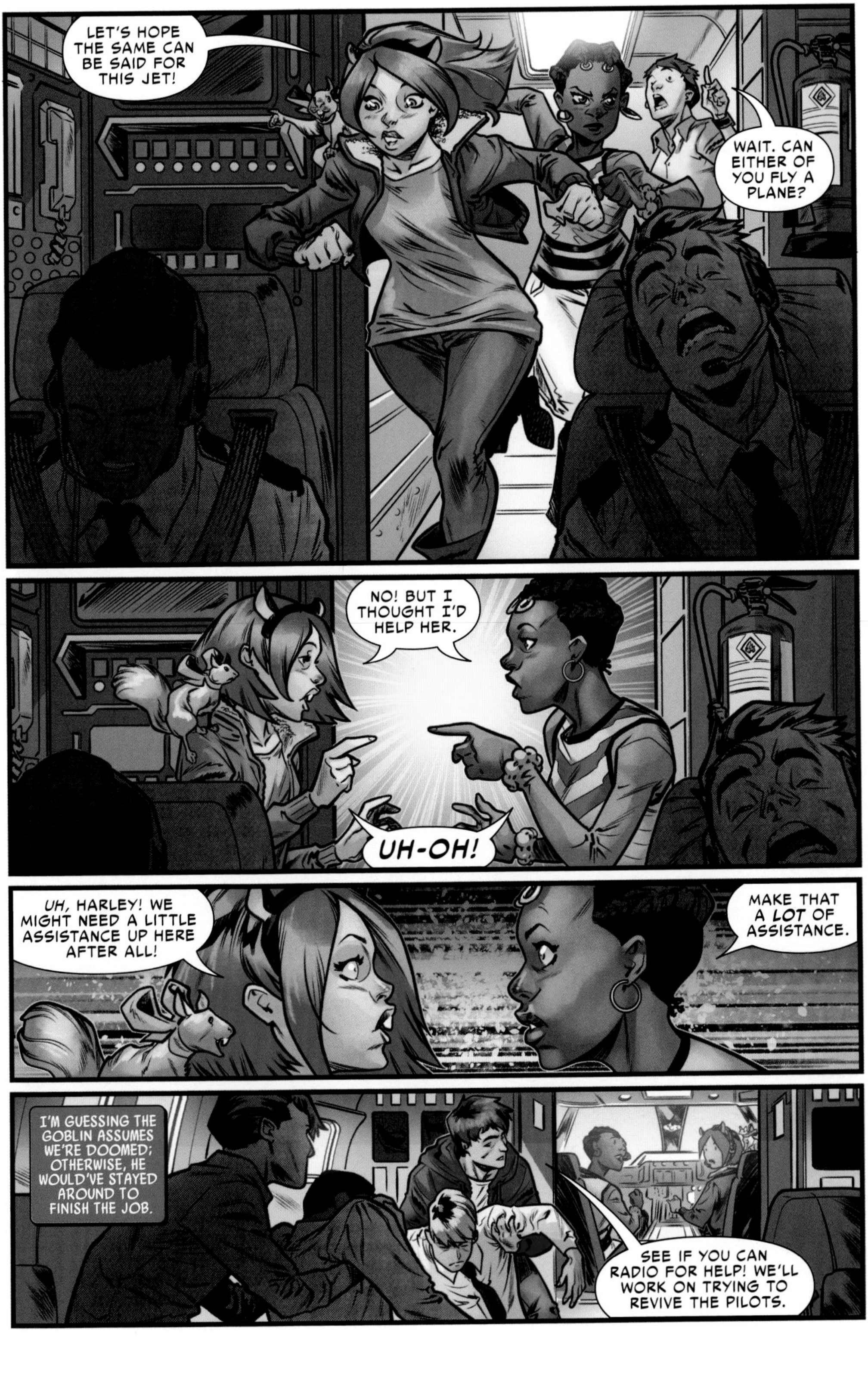
LET'S HOPE THE SAME CAN BE SAID FOR THIS JET!
WAIT. CAN EITHER OF YOU FLY A PLANE?
NO! BUT I THOUGHT I'D HELP HER.
UH-OH!
UH, HARLEY! WE MIGHT NEED A LITTLE ASSISTANCE UP HERE AFTER ALL!
MAKE THAT A LOT OF ASSISTANCE.
I'M GUESSING THE GOBLIN ASSUMES WE'RE DOOMED; OTHERWISE, HE WOULD'VE STAYED AROUND TO FINISH THE JOB.
SEE IF YOU CAN RADIO FOR HELP! WE'LL WORK ON TRYING TO REVIVE THE PILOTS.

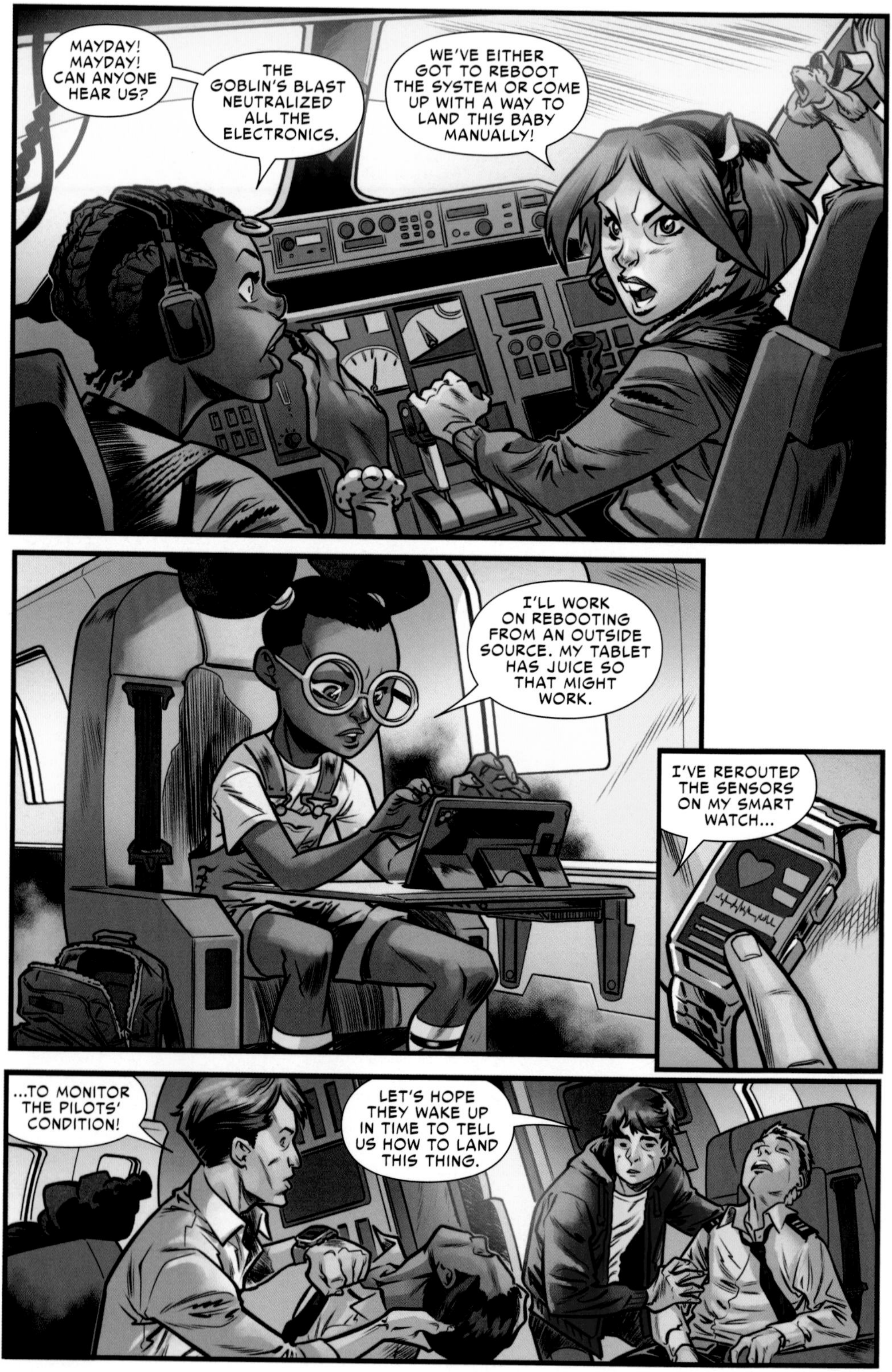
MAYDAY! MAYDAY! CAN ANYONE HEAR US?
THE GOBLIN'S BLAST NEUTRALIZED ALL THE ELECTRONICS.
WE'VE EITHER GOT TO REBOOT THE SYSTEM OR COME UP WITH A WAY TO LAND THIS BABY MANUALLY!
I'LL WORK ON REBOOTING FROM AN OUTSIDE SOURCE. MY TABLET HAS JUICE SO THAT MIGHT WORK.
I'VE REROUTED THE SENSORS ON MY SMART WATCH...
...TO MONITOR THE PILOTS' CONDITION!
LET'S HOPE THEY WAKE UP IN TIME TO TELL US HOW TO LAND THIS THING.

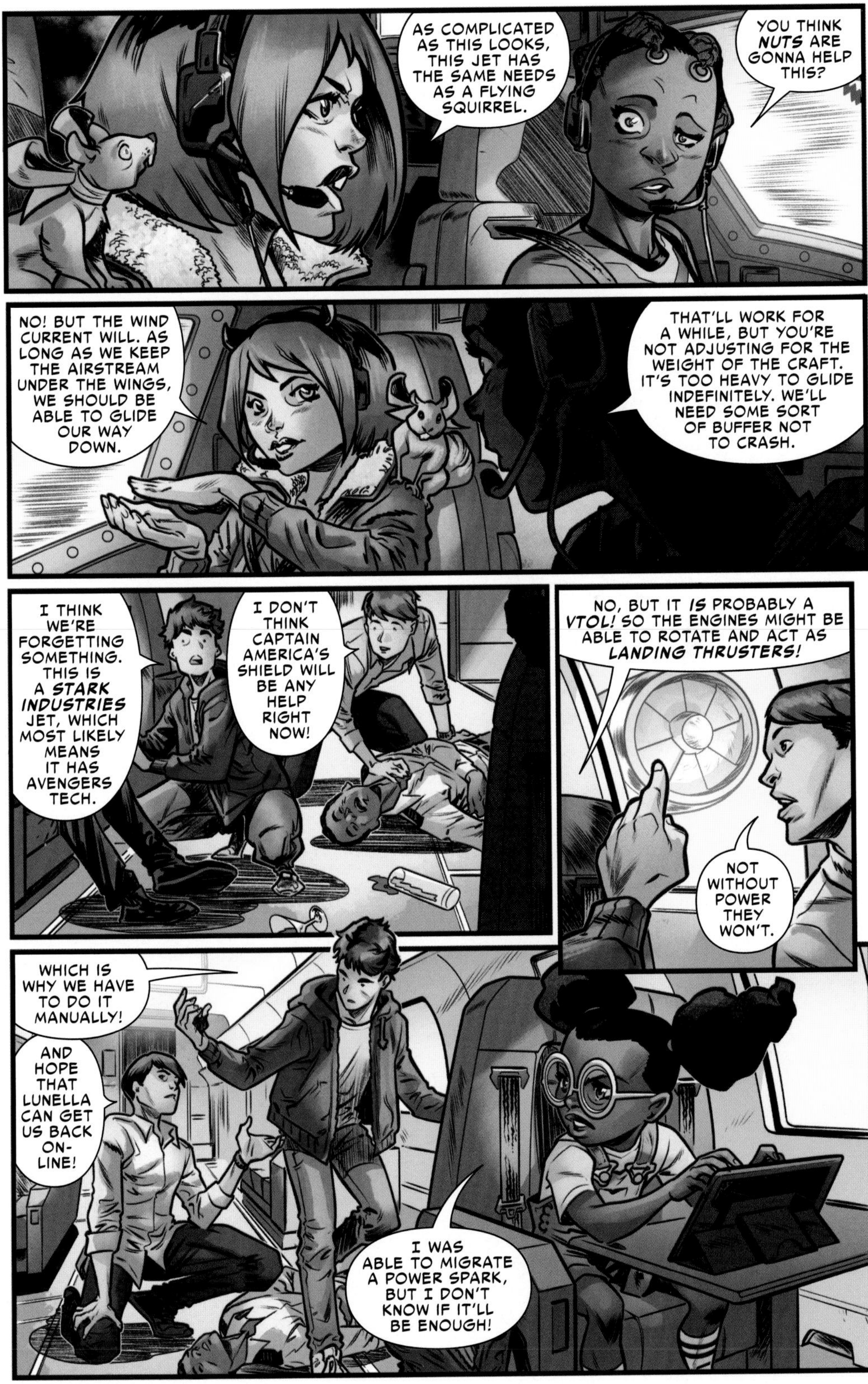
AS COMPLICATED AS THIS LOOKS, THIS JET HAS THE SAME NEEDS AS A FLYING SQUIRREL.
YOU THINK NUTS ARE GONNA HELP THIS?
NO! BUT THE WIND CURRENT WILL. AS LONG AS WE KEEP THE AIRSTREAM UNDER THE WINGS, WE SHOULD BE ABLE TO GLIDE OUR WAY DOWN.
THAT'LL WORK FOR A WHILE, BUT YOU'RE NOT ADJUSTING FOR THE WEIGHT OF THE CRAFT. IT'S TOO HEAVY TO GLIDE INDEFINITELY. WE'LL NEED SOME SORT OF BUFFER NOT TO CRASH.
I THINK WE'RE FORGETTING SOMETHING. THIS IS A STARK INDUSTRIES JET, WHICH MOST LIKELY MEANS IT HAS AVENGERS TECH.
I DON'T THINK CAPTAIN AMERICA'S SHIELD WILL BE ANY HELP RIGHT NOW!
NO, BUT IT IS PROBABLY A VTOL! SO THE ENGINES MIGHT BE ABLE TO ROTATE AND ACT AS LANDING THRUSTERS!
NOT WITHOUT POWER THEY WON'T.
WHICH IS WHY WE HAVE TO DO IT MANUALLY!
AND HOPE THAT LUNELLA CAN GET US BACK ON-LINE!
I WAS ABLE TO MIGRATE A POWER SPARK, BUT I DON'T KNOW IF IT'LL BE ENOUGH!

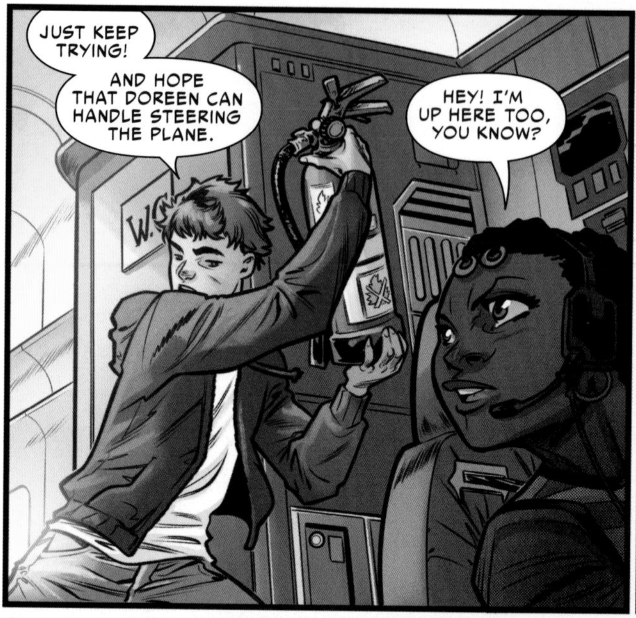
JUST KEEP TRYING!
AND HOPE THAT DOREEN CAN HANDLE STEERING THE PLANE.
HEY! I'M UP HERE TOO, YOU KNOW?
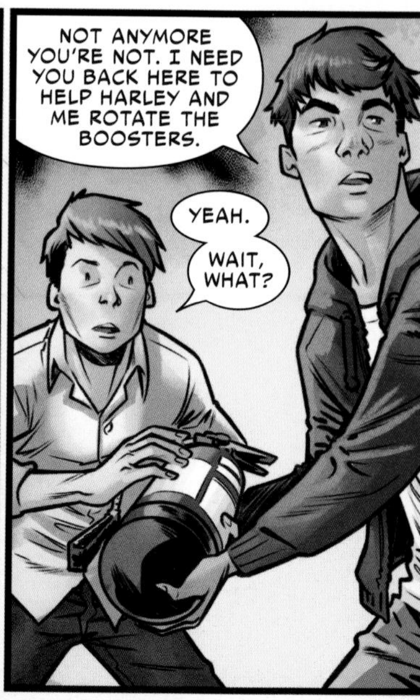
NOT ANYMORE YOU'RE NOT. I NEED YOU BACK HERE TO HELP HARLEY AND ME ROTATE THE BOOSTERS.
YEAH.
WAIT, WHAT?
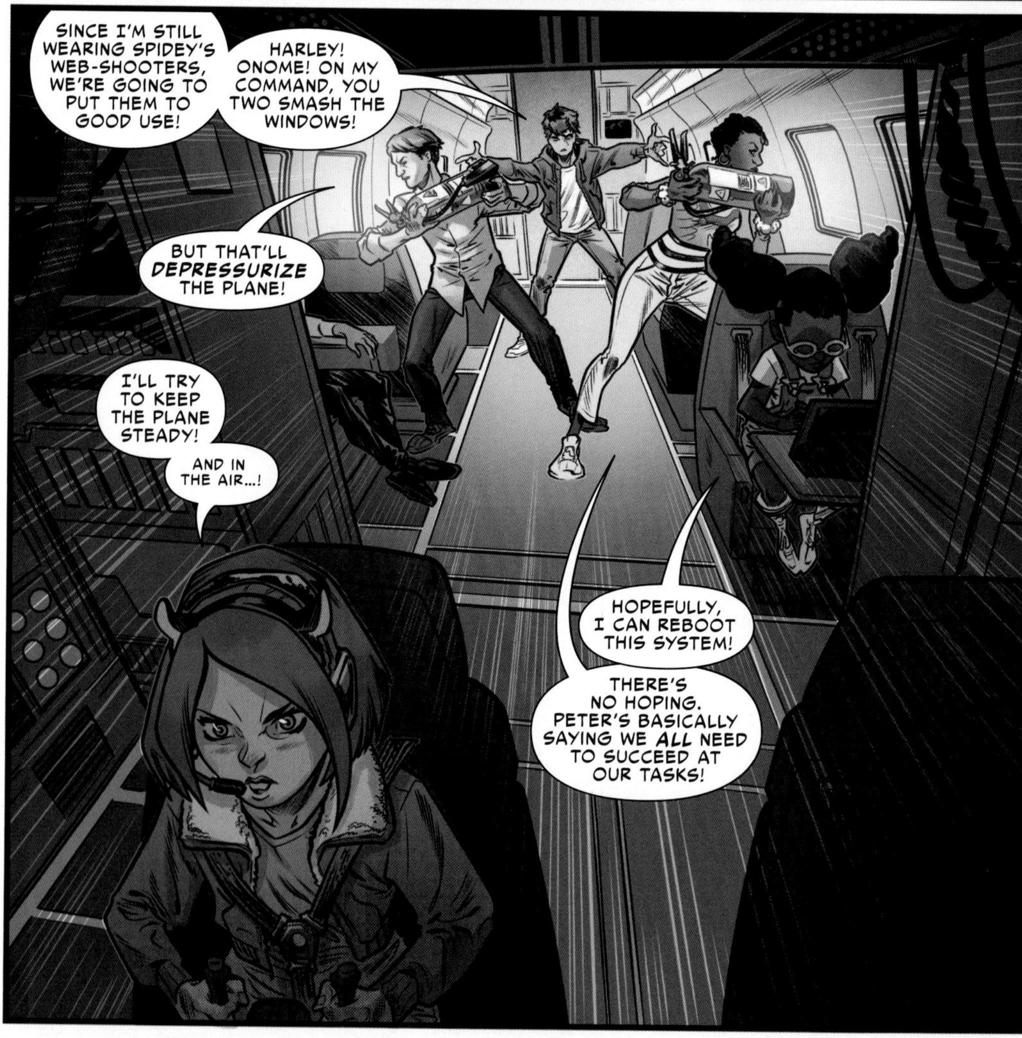
SINCE I'M STILL WEARING SPIDEY'S WEB-SHOOTERS, WE'RE GOING TO PUT THEM TO GOOD USE!
HARLEY! ONOME! ON MY COMMAND, YOU TWO SMASH THE WINDOWS!
BUT THAT'LL ***DEPRESSURIZE*** THE PLANE!
I'LL TRY TO KEEP THE PLANE STEADY!
AND IN THE AIR...!
HOPEFULLY, I CAN REBOOT THIS SYSTEM!
THERE'S NO HOPING. PETER'S BASICALLY SAYING WE ***ALL*** NEED TO SUCCEED AT OUR TASKS!

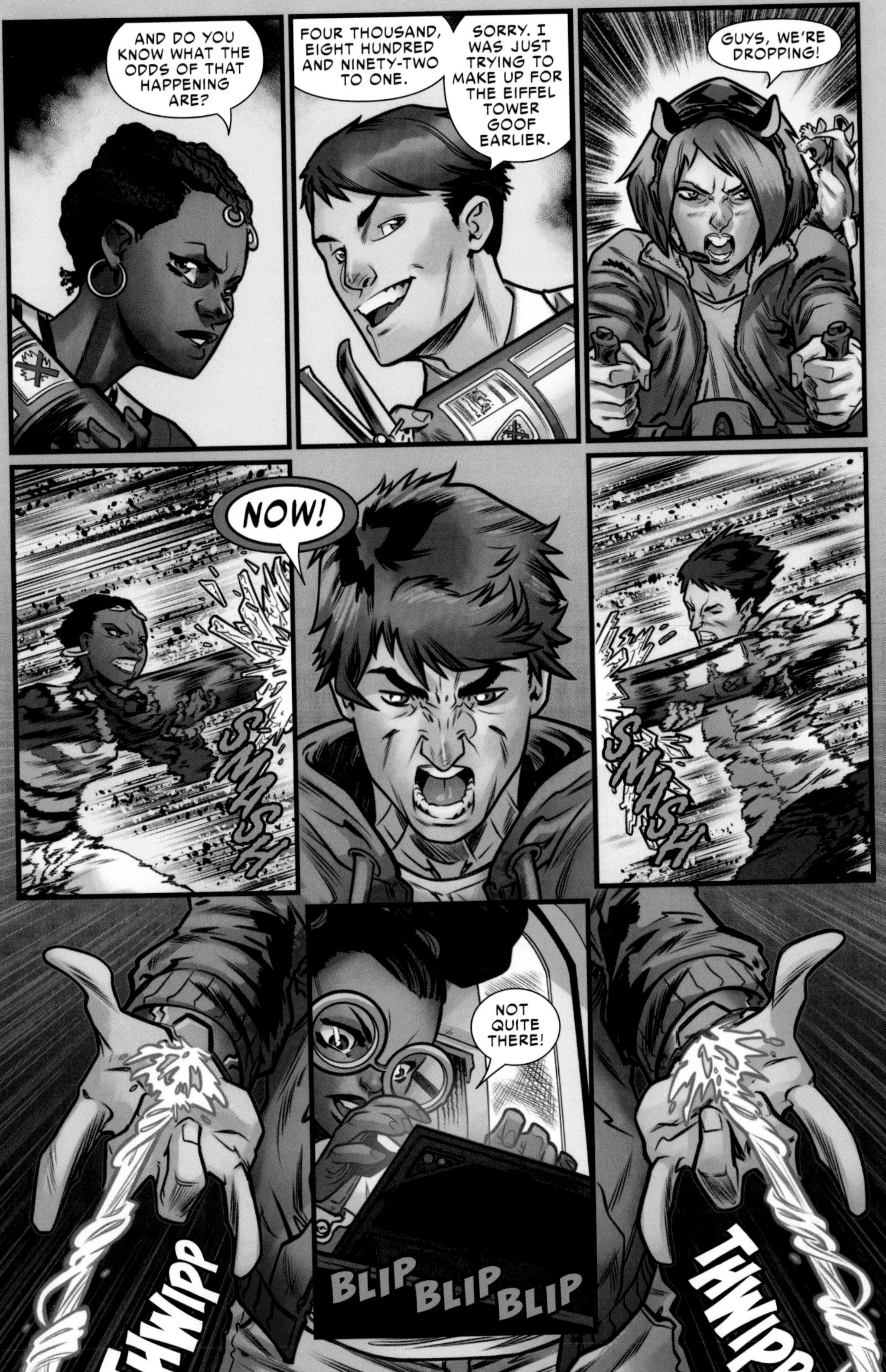
AND DO YOU KNOW WHAT THE ODDS OF THAT HAPPENING ARE?
FOUR THOUSAND, EIGHT HUNDRED AND NINETY-TWO TO ONE.
SORRY. I WAS JUST TRYING TO MAKE UP FOR THE EIFFEL TOWER GOOF EARLIER.
GUYS, WE'RE DROPPING!
NOW!
SMASH
SMASH
NOT QUITE THERE!
THWIPP
BLIP BLIP BLIP
THWIPP

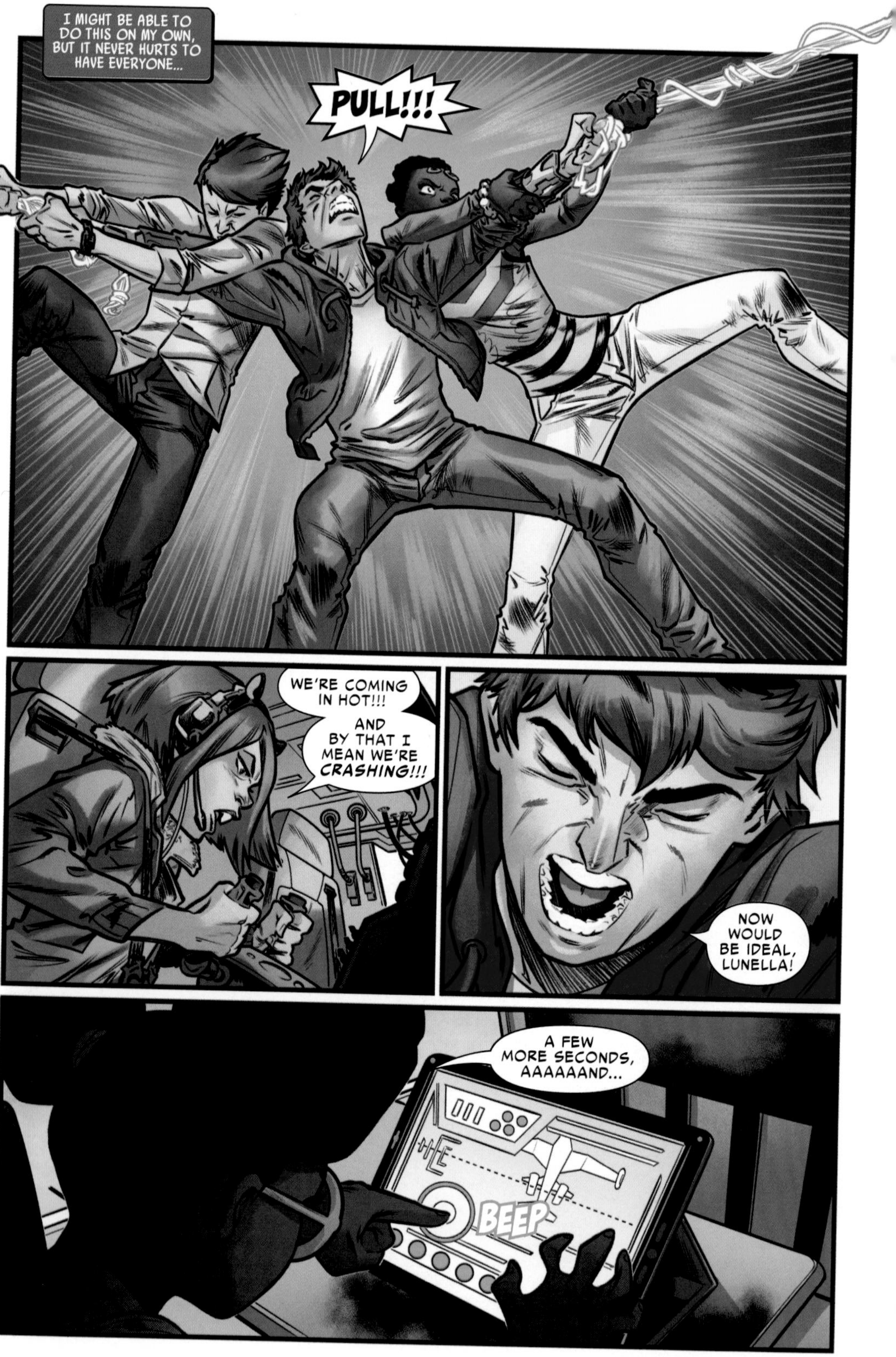
I MIGHT BE ABLE TO DO THIS ON MY OWN, BUT IT NEVER HURTS TO HAVE EVERYONE...
PULL!!!
WE'RE COMING IN HOT!!!
AND BY THAT I MEAN WE'RE CRASHING!!!
NOW WOULD BE IDEAL, LUNELLA!
A FEW MORE SECONDS, AAAAAAND...
BEEP

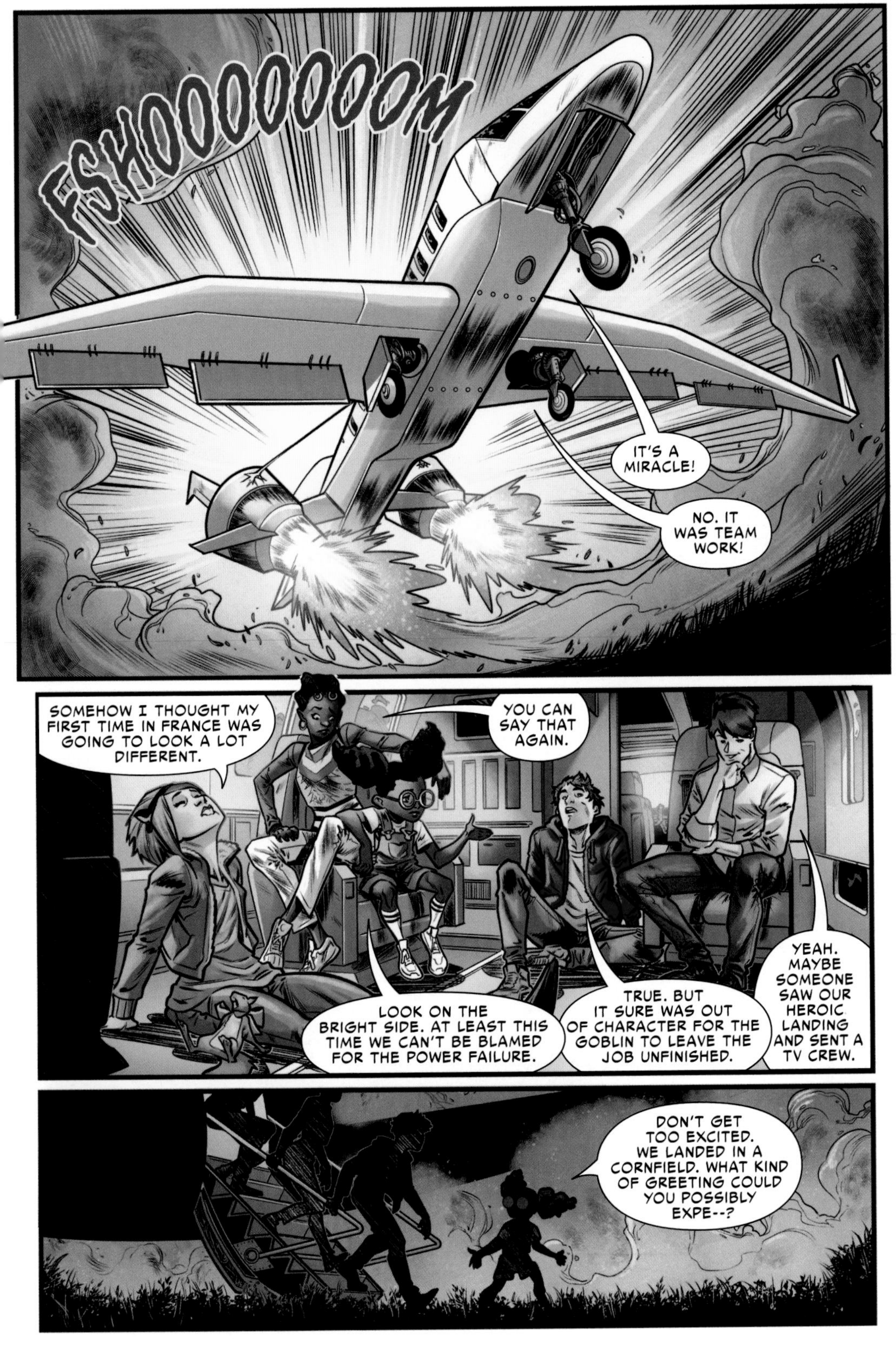
FSHOOOOOOOM
IT'S A MIRACLE!
NO. IT WAS TEAM WORK!
SOMEHOW I THOUGHT MY FIRST TIME IN FRANCE WAS GOING TO LOOK A LOT DIFFERENT.
YOU CAN SAY THAT AGAIN.
LOOK ON THE BRIGHT SIDE. AT LEAST THIS TIME WE CAN'T BE BLAMED FOR THE POWER FAILURE.
TRUE. BUT IT SURE WAS OUT OF CHARACTER FOR THE GOBLIN TO LEAVE THE JOB UNFINISHED.
YEAH. MAYBE SOMEONE SAW OUR HEROIC LANDING AND SENT A TV CREW.
DON'T GET TOO EXCITED. WE LANDED IN A CORNFIELD. WHAT KIND OF GREETING COULD YOU POSSIBLY EXPE--?

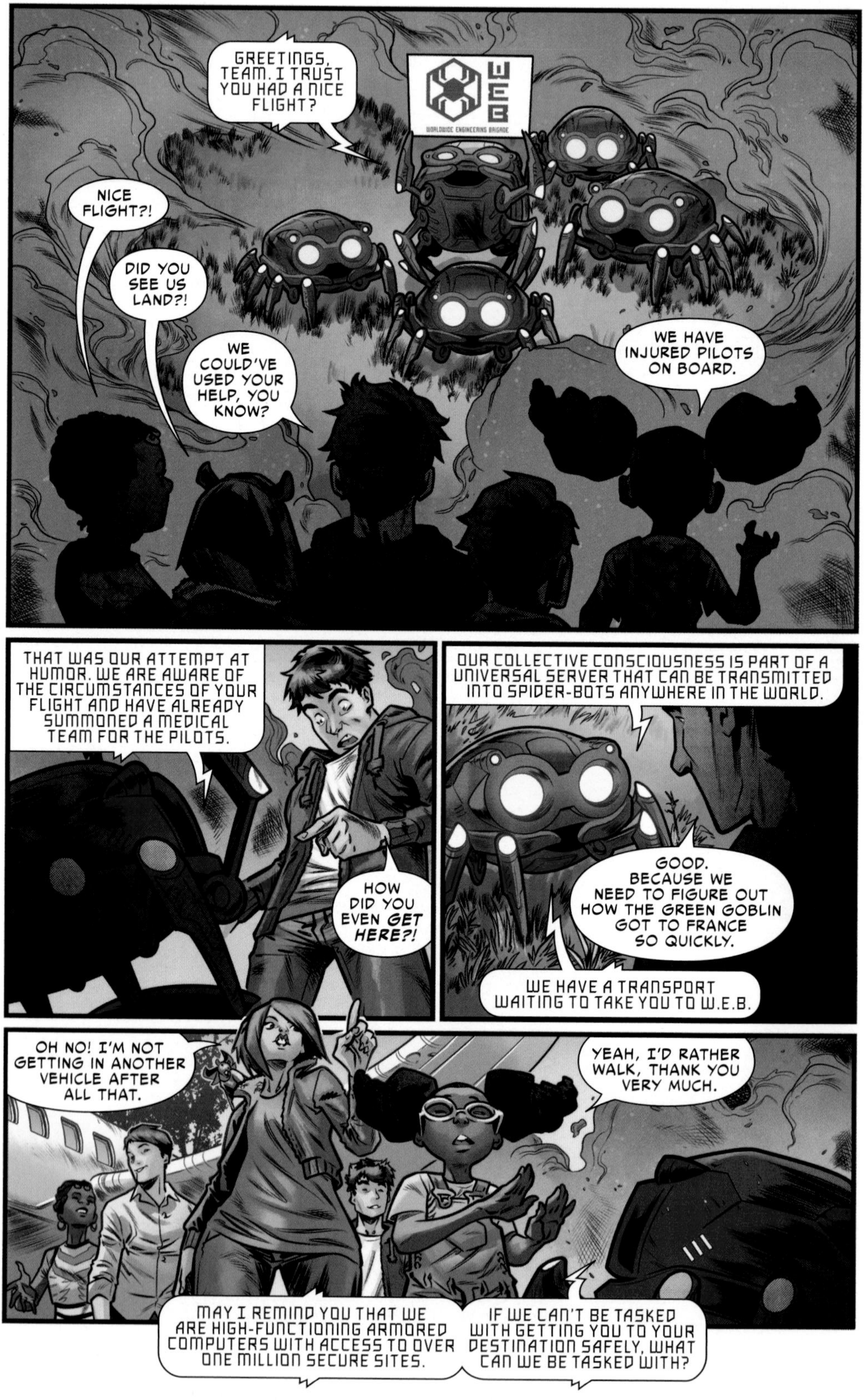
WEB
WORLDWIDE ENGINEERING BRIGADE
GREETINGS, TEAM. I TRUST YOU HAD A NICE FLIGHT?
NICE FLIGHT?!
DID YOU SEE US LAND?!
WE COULD'VE USED YOUR HELP, YOU KNOW?
WE HAVE INJURED PILOTS ON BOARD.
THAT WAS OUR ATTEMPT AT HUMOR. WE ARE AWARE OF THE CIRCUMSTANCES OF YOUR FLIGHT AND HAVE ALREADY SUMMONED A MEDICAL TEAM FOR THE PILOTS.
HOW DID YOU EVEN *GET HERE?!*
OUR COLLECTIVE CONSCIOUSNESS IS PART OF A UNIVERSAL SERVER THAT CAN BE TRANSMITTED INTO SPIDER-BOTS ANYWHERE IN THE WORLD.
GOOD. BECAUSE WE NEED TO FIGURE OUT HOW THE GREEN GOBLIN GOT TO FRANCE SO QUICKLY.
WE HAVE A TRANSPORT WAITING TO TAKE YOU TO W.E.B.
OH NO! I'M NOT GETTING IN ANOTHER VEHICLE AFTER ALL THAT.
YEAH, I'D RATHER WALK, THANK YOU VERY MUCH.
MAY I REMIND YOU THAT WE ARE HIGH-FUNCTIONING ARMORED COMPUTERS WITH ACCESS TO OVER ONE MILLION SECURE SITES.
IF WE CAN'T BE TASKED WITH GETTING YOU TO YOUR DESTINATION SAFELY, WHAT CAN WE BE TASKED WITH?

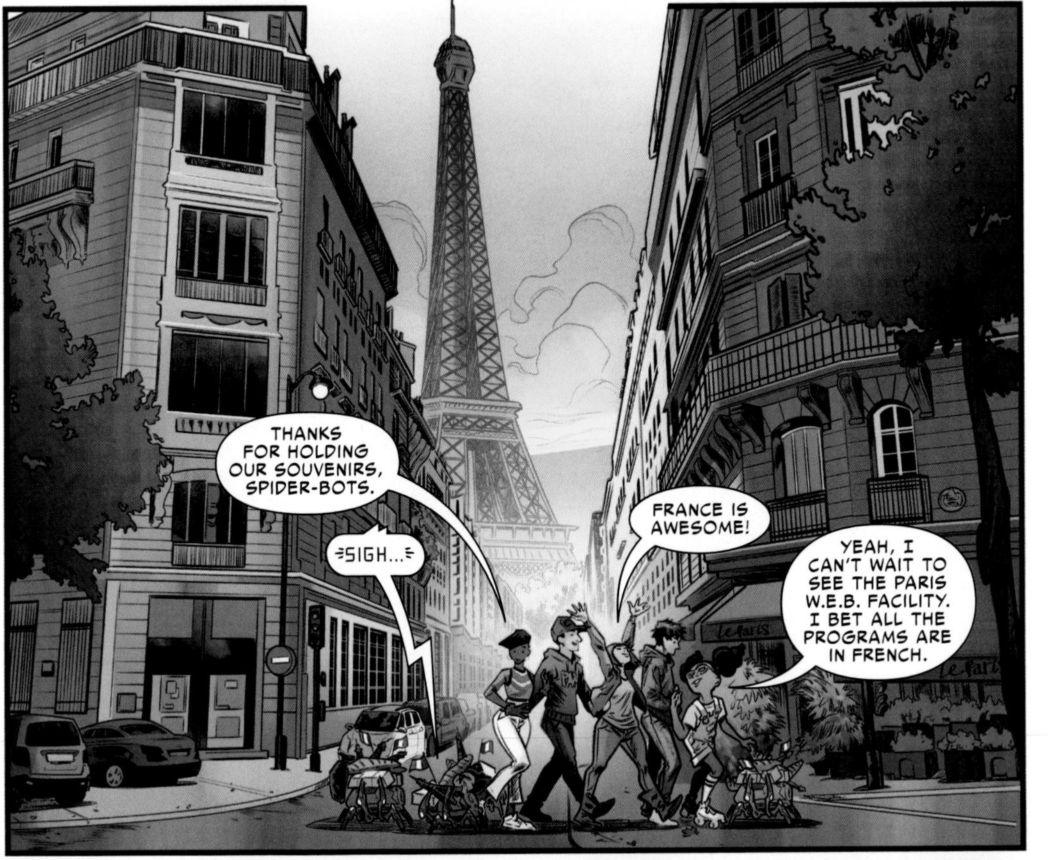
THANKS FOR HOLDING OUR SOUVENIRS, SPIDER-BOTS.
SIGH...
FRANCE IS AWESOME!
YEAH, I CAN'T WAIT TO SEE THE PARIS W.E.B. FACILITY. I BET ALL THE PROGRAMS ARE IN FRENCH.

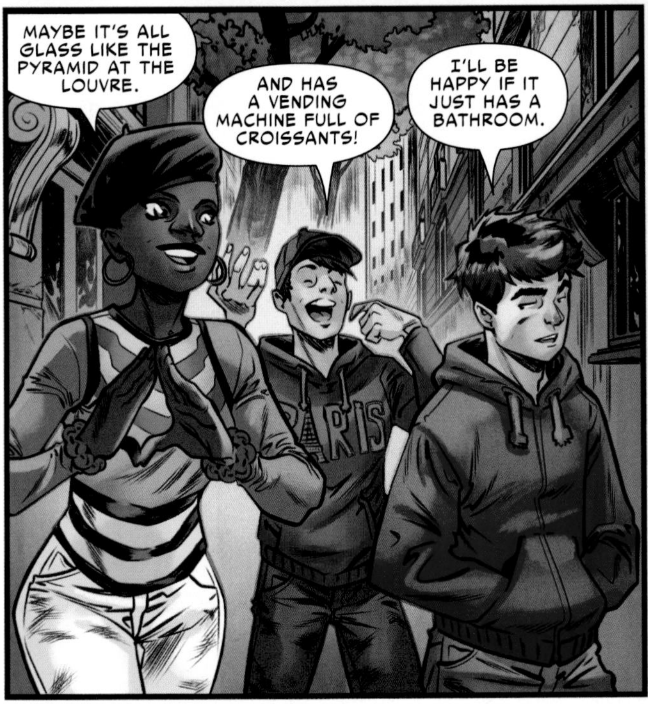
MAYBE IT'S ALL GLASS LIKE THE PYRAMID AT THE LOUVRE.
AND HAS A VENDING MACHINE FULL OF CROISSANTS!
I'LL BE HAPPY IF IT JUST HAS A BATHROOM.
PARIS

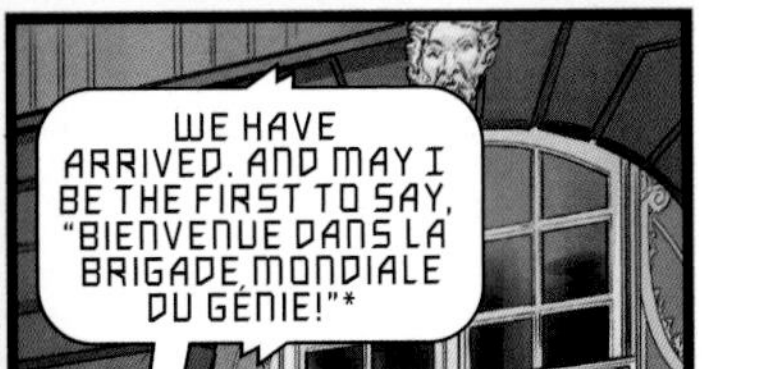
WE HAVE ARRIVED. AND MAY I BE THE FIRST TO SAY, "BIENVENUE DANS LA BRIGADE MONDIALE DU GÉNIE!"*
*TRANSLATION: WELCOME THE WORLDWIDE ENGINEERING BRIGADE.

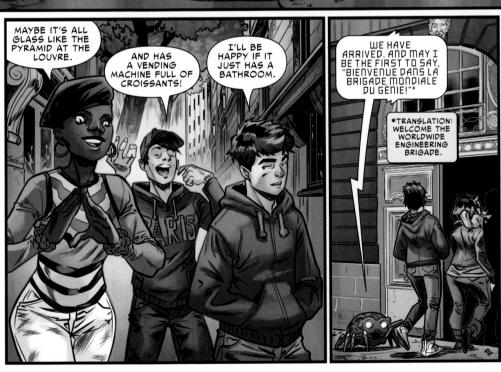

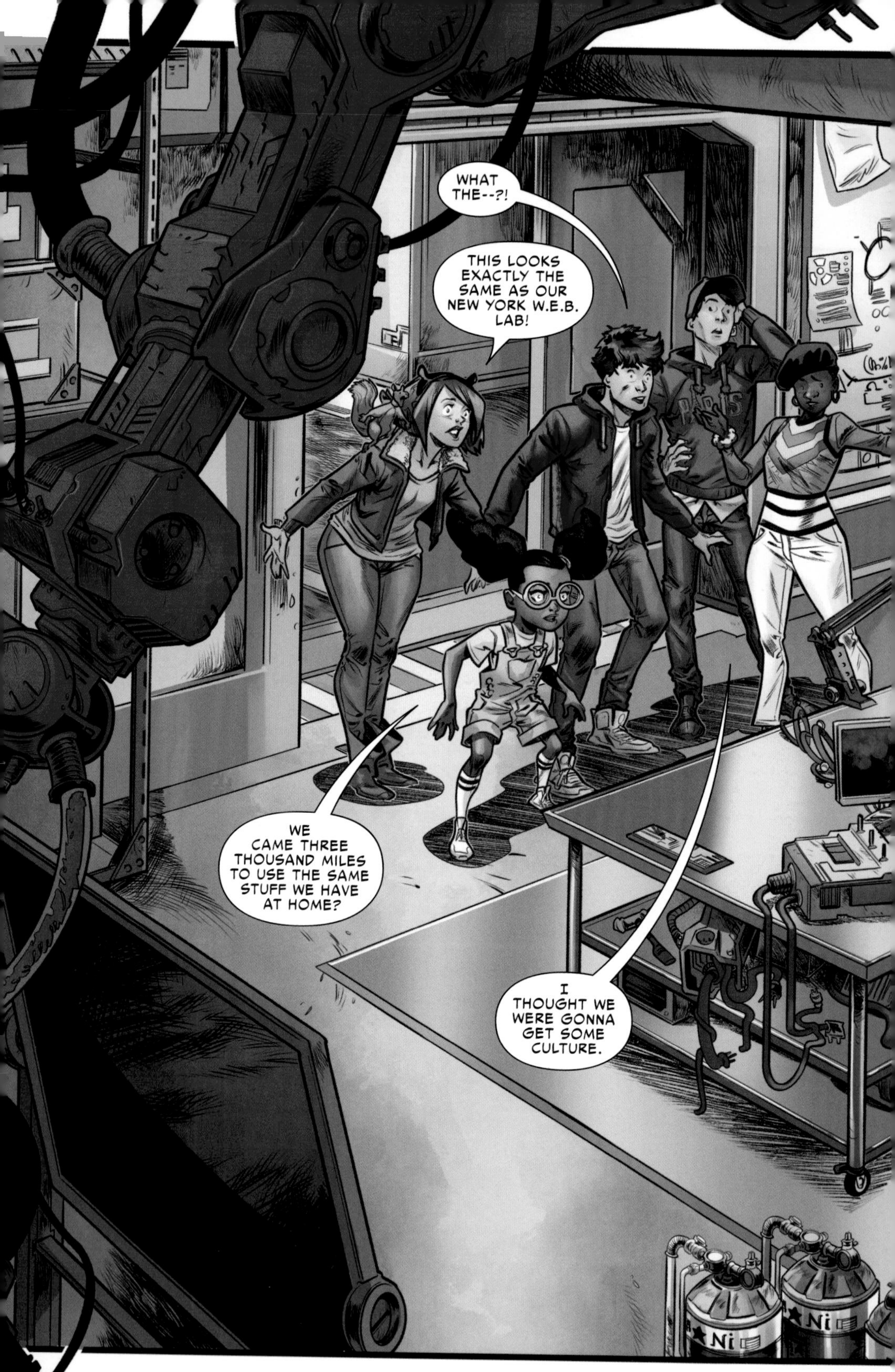
WHAT THE--?!
THIS LOOKS EXACTLY THE SAME AS OUR NEW YORK W.E.B. LAB!
WE CAME THREE THOUSAND MILES TO USE THE SAME STUFF WE HAVE AT HOME?
I THOUGHT WE WERE GONNA GET SOME CULTURE.

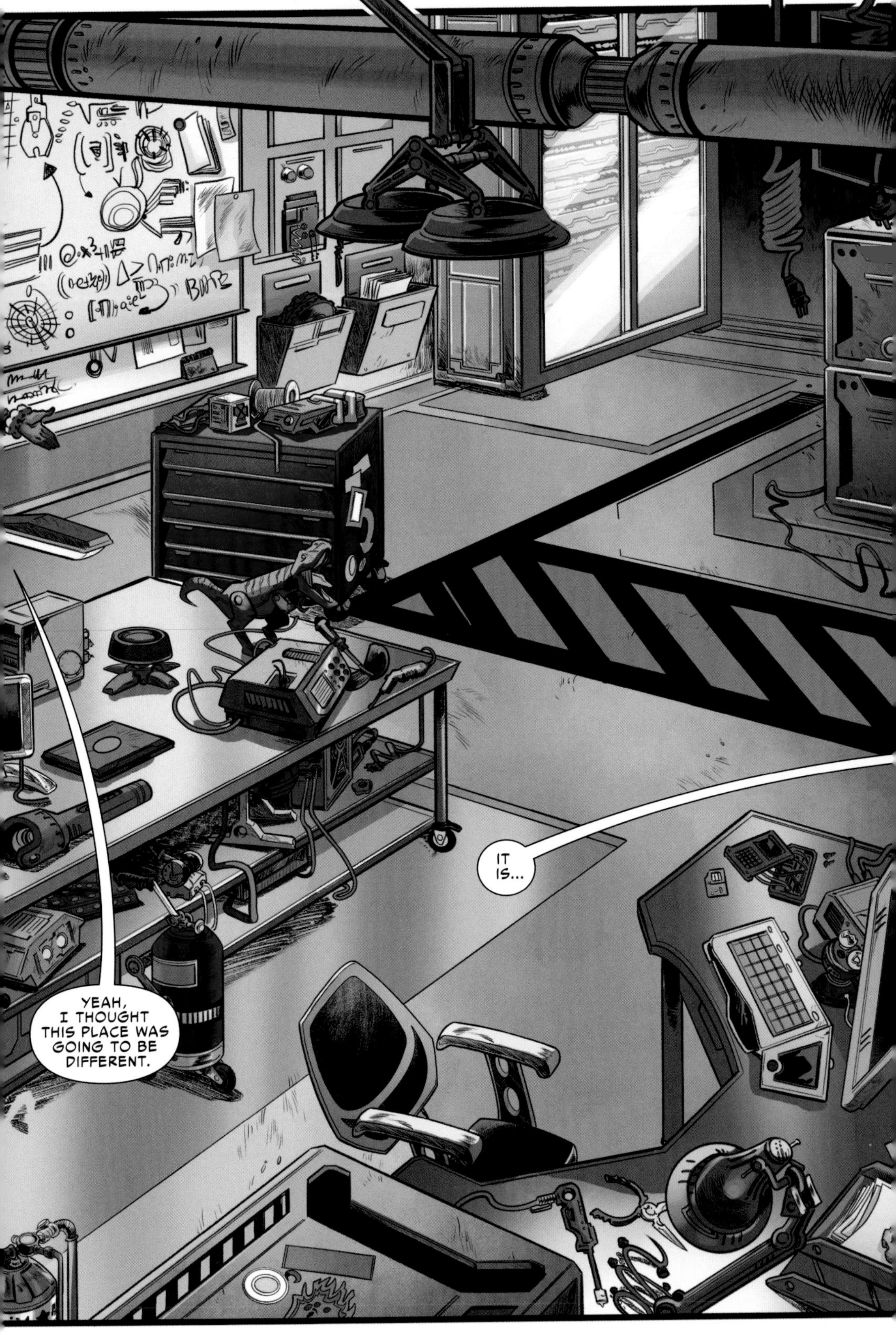
YEAH, I THOUGHT THIS PLACE WAS GOING TO BE DIFFERENT.
IT IS...

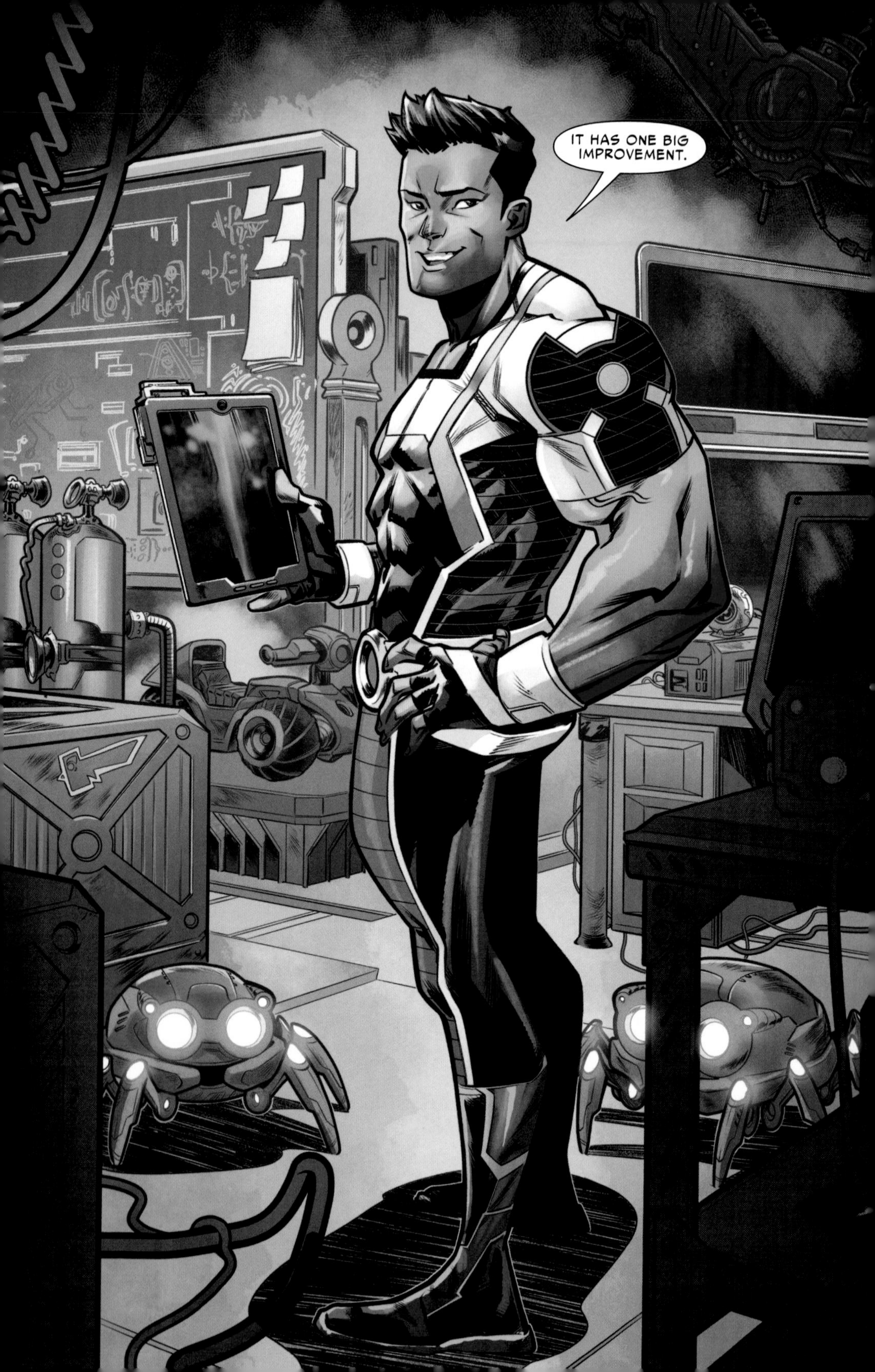
IT HAS ONE BIG IMPROVEMENT.

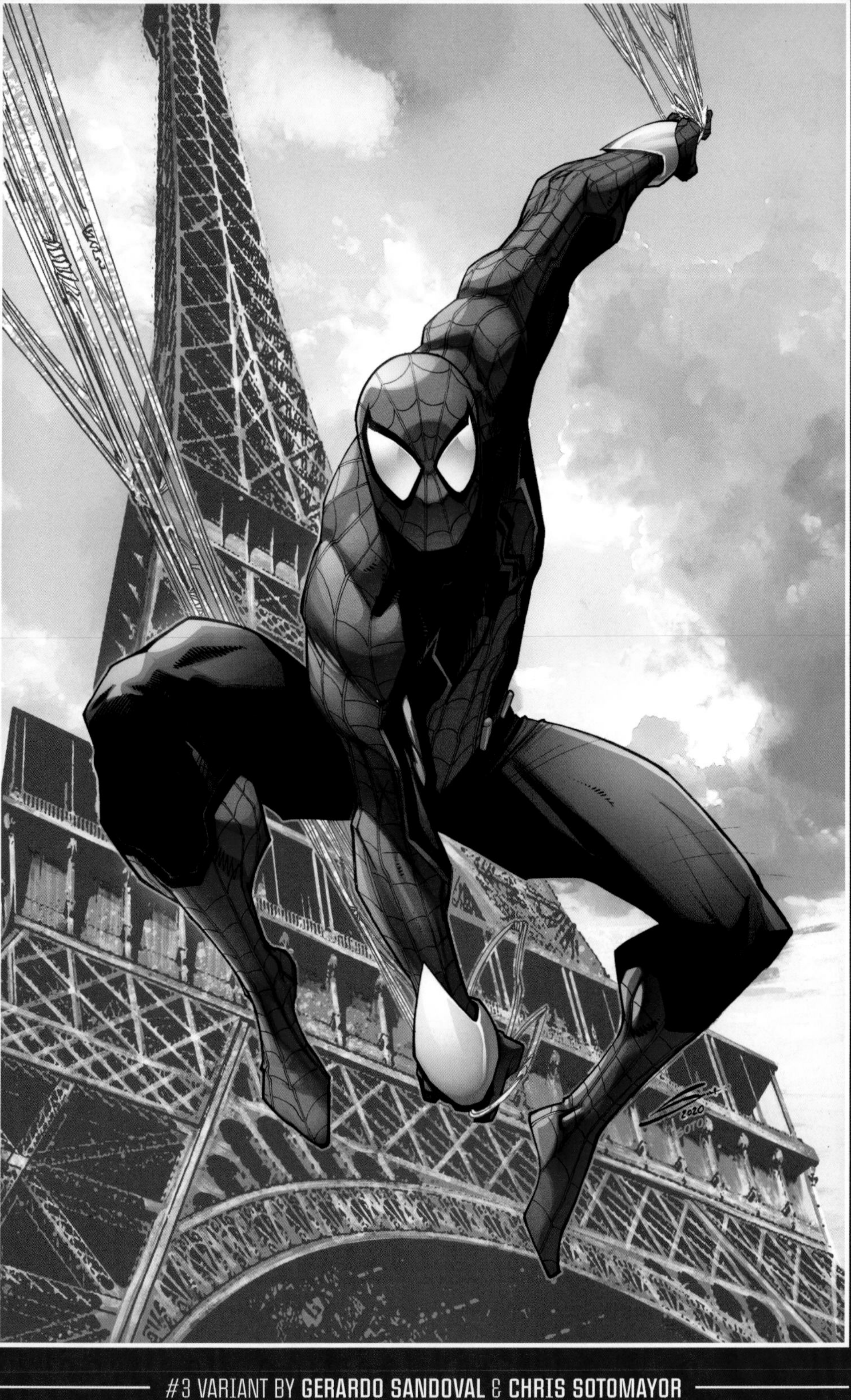
2020

#3 VARIANT BY **GERARDO SANDOVAL** & **CHRIS SOTOMAYOR**

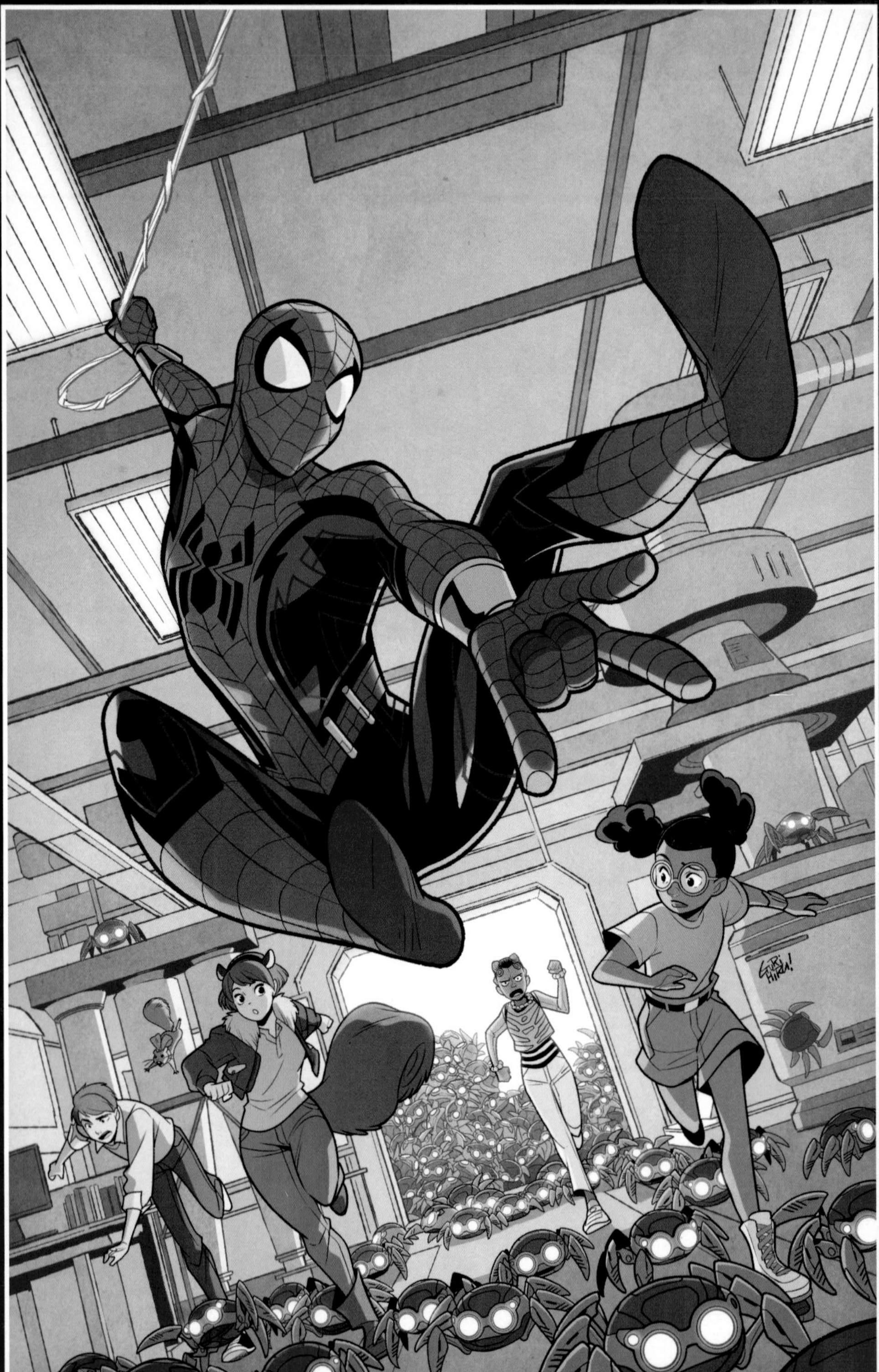

4

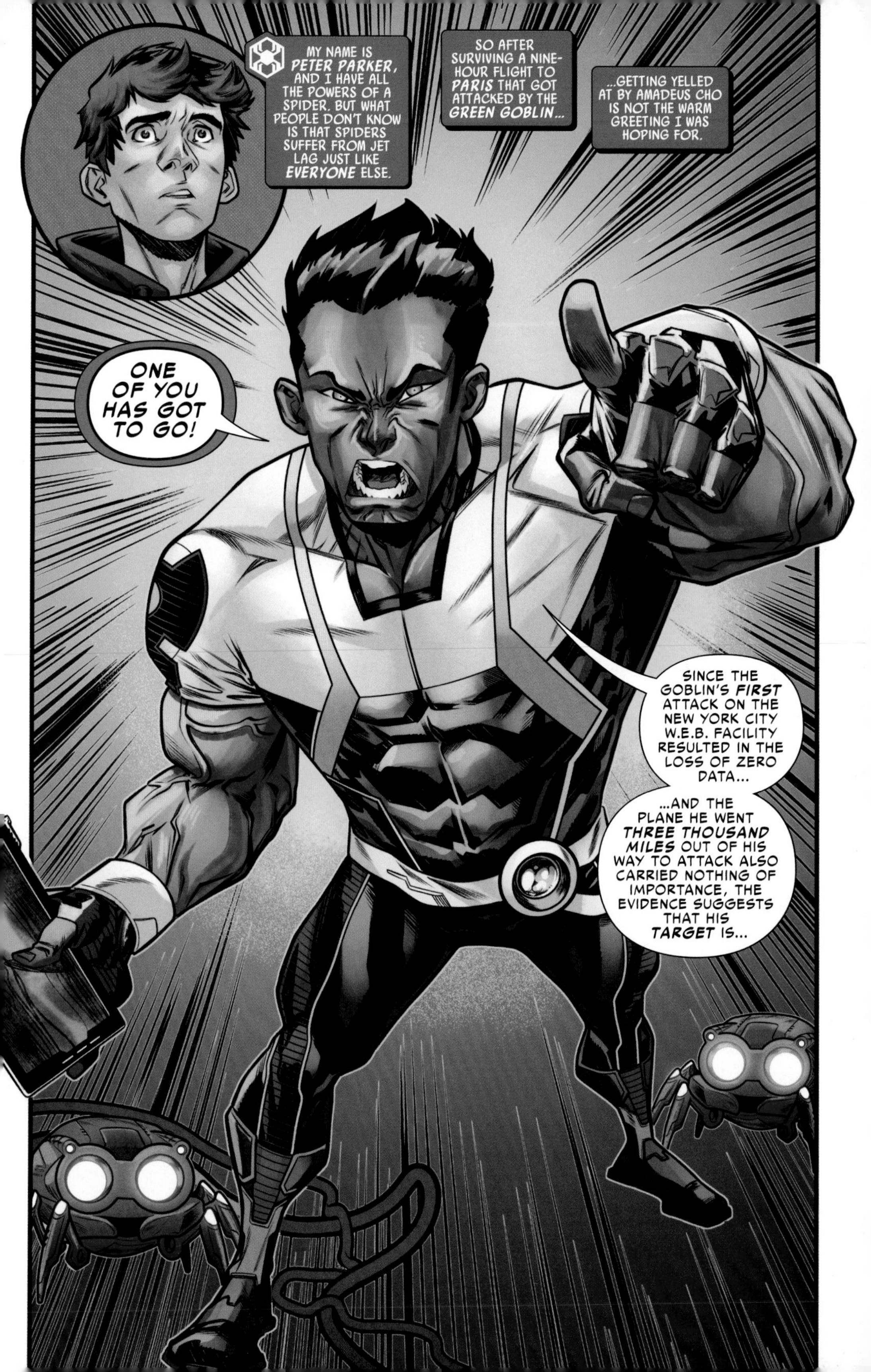
MY NAME IS PETER PARKER, AND I HAVE ALL THE POWERS OF A SPIDER. BUT WHAT PEOPLE DON'T KNOW IS THAT SPIDERS SUFFER FROM JET LAG JUST LIKE EVERYONE ELSE.
SO AFTER SURVIVING A NINE-HOUR FLIGHT TO PARIS THAT GOT ATTACKED BY THE GREEN GOBLIN...
...GETTING YELLED AT BY AMADEUS CHO IS NOT THE WARM GREETING I WAS HOPING FOR.
ONE OF YOU HAS GOT TO GO!
SINCE THE GOBLIN'S FIRST ATTACK ON THE NEW YORK CITY W.E.B. FACILITY RESULTED IN THE LOSS OF ZERO DATA...
...AND THE PLANE HE WENT THREE THOUSAND MILES OUT OF HIS WAY TO ATTACK ALSO CARRIED NOTHING OF IMPORTANCE, THE EVIDENCE SUGGESTS THAT HIS TARGET IS...

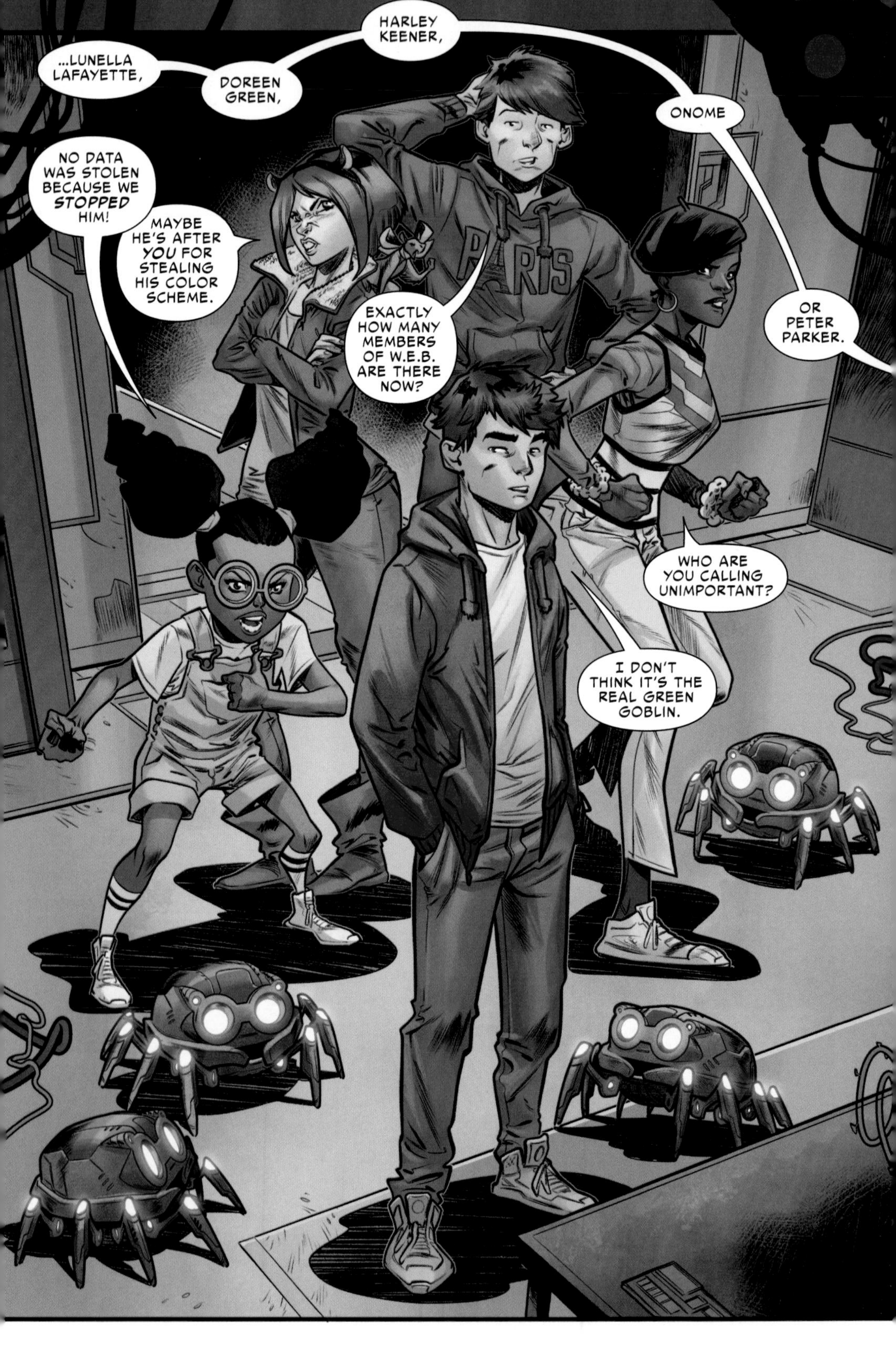

...LUNELLA LAFAYETTE,
DOREEN GREEN,
HARLEY KEENER,
ONOME
OR PETER PARKER.
NO DATA WAS STOLEN BECAUSE WE *STOPPED* HIM!
MAYBE HE'S AFTER *YOU* FOR STEALING HIS COLOR SCHEME.
EXACTLY HOW MANY MEMBERS OF W.E.B. ARE THERE NOW?
WHO ARE YOU CALLING UNIMPORTANT?
I DON'T THINK IT'S THE REAL GREEN GOBLIN.

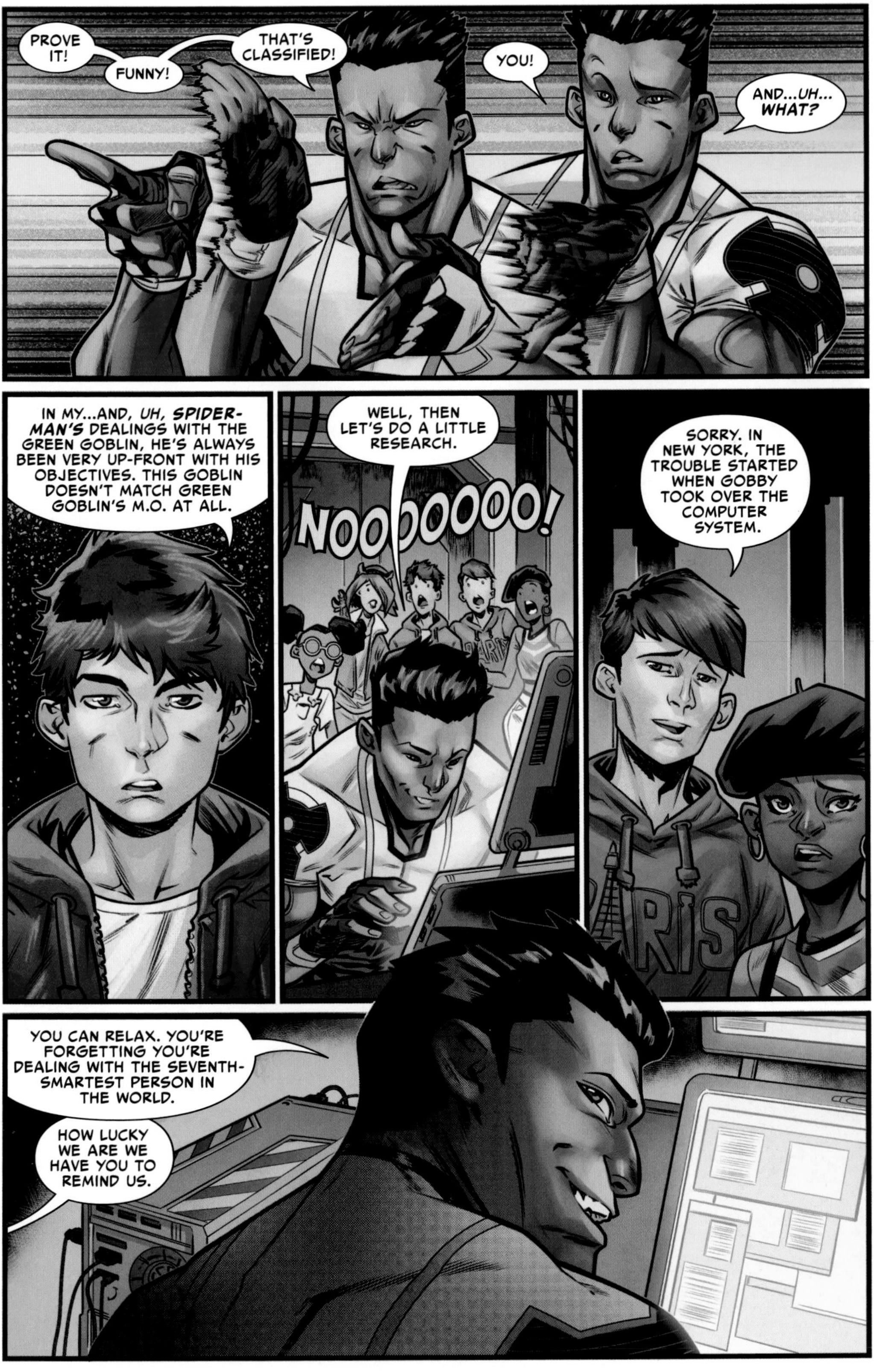
PROVE IT!
FUNNY!
THAT'S CLASSIFIED!
YOU!
AND...UH... WHAT?
IN MY...AND, UH, SPIDER-MAN'S DEALINGS WITH THE GREEN GOBLIN, HE'S ALWAYS BEEN VERY UP-FRONT WITH HIS OBJECTIVES. THIS GOBLIN DOESN'T MATCH GREEN GOBLIN'S M.O. AT ALL.
WELL, THEN LET'S DO A LITTLE RESEARCH.
NOOOOOOO!
SORRY. IN NEW YORK, THE TROUBLE STARTED WHEN GOBBY TOOK OVER THE COMPUTER SYSTEM.
YOU CAN RELAX. YOU'RE FORGETTING YOU'RE DEALING WITH THE SEVENTH-SMARTEST PERSON IN THE WORLD.
HOW LUCKY WE ARE WE HAVE YOU TO REMIND US.

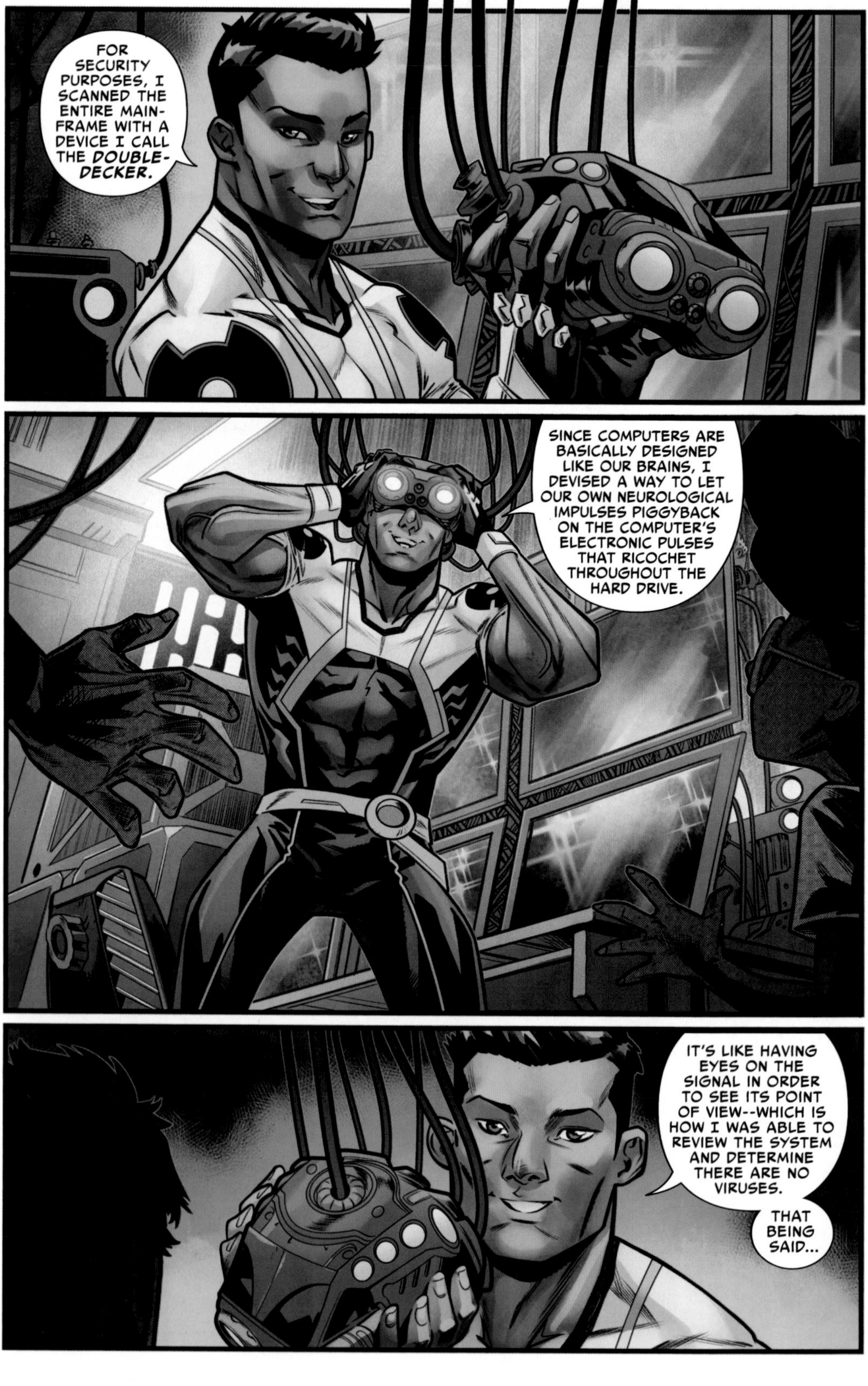
FOR SECURITY PURPOSES, I SCANNED THE ENTIRE MAIN-FRAME WITH A DEVICE I CALL THE *DOUBLE-DECKER*.
SINCE COMPUTERS ARE BASICALLY DESIGNED LIKE OUR BRAINS, I DEVISED A WAY TO LET OUR OWN NEUROLOGICAL IMPULSES PIGGYBACK ON THE COMPUTER'S ELECTRONIC PULSES THAT RICOCHET THROUGHOUT THE HARD DRIVE.
IT'S LIKE HAVING EYES ON THE SIGNAL IN ORDER TO SEE ITS POINT OF VIEW--WHICH IS HOW I WAS ABLE TO REVIEW THE SYSTEM AND DETERMINE THERE ARE NO VIRUSES.
THAT BEING SAID...

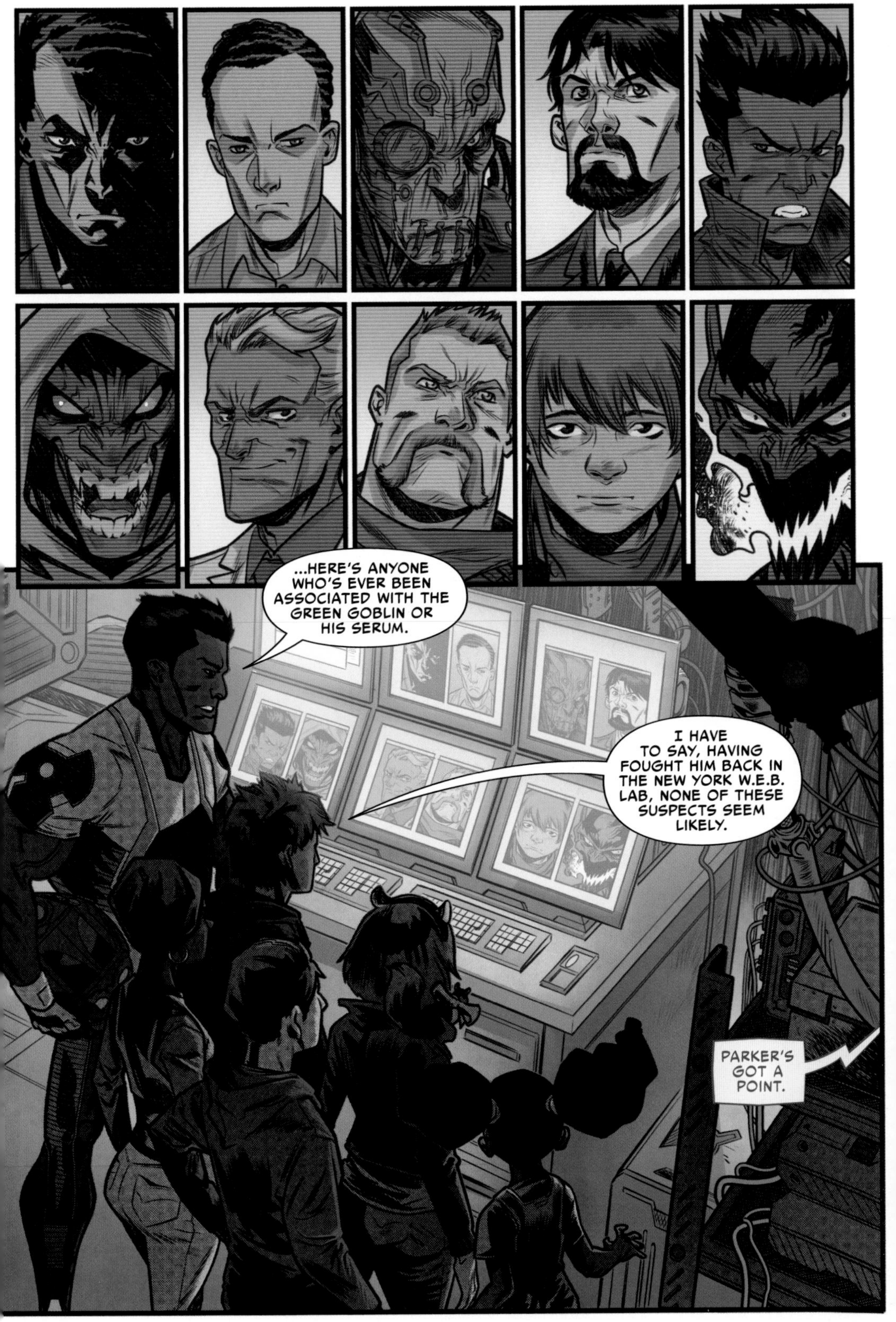
...HERE'S ANYONE WHO'S EVER BEEN ASSOCIATED WITH THE GREEN GOBLIN OR HIS SERUM.
I HAVE TO SAY, HAVING FOUGHT HIM BACK IN THE NEW YORK W.E.B. LAB, NONE OF THESE SUSPECTS SEEM LIKELY.
PARKER'S GOT A POINT.

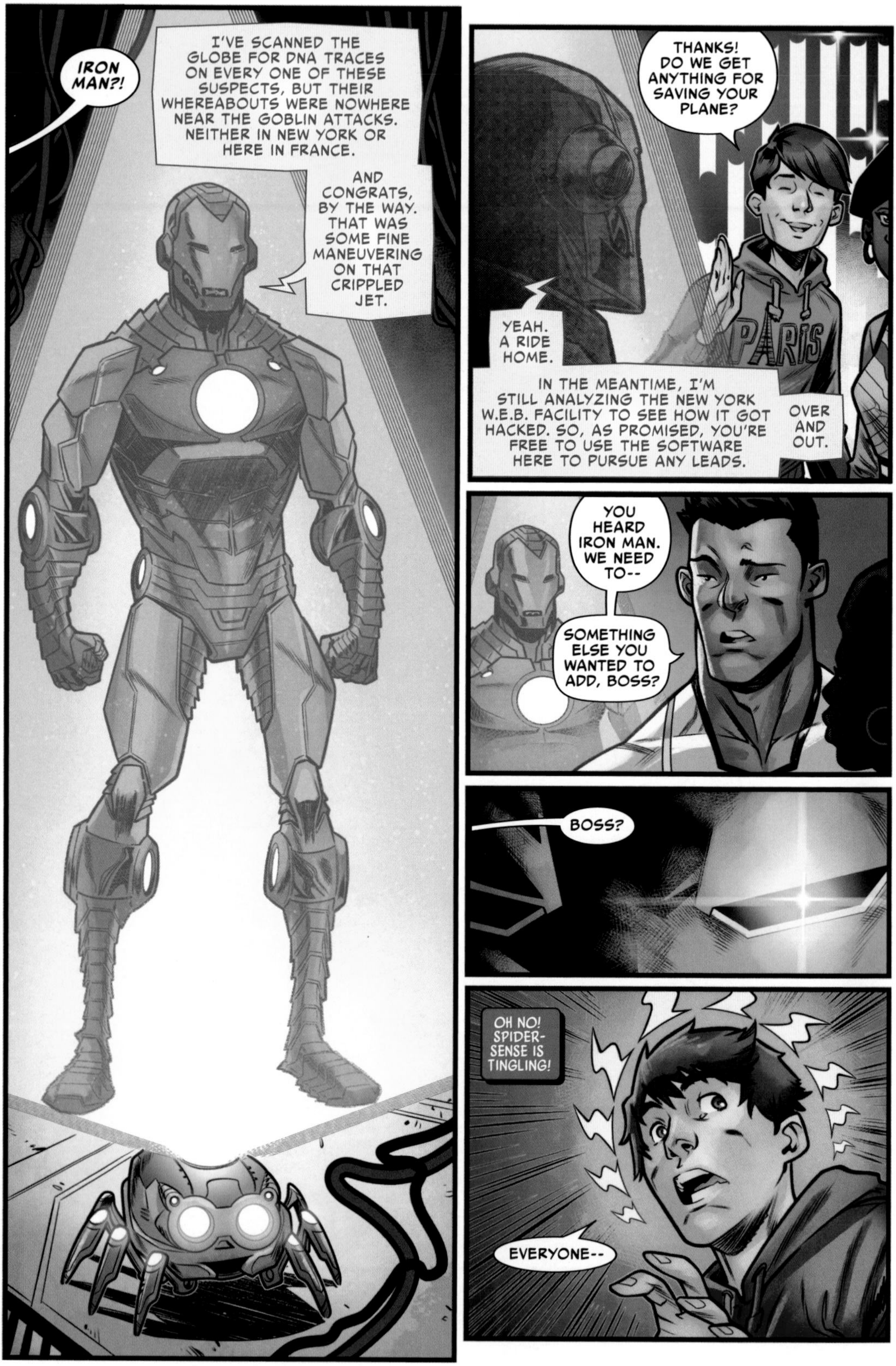
IRON MAN?!
I'VE SCANNED THE GLOBE FOR DNA TRACES ON EVERY ONE OF THESE SUSPECTS, BUT THEIR WHEREABOUTS WERE NOWHERE NEAR THE GOBLIN ATTACKS. NEITHER IN NEW YORK OR HERE IN FRANCE.
AND CONGRATS, BY THE WAY. THAT WAS SOME FINE MANEUVERING ON THAT CRIPPLED JET.
THANKS! DO WE GET ANYTHING FOR SAVING YOUR PLANE?
YEAH. A RIDE HOME.
IN THE MEANTIME, I'M STILL ANALYZING THE NEW YORK W.E.B. FACILITY TO SEE HOW IT GOT HACKED. SO, AS PROMISED, YOU'RE FREE TO USE THE SOFTWARE HERE TO PURSUE ANY LEADS.
OVER AND OUT.
PARIS
YOU HEARD IRON MAN. WE NEED TO--
SOMETHING ELSE YOU WANTED TO ADD, BOSS?
BOSS?
OH NO! SPIDER-SENSE IS TINGLING!
EVERYONE--

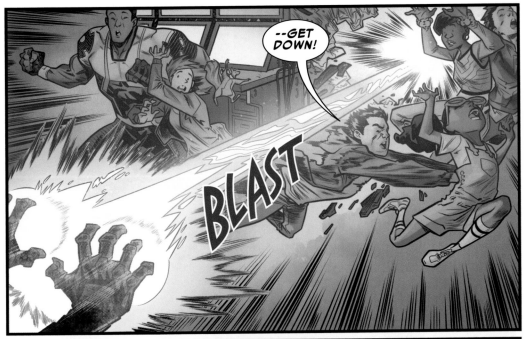

--GET DOWN!

BLAST

SOMEONE'S HIJACKED IRON MAN'S SIGNAL.

BUT I CAN'T LAND A PUNCH!

SWISHHH

TRUST US! WE'VE SEEN THIS BEFORE. W.E.B.'S BEEN COMPROMISED.

AGAIN!

BUT I SCANNED! THERE'S NO WAY ANYONE COULD'VE BROKEN IN HERE.

WHAT ABOUT BROKEN *OUT?* LIKE THE BUILDING ITSELF, THE FIRE WALLS ARE STRONGEST ON THE OUTSIDE TO PREVENT ENTRY. BUT MAYBE THEY'VE TARGETED THE WEAKER SIDE TO BREAK *OUT.*

WHY WOULD ANYONE WANT TO BREAK OUT OF W.E.B.?

UNLESS THEY WERE...

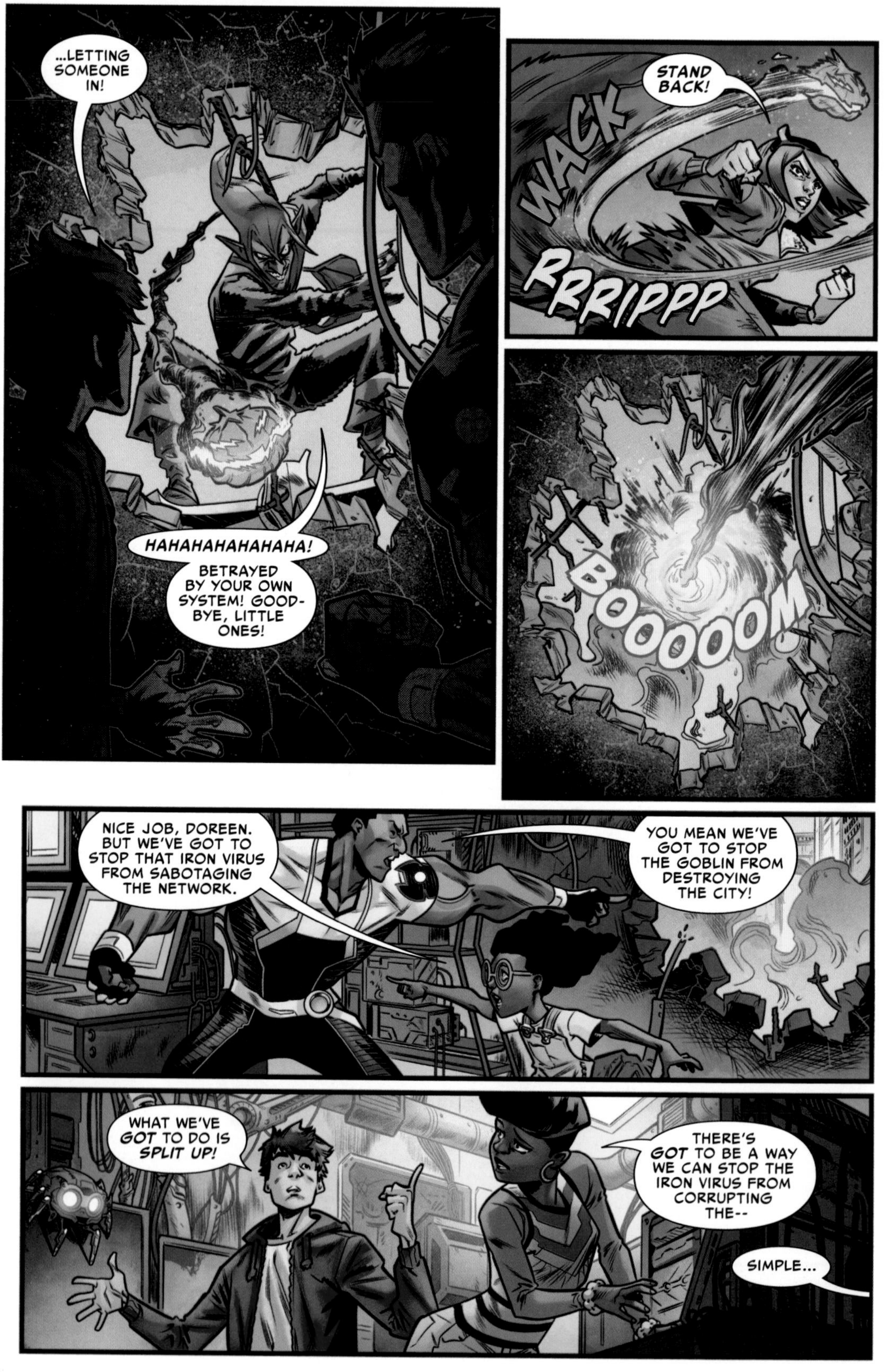
...LETTING SOMEONE IN!
HAHAHAHAHAHAHA!
BETRAYED BY YOUR OWN SYSTEM! GOOD-BYE, LITTLE ONES!
STAND BACK!
WACK
RRRIPPP
BOOOOOM
NICE JOB, DOREEN. BUT WE'VE GOT TO STOP THAT IRON VIRUS FROM SABOTAGING THE NETWORK.
YOU MEAN WE'VE GOT TO STOP THE GOBLIN FROM DESTROYING THE CITY!
THERE'S GOT TO BE A WAY WE CAN STOP THE IRON VIRUS FROM CORRUPTING THE--
WHAT WE'VE GOT TO DO IS SPLIT UP!
SIMPLE...

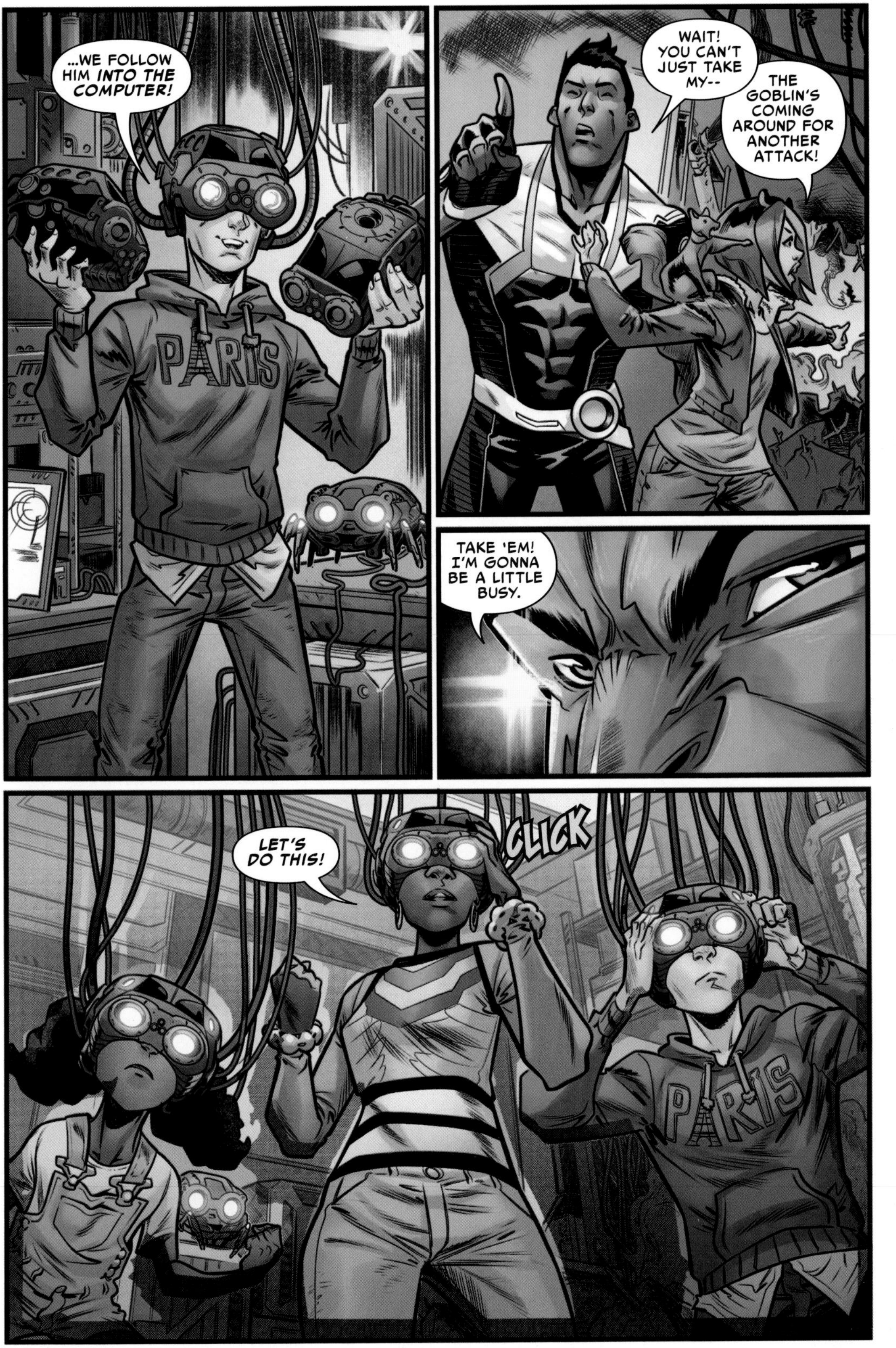

...WE FOLLOW HIM INTO THE COMPUTER!
WAIT! YOU CAN'T JUST TAKE MY--
THE GOBLIN'S COMING AROUND FOR ANOTHER ATTACK!
TAKE 'EM! I'M GONNA BE A LITTLE BUSY.
LET'S DO THIS!
CLICK
PARIS
PARIS

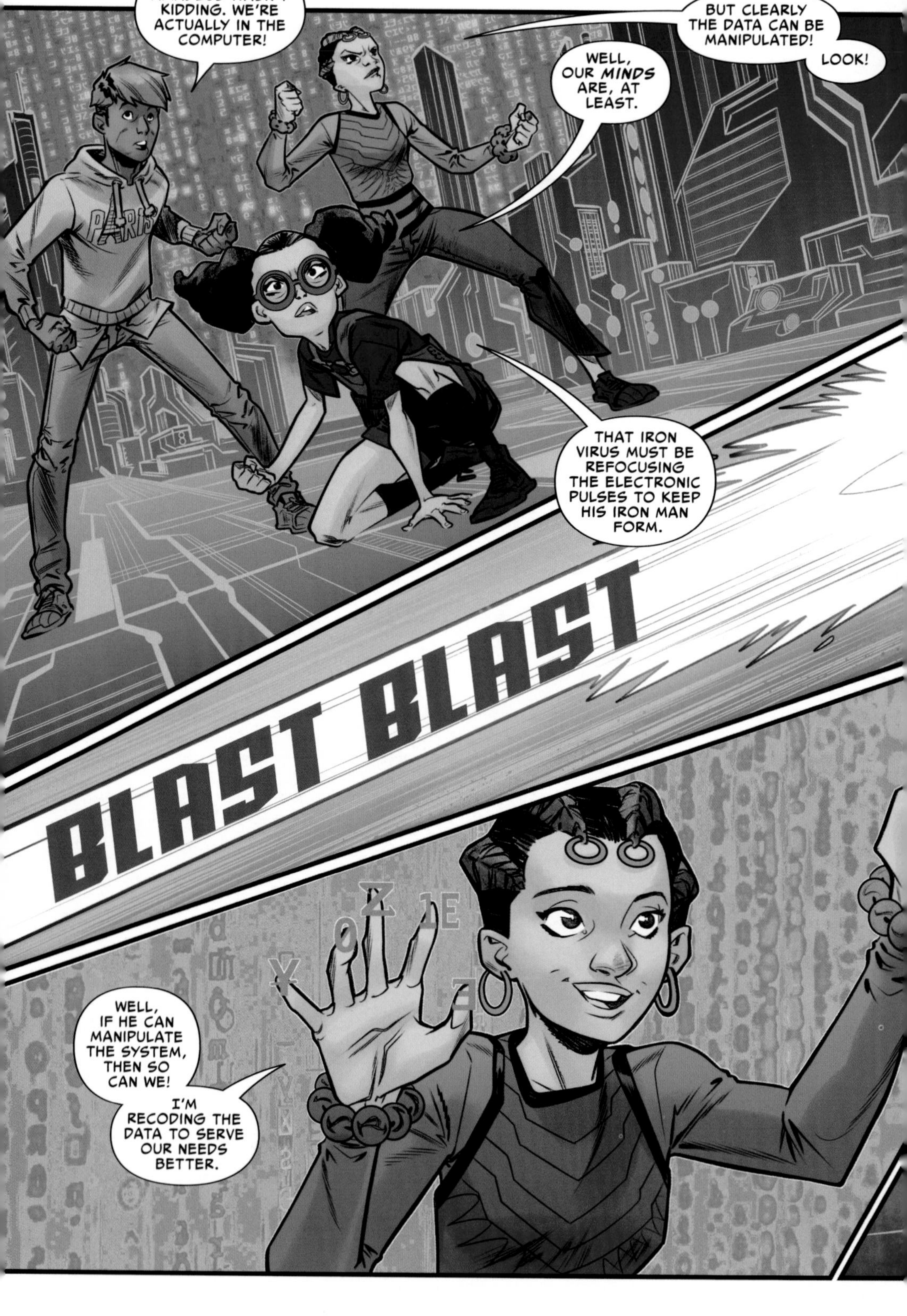
WHOA! AMADEUS WASN'T KIDDING. WE'RE ACTUALLY IN THE COMPUTER!
WELL, OUR *MINDS* ARE, AT LEAST.
BUT CLEARLY THE DATA CAN BE MANIPULATED!
LOOK!
THAT IRON VIRUS MUST BE REFOCUSING THE ELECTRONIC PULSES TO KEEP HIS IRON MAN FORM.
BLAST BLAST
WELL, IF HE CAN MANIPULATE THE SYSTEM, THEN SO CAN WE!
I'M RECODING THE DATA TO SERVE OUR NEEDS BETTER.

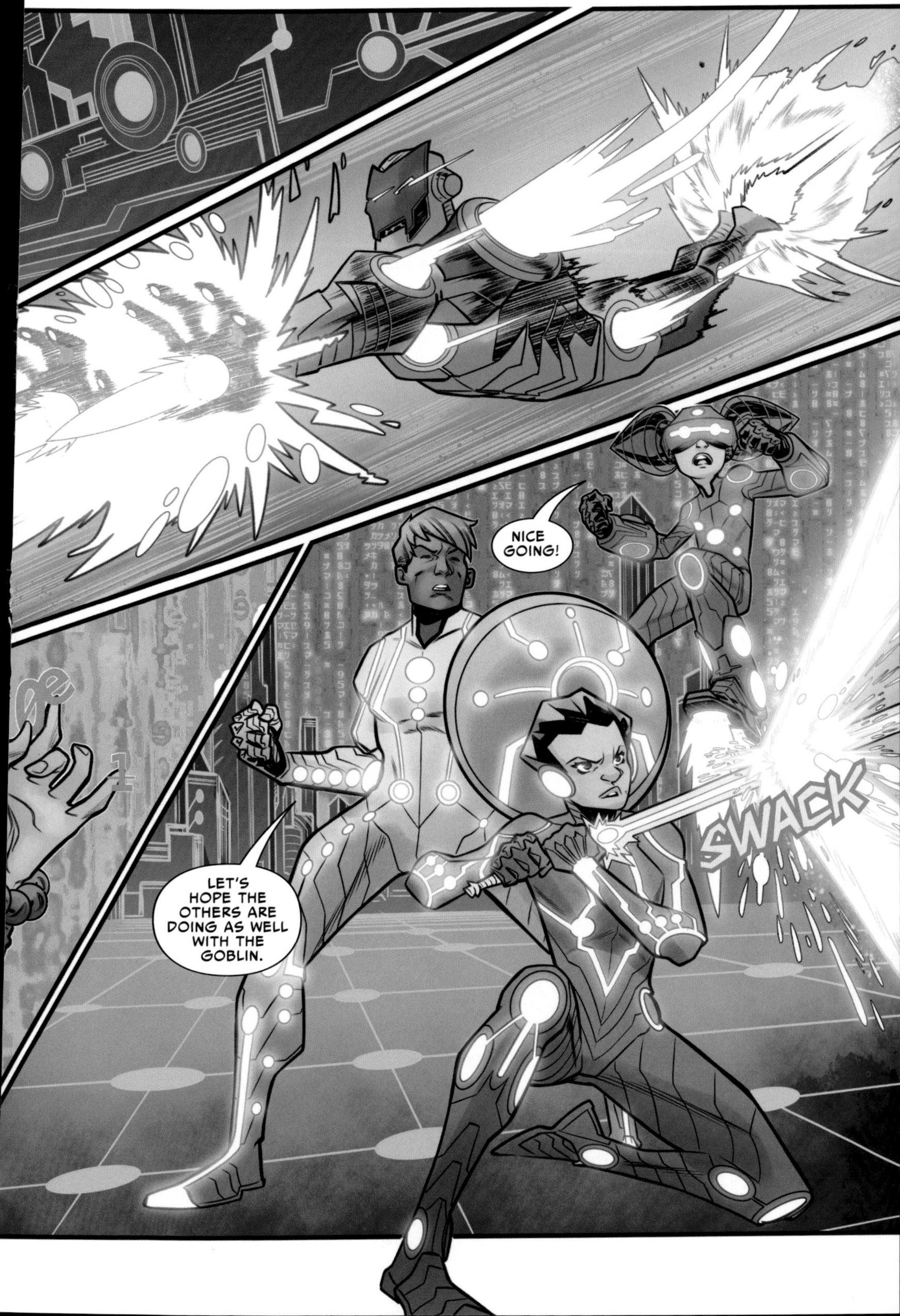
NICE GOING!
LET'S HOPE THE OTHERS ARE DOING AS WELL WITH THE GOBLIN.
SWACK

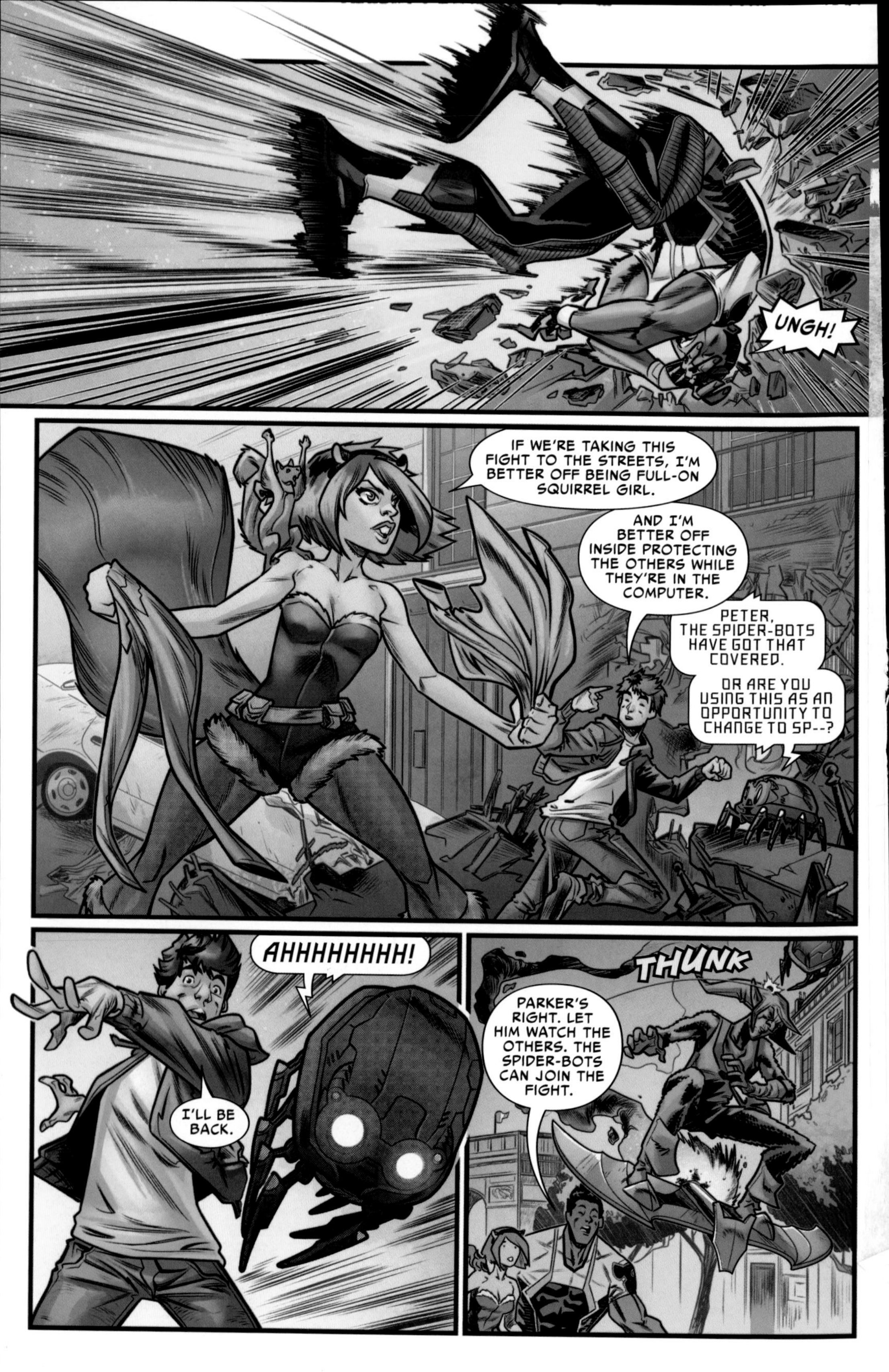
UNGH!
IF WE'RE TAKING THIS FIGHT TO THE STREETS, I'M BETTER OFF BEING FULL-ON SQUIRREL GIRL.
AND I'M BETTER OFF INSIDE PROTECTING THE OTHERS WHILE THEY'RE IN THE COMPUTER.
PETER, THE SPIDER-BOTS HAVE GOT THAT COVERED.
OR ARE YOU USING THIS AS AN OPPORTUNITY TO CHANGE TO SP--?
AHHHHHHHH!
I'LL BE BACK.
THUNK
PARKER'S RIGHT. LET HIM WATCH THE OTHERS. THE SPIDER-BOTS CAN JOIN THE FIGHT.

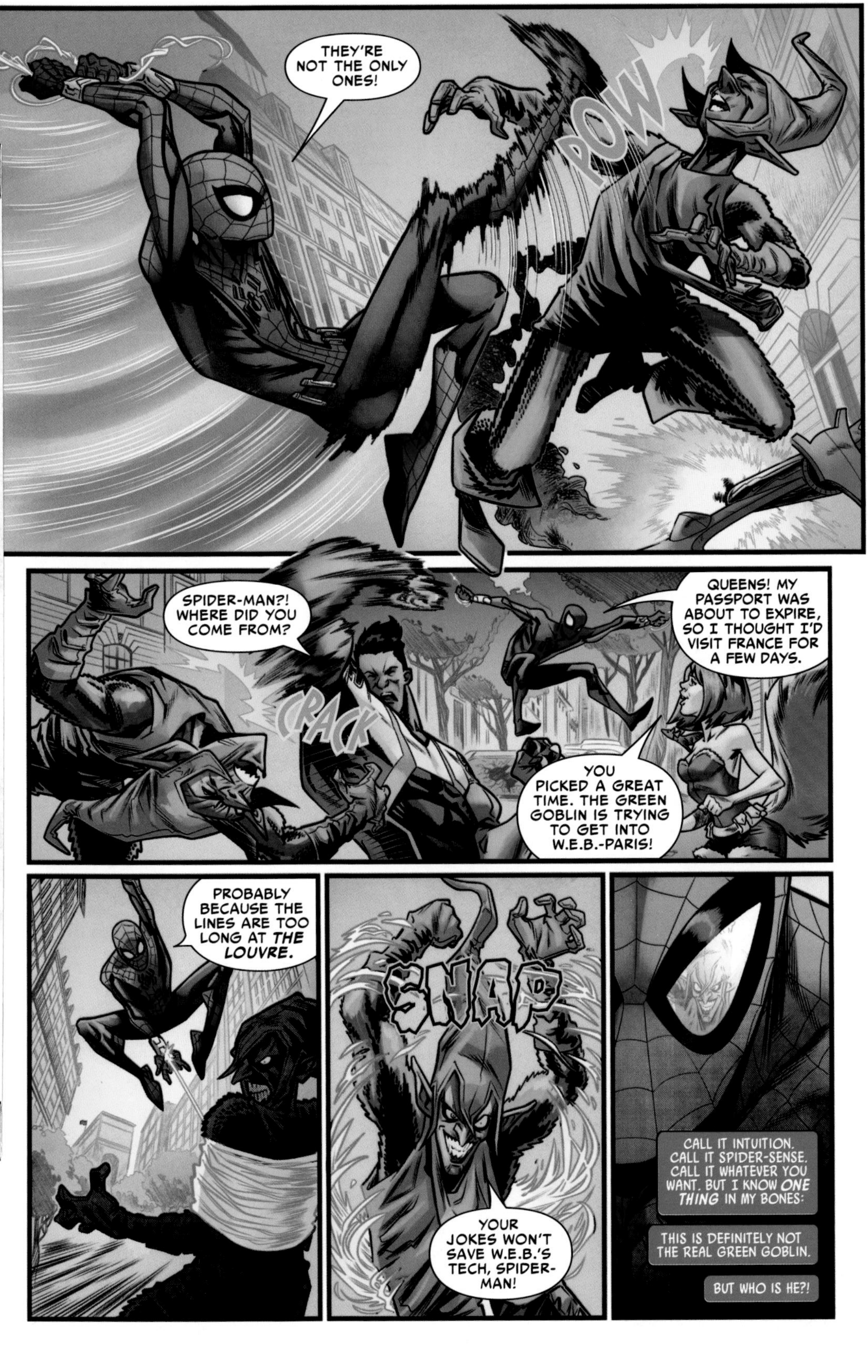
THEY'RE NOT THE ONLY ONES!
POW
SPIDER-MAN?! WHERE DID YOU COME FROM?
CRACK
QUEENS! MY PASSPORT WAS ABOUT TO EXPIRE, SO I THOUGHT I'D VISIT FRANCE FOR A FEW DAYS.
YOU PICKED A GREAT TIME. THE GREEN GOBLIN IS TRYING TO GET INTO W.E.B.-PARIS!
PROBABLY BECAUSE THE LINES ARE TOO LONG AT THE LOUVRE.
SNAP
YOUR JOKES WON'T SAVE W.E.B.'S TECH, SPIDER-MAN!
CALL IT INTUITION. CALL IT SPIDER-SENSE. CALL IT WHATEVER YOU WANT. BUT I KNOW ONE THING IN MY BONES:
THIS IS DEFINITELY NOT THE REAL GREEN GOBLIN.
BUT WHO IS HE?!

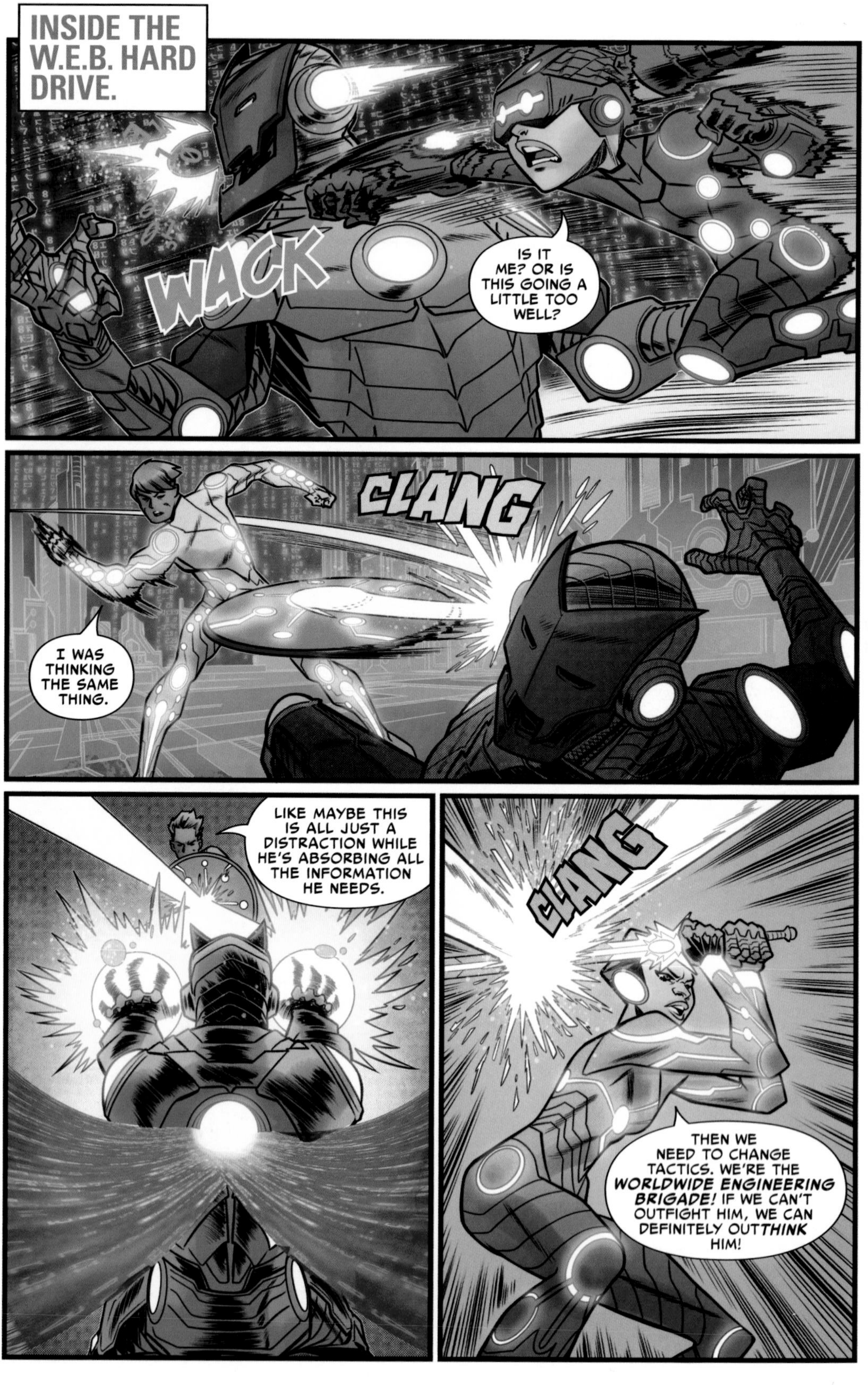

INSIDE THE W.E.B. HARD DRIVE.
WACK
IS IT ME? OR IS THIS GOING A LITTLE TOO WELL?
CLANG
I WAS THINKING THE SAME THING.
LIKE MAYBE THIS IS ALL JUST A DISTRACTION WHILE HE'S ABSORBING ALL THE INFORMATION HE NEEDS.
CLANG
THEN WE NEED TO CHANGE TACTICS. WE'RE THE WORLDWIDE ENGINEERING BRIGADE! IF WE CAN'T OUTFIGHT HIM, WE CAN DEFINITELY OUTTHINK HIM!

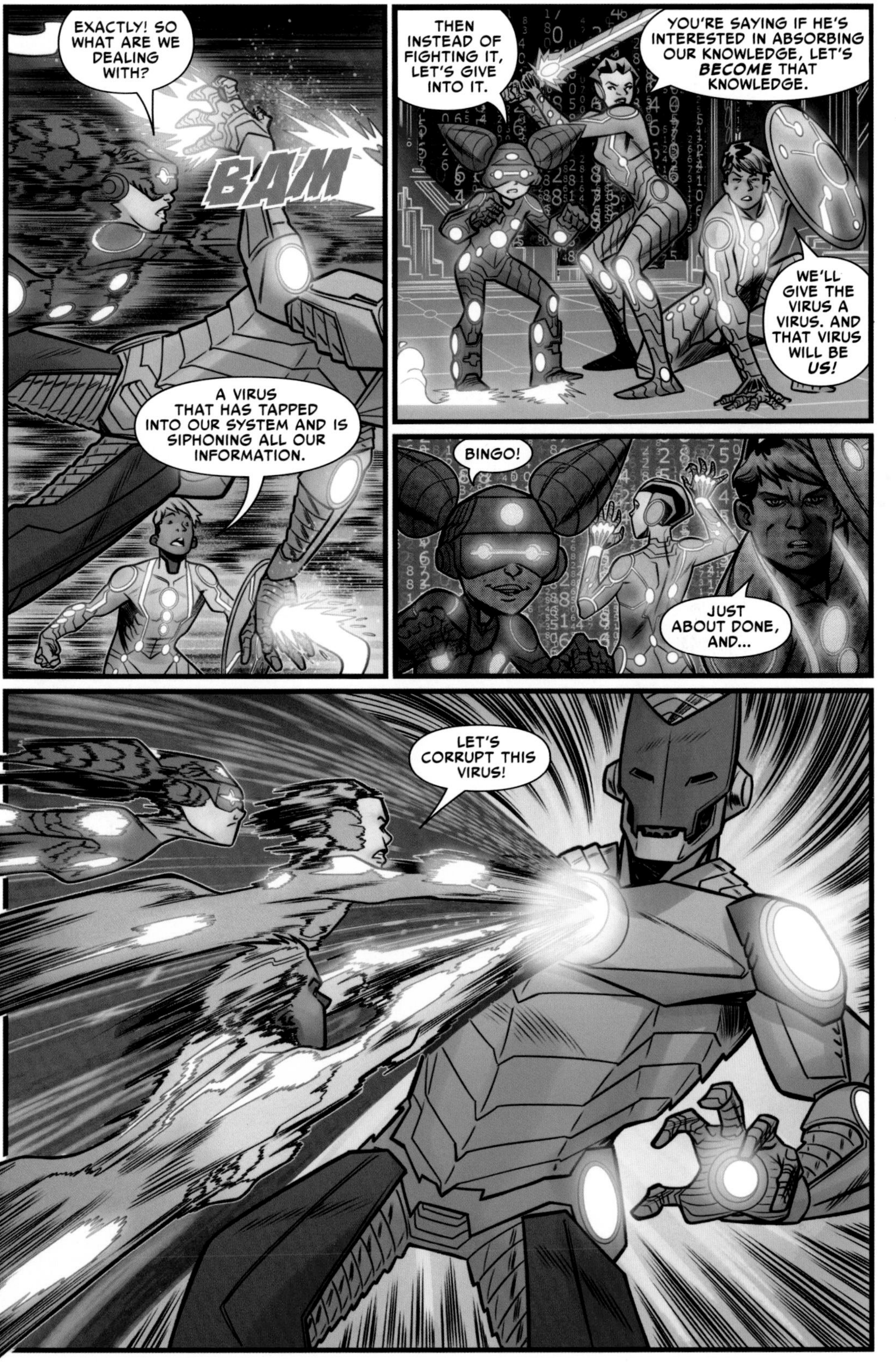
EXACTLY! SO WHAT ARE WE DEALING WITH?
BAM
A VIRUS THAT HAS TAPPED INTO OUR SYSTEM AND IS SIPHONING ALL OUR INFORMATION.
THEN INSTEAD OF FIGHTING IT, LET'S GIVE INTO IT.
YOU'RE SAYING IF HE'S INTERESTED IN ABSORBING OUR KNOWLEDGE, LET'S *BECOME* THAT KNOWLEDGE.
WE'LL GIVE THE VIRUS A VIRUS. AND THAT VIRUS WILL BE *US!*
BINGO!
JUST ABOUT DONE, AND...
LET'S CORRUPT THIS VIRUS!

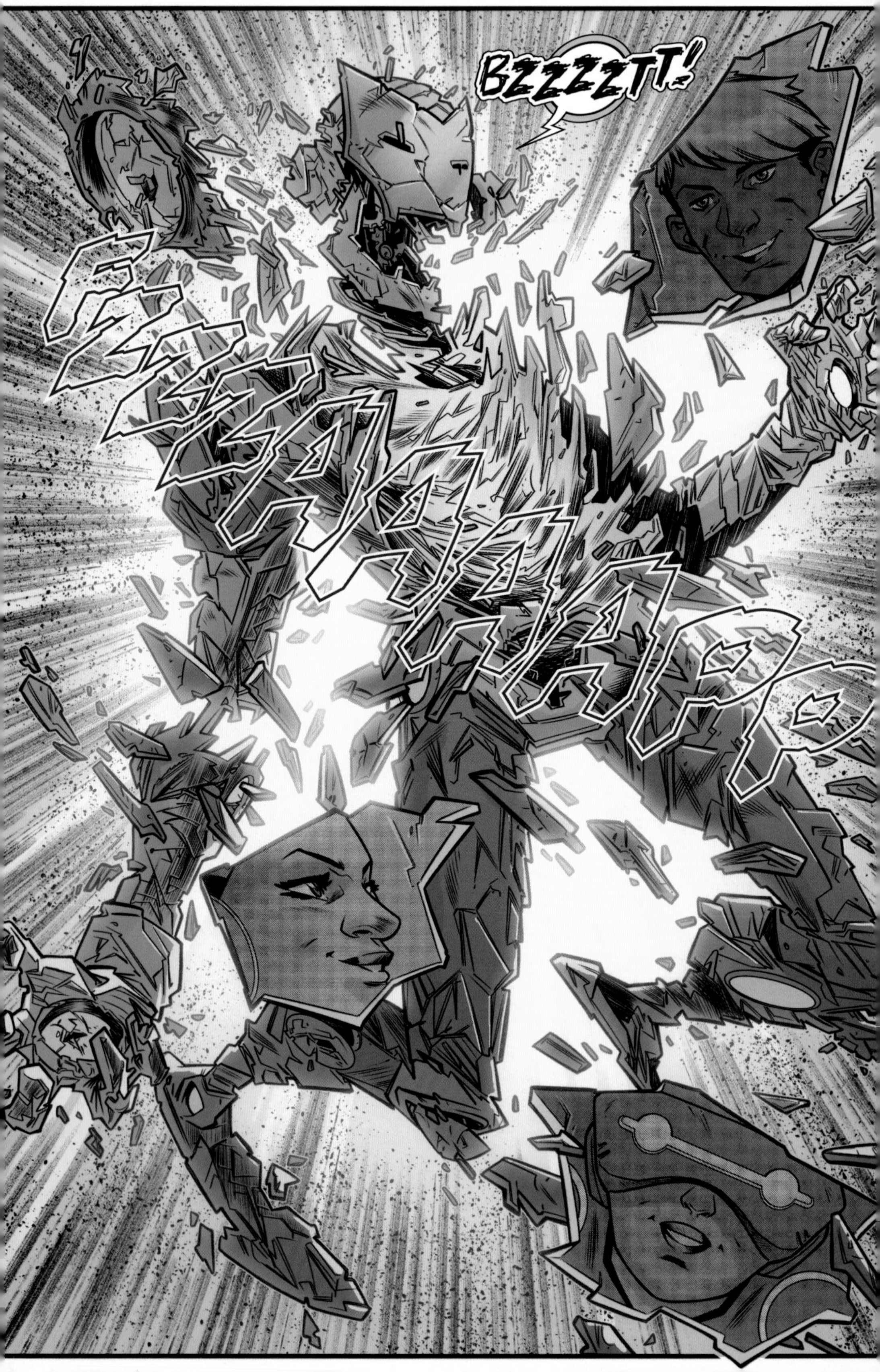
BZZZZZTT!

I'VE JUST BEEN ALERTED THAT THE OTHER MEMBERS OF W.E.B. HAVE SUCCEEDED!

ADDITIONAL SPIDER-BOTS ARE NOW LEAVING THEIR POSTS AND ARE ON THEIR WAY TO HELP US!

HOW DO WE KNOW THEY WON'T BE HACKED AS WELL?

EXACTLY! IN FACT, THEY'RE FLYING RIGHT PAST US.

GUYS, MY ENHANCED SQUIRREL-SNIFFING IS DETECTING AN ODOR THAT I'VE ONLY EVER FOUND IN THE FABRICATION OF ARTIFICIAL FLESH.

SO YOU'RE SAYING GOBBY ISN'T HUMAN?

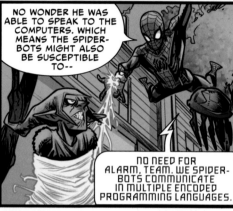

NO WONDER HE WAS ABLE TO SPEAK TO THE COMPUTERS. WHICH MEANS THE SPIDER-BOTS MIGHT ALSO BE SUSCEPTIBLE TO--

NO NEED FOR ALARM, TEAM. WE SPIDER-BOTS COMMUNICATE IN MULTIPLE ENCODED PROGRAMMING LANGUAGES.

SO WHAT YOU'RE SAYING IS, NOT EVERYONE NEEDS TO...

POW

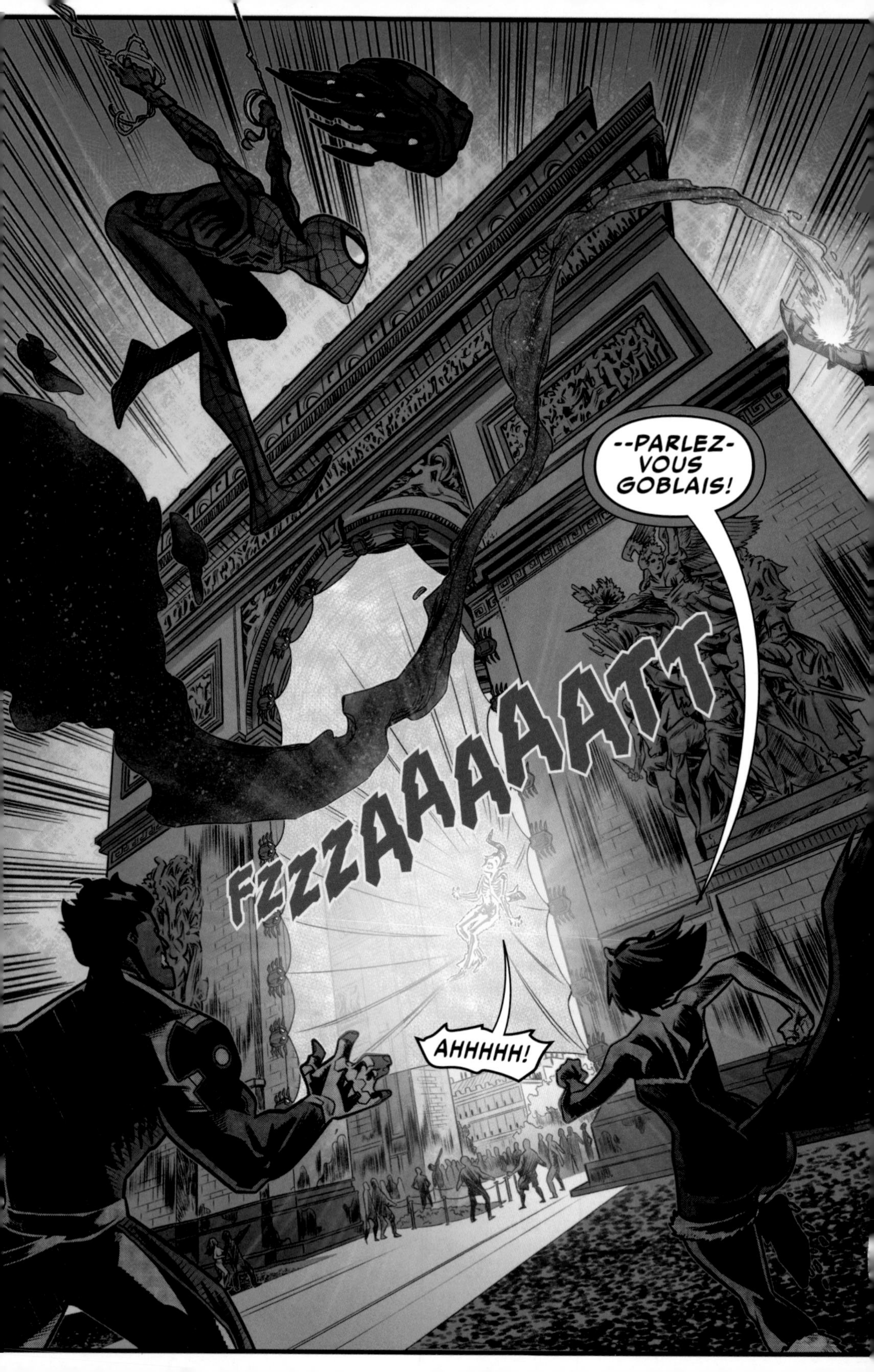
--PARLEZ-VOUS GOBLAIS!
FZZZAAAAATT
AHHHHH!

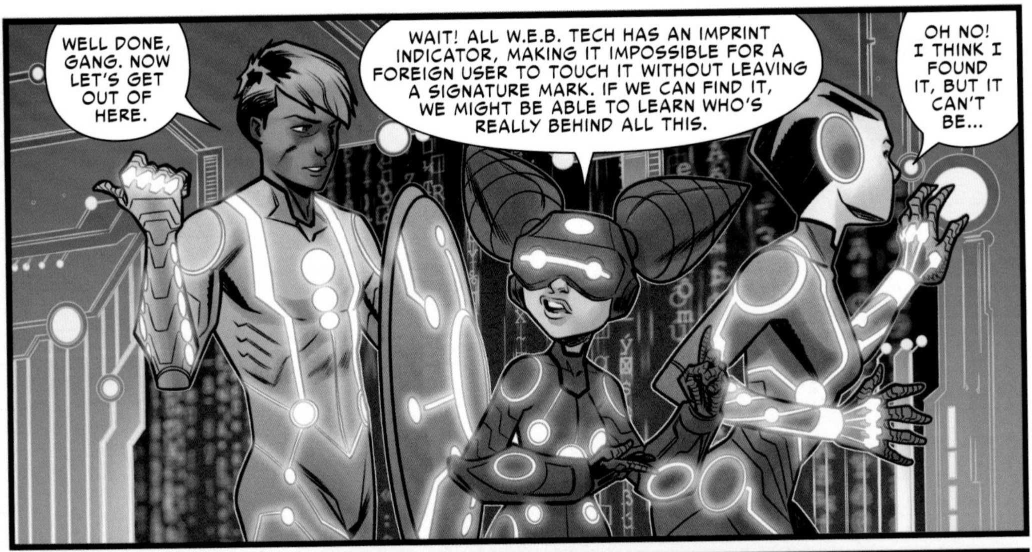
WELL DONE, GANG. NOW LET'S GET OUT OF HERE.
WAIT! ALL W.E.B. TECH HAS AN IMPRINT INDICATOR, MAKING IT IMPOSSIBLE FOR A FOREIGN USER TO TOUCH IT WITHOUT LEAVING A SIGNATURE MARK. IF WE CAN FIND IT, WE MIGHT BE ABLE TO LEARN WHO'S REALLY BEHIND ALL THIS.
OH NO! I THINK I FOUND IT, BUT IT CAN'T BE...

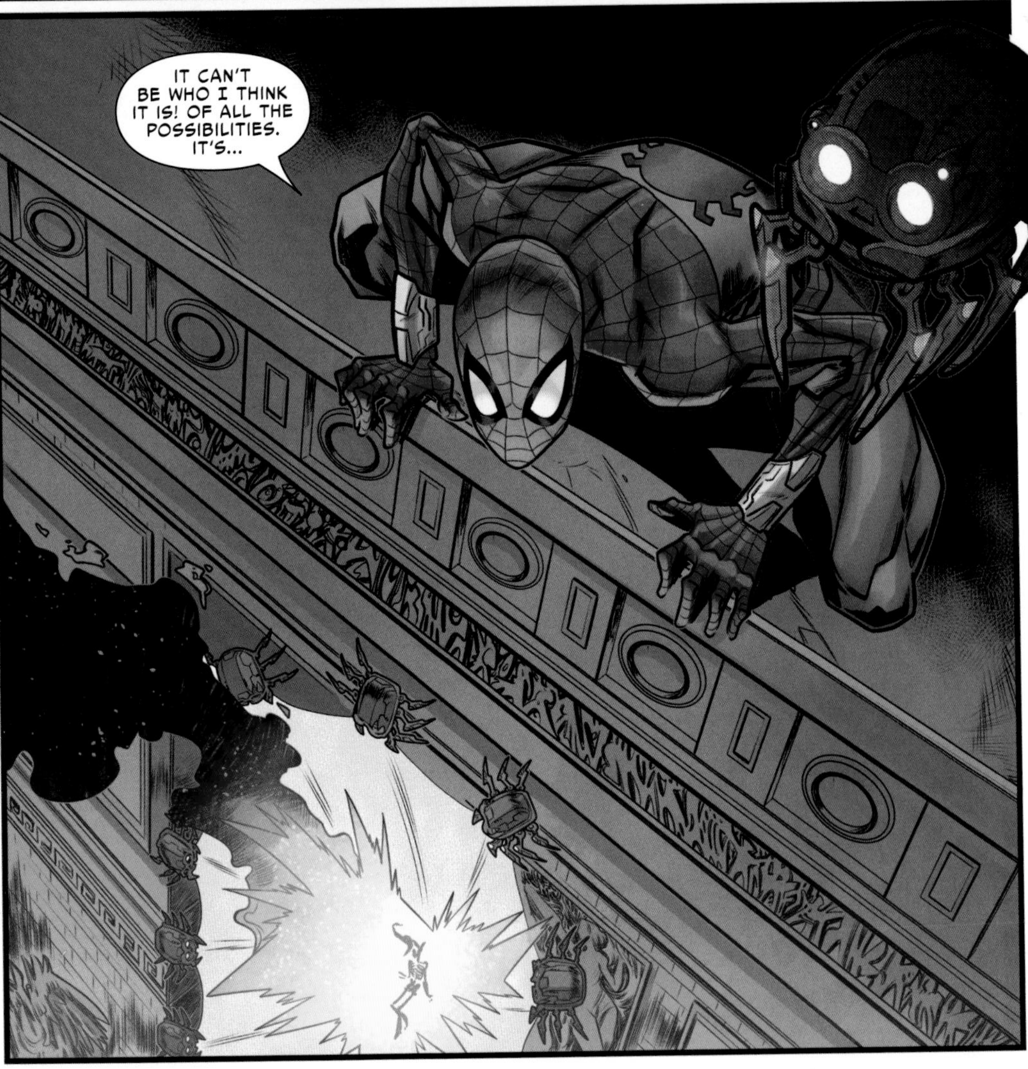
IT CAN'T BE WHO I THINK IT IS! OF ALL THE POSSIBILITIES. IT'S...

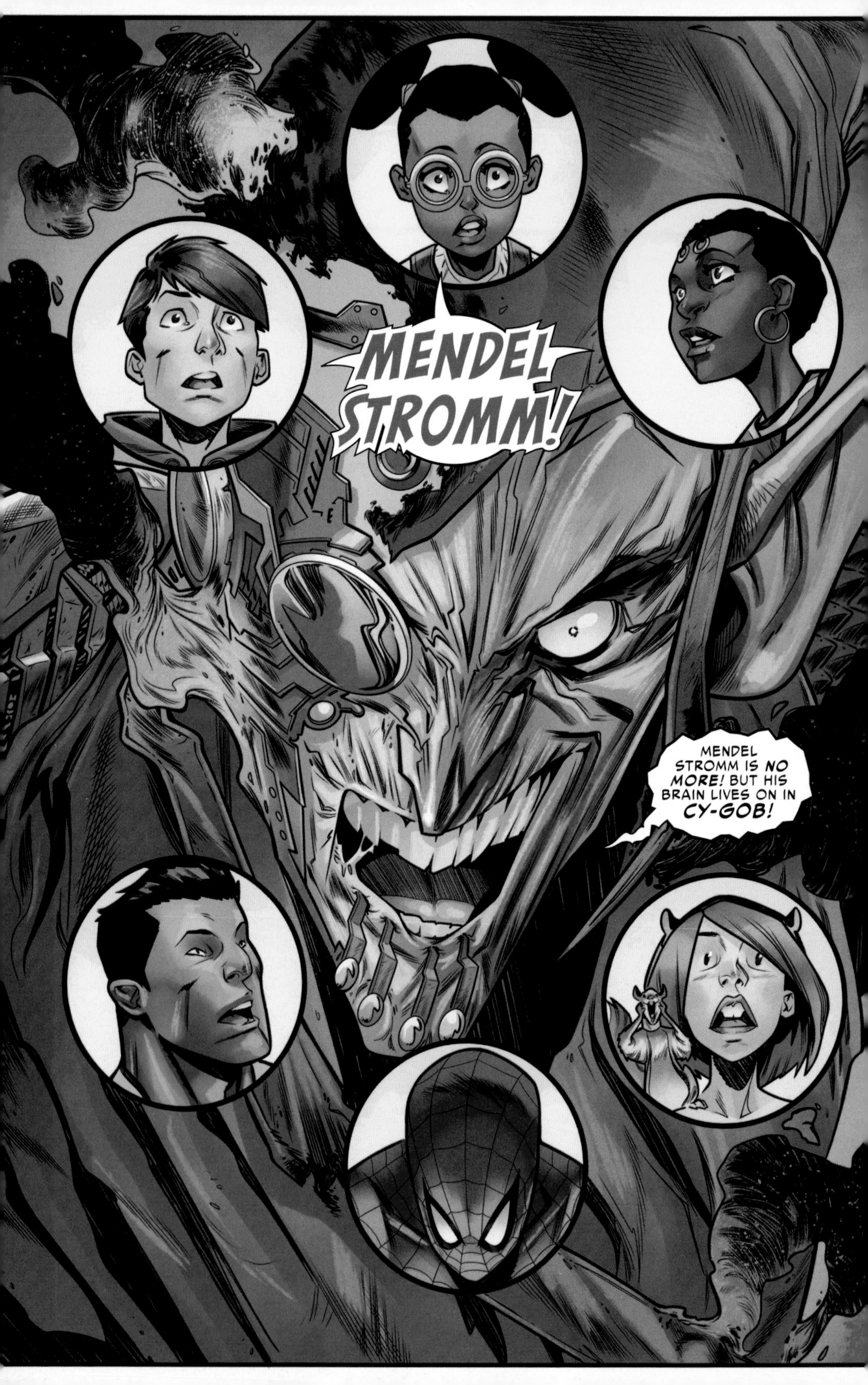
MENDEL STROMM!
MENDEL STROMM IS NO MORE! BUT HIS BRAIN LIVES ON IN CY-GOB!

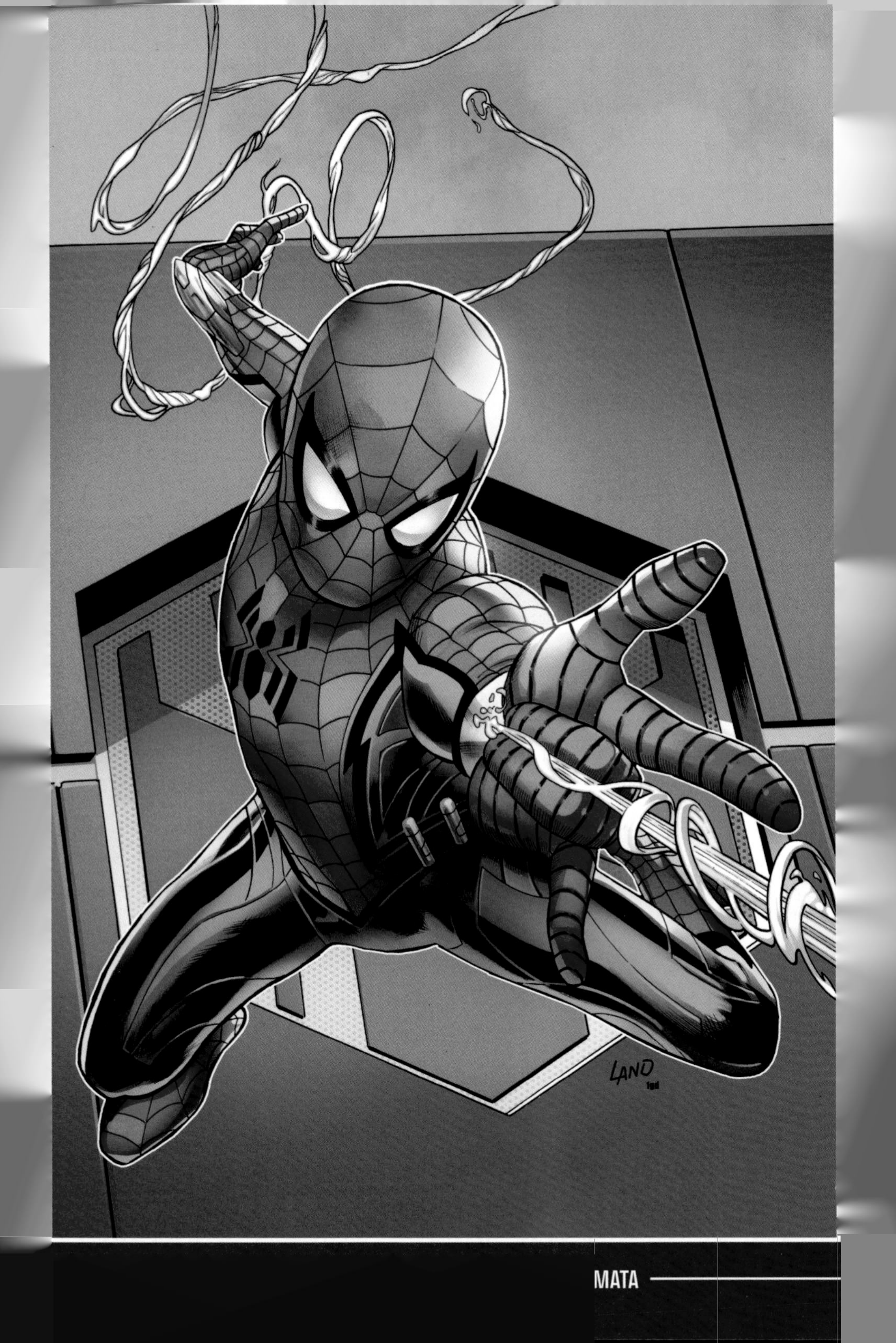
LAND

MATA

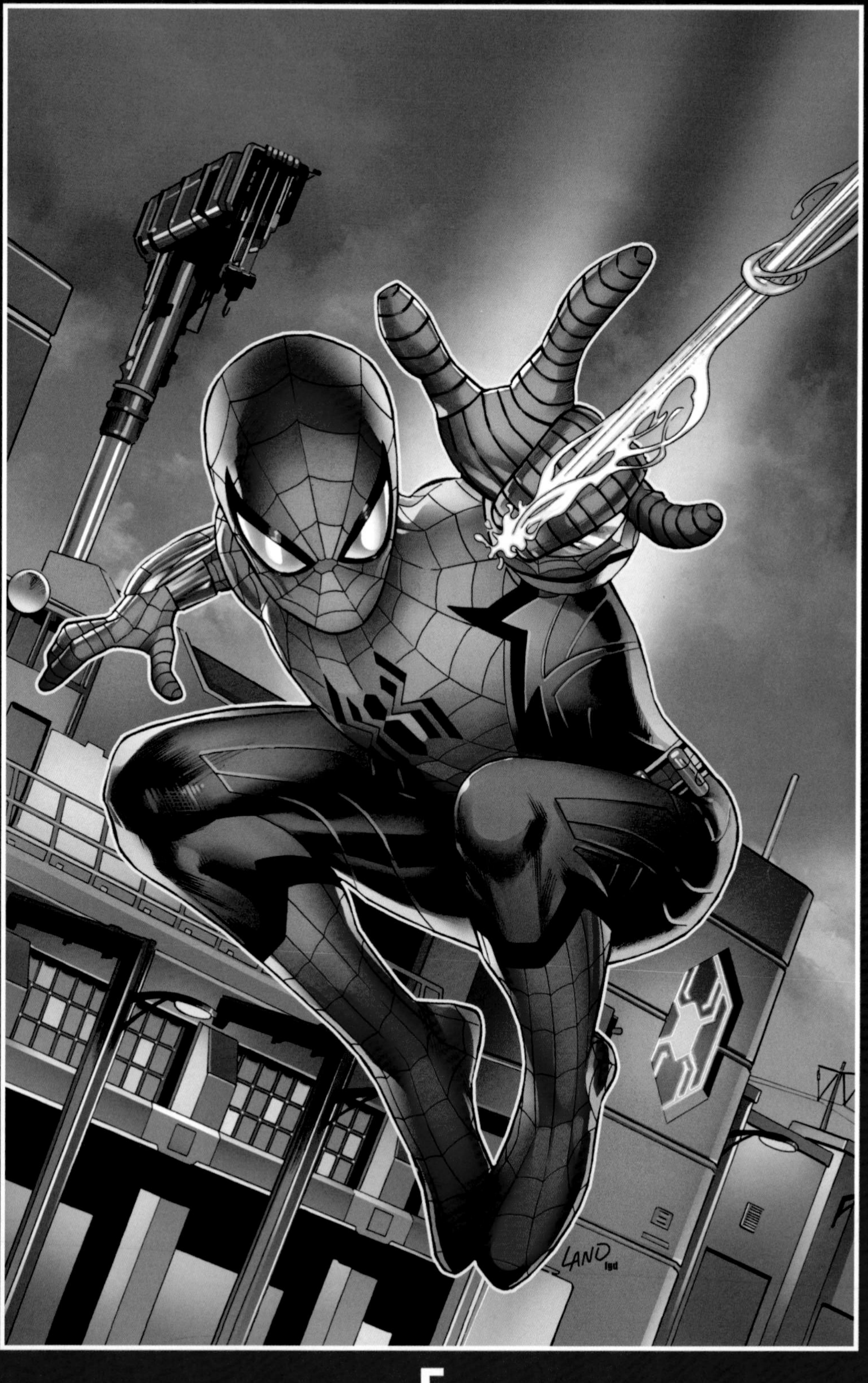

5

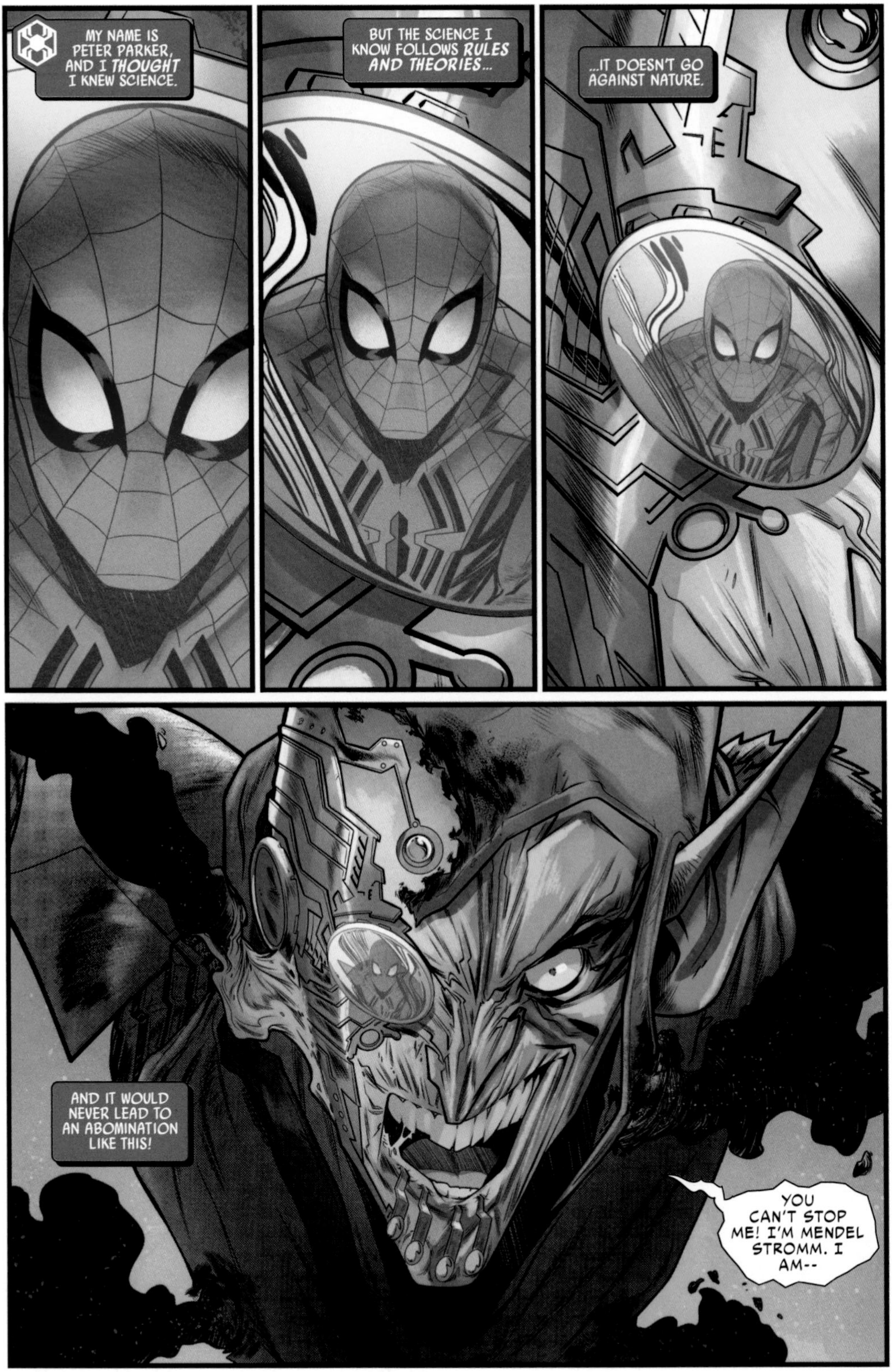
MY NAME IS PETER PARKER, AND I THOUGHT I KNEW SCIENCE.
BUT THE SCIENCE I KNOW FOLLOWS RULES AND THEORIES...
...IT DOESN'T GO AGAINST NATURE.
AND IT WOULD NEVER LEAD TO AN ABOMINATION LIKE THIS!
YOU CAN'T STOP ME! I'M MENDEL STROMM. I AM--

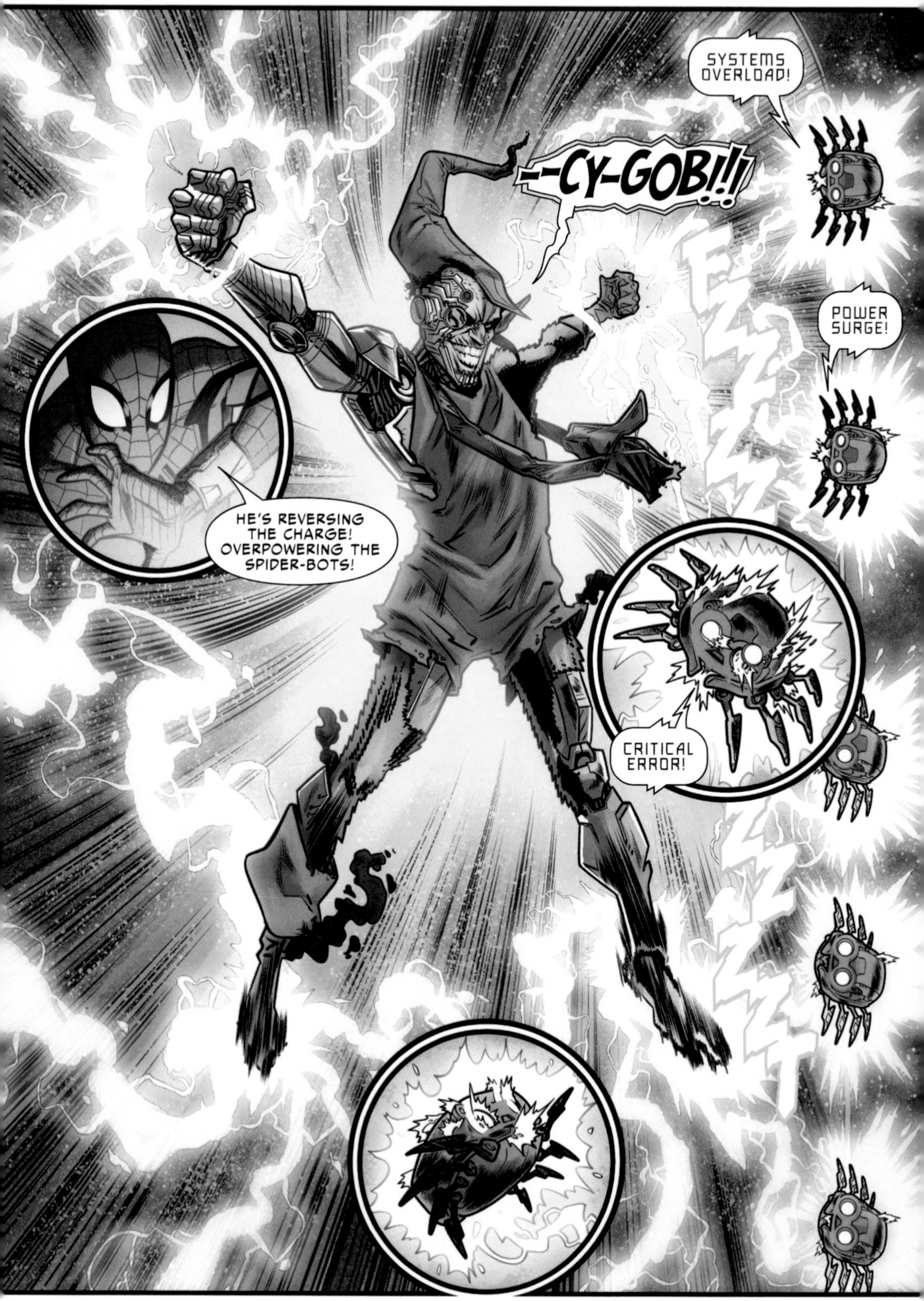
--CY-GOB!!!
SYSTEMS OVERLOAD!
POWER SURGE!
HE'S REVERSING THE CHARGE! OVERPOWERING THE SPIDER-BOTS!
CRITICAL ERROR!

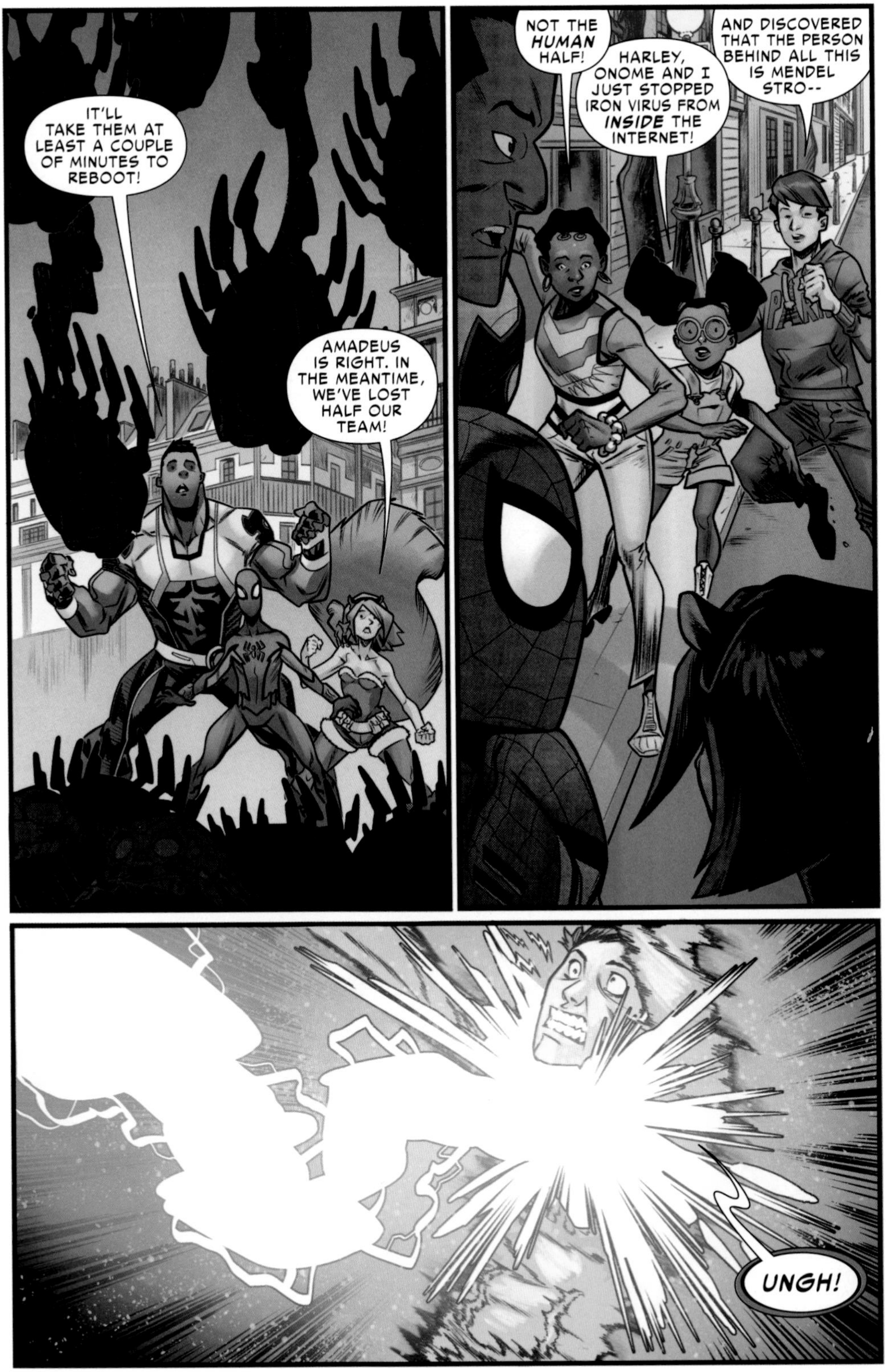
IT'LL TAKE THEM AT LEAST A COUPLE OF MINUTES TO REBOOT!
AMADEUS IS RIGHT. IN THE MEANTIME, WE'VE LOST HALF OUR TEAM!
NOT THE HUMAN HALF!
HARLEY, ONOME AND I JUST STOPPED IRON VIRUS FROM INSIDE THE INTERNET!
AND DISCOVERED THAT THE PERSON BEHIND ALL THIS IS MENDEL STRO--
UNGH!

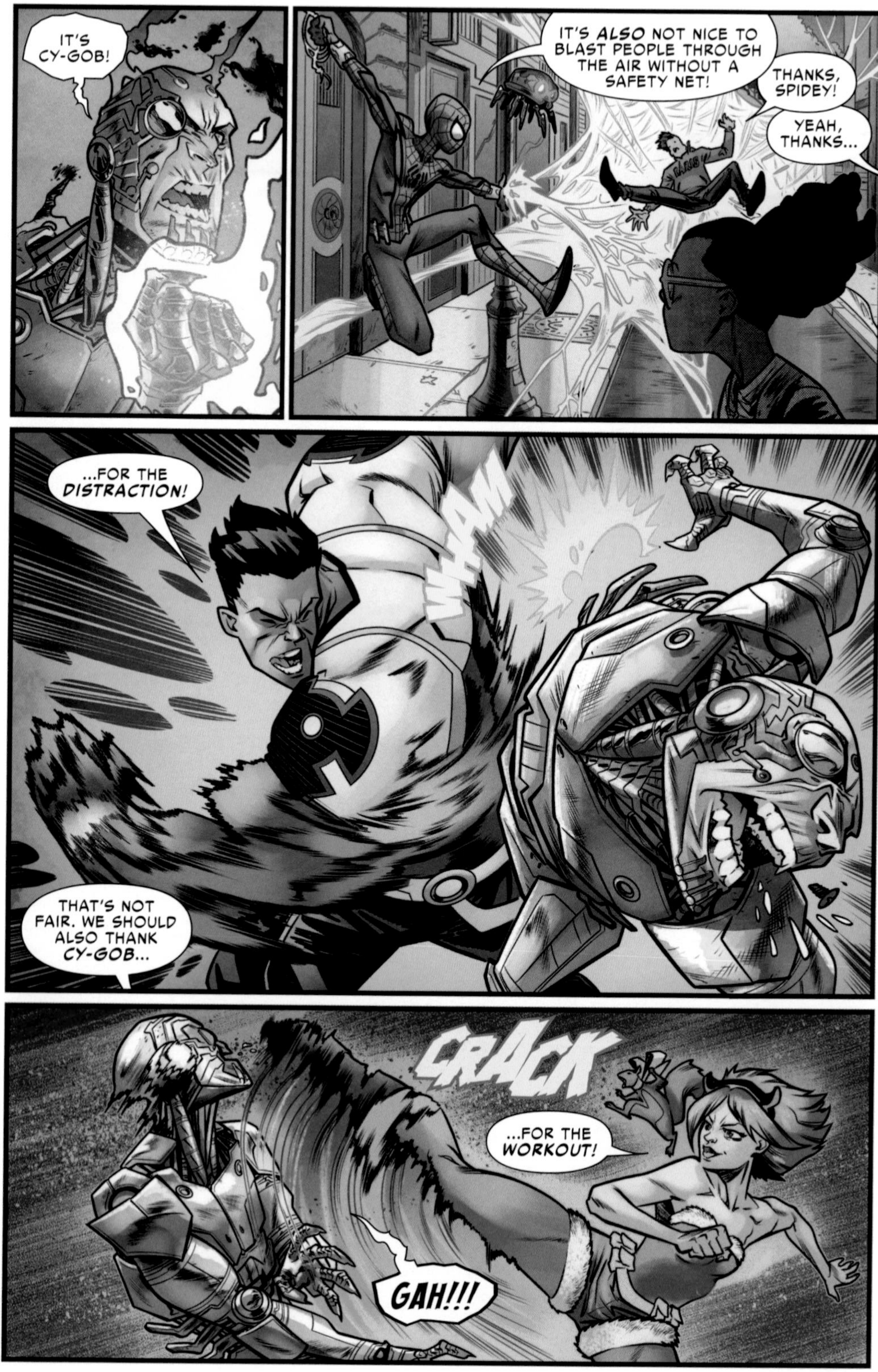

IT'S CY-GOB!
IT'S ALSO NOT NICE TO BLAST PEOPLE THROUGH THE AIR WITHOUT A SAFETY NET!
THANKS, SPIDEY!
YEAH, THANKS...
...FOR THE DISTRACTION!
WHAM
THAT'S NOT FAIR. WE SHOULD ALSO THANK CY-GOB...
CRACK
...FOR THE WORKOUT!
GAH!!!

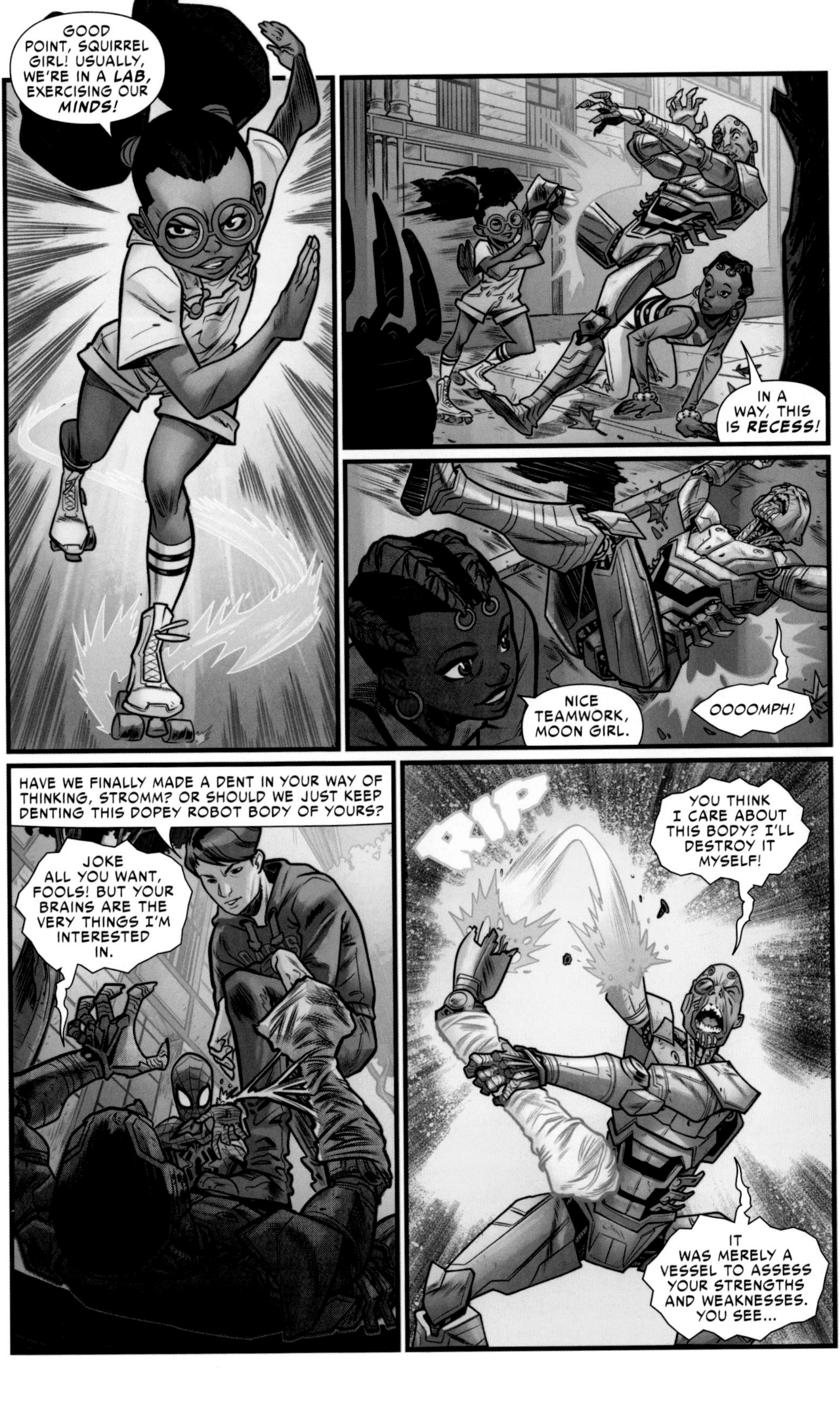
GOOD POINT, SQUIRREL GIRL! USUALLY, WE'RE IN A LAB, EXERCISING OUR MINDS!
IN A WAY, THIS IS RECESS!
NICE TEAMWORK, MOON GIRL.
OOOOMPH!
HAVE WE FINALLY MADE A DENT IN YOUR WAY OF THINKING, STROMM? OR SHOULD WE JUST KEEP DENTING THIS DOPEY ROBOT BODY OF YOURS?
JOKE ALL YOU WANT, FOOLS! BUT YOUR BRAINS ARE THE VERY THINGS I'M INTERESTED IN.
RIP
YOU THINK I CARE ABOUT THIS BODY? I'LL DESTROY IT MYSELF!
IT WAS MERELY A VESSEL TO ASSESS YOUR STRENGTHS AND WEAKNESSES. YOU SEE...

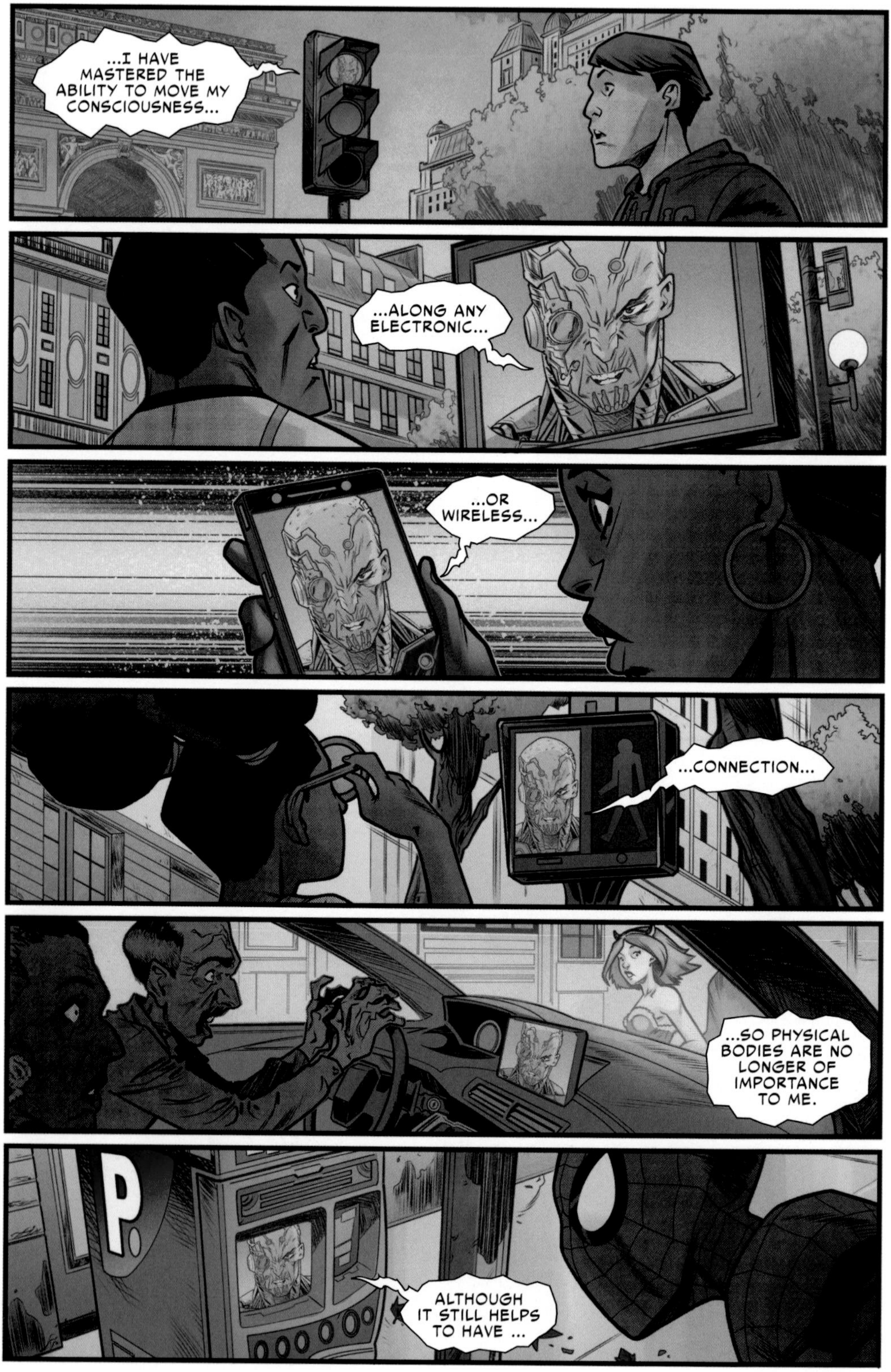
...I HAVE MASTERED THE ABILITY TO MOVE MY CONSCIOUSNESS...
...ALONG ANY ELECTRONIC...
...OR WIRELESS...
...CONNECTION...
...SO PHYSICAL BODIES ARE NO LONGER OF IMPORTANCE TO ME.
P.
ALTHOUGH IT STILL HELPS TO HAVE ...

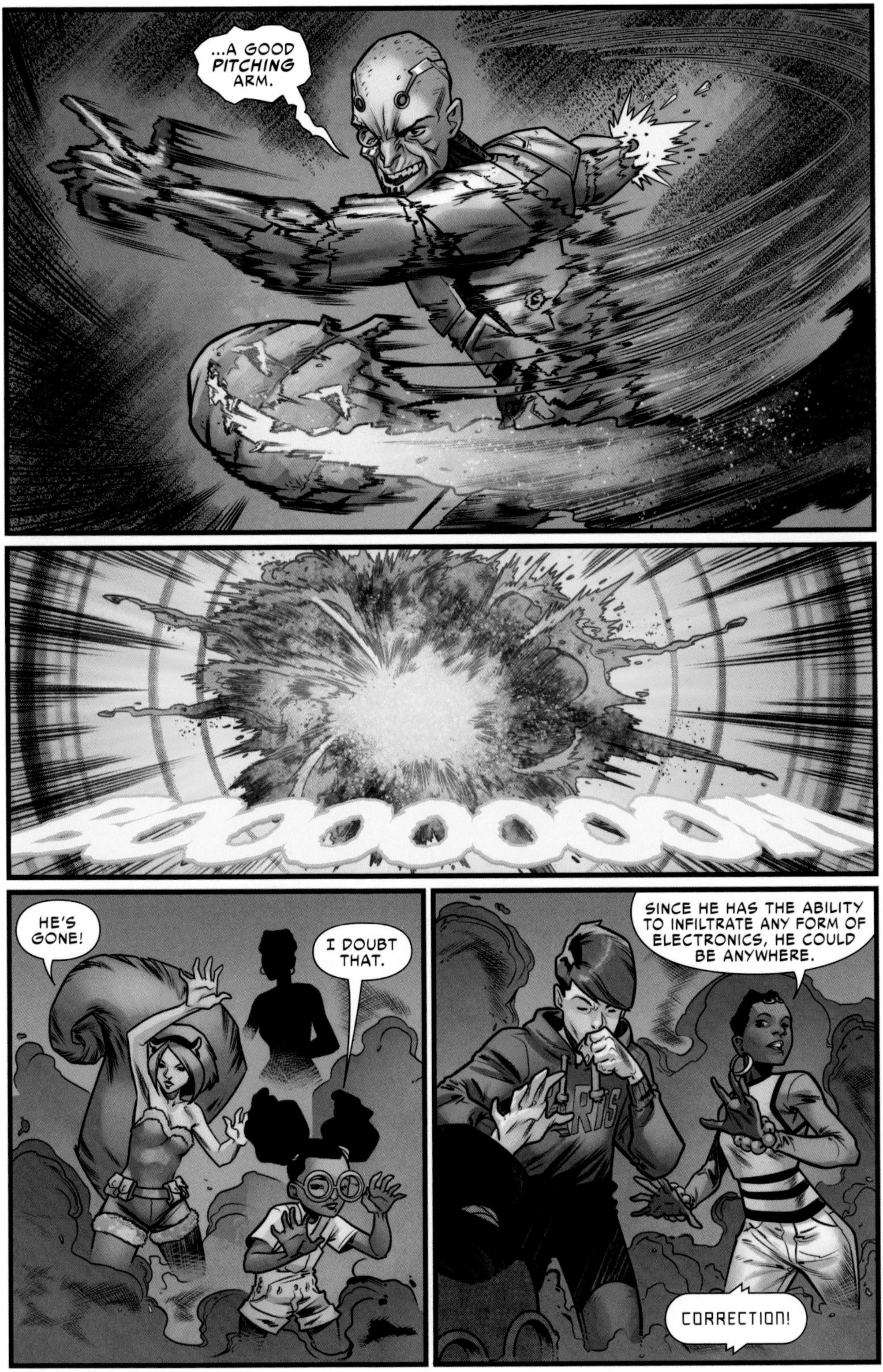
...A GOOD PITCHING ARM.
HE'S GONE!
I DOUBT THAT.
SINCE HE HAS THE ABILITY TO INFILTRATE ANY FORM OF ELECTRONICS, HE COULD BE ANYWHERE.
CORRECTION!

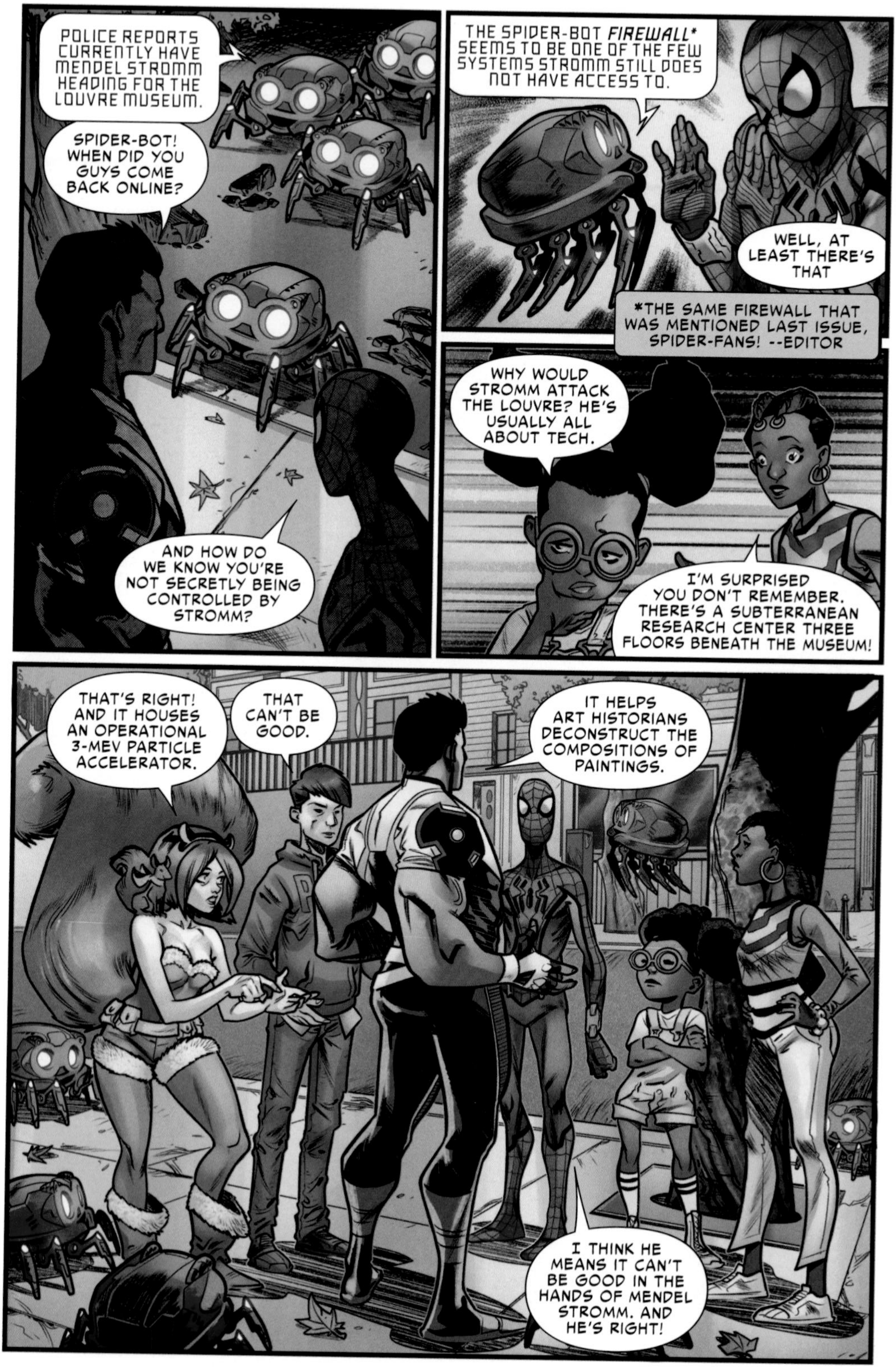
POLICE REPORTS CURRENTLY HAVE MENDEL STROMM HEADING FOR THE LOUVRE MUSEUM.
SPIDER-BOT! WHEN DID YOU GUYS COME BACK ONLINE?
AND HOW DO WE KNOW YOU'RE NOT SECRETLY BEING CONTROLLED BY STROMM?
THE SPIDER-BOT FIREWALL* SEEMS TO BE ONE OF THE FEW SYSTEMS STROMM STILL DOES NOT HAVE ACCESS TO.
WELL, AT LEAST THERE'S THAT
*THE SAME FIREWALL THAT WAS MENTIONED LAST ISSUE, SPIDER-FANS! --EDITOR
WHY WOULD STROMM ATTACK THE LOUVRE? HE'S USUALLY ALL ABOUT TECH.
I'M SURPRISED YOU DON'T REMEMBER. THERE'S A SUBTERRANEAN RESEARCH CENTER THREE FLOORS BENEATH THE MUSEUM!
THAT'S RIGHT! AND IT HOUSES AN OPERATIONAL 3-MEV PARTICLE ACCELERATOR.
THAT CAN'T BE GOOD.
IT HELPS ART HISTORIANS DECONSTRUCT THE COMPOSITIONS OF PAINTINGS.
I THINK HE MEANS IT CAN'T BE GOOD IN THE HANDS OF MENDEL STROMM. AND HE'S RIGHT!

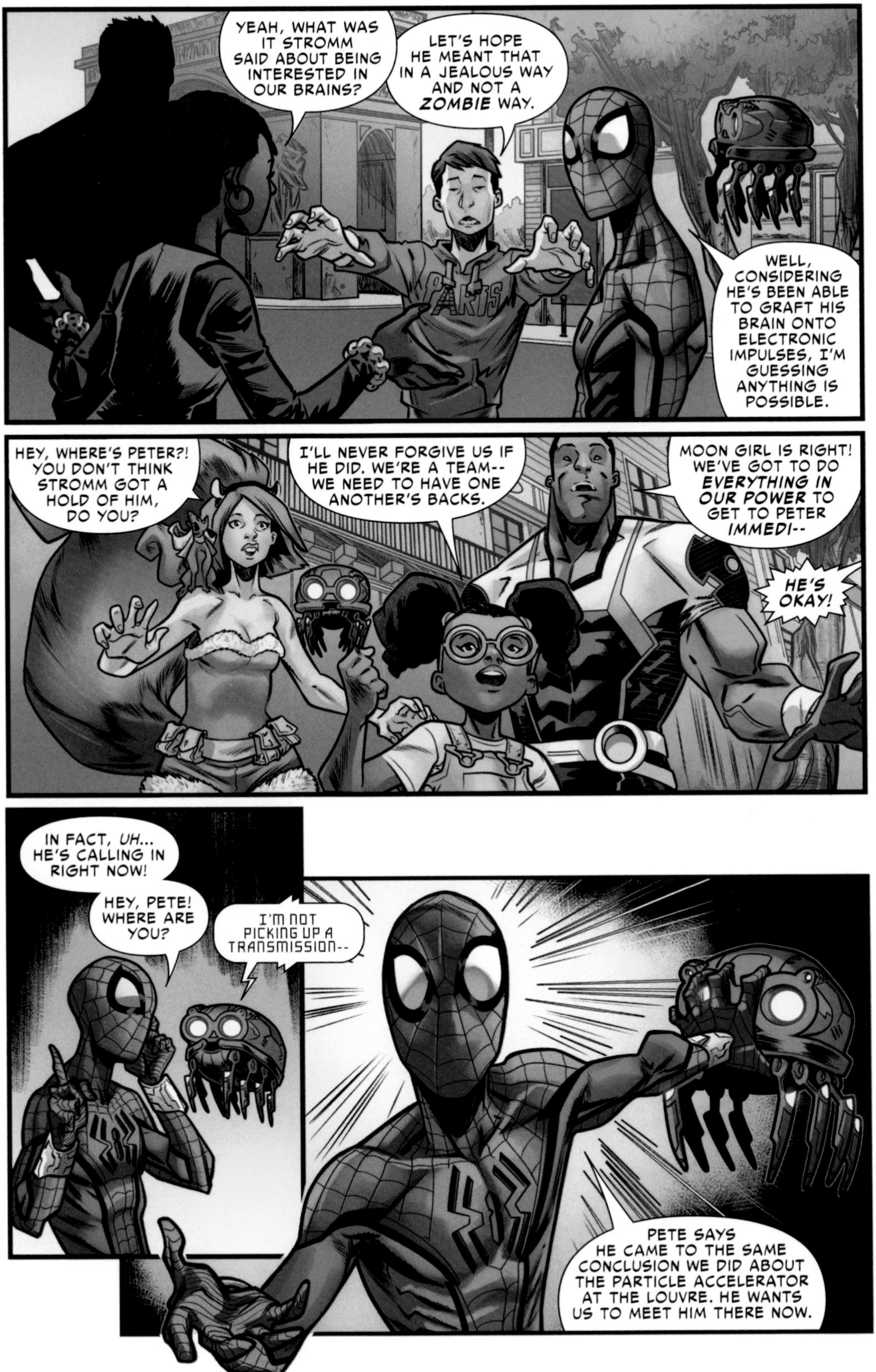
YEAH, WHAT WAS IT STROMM SAID ABOUT BEING INTERESTED IN OUR BRAINS?
LET'S HOPE HE MEANT THAT IN A JEALOUS WAY AND NOT A ZOMBIE WAY.
WELL, CONSIDERING HE'S BEEN ABLE TO GRAFT HIS BRAIN ONTO ELECTRONIC IMPULSES, I'M GUESSING ANYTHING IS POSSIBLE.
HEY, WHERE'S PETER?! YOU DON'T THINK STROMM GOT A HOLD OF HIM, DO YOU?
I'LL NEVER FORGIVE US IF HE DID. WE'RE A TEAM-- WE NEED TO HAVE ONE ANOTHER'S BACKS.
MOON GIRL IS RIGHT! WE'VE GOT TO DO EVERYTHING IN OUR POWER TO GET TO PETER IMMEDI--
HE'S OKAY!
IN FACT, UH... HE'S CALLING IN RIGHT NOW!
HEY, PETE! WHERE ARE YOU?
I'M NOT PICKING UP A TRANSMISSION--
PETE SAYS HE CAME TO THE SAME CONCLUSION WE DID ABOUT THE PARTICLE ACCELERATOR AT THE LOUVRE. HE WANTS US TO MEET HIM THERE NOW.

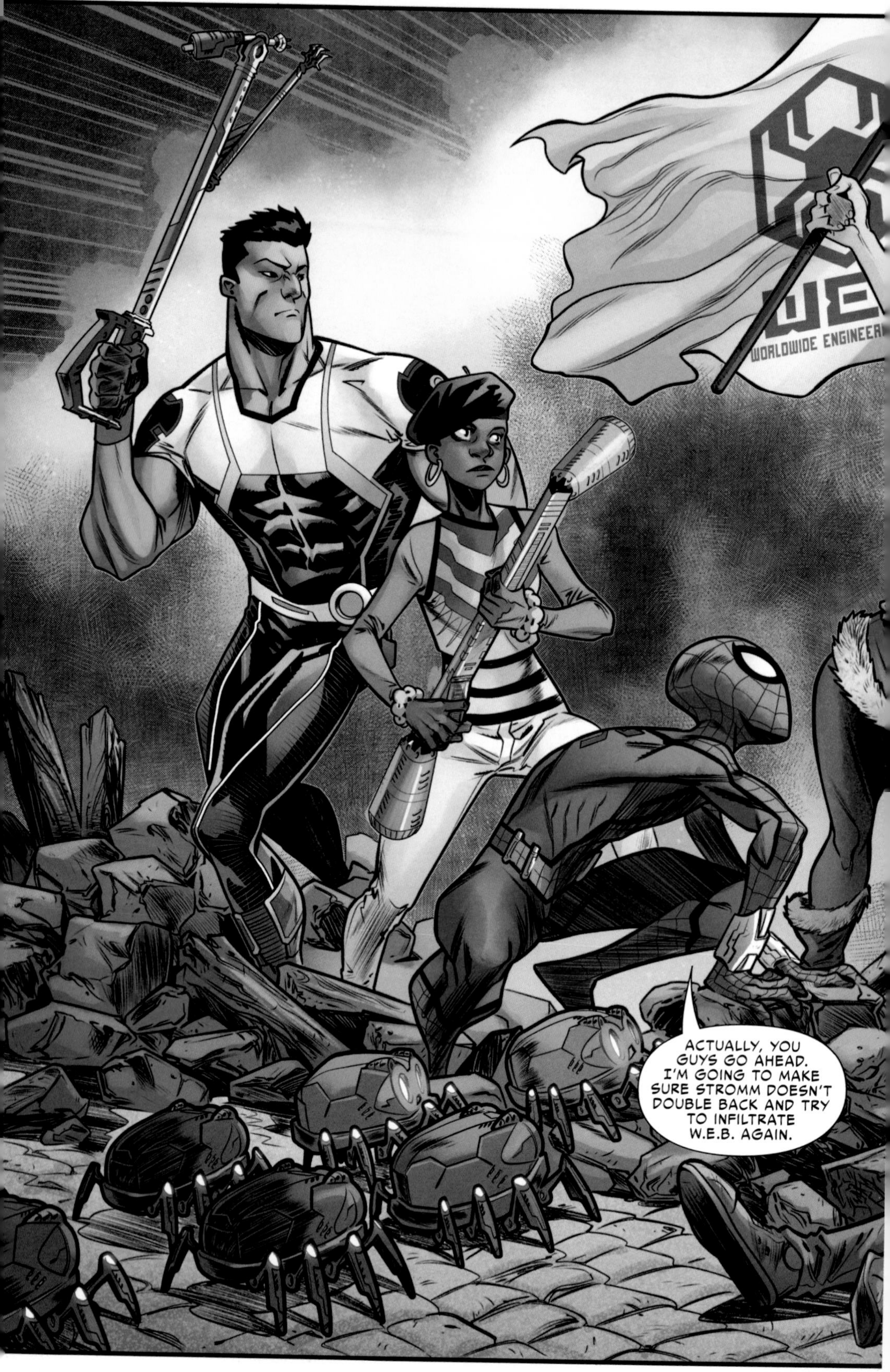
WORLDWIDE ENGINEER
ACTUALLY, YOU GUYS GO AHEAD. I'M GOING TO MAKE SURE STROMM DOESN'T DOUBLE BACK AND TRY TO INFILTRATE W.E.B. AGAIN.

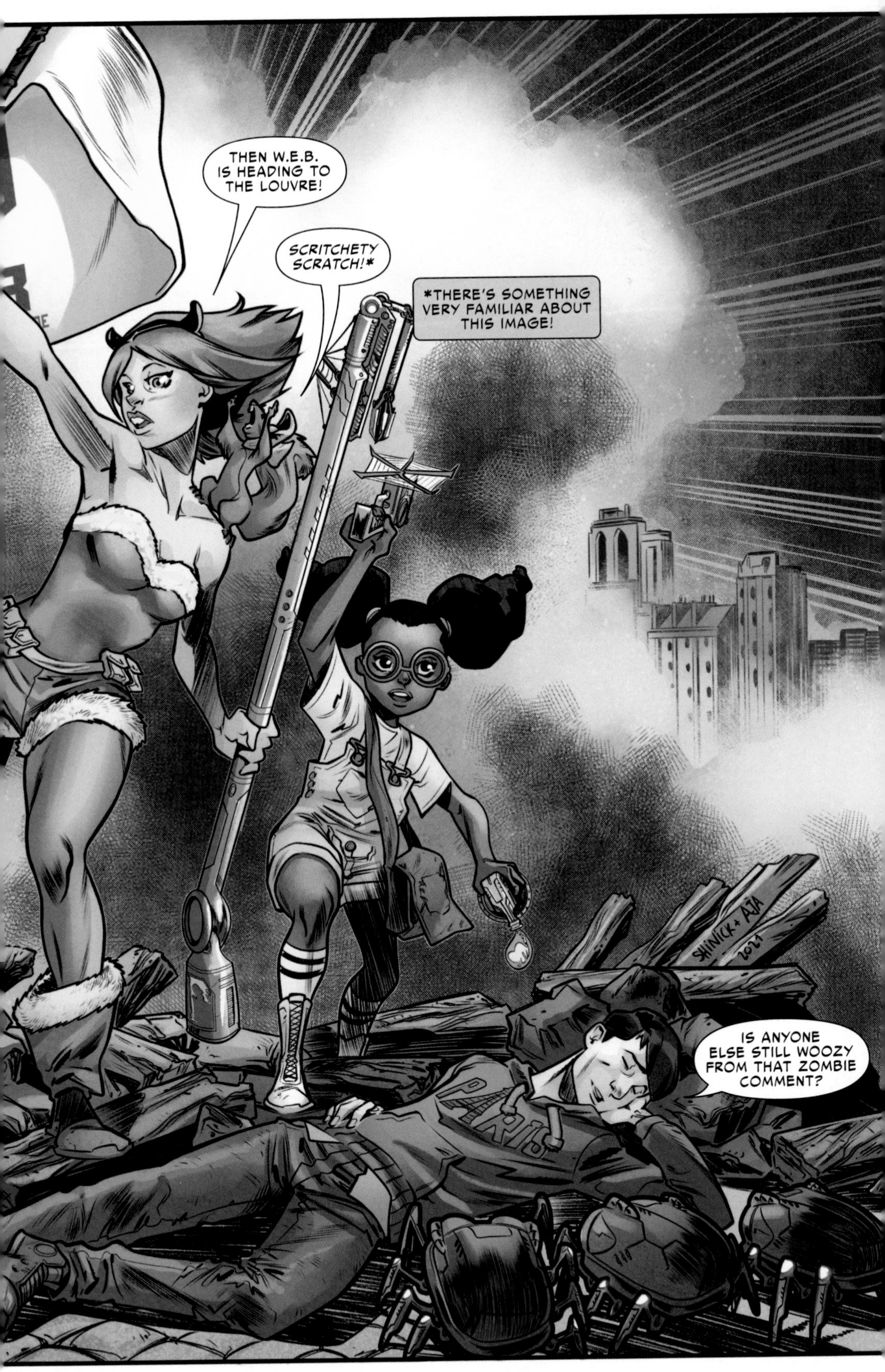
THEN W.E.B. IS HEADING TO THE LOUVRE!
SCRITCHETY SCRATCH!*
*THERE'S SOMETHING VERY FAMILIAR ABOUT THIS IMAGE!
IS ANYONE ELSE STILL WOOZY FROM THAT ZOMBIE COMMENT?
SHINICK + AJA 2021

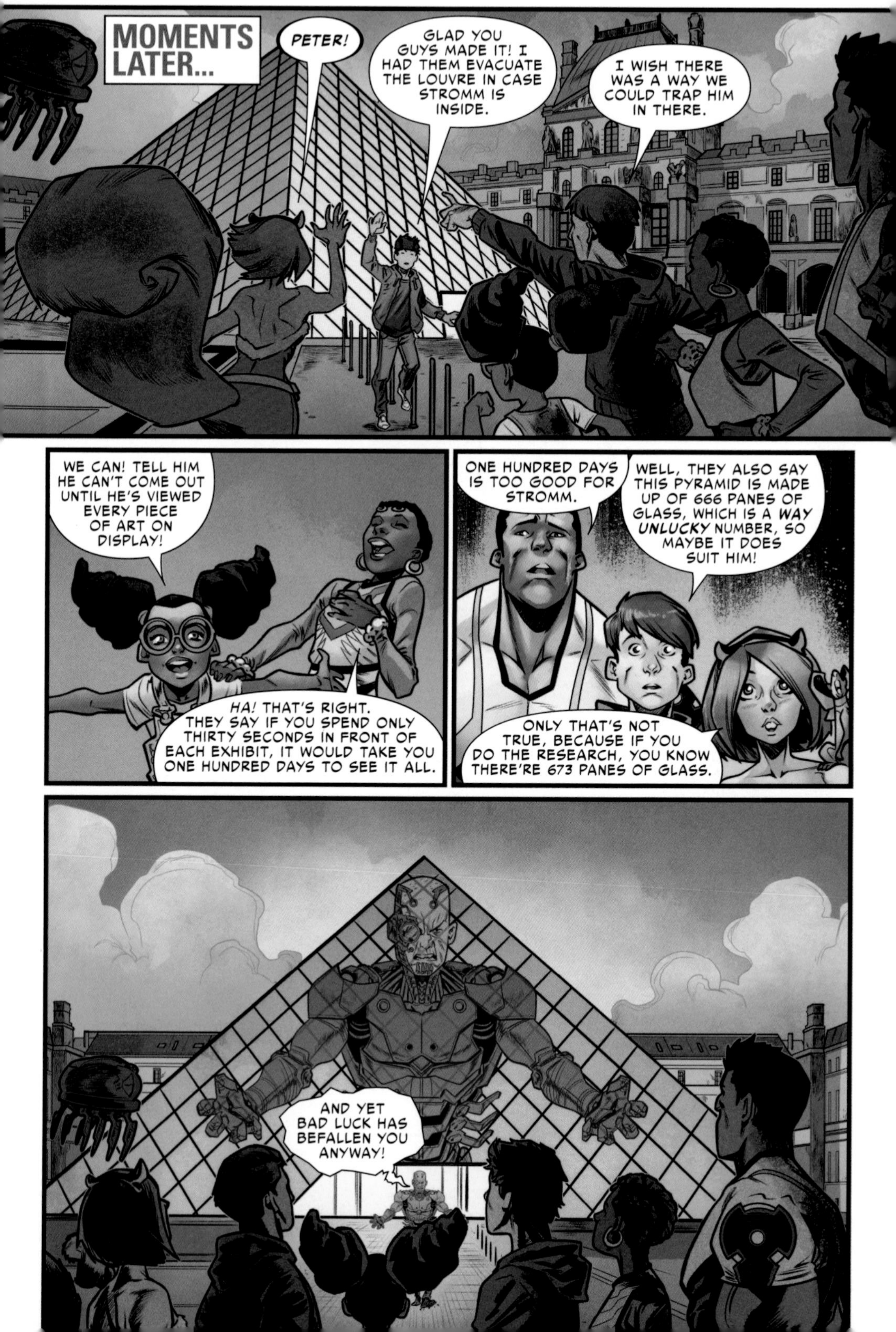
MOMENTS LATER...
PETER!
GLAD YOU GUYS MADE IT! I HAD THEM EVACUATE THE LOUVRE IN CASE STROMM IS INSIDE.
I WISH THERE WAS A WAY WE COULD TRAP HIM IN THERE.
WE CAN! TELL HIM HE CAN'T COME OUT UNTIL HE'S VIEWED EVERY PIECE OF ART ON DISPLAY!
HA! THAT'S RIGHT. THEY SAY IF YOU SPEND ONLY THIRTY SECONDS IN FRONT OF EACH EXHIBIT, IT WOULD TAKE YOU ONE HUNDRED DAYS TO SEE IT ALL.
ONE HUNDRED DAYS IS TOO GOOD FOR STROMM.
WELL, THEY ALSO SAY THIS PYRAMID IS MADE UP OF 666 PANES OF GLASS, WHICH IS A WAY UNLUCKY NUMBER, SO MAYBE IT DOES SUIT HIM!
ONLY THAT'S NOT TRUE, BECAUSE IF YOU DO THE RESEARCH, YOU KNOW THERE'RE 673 PANES OF GLASS.
AND YET BAD LUCK HAS BEFALLEN YOU ANYWAY!

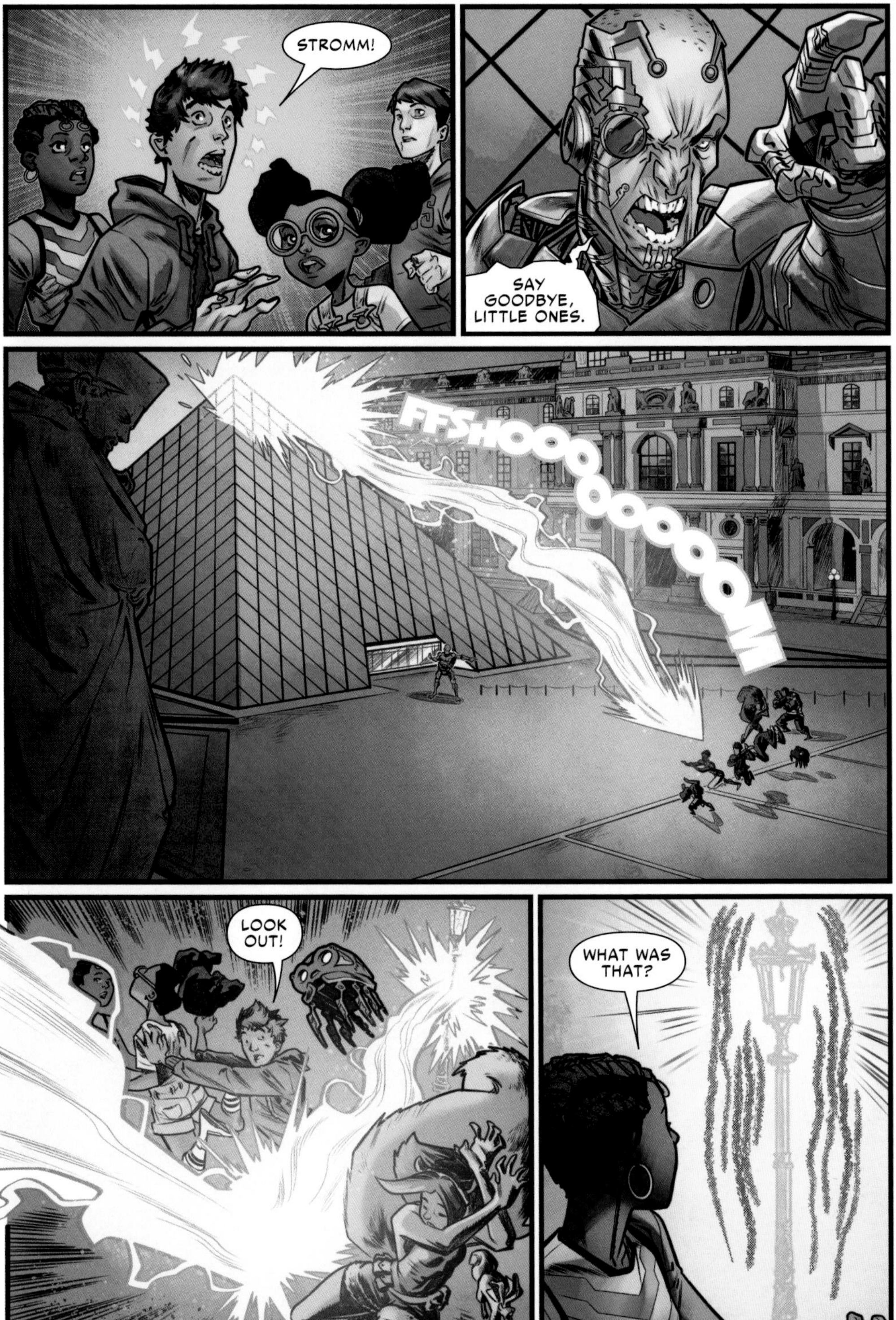
STROMM!
SAY GOODBYE, LITTLE ONES.
FFSHOOOOOOOOOOOM
LOOK OUT!
WHAT WAS THAT?

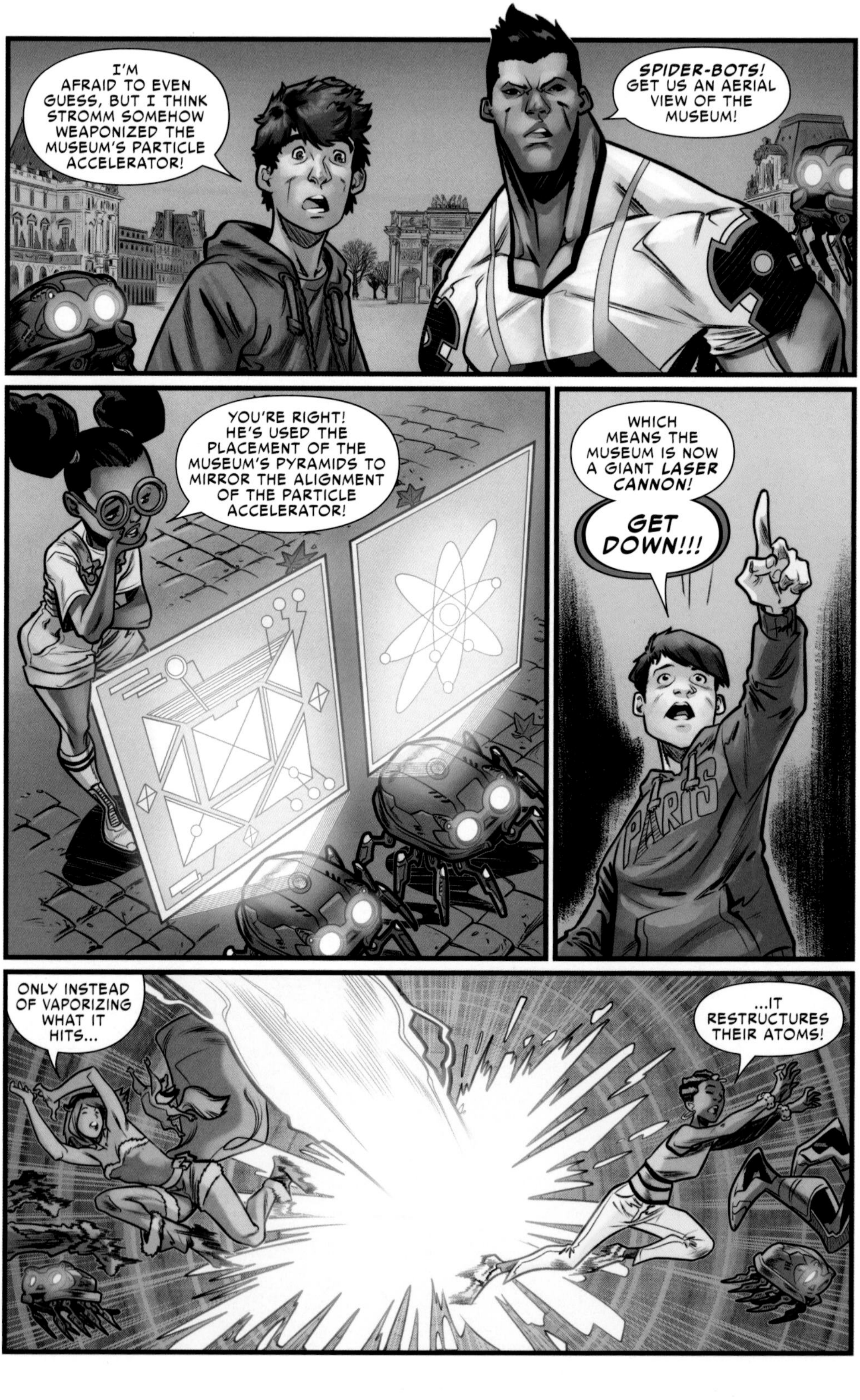
I'M AFRAID TO EVEN GUESS, BUT I THINK STROMM SOMEHOW WEAPONIZED THE MUSEUM'S PARTICLE ACCELERATOR!
SPIDER-BOTS! GET US AN AERIAL VIEW OF THE MUSEUM!
YOU'RE RIGHT! HE'S USED THE PLACEMENT OF THE MUSEUM'S PYRAMIDS TO MIRROR THE ALIGNMENT OF THE PARTICLE ACCELERATOR!
WHICH MEANS THE MUSEUM IS NOW A GIANT LASER CANNON!
GET DOWN!!!
PARIS
ONLY INSTEAD OF VAPORIZING WHAT IT HITS...
...IT RESTRUCTURES THEIR ATOMS!

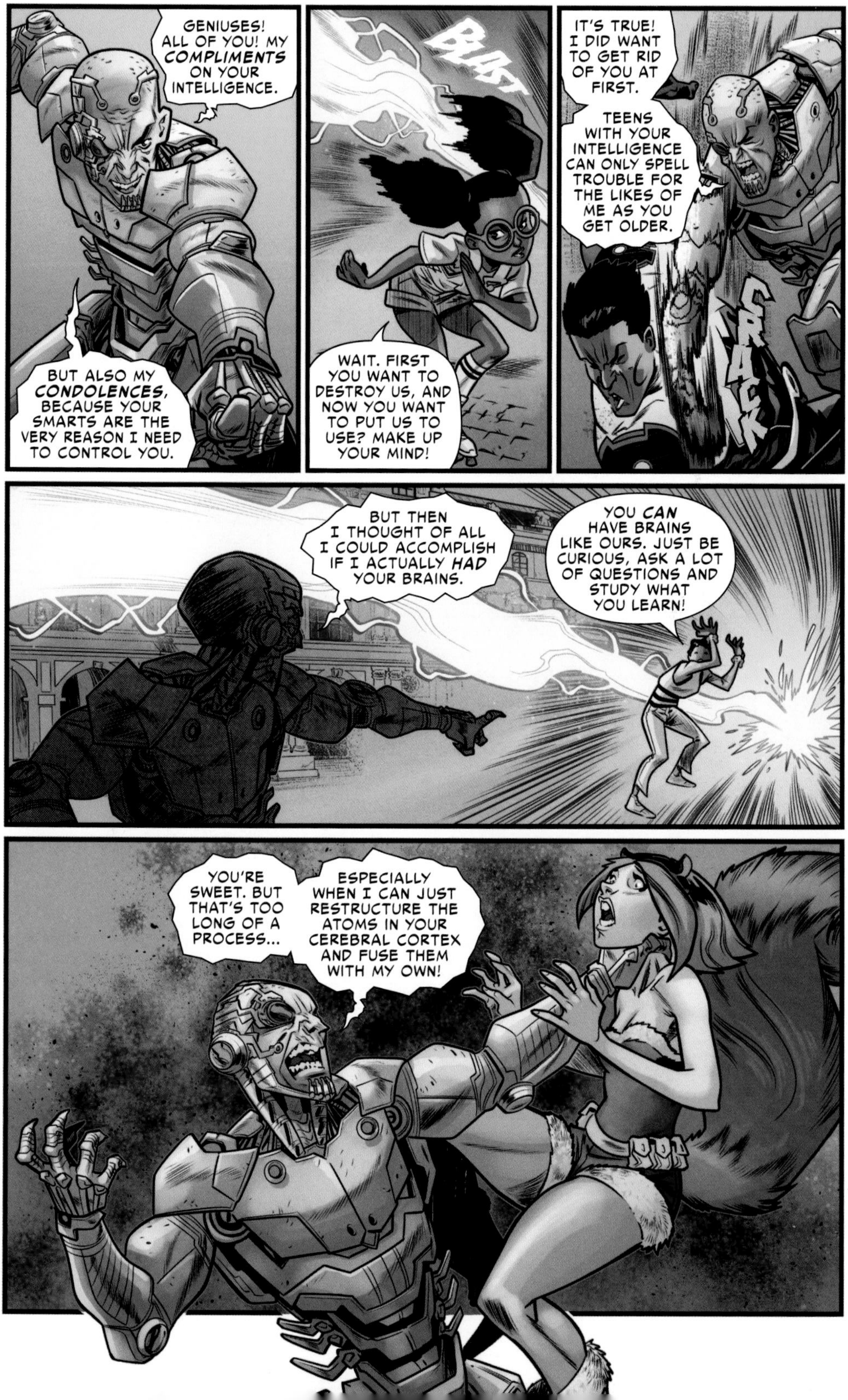
GENIUSES! ALL OF YOU! MY COMPLIMENTS ON YOUR INTELLIGENCE.
BUT ALSO MY CONDOLENCES, BECAUSE YOUR SMARTS ARE THE VERY REASON I NEED TO CONTROL YOU.
BLAST
WAIT. FIRST YOU WANT TO DESTROY US, AND NOW YOU WANT TO PUT US TO USE? MAKE UP YOUR MIND!
IT'S TRUE! I DID WANT TO GET RID OF YOU AT FIRST.
TEENS WITH YOUR INTELLIGENCE CAN ONLY SPELL TROUBLE FOR THE LIKES OF ME AS YOU GET OLDER.
CRACK
BUT THEN I THOUGHT OF ALL I COULD ACCOMPLISH IF I ACTUALLY HAD YOUR BRAINS.
YOU CAN HAVE BRAINS LIKE OURS. JUST BE CURIOUS, ASK A LOT OF QUESTIONS AND STUDY WHAT YOU LEARN!
YOU'RE SWEET. BUT THAT'S TOO LONG OF A PROCESS...
ESPECIALLY WHEN I CAN JUST RESTRUCTURE THE ATOMS IN YOUR CEREBRAL CORTEX AND FUSE THEM WITH MY OWN!

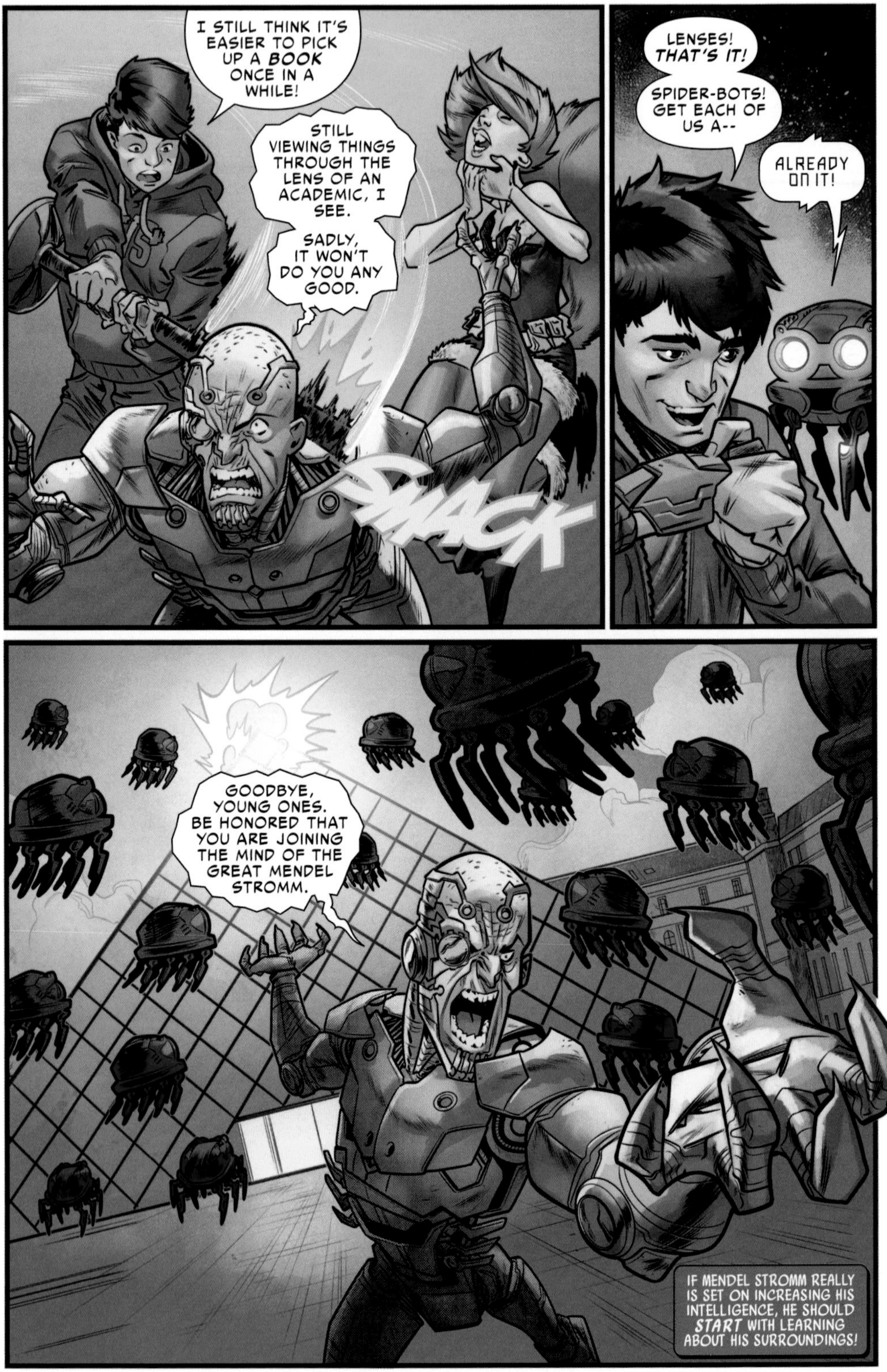
I STILL THINK IT'S EASIER TO PICK UP A *BOOK* ONCE IN A WHILE!
STILL VIEWING THINGS THROUGH THE LENS OF AN ACADEMIC, I SEE.
SADLY, IT WON'T DO YOU ANY GOOD.
SMACK
LENSES! *THAT'S IT!*
SPIDER-BOTS! GET EACH OF US A--
ALREADY ON IT!
GOODBYE, YOUNG ONES. BE HONORED THAT YOU ARE JOINING THE MIND OF THE GREAT MENDEL STROMM.
IF MENDEL STROMM REALLY IS SET ON INCREASING HIS INTELLIGENCE, HE SHOULD *START* WITH LEARNING ABOUT HIS SURROUNDINGS!

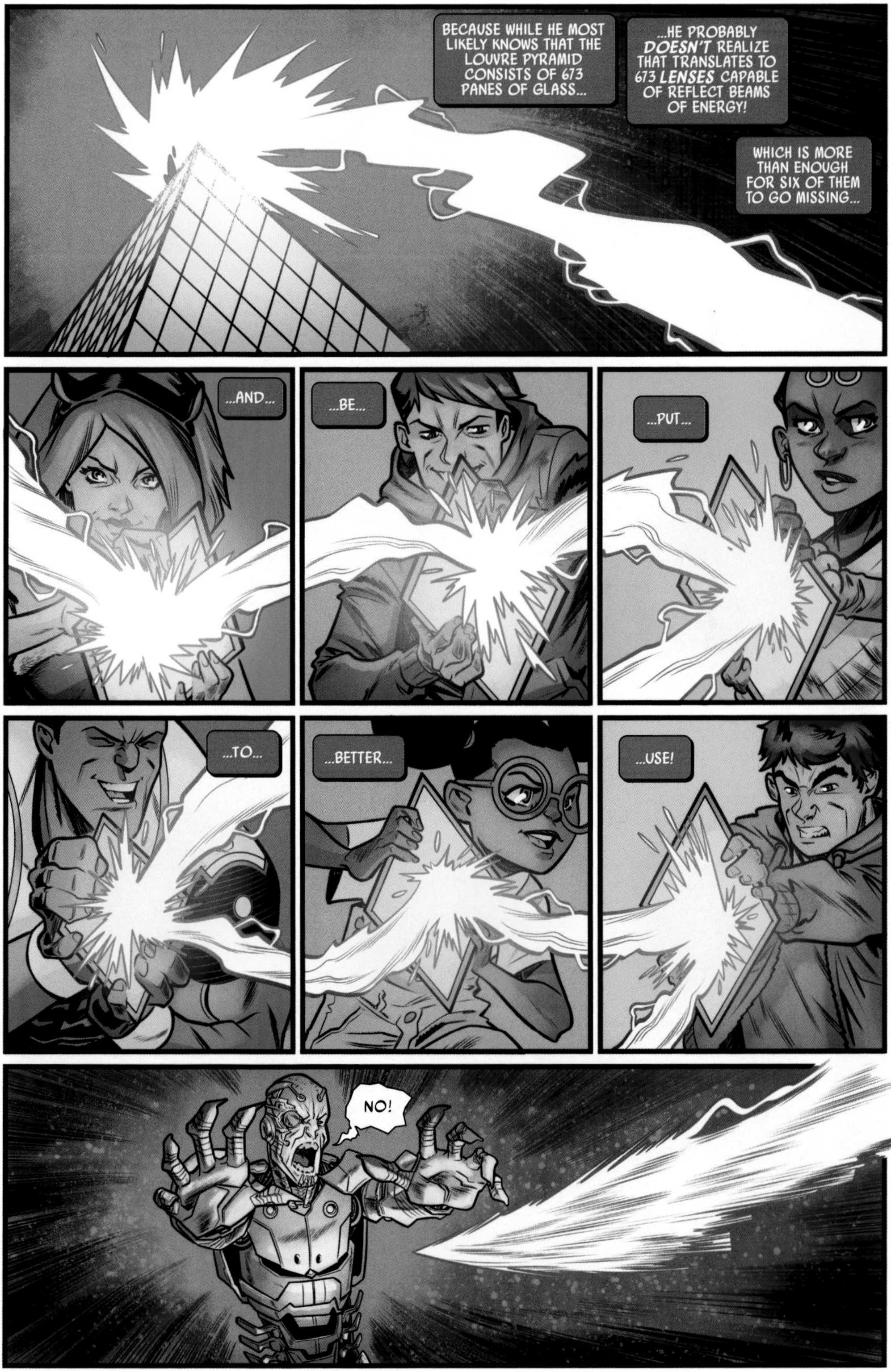

BECAUSE WHILE HE MOST LIKELY KNOWS THAT THE LOUVRE PYRAMID CONSISTS OF 673 PANES OF GLASS...
...HE PROBABLY DOESN'T REALIZE THAT TRANSLATES TO 673 LENSES CAPABLE OF REFLECT BEAMS OF ENERGY!
WHICH IS MORE THAN ENOUGH FOR SIX OF THEM TO GO MISSING...
...AND...
...BE...
...PUT...
...TO...
...BETTER...
...USE!
NO!

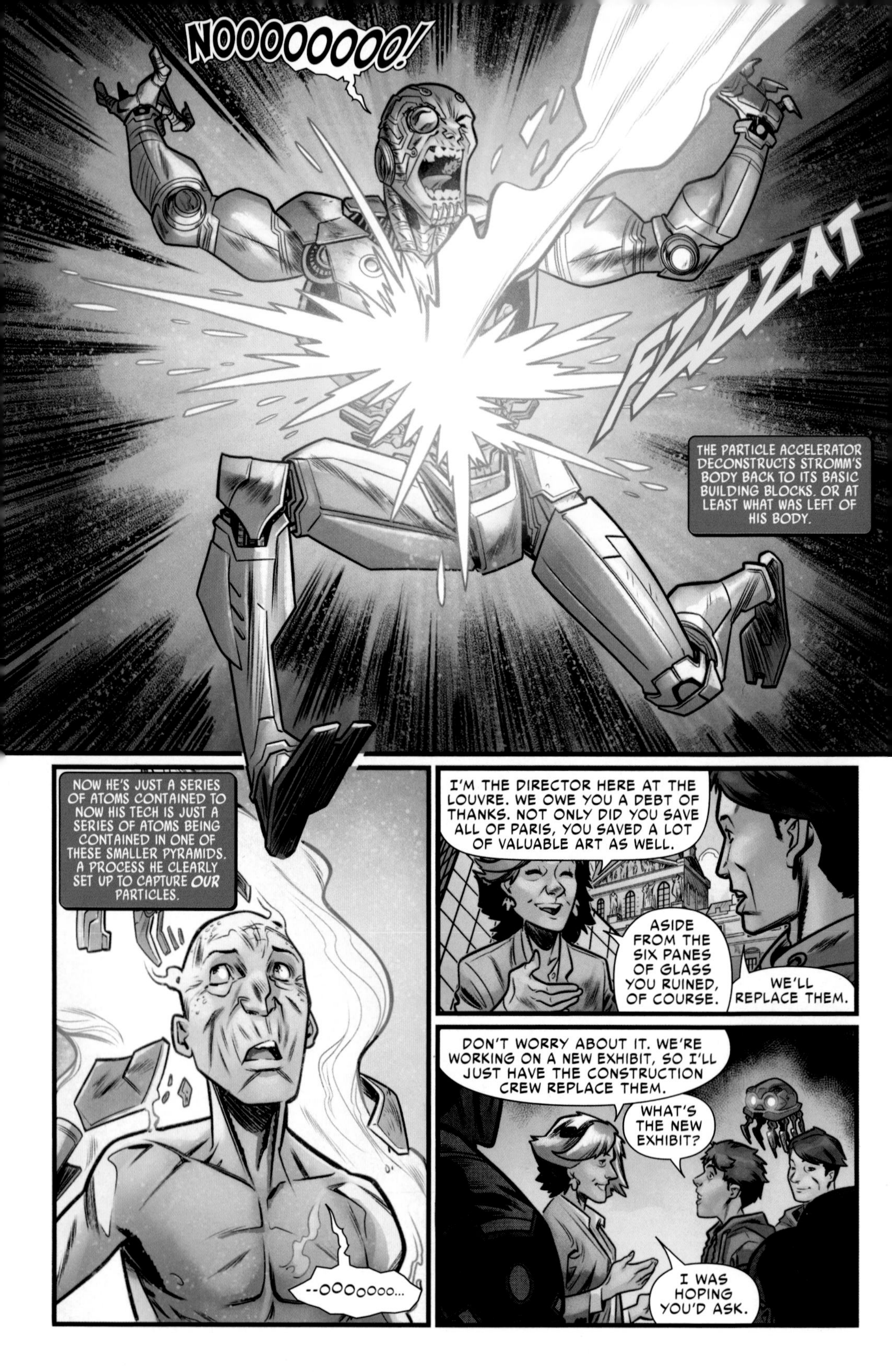
NOOOOOOOO!
FZZZZAT
THE PARTICLE ACCELERATOR DECONSTRUCTS STROMM'S BODY BACK TO ITS BASIC BUILDING BLOCKS. OR AT LEAST WHAT WAS LEFT OF HIS BODY.
NOW HE'S JUST A SERIES OF ATOMS CONTAINED TO NOW HIS TECH IS JUST A SERIES OF ATOMS BEING CONTAINED IN ONE OF THESE SMALLER PYRAMIDS. A PROCESS HE CLEARLY SET UP TO CAPTURE *OUR* PARTICLES.
--OOOoooo...
I'M THE DIRECTOR HERE AT THE LOUVRE. WE OWE YOU A DEBT OF THANKS. NOT ONLY DID YOU SAVE ALL OF PARIS, YOU SAVED A LOT OF VALUABLE ART AS WELL.
ASIDE FROM THE SIX PANES OF GLASS YOU RUINED, OF COURSE.
WE'LL REPLACE THEM.
DON'T WORRY ABOUT IT. WE'RE WORKING ON A NEW EXHIBIT, SO I'LL JUST HAVE THE CONSTRUCTION CREW REPLACE THEM.
WHAT'S THE NEW EXHIBIT?
I WAS HOPING YOU'D ASK.

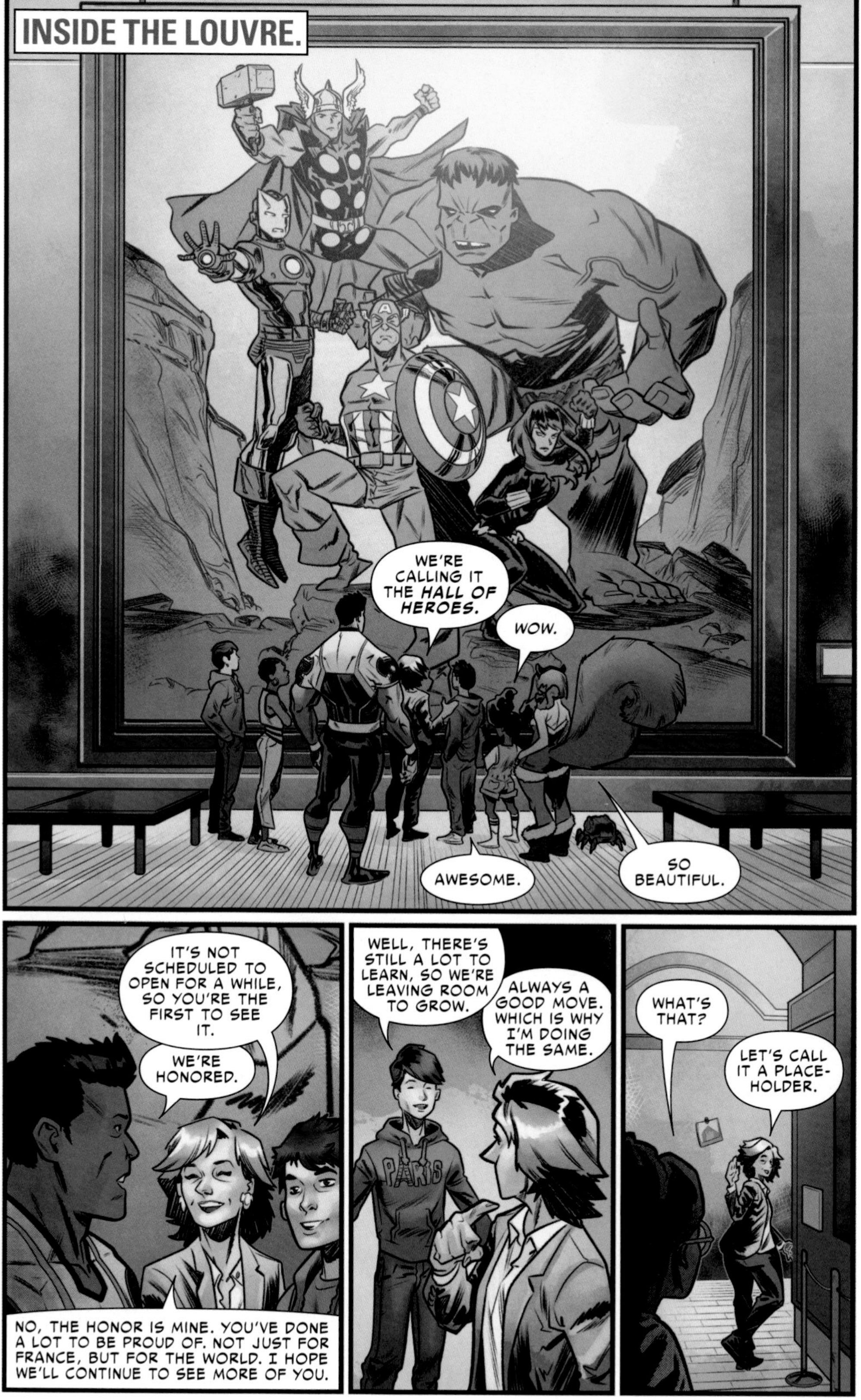
INSIDE THE LOUVRE.
WE'RE CALLING IT THE *HALL OF HEROES*.
WOW.
AWESOME.
SO BEAUTIFUL.
IT'S NOT SCHEDULED TO OPEN FOR A WHILE, SO YOU'RE THE FIRST TO SEE IT.
WE'RE HONORED.
NO, THE HONOR IS MINE. YOU'VE DONE A LOT TO BE PROUD OF. NOT JUST FOR FRANCE, BUT FOR THE WORLD. I HOPE WE'LL CONTINUE TO SEE MORE OF YOU.
WELL, THERE'S STILL A LOT TO LEARN, SO WE'RE LEAVING ROOM TO GROW.
ALWAYS A GOOD MOVE. WHICH IS WHY I'M DOING THE SAME.
PARIS
WHAT'S THAT?
LET'S CALL IT A PLACE-HOLDER.

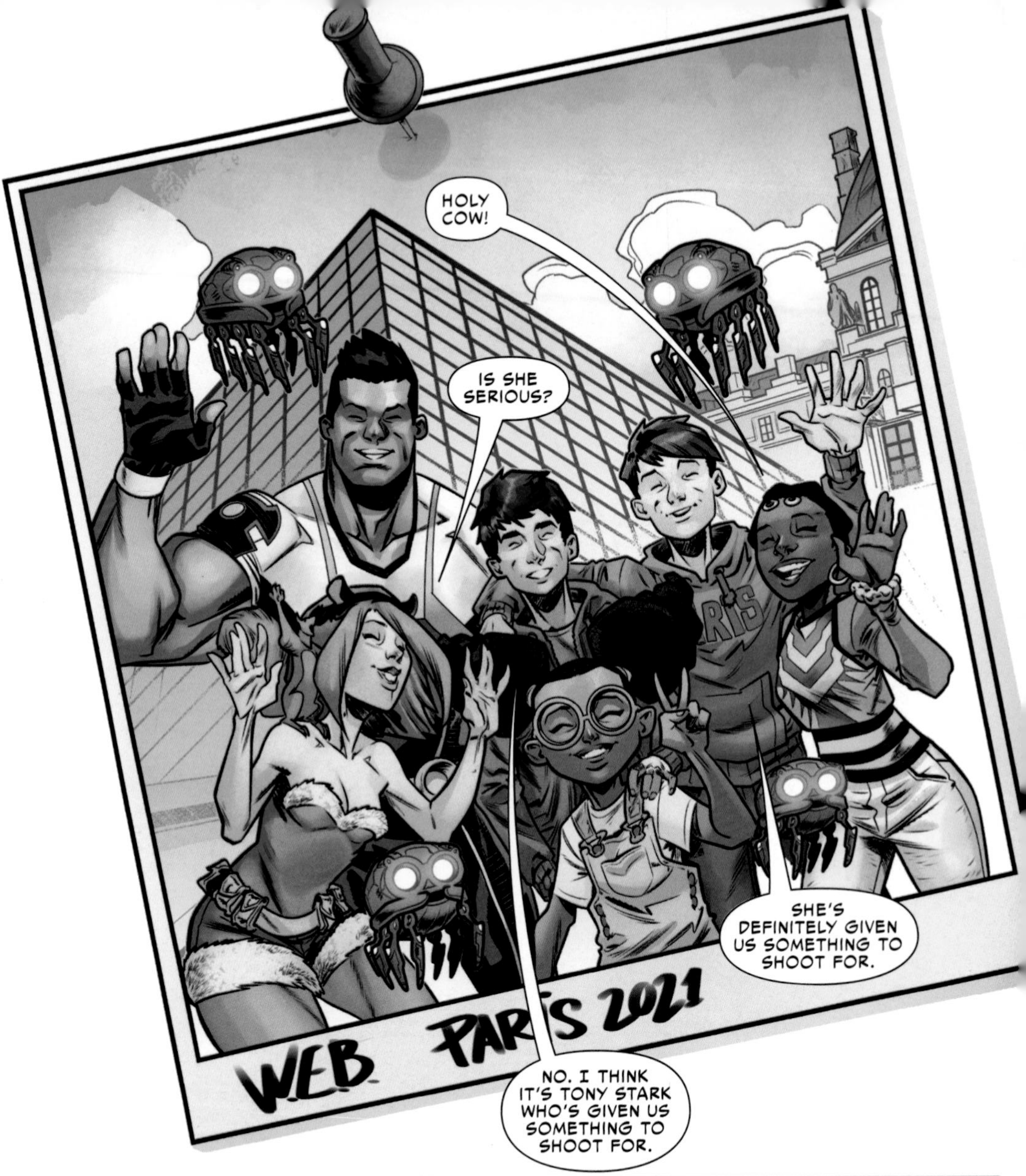
HOLY COW!
IS SHE SERIOUS?
SHE'S DEFINITELY GIVEN US SOMETHING TO SHOOT FOR.
W.E.B. PARIS 2021
NO. I THINK IT'S TONY STARK WHO'S GIVEN US SOMETHING TO SHOOT FOR.

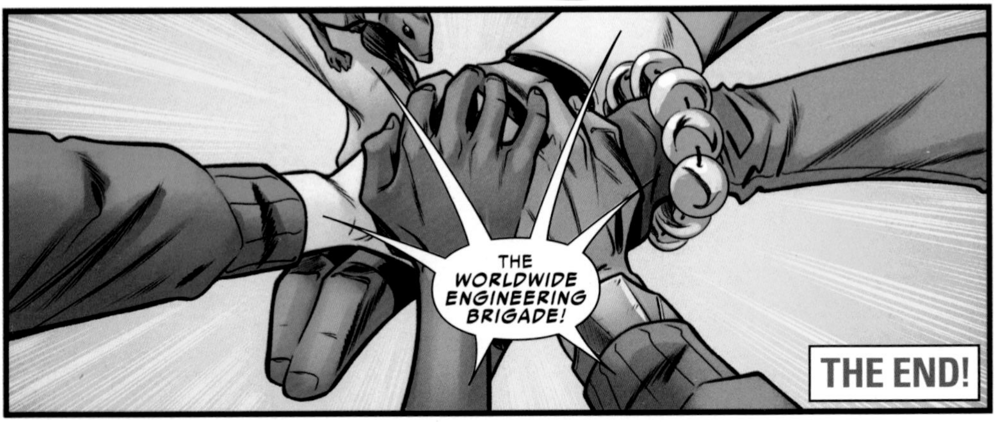
THE *WORLDWIDE ENGINEERING BRIGADE!*
THE END!